SILENCE
BREAKING

Silence
Breaking

Robert Thier

2018

Disclaimer:

This work is a work of fiction. All names, characters, businesses, places, events and incidents appearing in this work are fictitious. Any resemblance to real names, businesses, places, events and incidents, or to real persons, living or dead, is purely coincidental.

First Printing: 2018

ISBN: 978-3-962600594

This book is also available in eBook format. More information on this and any other subject connected with Robert Thier's books on: www.robthier.com

Dedication

I would like to dedicate this story to all my trilingual readers who figured out all by themselves what *Prince Utairah Jafri fi al Qurram Qumrah III, heir to the principality of Bakavāsa* means. I salute you and your language skills.

This volume is furthermore dedicated to my three fabulous proofreaders who've been helping to edit this series for quite some time now: Iris Chacon, Nela Korenica and Svasti Sharma. It is thanks to their ongoing help that this series has been published in the best possible condition. Thank you!

Last, but certainly not least, I want to thank all my loyal fans who have been enthusiastically supporting this series for four books in a row now. I wish I could thank every single one of you personally, but since I can't, let me invite you to a party in the principality of Bakavāsa! I'm sure Karim would be happy to welcome you.

CONTENTS

THE UNMENTIONABLE M

'For the last time, Sir: *when are we going?*'

'For the last time, Mr Linton – when the time is right.'

'And when will that be, Sir?'

'Soon.'

'How soon?'

'Quite soon.'

Across the miniscule carriage we were squashed into, I glared at my employer – to absolutely no effect. The perfect, chiselled face of Mr Rikkard Ambrose remained as stony and composed as ever, not a muscle moving. The only reaction I got was a look cold enough to freeze a volcano. Thank God I had developed immunity to frostbite after about a year in his employ.

'If you intend to pay your family a visit,' I explained for the umpteenth time, trying to keep my voice calm and patient and failing miserably, 'I need a date. That's what secretaries do. They ask their employers on which date they plan to do stuff, and then they write it down in things called "calendars" – look, like this little papery fellow I have here – so they can make all those pesky little arrangements their employers are far too important for.' *If you insert a 'self' before 'important', that is.* 'So, I ask again, Mr Ambrose, Sir: *when are we going?*'

His answer was the one he preferred to give in any and all circumstances: cold silence.

'Just one date. Come on. Just one measly little number.'

Silence.

'Do I need to get on my knees and beg?' Not that I would. I would sooner stab myself with my own pen. But I thought it might startle a response from him. Instead...

Silence.

'For goodness' sake! Why is it so difficult? It's just a date!'

He threw me another cold look. 'I am a very important man, Mr Linton. I have many demands on my time, and a lot of business to take care of before I can even think of leaving town.'

His left little finger made a nervous twitch.

And finally, it hit me. *Of course!* Why hadn't I seen it earlier? Slowly, a grin spread across my face. 'You're scared!'

'What? That, Mr Linton, is utterly ridiculous.'

'You're scared of your mother!'

His left little finger twitched again. 'I most certainly am not!'

'Ha! Liar, liar, pants on fire!'

'Not that it is any business of yours, Mr Linton, but my undergarments happen to be at quite a comfortable room temperature. I am no liar. I am, as I said, an important man. You cannot simply expect me to up and leave, merely because my bothersome relatives demand it. There is much important business–'

'Oh really?' I cut in, throwing him an innocent smile. 'Let's see what this "important business" is that you had to take care of during the last couple of days....' Crossing my legs, I leant back and started flicking through his calendar. 'Yesterday, a visit to the match factory to check the average sulphur content of medium-sized matches. The day before that, a visit to the East End warehouse to check the state of the building–'

'That was perfectly legitimate. There were important repairs needing to be done on that building.'

'There was *one loose shingle* on the roof.'

'You can never be too thorough. In my experience–'

I didn't let him finish. 'The day before that, we took a trip to that farm out in the country to check whether the furrows were straight enough for your liking. The day before that, we spent breathing smoke to determine the best plant for a tobacco plantation you might be planning to open *in two years*, once the land it's supposed to be on is cleared of forest, rocks, and the occasional mountain. The day before that–'

'All right, all right!'

He sent me another one of those looks meant to deep-freeze his conversational partner. I sent back another smile.

'You want a date? You can have a date. We'll leave the day after tomorrow.'

Yay! Victory! With effort, I resisted the urge to punch the air. With even more effort, I resisted the urge to punch him, which would have been much more fun.

'Our little excursion tonight will be the last piece of business I have to take care of before we leave. Tomorrow, we will pack, and you will make all the necessary arrangements. I expect you to be ready and waiting with an *inexpensive* coach in front of Empire House at six a.m. the day after tomorrow.'

'Yes, Sir!'

'Any delay in travel due to a lack of appropriate travel arrangement will be your responsibility, and I will deduct its cost from your wages.'

'Yes, Sir.'

'And no coachman will be necessary. Karim will be driving.'

'Ah. I should get a sturdy coach, then.'

To that, Mr Ambrose did not deign to give a reply, instead sinking back into the arctic fortress of himself.

Outside, street lamps whizzed by at a prodigious pace. It was too dark to see exactly where we were going, but since I knew we were heading east, there was relatively little chance that we were going to a spectacular ball or a thrilling theatre performance. Nothing good was ever to be found in the East End, unless you were looking for a good stab in the back or a good punch in the face.

Well, at least that was my opinion. But to judge by the light and laughter drifting from the three-storey house we were heading towards, other people had different views. A high-pitched shriek, followed by a giggle, escaped through one of the upper windows. A moment later, a bed started squeaking.

Turning to Mr Ambrose, I lifted an eyebrow. 'Just out of curiosity, Sir – what kind of "business" will you be conducting here tonight, exactly?'

When his dark eyes met mine, they were as unreadable as a coded dictionary at the bottom of the sea.

'Private business.'

No.

No, he wouldn't, would he?

Not while I was there? He wouldn't dare!

Of course he would. Mr Rikkard Ambrose would dare anything in the company of anyone.

But, on the other hand...

Again, a grin spread across my face. Mr Rikkard Ambrose might have no problems ignoring my presence and doing whatever the heck he wanted, but he would die before he would pay a woman for nothing but lying on her back all night. He found it galling enough to pay me, and I worked for him like a slave.

Secure in my knowledge, I leaned back in my seat. Nothing would happen. He would be perfectly safe.

And so, whispered a little voice inside me I did my best to ignore, *will your heart.*

With a squeal, the carriage came to a halt in front of the bawdy house.[1] Immediately, Mr Ambrose jumped out and strode towards the open door, and I followed, hesitantly. I had no particular desire to see this den of iniquity. The mere idea of women having to sell their bodies to men to survive made me shudder. I got enough of that feeling every morning when my sisters devoured the *Times* page with the wedding announcements. I didn't need any more of it.

But I was a world-class secretary, and so I stomped after my employer, although what I really wanted to do was set fire to the pants of every man within that building and paint 'Feminism Forever' in big, fat letters on the front door.

Inside, I was not greeted by the stench of chauvinism but by a mix of sweet-smelling perfumes. Flickering lamps on the wall illuminated a dingy salon, where hosts of unfortunate, fallen women sat on plush sofas, looking annoyingly content with their fate. As soon as they caught sight of Mr Ambrose, they looked even more content – like a cat who had just gotten a big, juicy mouse for Christmas. One of them actually licked her lips.

Hands off, ladies! He's mine!

The thought shot through my brain before I could help it, and I tried to stomp on it. But it was stubborn, and kicked back like a mule.

He wasn't mine. He wasn't.

He had been. Oh yes, he had been, once. Or twice. Or maybe three times? All right, maybe we had gotten a little bit carried away down there in South America. It had been even worse than that little escapade in Egypt. We had said things and done things that were hard to forget. But here in London...

Here it was even harder to forget that he was Mr Rikkard Ambrose, the richest, most powerful and most miserably miserly man of the entire British Empire, and I...

---

[1] Victorian expression for 'brothel'.

Well, I was Lilly Linton, his humble secretary, pain in the butt and *ifrit* extraordinaire.

Not that *I* harboured any delusions that he was above me. I knew perfectly well that I was worth just as much as any man, thank you very much. But I had my doubts that Mr Rikkard Ambrose agreed with that estimation.

I should just forget about him. I should forget what happened in South America, and Egypt, and in his office, and in that crate on that ship. And I would – as soon as all those bloody women stopped staring at him!

'Excuse me. Pardon me, Miss. Excuse me.'

Shouldering through the crowd – yes, a crowd had formed around him, and yes, it was exclusively composed of giggling females – I reached Mr Ambrose and latched onto his arm.

'Let's get this over with, shall we?' I suggested.

'By all means, Mr Linton.'

'What is this "business" you're here to conduct?'

'It is sitting over there.'

I glanced over – and my eyebrows rose. Where Mr Ambrose pointed, in a dark corner of the room, a smarmy little fellow with a hooked nose and bald head was sitting, smoking an opium pipe.

'Well, well, Sir. I never knew your tastes ran in *that* direction. Oh well, to each his own, I guess.'

Mr Ambrose threw me a chilling look.

'That, Mr Linton, is Mr Cox – the man whose shop I wish to purchase. He insisted on meeting here.'

I watched as a chubby woman slid onto the cushion beside Mr Cox and draped her arm around him. 'What a charmer.'

'Charm is not the issue here, Mr Linton.'

No, it wasn't. Money was. And I had been with Mr Ambrose long enough to instantly see why he had agreed to meet this little worm here. Mr Ambrose liked negotiating with people who were ravenously inhaling opium smoke. It made ripping them off so much easier.

'So...you really do have business here tonight? It's not just another ploy because you're scared of your mother?'

'Mr Linton?'

'Yes, Sir?'

'Stop. Saying. That.'

'What, Sir? That you have business here tonight?'

'No! That I am scared of my–'

He cut off abruptly and sent me a bone-freezing glare.

'Go on,' I encouraged him with a pat on the back. 'You can say it. It starts with "M".'

'Mr Linton?'

'Yes, Sir?'

'Be silent!'

'Yes, Sir. Right away, Sir.'

Mr Ambrose stalked off towards the sacrificial lamb that was to be slaughtered on the altar of Mammon. I followed, whistling to myself and trying to conceal my grin.

Mr Cox looked up when, only a few feet from his face, two lean, hard, black-clad legs came to a halt. His gaze met that of Mr Ambrose.

'Mr Cox.' That, and a curt nod, was all the greeting Mr Ambrose was willing to give.

'Ah! Mr Ambrose. Sit down, sit down.' He smiled at the plump woman and another female who had settled down on his other side. 'This, ladies, is the redoubtable Mr Rikkard Ambrose, who is going to make me a rich man tonight. Mr Ambrose, meet the Glamourous Gladys and... and Whatshername.'

Mr Ambrose gave the Glamorous Gladys a look. 'Leave. Now.'

I had never in my life seen a prostitute running so fast. It really was amazing how she managed it in that long dress, and while dragging her companion after her.

'Now what did you do that for?' Mr Cox protested.

'The business we have to discuss is confidential. This place is public enough without two eager ears listening in. People who sell other parts of their body will not hesitate to sell their ears and lips.'

Reaching into his tailcoat, Mr Ambrose half lifted something heavy out of a pocket and let it sink back again. I heard the tinkle of coins and rustle of banknotes. And so, to judge by the sudden light in his eyes, did Mr Cox.

'Now – to business. The ground plan to your shop, Mr Cox? The plans for the prototypes? You said you would bring them with you.'

'Oh yes.' The little man grinned. 'But be prepared. What I've got will change the world of mechanics as we know it. Are you sure you're ready?'

'I am afraid of nothing, Mr Cox.'

I cleared my throat. For some reason, my cough ended up sounding quite a bit like the word 'Mother!'

Without looking, Mr Ambrose stomped down on my foot.

He wasn't the only one who had noticed my little contribution to the conversation. Mr Cox looked up, eyeing me suspiciously.

'Who's that? I thought you said our dealings would be confidential.'

'This is Mr Victor Linton, my private secretary.'

Mr Cox studied my youthful, rounded features. As a 19-year-old girl, you might be able to pull off disguising yourself as a man – but you could never pull off making yourself manly. Slowly, his mistrustful expression changed into a grin of derision.

'A green lad, eh? You probably have trouble breaking him in.'

'You,' Mr Ambrose said in a very calm and neutral voice, 'have no idea.'

My mouth fell open in outrage. Mr Cox chuckled.

'Well, Mr Ambrose, I hope you don't take this the wrong way, but I don't particularly want our business discussed in front of a stripling like that, who's only just let go of his mother's apron strings.'

Mr Ambrose regarded me with a look that, if I hadn't known he was devoid of all emotion, I might have called self-satisfied.

'I don't either, Mr Cox. He's very new. Very unprofessional, at times, and takes too many liberties. But I can't send him back. The coach has already left.'

'Oh, that's no problem.' Mr Cox chuckled. 'Why don't we simply send him upstairs? I'm sure one of the girls would be all too happy to keep him entertained and make a real man of him in the process.'

My mouth was already open. But somehow I managed to unhinge my jaw and drop it another few inches.

Make a real man out of...

They couldn't mean what I thought they meant, could they?

But then I looked into the face of Mr Rikkard Ambrose, where 'revenge' was written in bold capital letters, and I realised: yes, they could.

'You know...' Mr Ambrose tapped his chin, 'I think that is an excellent idea.' He waved at me. 'Well, Mr Linton, what are you waiting for? Go ahead and amuse yourself.'

'You...you can't...'

'But no more than two or three girls at a time, no matter how much fun you might be having. We don't want you to overexert yourself, do we? Besides, prices here are quite steep.'

Before I could even think of an appropriate response to that, he made an imperious gesture with one single crooked finger. A slender arm slid around my shoulder, drawing me against something warm and soft.

'Hello there, big man,' a soft voice purred in my ear. 'My oh my...some lucky girl will have real fun with you tonight.'

A VALUABLE LESSON

Why me? Oh, dear Lord, why me?

That was the question I asked myself while I was skilfully and determinedly steered upstairs. The soft arm around my shoulder, it had turned out, belonged to the brothel madam. And while it was soft, it was also astonishingly strong and determined to make sure a potential client didn't slip away.

'No need to be nervous, lad,' she purred into my ear as she manoeuvred me down the corridor. I was dividing my efforts between trying to wrestle free and throwing venomous glares over my shoulder at the figure of Mr Ambrose. Neither seemed to have the least effect. 'I'll 'ave Amy take care of ye. She'll let ye do whatever ye want.'

Oh great! How about screaming and running away?

'And if ye're skittish, she'll take care of everythin'. Just lie back and relax, and she'll make ye scream.'

I don't doubt it! I'll scream bloody murder!

Still smiling, the brothel madam pulled open the door at the end of the corridor.

'Amy! Got a new gent for ye. This here is young Victor. Be gentle with 'im, will ye? It's his first time.'

And hopefully my last!

Gently but determinedly, the madam shoved me inside and closed the door. Immediately I whirled around, my hands going for the doorknob – but before I could reach it, I heard the scrape of a key in the lock. Bloody hell! The conniving little...

Well, I had to hand it to her: she was a good businesswoman. Even Mr Ambrose could not have handled a prospective client better.

'Victor, eh?' The voice coming from behind me was melodious, like a little bird sitting on a tree in spring. 'Well, ye certainly shall be the victor tonight. Why don't ye turn 'round and let me see yer handsome face?'

Taking a deep breath, I made sure that my belt buckle was tightly shut and turned around to face my doom.

My doom took the form of a small, slender young woman, probably only a year or two older than me, who regarded me with interest from a chaise longue in the corner. To my intense relief, she wore clothes. However, the big bed in the middle of the room suggested this happy circumstance might not be of long duration.

'I, um...Miss...'

'Amilia,' the slender girl whispered, her eyes twinkling. Was she laughing at me? 'But ye, young stallion, may call me Amy.'

Young stallion?

She *was* laughing at me!

Slowly, she rose from the chaise longue and started towards me. I retreated until I bumped into a corner.

'Now, err... look here, Miss. There's no need for that. We can just wait a little and go out again, surely? We don't need to...you know. I'll pay you anyway. I'll pay you anything you want!'

'That won't be no good.' She shook her head, her eyes sliding over me, assessing. 'Madam always knows if a customer ain't satisfied.'

'Trust me, I'd be a lot more satisfied if you let me sit quietly in a corner somewhere!'

'Oh, come on.' She gave a little laugh. 'Don't be shy. I'll take good care of ye and your little friend.'

'My *little friend*?'

'Or maybe 'e's big. Who knows?' She shrugged. 'Let's find out, shall we?'

And she reached for my trousers.

With a squeak, I jumped back – and slammed right into a wall.

'No! Let's not!'

'Oh, so ye're one of those who like the chase, are ye?' Her eyes sparkled, and she started towards me.

'No! No, I'm definitely not.'

'There ain't no reason to be ashamed. I'll be discreet.' And she leapt like a panther. Giving another squeak, I ducked out of the way just in time.

'No, please! You don't understand! You don't want to do this. I'm not what you think. I can't... I haven't...'

Her eyes widened in understanding. 'Oh dear.'

'Yes!' Relief flooded through me. Finally! She had understood. She had seen me for what I really was.

'Ye...ye are...'

'Yes.'

'...a virgin?'

What?

'Never dipped your wick before, 'ave ye, poor boy?'

No! No!

She gave me a smile that was probably supposed to be reassuring. 'Not to worry! Like I said, Amy'll take good care of your little friend. We'll start with something easy. Ye lie back, and I'll–'

I covered my ears with my hands just in time to prevent having to hear what exactly she planned to do. Not getting the message, she started towards me again. Frantically, I glanced from left to right – and suddenly spotted *it*. My way to freedom. My salvation. The window.

So what if we were two storeys up and I would probably break my neck? Desperate times demanded desperate measures. Leaping out of the reach of Amy the Terrible Temptress, I grabbed the window latch and wrenched it open. One thrust of my arm and the cold wind blew into the room through the open window.

'Stop! Remain where you are! Um...one foot nearer, and I, err... I plunge myself from the precipice! Yes, that's what I'll do! I'll plunge myself straight down, and my body shall be crushed out of the very form of humanity upon the stones of that courtyard, ere it become the victim of thy brutality!'

All right, maybe that was a little bit over the top. But it had worked for that girl in *Ivanhoe* backed into a corner by a lecherous Templar.

The girl frowned. 'Eh? What?'

'Stay the bloody hell away from me or I'll jump!'

'What?' Planting her feet a few feet away from me, the girl put her fists on her hips. 'Now listen 'ere, guv! I ain't that bad!'

'Oh. Um...I didn't mean to imply–'

'Just so you know, there's plenty a fellow who'd ask nicely and pay good money for a little romp with Amy!'

'I, err...am sure they would. It's just–'

'It's just what?' Her bright eyes bored into me like daggers, and suddenly she didn't look so much like a delicate songbird anymore. 'Ain't I pretty enough for ye? Someone 'as a pretty 'igh opinion of themselves here, eh?'

She started towards me, and before asking my brain about it, my legs started backing away. My hands rose pleadingly. 'No, it's not that. You're, um...quite pretty.'

Her eyes narrowed. 'Quite?'

'I meant to say very! Very pretty! Beautiful, in fact.'

'And ye don't think I'm ugly?'

'No! No, not at all.'

'Oh. Well, well.' Suddenly, she was grinning again. 'That problem's solved, then,'

And she leapt forward. Before I could move so much as a finger, she had me in her clutches.

'Aww,' she purred. 'Good, strong. Now, let's see...' And she reached for my crotch. Her fingers searched, once. Then twice. Then a third time. Slowly, her eyes, widening with shock, rose from my nether region to my face.

I did my best to conjure a smile.

'Surprise, surprise.'

~~**~*~*

'...and when we had all the gold loaded back onto the ship, we returned to London. And here's where I've been ever since, slaving away for His Mightiness, Ambrose the Miserly.'

Clearing my dry throat, I reached for a carafe of water on the bedside table and filled myself a glass. When I was done soothing my parched vocal cords, I looked over at Amy, and caught her wide-eyed stare.

'Ye...ye dressed up as a man to vote?'

'Yep.'

'And that man hired ye off the street as his...'

'His private secretary. Yes, he did.' I smirked. 'Though he was less than pleased when he found out that under my top hat, trousers and waistcoat I wasn't exactly the strapping young man he thought he'd hired.'

'But he kept ye. And ever since then, ye've bin gallivanting 'round the world with him, to Egypt and America and God only knows where!'

'Oh, I didn't see all of America. Just the South half. Argentina and Brazil, mostly.'

'And, of course, that's so little!' Amy shook her head, still staring. 'And under that getup, ye're really...ye ain't got no...you know.' Reaching out, she poked between my legs.

'Hey! Hands off! That's a restricted area.'

'Sorry. I just 'ad to be sure. 'ad to see whether you're really...you know.'

'I believe the word you're looking for is "female".'

She gave a little snort of laughter. Again, she let her incredulous eyes roam over my disguise. I had to admit, I was rather proud of it. I had come a long way since I first slipped into my Uncle Bufford's dusty Sunday best. I had bought my own clothes, with my own money. And quite nice ones they were, too, if I do say so myself.

'So ye've been running around behind yer guardians' backs for years, making money of yer own, in the company of men...'

'With my clothes on!' I reminded her.

Well, most of the time, anyway.

A giggle escaped her. 'I believe that! I ain't sure I could 'ave pried your clothes off ye with a crowbar! And all this time ye've been with 'im, ye've bin pretendin' to be 'is secretary?'

I raised my chin. 'I'm not pretending. I *am* his secretary.'

'But you squash yourself into a corset to 'ide yer boobies.'

'Ehem. Yes. I suppose I do that.'

'Bloody Christ!' Leaning back, Amy waved at herself, as if she was in danger of fainting. 'That's just...well, I don't know. I ain't got no idea what to say.'

I grinned. I had to admit, I was a tiny little bit pleased. I had never been able to brag of my exploits before, mostly because if my aunt learned of them she would rip my head off and pickle it in vinegar. This unexpected chance to share my experiences with a fellow victim of the patriarchy did give me quite a little bit of an ego boost.

'Wait!' Snapping her fingers, Amy suddenly shot straight again. 'Scratch that! I do know what to say! Bloody 'ell, yes I do. Or rather, I know what to ask.' She turned towards me with an evil grin. 'Ye've left something out.'

I blinked at her. 'I have?'

'Ain't no good playin' the innocent with me, missy! I know all the dirty tricks. So, out with it! What's goin' on between the two of ye?'

I managed to blink at her innocently, while inside, my stomach did a somersault. 'Going on? Why, he pays me for keeping his calendar in order, and filing his papers and–'

'Don't ye take me for a fool, missy!' Amy grinned. 'I know there's bin more exchanged between the two of ye than files and folders! Ye're sweet on 'im.'

My ears heated. Damn! 'No, I'm not! There's nothing between us! Nothing!'

'Nothin'...?'

I cleared my throat. My ears grew even hotter. 'Well...'

'Ha! I knew it! Ye've got it bad!'

'No need to overexaggerate. There might have been one or two instances...'

'One or two?'

'All right, maybe more than two.'

'Or maybe more than a dozen?'

I sent her a stern look which she answered with a cheeky grin. 'Instances of what, exactly?'

My eyes flicked to the door. Was it possible the madam could have had mercy on me and unlocked it by now?

Amy noticed the direction of my glance, and shook her head, her grin widening. 'No chance, missy! Ye ain't going nowhere before I know everythin'.'

My gaze was drawn to the window.

'Don't ye dare try!' Amy threatened. 'I'll drag ye back by yer hair.'

I believed her. Damn!

'We...kissed.'

'Ha! I knew it.'

'Repeatedly.'

'Ha!'

'Don't get me wrong, I didn't *plan* to! Not at all. Rikkard Ambrose is the most disgustingly chauvinistic miser on the surface of this earth. I would never have...could never have...well...it just sort of...happened.'

Amy patted me on the shoulder. 'No need to worry. I understand.'

My face brightened. 'You do?'

'Of course! I saw 'im from the gallery earlier. If I'd been workin' for a man who looks like that, I'd have seen to it that things "sort of happened" sooner or later, too.'

I threw her another glare, which she completely ignored. Instead of looking at me, she was staring into space, and had a contemplative expression on her face.

'So, tell me,' she mused. 'What 'ave ye done to catch 'im?'

I blinked. 'Catch him?'

'Of course! God, are ye daft? Ye don't let a man like that get away!'

'You don't?'

'Of course not!'

I met her gaze, and as I did, I realised she was right. I didn't want to let Rikkard Ambrose go. I didn't know what I wanted from him, exactly, but I knew I couldn't let anyone else have him. The mere thought made me want to strangle the world.

So...there was only one thing left to do: get him!

A tentative smile tugged at my lips. Who said it was only men who could chase women? I was a feminist! I could do anything I bloody well wanted. And I wanted him. He was mine! He just didn't know it yet.

Squaring my shoulders, I leant towards my co-conspirator. 'How do I catch him?' I enquired. 'With a net?'

She gave me a queer look. 'Ye ain't got much experience in chasin' men, do ye?'

'Of course I have! Plenty!'

'Aye?'

'In chasing them away,' I admitted, grudgingly. 'It always seemed the much more sensible option.'

She gave an evil little chuckle. 'It is, mostly. But in this case...'

'Yes.' I sighed. 'I know.'

'Has he said anythin' that tells ye he wants ye?'

'*Said anything*? You do realise you're talking about Mr Rikkard Ambrose, don't you?'

'Stubborn one, is he?'

'You can say that again!'

'Aye, well...' Rubbing her hands, she, too, leant closer until we were huddled together, the perfect little feminine conspiracy, ready to take over the world. 'We'll have to do something about that, then, won't we?'

Reaching into the bedside table, she pulled out a book with a plain black cover. When she let it fall open on her lap, I saw it was a book with illustrations. Lots of illustrations. And not the kind you'd find in children's books.

I stared, my eyes going wide.

'Good God! That man...is he...is that his? And how is he able to bend...? And her...Holy moly! She can't really be...'

Amy grinned. 'Practice makes perfect.'

I swallowed. She patted me on the back. 'Listen up, and listen closely, because we ain't got much time. I'm gonna tell you some things. And then, I'm gonna show you some things. And when ye and him are alone next time in a nice, quiet place...' She winked. It was the lewdest and most brilliant gesture I had ever seen.

'Then I cast my net?' I guessed.

'Ye won't need one. The best way to catch a man is to make him want to get caught.'

~~**~*~*

Forty-five very educational minutes later, I came down the stairs, just as Mr Ambrose was rising from beside the prone, opium-drugged figure of Mr Cox, signed contract in hand.

'Ah. There you are, Mr Linton.' He regarded me as if I were a chastened lap-dog. 'And? Was your tryst...entertaining?'

'Oh yes.'

'I trust you learned your lesson?'

'Oh yes.' Somehow, I managed not to smile an evil smile of anticipation. But it was very hard. 'I certainly did.'

THE ART OF IMAGINARY ELOPEMENT

As per my instructions, I began my preparations for leaving early next morning. First on the list were my dear relatives. When I told my aunt I was going away for a couple of weeks to visit distant cousins, she jumped with joy. Well, maybe that was overstating it a bit. She didn't exactly jump – more wrinkled her nose and gave me a 'why aren't you gone already?' look. But she certainly didn't object to my going. It was the middle of winter, after all, and all the eligible bachelors she planned to marry me off to were holed up in their comfy country estates, and wouldn't venture out into cold, old, rainy London Town until the beginning of the Social Season in April. So, if right now she couldn't get rid of me permanently, why not at least get rid of me for a while?

Loving relatives are such a comfort to a girl.

Whistling a merry melody, I started packing. Nothing much, really. Unlike most women, I didn't have to drag around whole crates with different dresses, bonnets and perfumes. I just packed what every elegant, modern young lady should have: my favourite books, two pairs of trousers, two shirts, a waistcoat and tailcoat, a corset for squashing my non-existent cleavage, a gun and a big bag of cartridges. The latter two I deemed particularly important. I had heard a little bit about Mr Ambrose's family, and so had gone out to purchase the necessary equipment. It was always better to be prepared.

But there was one thing I couldn't pack – because I didn't have it yet. A thing I'd only recently learned about last night.

Going down into the drawing room, I got some linen, thread, scissors and a needle out of the sewing basket, and settled myself down to work. I wasn't really an expert with needle and thread, but it couldn't be that difficult, could it? Let's see...

Approximately five minutes later, my blasphemous cursing attracted the attention of my little sister, Ella.

'Lill, what is the matter, are you – oh! You're trying to sew?'

'Yes, blast and damn!'

She gave me a warm sisterly smile. 'I'm so glad you're finally finding an interest in lady's work. I was worried about you, always running around saying you wanted to vote and work and God only knows what else. It isn't healthy to excite yourself like that, you know.'

I could have answered 'Oh, I've been working for nearly a year now, as a private secretary to a business mogul with whom I travel around the world. And did I mention we regularly get shot at by nasty business rivals?' But I didn't want to give my dear little sister a heart attack, so I simply made a noncommittal noise.

'How are you doing?' she enquired, peering over my shoulder.

'Bad! Worse! Worst! Worse than worst! The bloody things won't stay still when I stab at them, and the needle isn't nearly big enough.'

'How about if I help you a little?'

I gazed up at my little sister, unashamed pleading in my eyes. 'Would you? I wouldn't normally ask, but I have to get this done before I leave tomorrow morning.'

'Of course! What are sisters for? Let's see what you're making, shall we?'

Oops. Maybe this hadn't been such a good idea after all.

Slowly, Ella raised the long, tube-like linen objects to the light. She looked puzzled for a moment – then smiled. 'Glove fingers? Gloves! You're making gloves! How wonderful.'

'Errr...' I cleared my throat. 'Yes. Gloves. Absolutely.'

'But they can't be for you, can they? Whoever they're for must have really big fingers.'

'No, they are most definitely not for me.'

'All right. Let's see...Ah, there's the problem. Your stitches aren't regular enough, you see? You have to do it like that...and like that...and that.'

The next few minutes were spent in companionable silence while we sat and worked together – or, Ella worked while I made noises of applause and approval. Finally, we were finished, and Ella regarded our work with pride. But suddenly she frowned, and that confused expression returned to her face.

'Wait a minute, Lill...if those are for gloves, where are the pieces for the front and back of the hand?'

'Well, um...'

'And why are there thirty-two fingers?'

I smiled to myself. 'Let's just say I'm hopeful.'

~~**~*~*

'Away for *weeks*?' Eve stared at me aghast. 'But we wanted to stage a protest in Hyde Park next week! Don't you remember? We've already started to paint the signs, and Flora has been working for months on building up the courage to ask her mother to let her come!'

'I know, I know.' I hung my head. 'But I can't make it. I promise, I'll be back in time for our demonstration during the general election, but I have to leave for now. Something came up.'

'What?' Eve demanded. 'What could possibly be more important than this?'

'That's what I'd like to know, too,' Patsy chimed in. 'How can you forsake us in our hour of need?'

'I'm not. Honestly, I'm not. I'm just asking you to postpone your hour of need a little bit.'

'And why, exactly?' Patsy was relentless. 'What is so important that you have to forsake your friends, your principles, all that makes your life worth living?'

Not all. There's so much more you don't know about...

'I, um...have to take a little trip up north.'

'A *trip*?' I could almost see the steam rising out of Patsy's ears. 'You're forsaking us for a *holiday*?'

'No! Of course not!' Whatever my journey north would be – a holiday wasn't it. Mr Rikkard Ambrose would see to that. 'I would never! It's more...well...some important matter I have to take care of.'

Three pairs of suspicious eyes bored into me. Then, suddenly, Eve gasped, and her eyes widened in understanding.

'Of course! A trip north. Why didn't I see it right away?'

'See what?' Patsy demanded.

But instead of answering her, Eve turned to Flora. 'Flora – in those books you like so much, what is the only reason girls ever travel up north to Scotland?'

Flora blinked, taken aback – and then, suddenly, her eyes widened, too. 'Oh no!'

'Oh yes!' Triumphantly, Eve turned back to me. 'Our Lilly is eloping!'

My mouth dropped open.

'*What?*' The word that came out of Patsy's mouth was half harpy's shriek, half blood-thirsty warcry.

'Ooooh yes.' Eve was practically hopping up and down with excitement. 'Our Lilly has found herself a paramour, and she's going to run off with him, and they're going to travel all the way up the big north road to Scotland, you know, that little village right on the border called Gretna Green[2], where you can get married no matter where you're from or how old you are, and your parents or guardians can't do anything about it! And it's gonna be a big scandal, and she'll be infamous, and all of the people in the street will point at her and say "See? That's the girl who ran away!" and we'll be infamous, too, because we're her friends! And her aunt will throw herself from the rooftop because of the shame

---

[2] The southernmost village of Scotland, and first to reach via the great northern road. Due to its location, and because marriage in Scotland could, up until quite recently, be easily performed by any Scotsman you met on the street without any legal matters or paperwork to take care of, it was a popular place for runaway English couples to get married.

– oh, that will be great fun! – and her uncle will forbid her to ever come into his house again, and it will all be so exciting!'

Flora's eyes went even bigger. 'R-really? Lilly is going to run away with a man?'

'She's been corrupted by the insidious influence of patriarchy,' Patsy pronounced, sinisterly.

'Oh! That's so romantic.'

I had listened open-mouthed up to that point, but now it was high time to intervene.

'Now wait a minute, everyone.' I raised a hand. 'I most certainly don't plan to–'

'Romantic? No, it's not!' Patsy talked right over me, rounding on Flora. 'How can you say such a thing? Lilly is forsaking her friends, her life's work...and for what? For a man?'

'For love!'

'Love! Bah!' Patsy gave a snort like a knight's charger. 'Love is nothing but an illusion, a myth perpetuated by the patriarchy to gain women's willing co-operation for the slavery that is marriage! Oh, that I have to watch my best friend fall into that most insidious of masculine traps...'

'I'm not!' I protested. 'I swear I'm not!'

'...I can hardly bear the shame,' she continued, completely ignoring me. 'It is a black day for the feminist cause. A black day indeed.'

I tried a few more times to convince them that I was not being swept off my feet by a ravishing rake and carried to an impromptu altar in the wild north of Scotland – but to no avail. Patsy simply didn't listen, continuing to bemoan the loss of her best friend and the blow that was to the feminist cause. And as for Eve and Flora – they looked so crestfallen whenever I tried to convince them that I was not, in fact, eloping with my secret paramour, that I didn't have the heart to disabuse them.

Why try, anyway? I couldn't very well tell them the truth. Tell Patsy that I was going north with a man who regularly paid me money for accompanying him and had taken me for a nice little visit to a whorehouse yesterday? Yep, that would be just great. Mr Ambrose wouldn't survive the day. I could see the headline now: *Businessman stabbed to death with sharpened parasol. Investigation ongoing.*

So why not just let them believe the horrifyingly romantic hogwash? They would realise the truth as soon as I came back without a ring on my finger.

Unless...

I stomped down on that thought before it could go anywhere. Unless nothing! Nothing whatsoever! I didn't have time to think about unless. I had work to do.

After a day filled with packing and organising, I said my final goodbyes to my family and friends that evening. Patsy was still outraged, but instead of punching me, she simply tried to hug me to death. Eve and Flora did a lot of giggling and squealing, and insisted on giving me an endless stream of wedding advice – quite impressive, considering that neither of them was actually married. Ella cried and clung to me and made me promise to write as often as I could buy, borrow or steal paper and ink. My other sisters, Gertrude, Lisbeth, Anne and Maria, were far less effusive in their affections for me, the former two because they didn't like to show them, and the latter two because they didn't have any. Aunt Brank gave me another 'why aren't you gone already?' look, and dear old Uncle Bufford...

Well, he didn't actually come out of his upstairs study, so I had no idea what his reaction was. But I'm sure he gave at least a friendly grumble into his beard. The two of us had started to get along quite well since I'd informed him I didn't need him to pay me an allowance anymore.

Finally, I went to bed, expecting to get a good night's sleep before my big trip tomorrow – but no such luck. The moment my head touched the pillow, a million pictures, possibilities and unanswered questions started to rise up inside me.

Mr Ambrose opening his watch, a noble family's crest engraved upon the lid...

Mr Ambrose and Lord Dalgliesh shaking hands like they wanted to break each other's bones...

The Ambrose family name in an edition of Burke's Peerage...

Years and years of letters from Mr Ambrose's mother – all unanswered.

There was too much unanswered all around. Questions, especially. Why this distance between Mr Ambrose and his family? Where did the enmity with Lord Dalgliesh stem from? What in God's name was the name of the very much self-made businessman Rikkard Ambrose doing in Burke's Peerage? And, most importantly: what would happen once Mr Ambrose and I were ensconced in the carriage, all alone, huddled close together on our way up north?

The mere thought made my heart dance a galop.

One thing was for sure: the north held answers. About Mr Ambrose. About me. And maybe, just maybe, about the two of us together.

That was my last thought before, finally, darkness claimed me and I drifted off to sleep.

The next morning, I got up on tiptoes at the ungodly hour of five a.m. and was about to sneak downstairs so I wouldn't wake anyone – only to find Ella and my three best friends all waiting to ambush me at the back door. Phew, was I glad I hadn't changed into my tailcoat and trousers yet!

'You didn't really think we'd let you slip away without a last goodbye, did you?' Ella demanded, tears shimmering in her eyes. Throwing her arms around me, she pulled me close. 'Safe journey, Lill! Do you have everything? Warm woollens? Something to eat on the road? Your gloves?'

'My glo– oh.' I cleared my throat. 'Oh, yes. I have my, um, gloves.'

'Well, whoever they are for, I hope they fit well.'

I felt my ears grow hot. 'I certainly do so, too.'

'And when you're back, you'll tell me everything, all right?'

'Well...maybe not *everything*.'

Patsy chose that moment to shoulder Ella aside and enfold me in a vice-tight grip. 'It's not too late! You can abandon that fool of a man and come to your senses.'

I gave her a sad little smile. 'No, I don't think I can.'

Patsy gave me another hug, and a grim pat on the back. 'Nice knowing you.'

Next I was engulfed by the squealing whirlwind that was Flora and Eve. It went on like that for quite a while – Patsy uttering curses against the patriarchy, Ella sniffling into her handkerchief, and Eve and Flora showering me with their best wishes for my health and happiness, which earned them a few confused looks from my little sister. I hugged everyone at least three times, and when I finally had gotten Patsy to let go of me, I hurried down the street, trying to tell myself that, no, those were *not* tears threatening at the corners of my eyes. It had simply rained on my face at some point during the day, and I hadn't noticed up until now.

~~**~*~*

Ten minutes later, I stood in Smithfield Market in Clerkenwell, London, beside the most rickety, uncomfortable, and, most of all, cheapest rental carriage within the entire United Kingdom of Great Britain and Ireland. In front of the coach stood a team of four horses, led by the irritable old nag that had drawn Mr Ambrose's chaise since I could remember. I had changed in the garden shed before setting out, and now wore my usual tailcoat, pinstriped trousers and peacock vest. And I was stomping my feet, profoundly wishing I was wearing more. It was freezing outside, the winter chill biting into me from all sides, snow and slush spattered all over my trousers.

And do you want to know why I was out here, freezing my butt off? Why I wasn't already in the coach and on my way?

Yep, that's right: Mr Ambrose was late. Mr Rikkard 'knowledge is power is time is money' Ambrose was *late*!

'Blast him!' I managed to get out through my chattering teeth. 'Blast him all the way to hell and back! All this because he is afraid of his mo–'

'Yes, Mr Linton?' came a cool voice from right behind me.

I shut up.

I swallowed.

Slowly, I turned around and faced him. He was standing there, not a speck of snow on his impeccable black trousers, his cold eyes glinting as if he were the Prince and Supreme Ruler of this frozen world.

'You're late,' I told him.

Reaching into his pocket, he let his watch snap open. 'Six a.m. precisely. Your watch must be fast. Kindly correct this deplorable imprecision.' And without another word, he stepped past me into the coach. A set of heavy footsteps approached, and there was Karim, Mr Ambrose's personal bodyguard and beggar-deterrent. The huge Mohammedan gave me his customary greeting – a sinister look and a growl – and swung himself up onto the box, gripping the reins.

'What are you waiting for, Mr Linton?' Mr Ambrose called from inside. 'The road awaits!'

Squaring my shoulders, I straightened, and stepped towards the carriage with a smile. *You have no idea. The road isn't the only thing that awaits you...*

SOUTH AND NORTH

'So...where does this family of yours live, exactly?'

'In the North.'

I gave him a look. 'I had surmised as much from the fact that we're travelling on the Great Northern Road.'

'Indeed?'

'Yes, indeed, Sir.'

I waited for more. Nothing came. Nothing but the pictures my own imagination could conjure up. In the beginning, from the moment Mr Ambrose had first hinted he came from the North, I had always pictured some ice-cold, windy Scottish castle on top of a cliff, with no glass in the windows, and an underground vault filled with a life's worth of hoarded treasure. However, when I had voiced these theories, Mr Ambrose had looked at me as if I were a particularly repellent cockroach and informed me coolly that he had not and did never intend to live in Scotland, that he was a one hundred per cent English gentleman and did not appreciate my suggesting anything to the contrary.

Of course I didn't believe a word. The man had to be Scottish! He had to be! He hadn't bought new underwear in over ten years. If that didn't scream 'Highlander', I didn't know what did.

Still, it was a sensitive subject, so it might be best to proceed with caution.

'Okay, let's start crossing off possibilities,' I murmured. 'Do your parents live in a castle?'

'No.'

'A palace?'

'No.'

'A townhouse?'

'No.'

'A henhouse?'

No answer.

'Ah. So a henhouse it is, then.'

Mr Ambrose raised his gaze from the papers he had been studying. 'They do not live in a henhouse, Mr Linton. They live in...' A muscle in his cheek twitched. It was over and done with in a fraction of a second, but I saw it all right. Oh yes, I did. '...in a manor in the country.'

I casually leant closer, and enquired, 'In which part of Scotland?'

A moment of silence.

A long one.

'Mr Linton?'

'Yes, Mr Ambrose, Sir?'

'You know perfectly well that they do not live in Scotland! For the last time, I am not Scottish, and neither are they, and the same applies to my grandparents and their parents before them.'

I raised an eyebrow. 'That's what you say. I still doubt it's physically possible for anyone to be as stingy as you are if they don't have at least a drop of Scottish blood running through their veins.'

'I resent that implication, Mr Linton.'

'Indeed, Sir?'

'It is perfectly possible for an Englishman to be as frugal, prudent and economical as any Scotsman.'

'If you say so, Sir.'

With a cool look, he returned to studying his papers. I, for my part pulled out a book I had acquired as a little light reading for the journey: *The Stingy Scotsman – One-thousand Hilarious Jokes.* It really was hilarious reading, particularly if, like me, you had a pencil with you, and busied yourself replacing the words 'a Scotsman' with 'Rikkard Ambrose'.

This led to some quite interesting results...

What is Rikkard Ambrose's recipe for tomato soup? Heat a quarter gallon of water, and then fill it into red bowls.

Or how about this one:

Rikkard Ambrose accompanies a friend to the doctor. The doctor tells him, 'Your friend needs fresh sea air to get well again.' Mr Ambrose is very concerned, so the very next day, he gifts his friend with a free treatment: a full-time, unpaid job in his fishmonger business.

Another one on the great value of a wonderful friendship:

Mr Rikkard Ambrose's friend is dying. Rikkard Ambrose kneels beside his bed and gently takes his hand. 'Anything I can do for you? Any last requests?' His friend points towards the table next to the bed, where a meal is prepared. 'J-just one bite of that cake....please...' Mr Ambrose shakes his head, sternly. 'Now, really! You know very well that's for the funeral reception. I can't waste money buying another one.'

Or, a sweet, romantic one:

Why would Rikkard Ambrose love to marry on February 29? Because then he'd only have to pay for an anniversary gift every four years.

And my current favourite:

At an auction, a wealthy lord announces that he has lost his wallet containing £10,000 and will give a reward of £100 to the person who finds it. From the back of the crowd, Mr Rikkard Ambrose calls, 'I bid a hundred and ten!'

'Something funny, Mr Linton?'

Glancing up, I saw Mr Ambrose was staring at me – and only then did I realise I had been giggling.

'Um...no, Sir. Nothing. Nothing at all.'

'Indeed?'

A blast of cold wind hit the carriage, and I drew my tailcoat tighter around me. Bloody hell! This carriage was about as warm and comfortable as a can of sardines. But I should be glad that Mr Ambrose agreed to rent a carriage with a roof for the journey. It had taken quite some time to convince him that being caught in the middle of a snow storm in an open chaise wasn't a good idea.

Well, as long as it was cold, why not use it to my advantage?

Putting aside my book, I rose. Mr Ambrose showed no sign of noticing that I was moving until I settled myself down on the other bench, right next to him.

'Mr Linton!'

'Yes?'

'What are you doing?'

'Keeping warm, Sir.'

'Keeping wa–?'

His voice cut off abruptly as I leant against his hard, muscular side and snuggled into his warmth. Amazing how a man with a heart of ice and face of stone could be this warm.

'Mr...Linton...'

'Mmmmh?'

'I...you...'

I slid an arm around him, pulling him close, and his words drained away. I snuggled closer, revelling in his warmth, and a few minutes later, the world followed his words, slipping away into nothingness.

~~**~*~*

'Mr Linton?'

'Mmmm...'

'Mr Linton!'

''ts not time to get up yet, Ella... Let me sleep a little longer.'

'Mr Linton, wake up! We have stopped.'

Blinking, I yawned, dragging in cool winter air. The cold revived me a little – but only a little. Getting up at five a.m. was showing its effects. It was only then that I realised my head was resting in Rikkard Ambrose's lap. I blinked up at him.

'Oh. Hello there.'

'Good afternoon, Mr Linton.' He nodded to me. His body was as stiff as a board. 'Your head is lying on my papers. You are obstructing my view.'

'Then why didn't you wake me earlier?'

'I...' A muscle in the side of his face twitched, and I realised that he had one arm around my waist, holding me against him. He, too seemed to suddenly notice that and let go as if I were on fire. 'I cannot have you sleep-deprived. I need you at your full capacity when we arrive.'

'Oh. That's it, is it?'

He slid out from under me, letting my head thud onto the bench. 'Yes.'

'I see.' Groaning, I sat up straight and pulled the blinds partly aside. 'Why have we stopped?'

'The horses need rest. And the rest of us have certain business to take care of, too, I believe.'

I stared at him. 'Here? You want to hold a business meeting out here, in the middle of the country on the Northern Road? Mr Ambrose, dedication to work is all well and good, but this-'

'Not *business* business, Mr Linton. A...well...another kind of business.'

I stared at him for a few moments – but then, when the full feeling in my lower regions started to call attention to itself, I got it.

'Oh! Oh, I see.'

'Indeed.'

I stared at him. '*You* have to pee?' I asked, morbidly fascinated. I had always assumed he lived on the smell of money alone and had no digestive organs.

He gave me a cool look. 'I have to fulfil the same bodily functions as any other adult male.'

'And you're planning to do it here?' I glanced out of the window again. Outside, it was snowing heavily, and the wind was howling. 'Bloody hell! You'll be lucky if you don't freeze off your-'

'Finish that sentence the wrong way, Mr Linton, and it will cost you a week's wages.'

' – fingers.' I threw him a grin. 'Well then, good luck.'

'Good luck yourself, Mr Linton. You're going first.'

I blinked at him. 'You're not serious.'

'When and how exactly have I given you the impression that I tend to joke?'

'But...aren't we stopping at an inn, later?'

'No. It's a ten- to twelve-hour drive up to the North, well manageable within one day. Why waste money on an inn if we don't have to?'

'Because...how to put this delicately...no matter how often you call me "Mister", there are still a few anatomical differences between me and the average man, differences which make relieving myself while standing rather difficult. So if you don't want me to greet your mother in wet and smelly trousers, we should definitely stop at an inn.'

'Oh.'

The expression on his face was priceless. I tried my best to disguise my grin – but failed. He couldn't get out of the coach fast enough. As soon as he'd left, I fell over, collapsing in hopeless giggles. Minutes later, when Mr Ambrose returned to the coach and ordered Karim to start driving, I was still smiling. God bless the female bladder! I had no intention of driving all the way through to the North in one go. Oh no. I had plans that involved me, Mr Ambrose and a cosy little room at an inn somewhere, where we could huddle together and....

Well, you get the picture.

~~**~*~*

'There! There, do you see? I see lights right up ahead. That has to be an inn.'

'I suppose so.' Mr Ambrose gave me a cool look. 'And you really can't manage the last twenty miles or so?'

'You don't want to see – or smell – what happens if I try.'

'Indeed.' Mr Ambrose slammed his cane against the roof. 'Karim? Stop at that inn!'

It was early evening and the sun had just begun to set as we drove into the inn's courtyard. Through curtains of falling snow, I saw the landlord and a maid standing at a window, their noses pressed against the glass, staring out at us with eyes as big as saucers. They probably didn't get many visitors up here this time of year, and even fewer who were being driven around by a big Indian with a turban on his head.

'Karim?'

At Mr Ambrose's call, the big Mohammedan slid off the box, landing in the snow with a dull thud. A moment later, he appeared beside the blind-covered window. 'Yes, *Sahib*?'

'Go ahead and see if they have a room free, and if everything is secure.'

'Yes, *Sahib*.'

And he was gone. A moment later, I heard the front door of the inn squeak, and all chatter inside ceased immediately as the huge sabre-bearing bodyguard stepped inside. There was a moment of silence during which you could have heard a pin drop, then Karim's gravelly thunder of a voice proclaimed: 'My master has arrived. You there, fat man – you have a free room for him. If not, make one free *now*.'

You had to love Karim. He was simply so nice and sociable.

'I shall search this building now. Anyone harbouring malicious intent against the *Sahib*, make your peace with your God!'

And the door slammed shut.

I raised an eyebrow at Mr Ambrose. '*Check to see if everything is secure*? Right smack in the middle of the United Kingdom?'

'I have my reasons.' And I noticed that his hand hovered just over the place where he usually carried his gun.

Holy moly! What kind of family reunion is this going to be?

'The estate,' Mr Ambrose said, very slowly and precisely, as if he had to force every word out, 'of Lord Daniel Eugene Dalgliesh is only a few miles away from that of my parents.'

Oh.

That piece of information would have been kind of nice to have earlier. Like, for instance, before I nagged him into coming here?

Too late now, Lillian. You dug your own cesspit, so you'd better jump in.

Karim reappeared before the window. 'Everything secure, *Sahib*. I have spoken to the fat man with the apron and secured accommodations for you and–' he threw a look at me '–and your companion.'

'You didn't waste money on more than one room, did you?'

'Certainly not, *Sahib*. They only have one free room in any case. The others, the fat man tells me, are full of winter supplies. They were not expecting guests.'

'Then where will you sleep?' I demanded. Sharing a bed with Mr Ambrose was one thing, but Karim and his beard was where I drew the line!

Karim straightened to his full height, puffing out his chest. 'In the stables. I am strong and resilient and do not fear to suffer in Ambrose *Sahib*'s service.'

And he strutted away, very satisfied with himself for freezing his toes off and in the process saving his employer a few pence.

'Come on.' Gripping the door, Mr Ambrose pushed it open, letting snow swirl inside on a gust of cold wind. 'Let's go, Mr Linton.'

And, leaping down into the snow, he started toward the inn, his long legs eating up the distance fast. Grabbing my suitcase from the top of the carriage – of course, Karim had stowed away Mr Ambrose's luggage and left mine to soak in the snow – I hurried after him.

Inside the inn, we were greeted by a collection of patrons frozen solid into statues, all staring at the giant Indian who was standing guard next to the door, glaring at them as if any of them might draw a dagger at any moment and rush towards Mr Rikkard Ambrose. They didn't seem to me to be very intent on doing any rushing – except maybe out of the room. But nobody dared to move. Ale dropped from half-raised mugs. Somewhere in the background, a tea kettle whistled in shrill protest.

Mr Ambrose let his gaze wander over the assembled crowd – then turned away without a word, facing the innkeeper.

'One room. One night. No food.'

'Ah, um...yes, Sir.' The innkeeper fumbled with his apron. 'Your man already explained your requirements.'

'Adequate. Oh, and my employee here needs to use your facilities. If you would have a servant show him the way...'

'Certainly, Sir! I'll call Tom and–'

The innkeeper cut off as, suddenly, there was a movement in the small crowd of patrons. At the very back, an old man leant forward, frowning at Mr Ambrose – then suddenly, his eyes went wide, and he shot to his feet.

'No! It can't be! Master...Master Rikkard?'

Plans Gone Awry

'Master Rikkard?' The old man stepped towards us, staring. Karim made a threatening step forward, his hand on the pommel of his sabre, but Mr Ambrose held him back. His gaze was riveted to the old man as if looking at a ghost. His face twitched, breaking his usual cold mask. 'Elsby?'

'It *is* you, Master Rikkard!'

He started forward with arms outstretched as if to hug – yes, hug! – Mr Rikkard Ambrose, but then he realised that all eyes in the room were on him. His gaze flicked from the other patrons, over me and Karim, to Karim's sabre, where they stayed for a long, long moment.

He froze.

'Ah yes.' In an instant, Mr Ambrose's face smoothed out, and he was back to his cool, impenetrable persona. 'Let me introduce you. Karim, Mr Linton – this is Charles Elsby, my father's steward. Mr Elsby, this is Mr Linton, my private secretary, and Karim, my bodyguard.'

'Um...charmed.' Elsby's gaze was still on Karim's sabre. Slowly, he raised his eyes to those of the Mohammedan and gave him a weak smile. Karim didn't smile back.

Finally, Elsby's gaze returned to Mr Ambrose. Swallowing, he took another step forward – and stopped. It seemed like he had much to say and no idea how to say it in front of so many people and one very sharp sabre.

'Making the rounds of the tenant farms, I suppose, Elsby?'

'I was.' Taking a deep breath as if he'd just come to a decision, the old man stepped towards the door. 'But not any longer. I'm heading straight home to let His Lordship know you're coming.'

My ears pricked up. His Lordship? Not Lord Dalgliesh, surely!

Hopefully?

Please, please, please?

'I hardly think that is necessary.' Mr Ambrose's voice was a whip of biting ice. Elsby flinched, but then squared his shoulders and opened the door.

'Begging your pardon, Master Rikkard, but oh yes, it is.'

And with that, he left the inn, shutting the door behind him. A few errant snowflakes that had fluttered inside drifted to the ground, where they melted instantly. Mr Ambrose didn't melt. He just stood there, frozen like a block of ice – then suddenly whirled around and marched across the room and up the stairs. Somewhere above, a door slammed hard.

For a moment or two, utter silence reigned in the common room. Finally, the landlord stepped forward with a kettle in hand and a desperately hopeful smile on his face.

'Um... hot tea, anyone?'

~~**~*~*

I took some time to empty and refill myself. The inn not only had decent lavatories, but, astonishingly, decent cooking, too. True, I had to pay for both out of my own pocket, but so what? I could afford it. And besides, I had some time to kill. I couldn't go upstairs yet. I suspected Mr Ambrose needed some time to himself.

After three helpings of roast ham, I finally put my fork down, nodded at the landlord and started upstairs. The inn was quiet, any sound from outside dampened by the softly falling snow. Our room was at the very end of the corridor, far away from any prying eyes and curious ears. I hesitated in front of the door, Amy's words echoing in my mind.

And when ye and him are alone next time in a nice, quiet place...

Was it time?

I wanted him. Was here and now the right time to take what I wanted?

Bad Lilly! You saw how upset he was! You can't coldly and ruthlessly take advantage of him in a situation like that just to get what you want, can you?

Of course I could. I had learned from the best, after all.

I took the last few steps to the door. When I cautiously cracked it open, I expected Mr Ambrose to be asleep or pouring over his papers as usual, but he was doing neither. Instead, he was marching in circles, his back ramrod straight, every step like a punch to the poor wood floor.

The door slid shut behind me.

All right. If I wanted to make my move, now was the time. We were alone in his room together. It was a cold winter night. And with the state he was in right now...

Watch carefully, I heard Amy's voice whisper in my ear. *Wait. And when the time has come, when he's weak and defenceless – pounce!*

I licked my lips. Now was time. I had to pounce! Now! I had to pounce, now!

So why wasn't I pouncing?

Damn! Why hesitate, Lilly? Do it already!

But he just looked so...so alone. So terribly alone.

Well, go and do it! He won't feel alone once his clothes are off, and you and he...

Wouldn't he?

I glanced away from him. As if by magic, without asking my permission, my legs carried me over to the bed and I slid under the thin blanket, fully clothed. Shivering, I curled up into a ball. Out of the corner of my eye, I glimpsed Rikkard Ambrose: he was standing in front of the window now, his arms behind his back, his posture as stiff as a rod of iron.

I felt a tug at my heart.

Dammit, Lilly! Your heart is not the part of your anatomy you wanted to focus on tonight.

I couldn't help it. I was forgetting all about my insidious seduction plans for the night.

Finally, he unfroze from his post at the window and silently moved towards the bed. Another tug at my heart – he was being quiet because he didn't want to wake me. Mr Rikkard Ambrose being thoughtful? Impossible! And yet...

Stiffly, he lifted the other end of the blanket and slid into bed.

Now! Now's your chance. Jump him! Make him see you. Make him want!

Instead, all I did, was whisper softly into the darkness: 'Feeling a bit restless?'

He gave a little jump as he realised I was still awake. For a long time, no reply came. Then...

'Yes.'

I bit my lip. 'Nervous about seeing your family again?'

'Yes.'

It was on the tip of my tongue to ask why, to demand answers to all my questions, or better yet, demand that he take his clothes off and let me ravish him.

Instead, I simply turned towards him and, reaching out into the dark, found his hand.

For a moment, he stiffened like a spring under tension – then slowly relaxed under my touch. Oh, how I wished it wasn't so dark. What I wouldn't give to see his eyes right now...

'Don't worry.' The words seemed to be pulled from my mouth without my knowing how or where they came from. 'I'm here.'

His grip on my hand tightened. 'I know. I...'

'Shh.' Sliding over, I snuggled up against him. 'No words. Just... I'm here. Always.'

The last thing I felt before sleep claimed me was his arm sliding around my waist, holding me close.

~~**~*~*

Light. Bright, white light. That was the first thing I saw when, with all my might, I managed to drag up one eyelid the next morning. Yawning, I rolled over. My hand reached out – only to find that I was alone in bed. From downstairs, I could hear a familiar cool voice barking orders, and smiled into the cushion.

With another yawn, I pulled myself up and slid out of bed, padding over to the window on unsteady feet. The sight that greeted me took my breath away.

Out there lay a winter wonderland. Over rolling hills and high-rising trees lay a sparkling blanket of snow, painting everything in an angelic white. The sun, peeking through the trees at the horizon, was just beginning to tinge the land in a faint hue of gold. A deer stuck its head out of the forest, blinking in the morning light – then dashed off across the fields, leaving its tracks on the virgin snow.

Daring. Wanting to leave its mark.

I smiled.

'Mr Linton?' came a familiar voice from downstairs. 'Mr Linton, I know you're awake! Stop wasting time and get your posterior down here. We're leaving.'

My smile widened.

'Coming, Sir!'

And I was. Whatever dangers awaited us out there in the cold – we would face them together. Grabbing my suitcase, I took just enough time to straighten my clothes in the hope it wouldn't be quite so apparent I had slept in them, then exited the room and started down the stairs. When I arrived in the common room, the innkeeper was just trying to persuade Mr Ambrose to stay for breakfast.

'But Sir, you can't go to Battlewood this early! His Lordship and Her Ladyship won't even be up yet.'

'They'd better be,' was Mr Ambrose's curt reply. 'I didn't travel all this way for nothing.'

'Sir! I don't know who you think you are, but this is the Marquess and Marchioness Ambrose we are talking about! You can't simply appear on their doorstep at this ungodly hour of the morning!'

'Oh, I can't, can't I?' Reaching out, Mr Ambrose shoved the fat little man aside. 'Mr Linton?'

'Right here, Mr Ambrose, Sir!'

'We're going. Come!'

The innkeeper had gone very white in the face. 'A-Ambrose?'

I gave him a pat on the head in passing. 'I don't think the marchioness will mind terribly if we're a bit early. Mothers usually like it when their sons come to visit.'

And I followed Mr Ambrose outside into the sparkling snow.

The coach was waiting for us, freed of snow, all four horses ready and waiting, and Karim standing next to them like an extremely large, extremely bearded watchdog. He held open the coach door for Mr Ambrose, then slammed it shut so I had to open it again myself. Ah, the manners of a true gentleman...it was a wonderful thing to experience. Simply wonderful.

The moment the door shut behind us, Mr Ambrose slammed his cane against the roof. 'To Battlewood!'

And despite the beautiful winter world around us, I couldn't help feeling the name of the place would turn out to be an omen.

We rolled out of the yard, and, glancing back, I saw the landlord standing in front of the door, surrounded by a gaggle of servants and curious guests, wildly gesticulating after us. Over the rattle of the carriage wheel, I could just hear the words 'Ambrose' and... 'air'?

Were they complaining about the cold air?

No. Not 'air' I realised with a sudden, chilling certainty. 'Heir.'

Slowly, my eyes wandered over to Mr Ambrose, sitting stiff as a poker on the other bench. Not just a son, then. *The* son.

Silence reigned all around as the coach whizzed through the winter wonderland. Sparkling crystals of freshly fallen snow whizzed up into the air on either side, surrounding us with a glittering halo. Soon, the path we were travelling on was engulfed by a tall, proud forest, interspersed with beautiful clearings and glittering, frozen lakes. Game abounded everywhere, deer and rabbits poking their heads out of the trees right and left. Dear God... did all this country belong to his family?

Finally, the forest opened up and we rolled out onto a broad, snow-covered meadow on the other side of which stood a low stone wall. In its centre, a tall cast iron gate rose towards the sky. And in front of the gate, ready and waiting, stood old Elsby, a younger servant slouching against the wall behind him.

The moment they caught sight of the coach, Elsby took a deep breath and the young servant jerked up, as if right up until then, he hadn't believed anyone was actually coming.

'Move, boy!' The old man gave his young companion a whack. 'Get the gate open! And then run up to the house and tell Her Ladyship that our guests are here. Master Rikkard has come home!'

The gate swung open, and we rolled up the driveway. The coach came around a bend, and another. Finally, I caught sight of smoke rising in the distance. Chimneys! We were approaching the house. Slowing down, the coach rolled around a final bend and...

Oh, dear merciful Lord!

(Motherly) Love

What sort of house would you expect Rikkard Ambrose to have grown up in? Something massive and austere, maybe. Something like Empire House, where all the walls were bare grey stone and the only decorations were the skid marks of busy feet on the hard floor. But *this...*

Battlewood Hall was a palace. There simply was no other way to put it. A palace.

On either side of a portico held up by six tall Corinthian columns, the wings of the house spread out like those of a giant eagle. Colonnades ranged along both wings, interrupted only by the glitter of glass where a winter garden dared to boldly rise out of the snow, defying the winter's cold with its lush green vegetation and beautiful, colourful blossoms. The wings of the Hall stretched around a wide courtyard, in the centre of which rose a sculpted fountain bigger than any I had seen in London. In summer, I was sure, it would have been spraying sparkling jets of water in every direction. In winter, laden with snow, it rose towards the sky like the world's largest, most beautiful ice sculpture.

Figures were arrayed before the entrance. As the coach rolled closer, I could see that most were clad in the uniforms of footmen and chambermaids. The line of servants stretched for at least thirty yards. On the stairs in the shadow of the portico, I glimpsed a figure in a familiar pink dress, and beside her another, slimmer, taller figure with her raven hair falling in wild curls down her back.

'Ho!' with a rumble, Karim reigned in the horses and, driving a half-circle around the frozen fountain, came to a halt directly in front of the line of servants. White glitter sprayed up, giving several of the footmen a sugar coating.

One of the servants – presumably the butler – stepped forward to open the door of the carriage, but then he caught Karim's look, and retreated quicker than Napoleon at Waterloo. Turban raised proudly, Karim marched to the door and pulled it open.

'*Sahib?*'

'Why, thank you.' Giving him a broad smile, I slid out of the coach. 'So kind of you.'

Karim muttered something in a language I – and thankfully everyone else, too – did not understand. Ignoring him, I stretched, breathing in a lungful of fresh air and eying the staff who, in turn, were regarding me with wagonloads of veiled curiosity. I heard whispers, too low to understand but loud enough to send a shiver down my back.

The looks, the whispers – it all stopped the instant the door of the coach creaked behind me and Rikkard Ambrose stepped out into the open in all his chiselled, austere beauty. His face was as impassive as ever. He surveyed the scene in front of us as if he was looking at a cheap two-storey pub in the East End of London. Deadly silence reigned.

'Who is in charge here?' he demanded.

A man in a butler's uniform that looked ten times as new and shiny as Mr Ambrose's tailcoat tentatively stepped forward, clearing his throat.

'Mr Elsby, as steward, is the highest-ranking member of the staff, My Lord. But I handle most of the day-to-day running of the house. I'm the butler. Hastings is my name, My Lord. Welcome home. May I introduce the staff to you?'

'No,' Mr Ambrose told him. 'And do not call me "My Lord".'

'Um...'

'Karim will show you where our luggage is kept. I expect everything to be in my room and unpacked in ten minutes maximum. There are some very important papers I must go through before noon. Understood?'

'Y-yes, My Lor– Your Lo– Sir. Yes. Definitely, Sir.'

'Adequate. Come, Mr Linton.'

And we strode past the line of now openly gawping servants, towards the portico. The two figures waiting in its shadow now moved for the first time, shifting, leaning forward. I looked up and, yes, it was indeed her. Samantha Genevieve Ambrose, the mother of Rikkard Ambrose and mistress of this house. Although the tall, raven-haired young woman standing beside the little lady in the pink dress looked far more like she was in charge than her mother.

His sister.

Mr Ambrose had a sister. And a mother. And a father, too, if things had worked the normal way when he had been brought into this world. It was still a difficult concept to wrap my mind around.

The marchioness stood there on the top step, trembling, hardly able to stand still. My heart ached for the mother clearly desperate to enfold her son in her arms. The instant we were past the servants, she rushed forward, down the steps, straight towards us, and threw her arms around–

–me?

Sweet, innocent little me! What had *I* done to deserve this? And what was I supposed to do now? I hadn't been hugged by any creature that was remotely motherly since my own mother had died when I was five years old! Panic shot through me. What in God's name should I do? How did one respond to a motherly hug? I hardly doubted that the response I gave when hugged by my friends – a pat on the back and a friendly jab with my parasol – would be suitable in this situation. Anyway, I didn't even have my parasol, and I was being engulfed in all this warm, soft, motherly pinkness and...and... oh, what should I do? Where should I put my hands? And what, oh what had I done to deserve this?

'Thank you!' she sobbed into my peacock vest. 'Thank you for bringing my son home.'

Oh. That. Right.

'I have legs and a brain, Mother,' came a cool voice from outside the cocoon of pinkness that engulfed me. 'I can move without Mr Linton's assistance.'

Letting go of me – *Thank you, merciful God! I'll start going to church again!* – Lady Samantha whirled on her son and stabbed an accusing finger into his gut. 'What took you so long?'

'I had business in town to conclude. I–'

Not letting him finish, she threw her arms around him, too, smothering his words with motherliness. 'Oh, Rick, I...I can't believe that finally...!'

He stiffened, disapproval practically oozing out of his ears. 'Marchioness! You forget yourself.'

'Don't you marchioness me, boy! You are my son, and I am your mother. Oh, thank the Lord you're finally back again! We're going to hold a big ball in honour of your return. Everyone will know that the heir of Battlewood, my son, has returned.'

He tried to squirm out of her grip, but Lady Samantha seemed to possess supernatural strength when in mother mode. Her slim arms remained firmly fixed around him. 'That's really not necessary, Mother. I don't think that–'

'Poppycock! This house hasn't seen a proper feast for over a decade! And who else deserves a celebration if not my only son? Besides, it'll be Christmas soon. Who doesn't celebrate Christmas?'

Mr Ambrose opened his mouth – presumably to start listing people who didn't, beginning with him – but was cut off when his mother pulled him into another hug.

I was so busy staring, I didn't realise someone else had approached me until that someone cleared her throat. Glancing up, I noticed the tall, proud, black-haired girl standing in front of me with a chagrined expression that she clearly had to work hard to maintain.

'Mr Linton, is it? Mother told me what you did,' she murmured. 'How you helped her get through to my brother. I'm sorry if I came off a bit...gruff during our first meeting back in London.'

I smiled at her. 'No problem. Confident, strong-minded women are the future of this world.'

She blinked. 'You really believe that?'

'Oh yes.'

'What a refreshing change to meet a man with sense for once. You and I,' she declared while, behind her, her brother was trying to pry free of the tentacles of the Pink Mother Kraken, 'are going to be great friends.'

Turning to the servants she clapped her hands. 'All right! Have the doors opened, Hastings. Everyone inside. Mr Linton, let me introduce you to the staff, since my brother thinks himself too high and mighty to bother.'

We started up the stairs, surrounded by a gaggle of servants. I glanced back once at Mr Ambrose, who still seemed to be wrestling with an overdose of motherly affection, and wondered whether I should go rescue him. But he was a big boy. He could take care of himself. Probably.

'Well now...let's get the introductions out of the way – first of all my own, since I neglected introducing myself the first time we met. My name is Lady Adaira Louise Jannet Melanie Georgette Ambrose. But since I don't want to give you a headache, Lady Adaira will be fine. Now, as for the staff...Elsby and Hastings you've already met, I believe. This is Sally, along with her fellow housemaids, Ethel, Grace, Edna and Mabel. Then we have the parlourmaids, Ada, Cora, Jennie and Daisy; the chambermaids, Kathryn, Eva, Jennie – not to be confused with the other Jennie! – and Frances; the footmen, Jack, Oscar, Willie, Roy, Reginald and Allen; the second footman, Albert; the first footman, Floyd...'

Soon, my head started buzzing with names, and I didn't even try to pay attention anymore. It was hard enough to hold on to any of their names, let alone all of them. What did it matter if I was a little inattentive in regard to the servants? It wasn't as if this was life and death situation, right?

Boy, was I ever wrong.

'...and this is Marsden, who will be attending to your personal needs.'

Screech! Halt! Complete and utter brain stop! What did she just say?

'Um...' I cleared my throat. 'Attending to my personal needs?'

She gave me a smile. 'Yes. While you're our guest, he'll be your valet.'

'My valet. As in...the man who will help me dress every morning and undress every evening?'

'Yes.'

I glanced at Marsden, an older, friendly-looking man with a bald spot on his head and a slightly vague smile on his face. I didn't think he was prepared for what would pop out when he helped me undress in the evening. And to be honest, neither was I!

'I, um...don't think that will be necessary, really. I, err...am very self-sufficient. Besides, I am not really a guest. I am part of the staff myself. I should stay in the servants' quarters.'

'Aww! Do you hear that?' Suddenly, Lady Samantha was beside me, squeezing my hand. 'Such a nice, modest young man! Wherever did you find him, Rick?'

Mr Ambrose muttered something that sounded suspiciously like 'in the madhouse.' His mother ignored him, instead smiling up at me.

'Really, Mr Linton, you must think of yourself as a guest. Without you, this reunion would never have happened.'

'Very true,' came Mr Ambrose's cool voice from behind us. Everyone ignored him.

'I won't hear of you staying anywhere else but with the family,' Lady Samantha was telling me, patting my hand. It made me feel oddly warm and squishy inside. 'I won't force Marsden on you if you're used to getting along on your own, but you'll be in our second-best guest chamber, right next to Rick.'

Oh? So I'll be right next to Rick, will I?

I smiled. 'That sounds like an excellent arrangement.'

Behind me, Mr Ambrose muttered something too low to understand. Maybe it was better that way.

~~**~*~*

Once I'd seen my room, I decided that fate had to be in a good mood right now. It was a palatial place with a king-sized four-poster bed, damask curtains, wood panelled walls decorated in gold and silver, and, most important of all: a connecting door to the rooms of Mr Rikkard Ambrose. *Without* a lock.

A fact which he, happily, hadn't noticed so far, being far too busy with aggressively *not* answering his mother's questions about life in London.

Fifteen years!

I couldn't imagine being a mother. But if I were, and if my child were away from me for that long...

I shuddered.

What on earth could have happened?

I had no idea. But I knew this much: it had been something bad. I saw it every time tears glittered in Lady Samantha's eyes or she stumbled over words and suddenly broke off in the middle of a sentence. I saw it every time her daughter bit her lip in anger and held back irate comments. And I saw it in the big, empty hole that was left by the person who wasn't even there to greet Mr Ambrose: his father.

Lady Adaira and her mother did their best to conceal it, dragging him into the drawing room and peppering him with endless small talk, which he icily ignored, but after an hour or so it was becoming painfully obvious that his father had no intention of coming down. Mr Ambrose didn't demand to know what was going on, didn't question the servant about whether his father was out riding – but he did stand up and march to the window that overlooked the stables. Sure enough, there, in front of the place where both horses and coaches were kept, lay smooth, untouched snow. And it hadn't snowed since last night. Nobody was out. His father was in the house.

The muscles in Mr Ambrose's jaw tightened.

Hours dragged by. We sat in tense silence, waiting for a royal summons. I exchanged nervous glances with Lady Samantha while Lady Adaira muttered unladylike things under her breath, and Mr Ambrose got colder and colder, harder and harder, with every passing minute. Finally, Hastings the butler descended from upstairs and, approaching Mr Ambrose, bowed.

'His Lordship is ready to receive you now, Sir.'

'Indeed?' Mr Ambrose's face didn't show a spark of emotion. It was a mask of cold stone, with not a crack anywhere in sight. 'But I am not. Pray tell his Lordship that *I* shall be ready to receive *him* in half an hour. I shall await him in the small green drawing room.'

And with that, he turned and strode away, leaving the butler standing openmouthed.

My fingers clenched into a fist, and I couldn't suppress a grin. *Bravo! Show him!*

My warm glow of pride lasted about as long as it took me to glance at Lady Samantha's face.

The day didn't exactly get better from there. Mr Ambrose didn't show up for lunch, and neither did his father. In a weird way, it made sitting at the huge table in the dining room feel almost like home: all the ladies gathered around the table, with the male population of the house off stewing in their rooms somewhere.

More time passed, and dinner arrived. Once more, the three of us gathered around the table, trying desperately not to stare at the empty seat at the head – that is, until Mr Ambrose strode in and sat down in it.

'That is father's chair!' Lady Adaira exclaimed.

Mr Ambrose met her eyes, coolly. 'He doesn't seem to be using it, does he?'

'Yes, but–'

'Besides,' Mr Ambrose continued, his gaze hardening, 'are you so sure the chair truly belongs to him?'

He held her gaze for a moment – then she looked away.

What was that all about?

I was dying to ask, but didn't dare.

Dinner was – surprise, surprise – a rather tense affair. Mr Ambrose sat there, practising his master craft of silence, while we raw beginners sat around and somehow, while saying not a word, didn't manage to be nearly as silent as he was. Every breath he took seemed to suck sound and warmth from the air, and Lady Samantha was looking more miserable with every second.

I didn't understand this! From the bits and pieces I had heard, whatever had happened to separate the family, it hadn't been Mr Ambrose's fault, had it? This was so infuriating! I wanted to go up there and shake some sense into the old man who didn't swallow his pride to welcome home his son.

Plus, if the marquess thought that Mr Ambrose would be the one to swallow *his* pride, he hadn't reckoned on two things:

1.   The size of Mr Ambrose's pride relative to that of his throat.
2.   The infrequency with which Mr Ambrose opened his mouth for any reason, including swallowing.

'It has been a long day.' Shoving away his plate, Mr Ambrose rose to his feet. 'And I still have much work to finish. If you will excuse me, Mother, Lady Adaira, Mr Linton.'

'No, wait–' Lady Samantha reached out, but too late. He was already gone. She slumped in her chair.

Adaira stared after him. 'He called me *Lady* Adaira. What has he been feeding on since he left home? Ice cubes and starch?'

'Mostly,' I sighed. 'But currently, he's on a diet of gravel and cobblestones.'

Adaira, who had just taken a sip out of her glass, nearly sprayed its contents all over the table.

'Don't you laugh!' Lady Samantha admonished her daughter. 'This is no laughing matter!'

Coughing, Adaira shook her head. 'I disagree. Because you have just two options: you can either laugh or cry about it. I mean, honestly! The two are behaving like children! And over what? Only–'

Lady Samantha shook her head. 'You were too young back then. You don't remember how it was.' She shuddered. 'I'll never forget that night as long as I live. If only...'

By this time, I was quite ready to grab someone by the throat and start squeezing, yelling: 'Just tell me already! Tell me what is going oooon!'

But I was a gentleman – or at least dressed up as one. So, instead, I said: 'Some more tea, Lady Samantha?'

'No, thank you.'

She looked so despondent, the words slipped out of my mouth before I could help it: 'Isn't there anything I could do?'

Abruptly, her head rose. 'Well...yes, there is, actually.'

'Oh?' I hadn't reckoned on this.

'I know I'll be able to talk my husband around eventually. I just need time – but I'm afraid I don't have it. Rikkard...when he was younger, he was such a sweet, patient boy.'

Oh he was, was he?

'But the man who has come back today...I hardly recognised him. I don't think he would wait. Not for me. Not for his father. Not for anyone.' She threw me a pleading look. 'I just need a little bit of time. Could you distract him? Come up with something – papers to sign, news to read, anything – that would keep him distracted for a few days so he doesn't think about leaving?'

'Well...I don't know...'

'Please. I just want my family back together again.'

Her blue eyes looked so helpless, so pleading...

Damn!

'All right. I'll see what I can do.'

'Oh, thank you, Mr Linton!' Reaching over, she grabbed my hand and squeezed it. 'You're the best of men!'

'Trust me, I am many things – but not that.'

And with a small smile at the two women, I rose and left the room, on the tracks of Mr Rikkard Ambrose. I found him, or rather the sound of his marching feet, in his room. Every step hit the floor like the crack of a whip. I sat in my room and listened while he punished the floor for things he couldn't punish anyone else for, dark things in the past that I didn't know anything about. What an unusually unproductive waste of his time. Especially when I could think of much better things for the two of us to do.

He was stuffed full to the brim with tension right now – and I knew just the way to release it. Besides...I had official permission, didn't I? His mother had asked me to distract him. So distract him I would. Only, maybe not quite the way she'd had in mind.

Smiling to myself, I sat by the window and watched the sun go down while I waited. Finally, the footsteps in the other room subsided, and silence reigned. He had gone to bed.

It was time.

Rising to my feet, I crept over to the door and, like any upstanding rake bent on despoiling his innocent victim, peered through the keyhole. It was dark on the other side. I could just make out a shadowy figure standing beside the bed, then raising the covers and sliding in.

Oh yes. Relax. Close your eyes. Say goodbye to your innocence. Tonight is the night.

I waited, listening until his breathing had calmed. Slowly, my hand wandered over the wood until it found the knob and twisted.

Click.

Biting my lip, I waited with bated breath for a reaction – but none came. I breathed out. Slowly, excruciatingly slowly, I began to push the door open. It slid open silently, as if on the wings of dark angels. Taking a deep breath, I stepped into the room.

34

As soon as I entered, I felt the cold. Not metaphorical cold from Mr Ambrose – oh no, this was real and tangible. The window was thrown open, letting in gusts of arctic air. Cold moonlight spilled across the room. And there, right in the middle of the bed, his back to me, lay Mr Rikkard Ambrose, his hands opening and closing convulsively as if he were dreaming of strangling someone. But he wasn't dreaming. He was still very much awake.

'Damn him!' he growled. 'Damn him to hell!'

Stepping up to the bed and slipping in behind him, I pressed close. 'Who?'

'What the–!'

He moved so fast I didn't even have time to blink. In an instant, he had thrown himself around, one of his hands suddenly encasing both my wrists in a tight grip, his free arm above my throat, about to crush down, his heavy body pressing me in the mattress.

I had to say, apart from the imminent throat-crushing, I wasn't at all averse to the situation.

'Mr Linton!'

'Hello to you, too, Sir,' I croaked.

The pressure on my throat eased. 'What are you doing here?'

I smiled up at him, sweetly. 'It seemed wasteful for us to be using two such big beds when we would both fit easily into one. So I thought I'd do a bit of economizing.' Leaning up, I brushed my cheek against his. 'It's much more comfortable like this. Don't you agree, Sir?'

A muscle in his rock-hard jaw twitched. 'Mr Linton! Be serious. This isn't about economy.'

'True. It's also about warmth. For some reason,' I glanced at the wide-open window, 'It seems to be unseasonably cold in here. We could share a little warmth, just like in the coach. There's no harm in that, surely.'

His sea-coloured eyes flared. 'More harm than you might think. You're playing a dangerous game, Mr Linton.'

'No, Sir.' I let the smile slide from my face and bared myself. Looking straight into his eyes, I let him see everything. Who I was, why I had come here, and what I wanted. 'I'm not playing at all. I...I need warmth. I've needed it for a long, long time. And I think you need it, too.'

He opened his mouth, but no sound came out.

'Well, Sir?'

'If...' He cleared his throat. 'If you need warmth, I'll light you a fire.'

Stretching up, I once more brushed my face against his, letting my lips slide in a gentle caress over his cheek. 'A fire won't warm me. A furnace won't warm me. But you will.'

And instantly, his eyes, cold as the ocean floor a moment ago, burned with blue-green fire. Heat flooded over me. Then cold. Then heat again. I shivered, and it was not from the long-forgotten open window. His face began to lower towards mine.

'Mr Linton...'

Tearing my arms free of his grip, I placed a gentle finger on his lips, cutting him off.

'For the next few hours,' I told him, my voice low and demanding, 'you are not allowed to call me "Mister".'

And, taking hold of him, I pulled him down to claim his mouth with mine.

The Not So Silent Storm

I did it.

I kissed him.

I kissed Mr Rikkard Ambrose. And the moment my lips touched his, all the fantabulous advice Amy had given me about how to do it well, how to draw a man in, just flew right out of my mind. It felt like our very first time – like a first kiss was supposed to feel. Soft, and hesitant, and you still can't quite believe that this is happening, that he wants this as much as you do, but he does, and he's here with you, and he's kissing you, kissing you, kissing you until all the breath is gone from your lungs.

His arms wrapped around me like irons and he lowered himself down, pinning me to the mattress, answering my kiss in a silent shout of *Yes! Yes!* that roared out the window and echoed from the snow-clad hills. For a few precious, blissful moments, we weren't two people desperately searching for something, we were one, and we were warm inside.

Then, suddenly, his mouth was torn from mine. Panting, and blinking into the suddenly empty darkness above me, I was, for a moment, unable to move or even think.

'Why?' Rolling around, I saw Mr Ambrose at the utmost end of the bed, crouching like a predator, ready to spring. But...away from me, or towards me?

'Why? You really have to ask me that?' His eyes were in shadow, but I could see them glitter, see them burn. Fire and ice mixed together, each as deadly as the other. 'After what you just did? God! If you touch me one more time, I won't be able to stop myself!'

Slowly rising on my hands and feet, I scooted towards him. 'Who says you have to stop?'

That muscle in his jaw was beating a staccato rhythm. He was close to the edge. 'I do!'

I was almost there. Almost with him. 'Why? It's not as if we haven't done much more than this before.'

Suddenly, the cold mask of his face cracked, and through the gap, I could see the naked truth underneath. 'Yes! Yes, we have. But...'

But.

I knew exactly which 'but' he meant.

But that had been on another continent, a world away from England, with its rules, regulations and gossiping mouths. *But* that had been in wild exotic places, so far away, so very unreal.

This, on the other hand, was very real. As real as it could get. We were in the middle of civilisation, in a palatial mansion, surrounded by people who knew our names. We were in his parents' home, for heaven's sake! If we did this, was there a way back for us?

I didn't think so.

So there was only one thing to do.

I lunged forward. Grabbing a fistful of the hair at the back of his head, I pulled him towards me and kissed him. Kissed him hard. Kissed him until there was no tomorrow.

And he?

He kissed me back with ten times the force, a hundred times the need! Kissed me as if he lived for me instead of money. It was a nice thought to have, no matter how unlikely. When we finally broke apart and lay there, staring into each other's eyes, I didn't know what to say. But he did.

'My little *ifrit*...'

A grin spread across my face. 'Have my flaming wings impressed you?'

Reaching out, he stroked my cheek with the tips of his fingers. 'They have, nearly as much as the fire inside you.'

How could it be that here, in the cold and the dark, suddenly, poetry flowed from the lips of the master of silence?

Because he's never been silent for you, Lilly.

My fingers tightened in his hair, and I moved towards him. 'Well then...prepare to be burned!'

His eyes held mine with an iron grip. 'So, you have plans for me, Mr Linton?'

I froze.

Mister Linton?

I had warned him about that.

You want to know whether I have plans for you? Well...right up until now, I had. But after what you just said, there's been a little plan change.

Tightening my grip even more, I pulled his face down towards me. 'I told you,' I whispered, 'Tonight, you are not allowed to call me that!'

'Indeed?'

'Oh yes, indeed, Sir.' Closing the distance between us, I brushed my lips against his in the lightest, most terribly teasing of kisses. He groaned. 'You know what? I think it's time I gave you a little lesson.'

He cocked his head. 'Oh yes?'

'Yes. Nothing difficult, don't worry. I won't overtax your talents.'

Iron and ice flashed in his beautiful eyes, and I felt his grip tighten on me. 'There's nothing you can teach me!'

'Really? How about a little onomastics?'

He froze, blinking up at me. 'Pardon?'

'Onomastics. The science of names.' Moving my mouth to his ear, I whispered, 'Say my name, Sir. Go on.'

'Y-your name?'

Had Mr Rikkard Ambrose just stuttered?

'Yes. My name. And I don't mean "Victor".' My lips caressed his earlobe, making him tremble. 'Say my *real* name.'

Silence. That was all I heard from him. Utter, unbreakable silence.

'Say it,' I encouraged. 'Say my name.'

Again – silence.

'What?' I baited, gently biting his earlobe. 'Afraid?'

His muscles hardened, his hands clenching around me. His lips moved – but still, no sound came out.

'*Lillian*,' I whispered into his ear. 'Try it. It's easy. Just three syllables.'

He was breathing heavily. I could feel him tremble above me. To anyone else, it might seem laughable. Ridiculous even. Why be this upset about a bloody name?

But I understood. This was about reality. About the real me – which, up until now, he had never allowed himself to see. If he did this, if he truly acknowledged who and what I really was – a girl in his arms – and, more importantly, what I was *to him*, then there would be consequences. Rikkard Ambrose was a real man. A man who dealt in cold, hard facts and unshakable decisions. Once he acknowledged me, acknowledged *us*, there would be no turning back.

In the moonlight, I saw him wet his lips. He swallowed once, hard. Then he parted his lips.

'*Lillian*.'

The word was a whisper, a cool breath against my skin.

Sighing, I pressed myself into him, feeling a tug in my chest. 'Again.'

'Lillian.' His arms tightened, and he pulled me so hard against him it was almost painful. But I would rather have died than protested. 'Lillian!'

Suddenly, he pulled back far enough so he could see me. His eyes were searing into me with cold fire. 'Now you! Say my name!'

'Of course...' Grabbing his face, I pulled him back towards me until his ear was once more beside my lips – and smiled, wickedly. '...*Mr Ambrose, Sir.*'

A half-growl, half-laugh erupted from his chest. In an instant, he had rolled me over and claimed my mouth, saying with silence what he was not yet ready to say with words.

~~**~*~*

I didn't need to use any 'glove finger' that night. We were too busy kissing, too busy revelling in the newness of it all, whispering our names to each other and lying in the darkness, to think of the possibilities beyond.

Sometime during the night, we fell asleep in each other's arms, until...

Knock, knock, knock.

'Sir?'

'What is it, Mr Linton?' Mr Ambrose mumbled.

'Err...' I blinked in the morning sunlight flooding in through the open window. 'That wasn't me. I didn't say anything.'

'*What?*'

Knock, knock, knock.

Both our heads snapped around to the door, where the sound was coming from. 'Sir?' called a female voice from outside. 'The marchioness thought you would be exhausted after a day like yesterday. She asked me to bring you breakfast in bed. May I come in?'

'No!' Mr Ambrose barked. Swiftly, he threw a blanket over me and shoved me off the bed. I landed on the thick carpet with a thud.

'Oomph!'

'Sir?' The voice from outside sounded worried now. 'What was that noise?'

'Nothing,' Mr Ambrose stated, as cool as a cucumber, and shoved me under the bed. 'Absolutely nothing.'

Thank you so much for the compliment!

'May I come in now, Sir?'

'Yes, you may. What is for breakfast?'

From inside my white cocoon, I heard footsteps enter the room. Then followed a scrape, as if from the lid of a breakfast tray being lifted. 'Bacon, eggs, kippers, sausage, baked beans, fried tomatoes and mushrooms, black pudding, toast and pork chops, Sir.'

'I see. And for whom did the marchioness intend that breakfast, me, or a starved regiment of the British Army?'

'I believe Her Ladyship's exact words were "He's a growing boy and needs to eat", Sir.'

'Indeed?'

'Yes, Sir.'

'Tell the marchioness that I ravenously devoured every single morsel. You're dismissed.'

'Yes, Sir.'

I waited with bated breath until the door had slid shut with a click, and I heard footsteps receding down the corridor. I waited, and waited – then they were gone. Finally! Struggling free of the blanket, I stuck my head out from under the bed and gazed up at Mr Ambrose, who was just busy buttering a small piece of toast.

'You know,' I panted, 'now that we finally agree on my gender, I think it's time we work on your gentlemanly behaviour towards ladies.'

He placed a slice of kipper on his toast. 'Indeed?'

'Oh yes, indeed, Sir!'

I didn't have a chance to instruct him, however – because, at that very moment, I heard a noise through the connecting door. And not just any kind of noise: a knock. Apparently, Mr Ambrose wasn't the only one who the marchioness thought deserved a breakfast in bed this morning. Crap!

Jumping to my feet, I nearly fell flat on my nose because I'd forgotten my feet were still wrapped in the sheet. Struggling and cursing, I hopped to the connecting door and pulled it open.

'Um...is something the matter, Sir?' came the hesitant voice of a maid from outside.

'Nothing! Nothing whatsoever! Wait just a minute, I'm... I'm...well, just wait!'

'Certainly, Sir.'

I struggled free of the sheet and hurled it behind a screen in the corner. Slipping into bed, I pulled up the blanket far enough to cover the fact that I was still wearing yesterday's clothes.

Or at least most of them.

'Come in.'

~~**~*~*

I had to admit, breakfast in bed was a treat. But as for the rest of the day...

Did it go any better than the last one? Did it lead to a big, happy family reunion?

Well, not exactly.

Imagine the biblical story of the prodigal son: the son, who has broken with his father and foolishly ventured out into the world, returns, and the father prepares to hear his son's desperate pleas for help – only to discover that his son has come back with a buttload of cash, is now richer and more important than his father ever was, and knows it, too.

This, apparently, was a rough description of the problem that existed between Mr Ambrose and his father. The marquess was waiting for his son to ask for forgiveness, and Mr Ambrose – well, he wasn't in the habit of asking for anything. If anyone wanted him, they had better come to him, or get stuffed.

So the marquess remained up there in his study, waiting for his son to come up, and Mr Ambrose remained in the guest chamber, waiting for his father to come down. Whenever I thought about it, I had to fight to keep a straight face. Especially in the company of the marchioness, who was clearly upset by this unexpected development.

Luckily, there was more than enough going on to distract her: preparations for the ball were turning the entire household upside down. All rooms were cleaned and aired, the windows polished, the winter garden filled with new plants brought especially from the South, and, and, and. I thought it was all a bit much for just one ball, and mentioned this to the marchioness – who blushed a deep, guilty pink.

'Marchioness?'

'Well, Mr Linton...' She cleared her throat. 'I might not have been entirely honest when I said we were holding a ball.'

I raised an eyebrow. She blushed even deeper.

'Promise me this won't go any further? Promise me you won't tell anyone?'

'Trust me,' I told her, my voice deadpan. 'I'm very good at keeping secrets.'

She breathed a sigh of relief. 'All right. I'll tell you. Maybe it will be a relief, letting someone else in on my plans. But please don't tell anyone – especially not my son!'

My, my, this was getting interesting. 'I promise. Go on.'

'Well...what I am planning...it might be slightly more than just a ball.'

'Indeed?'

'In fact...maybe a lot more than that.'

'You don't say.'

'There'll be extended festivities stretching over several days, with hunting and dancing and picnics in the winter garden. I'm going to invite all the family's old friends and neighbours, and the officers of an army regiment quartered nearby for the winter, and, um...'

'Yes?'

'...and all the eligible young ladies of the county.'

My eyes went wide. 'You mean...'

'Yes.'

'Dear me! There really *is* going to be hunting, isn't there? It'll be open season!'

Lady Samantha's cheeks turned pink. Her eyes shone with moisture. 'My son has been alone for so long, Mr Linton. Too long.'

Fire rose inside me.

He's not alone! He has me!

I almost said it out loud – until I remembered the death sentence prescribed for certain practices by the Buggery Act of 1533. It might be wise to keep my mouth shut on that subject while I was wearing trousers and a tailcoat.[3]

'Um...do you really think something will come of it, Your Ladyship? You know that your son, while having excellent qualities–' *Although I can't think of any right now.* '–can be rather, err...frosty.'

She smiled at me, tremulously. 'A mother can dream.'

Yes. Nightmares. Terrible, horrific nightmares.

At least from my perspective.

Crap, crap, crap! What was I going to do?

'You'll help me, Mr Linton, won't you?' Taking my hand, she gazed up at me with those oh-so-motherly blue eyes. 'You know my son, and are such a loyal friend to him. You'll help me find the right girl?'

'Don't worry.' Swallowing down all my squirming anxieties. I squeezed her hand and gave her the smile of a fiery *ifrit*. 'I will make a hundred per cent sure that your son ends up with the one and only girl who's right for him. I swear it.'

Unnatural Selection

The marchioness didn't waste any time. The preparations for the big festivities began that very day. Missives were dispatched to villages all around, hiring additional staff. When the carriages returned, they weren't just laden with additional staff, but also with all sorts of delicacies of the season, from goose and turkey over gravy to treacle, cinnamon, nutmeg, cloves, ginger, and all the other ingredients needed for a Christmas pudding.

---

[3] This is a historical fact. The *Buggery Act 1533* (officially named *An Acte for the punishment of the vice of Buggerie*) made homosexual acts of sex punishable by death. It remained a capital offence until 1861, about two decades after the events of this book, and a criminal offence in some parts of the United Kingdom until 1982.

A real Christmas pudding...

The thought alone brought a smile to my face. I hadn't had one of those since my parents had died. Uncle Bufford's idea of celebrating Christmas was to let down all the blinds and put an extra sturdy lock on the door as protection against carol singers.

From the way Mr Ambrose's left little finger was twitching at the sight of servants bustling through Battlewood, polishing, cleaning and preparing, I could tell he had similar urges. But, like the strong man he was, he kept them in check.

The next few days were a whirlwind. People streamed into the manor house like mice into a pot of sugar. Everything was being cleaned, rooms were being aired that hadn't been used or even opened for years. Thousands of candles were fetched out of secret stores in the cellar, and soon the chandeliers throughout Battlewood shone in tripled glory. And it wasn't just the servants who did all the work: I was in the front ranks, along with Adaira and Lady Samantha, acting as generals of an army of little Christmas elves in maid and footman uniforms.

At my suggestion, Mr Ambrose was roped into the preparations and given the task of acquiring the decorations for the approaching Christmas celebrations. Ostensibly, the reason behind my suggestion was keeping Mr Ambrose too busy to think about leaving, but the real reason was that I simply really enjoyed watching the muscle in his jaw twitch maniacally while he chased servants through the snowy woods on the search for a suitably towering tree and stood on a ladder fixing mistletoe to chandeliers.[4]

I, meanwhile, had a bigger role to play than simply general of the Christmas elves: I had become Lady Samantha's official advisor on all things Rikkard Ambrose.

'I need you, Mr Linton,' she explained, looking up at me with a half-sad, half-hopeful expression on her face. 'When my son left, he was an open, cheerful boy. Today...' She shook her head. 'Sometimes I look into his eyes, and I wonder if it's really him, until I look deeper and know it is my son. It is definitely him. But I don't know him anymore. You are the closest thing my son has to a friend. If he is going to relax and enjoy during our festivities, I need you to help me. Tell me, what should I include in my plans for Christmas? What does my son enjoy?'

I considered for a moment. 'Err...making money?'

'No, no. I mean what does he do for fun, Mr Linton?'

'Work. A lot.'

---

[4] In case anyone was wondering about the tradition of the Christmas tree in Victorian times, here is a short history: while popular myth says that Prince Albert, husband of Queen Victoria, brought the tradition over from Germany in the 1840s, it was actually Queen Charlotte, the German wife of George III, who put up the first Christmas tree in England in 1800. True, Prince Albert was hugely influential in popularizing the tradition among the middle class, but by that time it was already well-established as a tradition among the British aristocracy.

'And other than that?'

'Um...bully employees into working faster?'

'So...what you are telling me is that my son most enjoys doing all the things in this world that are not meant to be enjoyed?'

'Exactly, Your Ladyship. You hit the nail on the head.'

'So what do you suggest we do?'

'Well, do you have more rooms in this house that aren't decorated yet?'

'Dozens. But they won't really be used.'

I smiled. 'He doesn't need to know that, does he? Keep him busy. That's the best thing you can do.' *Plus, it's just so much fun to watch.*

'Oh, thank you, Mr Linton! Thank you!'

'You're most welcome, Your Ladyship.'

The preparations continued in a wild whirlwind. With every day, things were better: the winter-blooming flowers in the winter garden opened, more sparkling snow fell, promising a perfectly white Christmas, and Rikkard Ambrose ran all over the place, chasing about tree-decorators and mistletoe-hangers, his jaw muscles now suffering from chronic twitches. In short: life was busy and life was good.

Until, one day...

'Mr Linton?'

'Yes?' Looking up from the mirror I had been inspecting for specs of dust, I saw Lady Samantha hurrying towards me, a stack of newspapers in her arms. The uppermost was open to the social pages, showing the engraving of a beautiful young lady.

Uh-oh...

'I, um...have been preparing for the *other part* of the festivities,' the marchioness whispered, glancing around as if she feared Mr Ambrose might suddenly jump out from behind one of the mirrors on the walls. 'Can we talk?'

'Of course, Your Ladyship. Is there somewhere private?'

'Come with me.'

She led me into a little chamber that had nothing in it but a table, a few chairs, and a lock on the door. The latter the marchioness now locked behind us. Then she went to check the windows and lower the blinds.

'You remember what I mentioned about the...special possibilities of this occasion?'

'Oh yes. I remember.'

'Well...' Depositing the papers on the table, she started spreading them out. 'I've collected the most recent issues of local papers – especially the social pages, with engravings of various young ladies that made impressions at balls in the vicinity.' A dreamy gleam entered into her eyes as she gazed down at the table. 'Look at them! Aren't they beautiful?'

'Yes,' I groaned. 'They are.'

'Mr Linton? You sound a little off. Are you feeling quite well?'

'Yes, yes, thank you. Please continue.'

'Well, I was going through these, trying to decide whom to invite, and I thought you could advise me. You've been such a tremendous help, and such a good friend to my son. Besides, it would be so helpful to get a man's perspective.'

'You don't say.'

'Yes.' She pointed down at the spread-out newspapers. 'So, which of these young ladies do you find most attractive? Which would you be inclined to marry?'

I cleared my throat. 'Well...that isn't an easy question to answer.'

'I know.' She sighed. 'They're all so lovely.'

'Well, um...yes. Of course. Lovely.' I cleared my throat again. 'But aren't we asking the wrong question? I mean, it is not about what I, a humble secretary, would prefer in a wife. Trust me, you would not want the kind of spouse that I am looking for for your son.'

'Are you sure?'

'Absolutely!'

'Well... I suppose you are right. Rick is the son of a marquess. The two of you belong to different worlds.'

'That, and he is a completely different person from me. We need to find the perfect woman for him, specifically.'

'You're right, of course.' She threw me a grateful smile. 'I'm so glad I have you to advise me.'

'So am I, Your Ladyship, believe me. So am I.'

'So...which of these young ladies do you think would make a good wife for my boy? Here are a few I picked out. Have a look and tell me what you think.'

She handed me a couple of newspaper cut-outs with more printed engravings. I looked at the first – and pulled a face.

'Ugh!'

'What?' Lady Samantha looked crestfallen. 'You don't like her? But she's so beautiful!'

My point exactly.

But I had a feeling I'd better not say that out loud. So instead, I cleared my throat. 'Well...yes. But she has blonde hair.'

A puzzled frown spread across Lady Samantha's face. 'Is that a problem?'

'Definitely! Any candidates for the post of your future daughter-in-law can't be blonde – or black-haired, for that matter. Mr Ambrose only ever looks with interest at brunettes.'

'Really?'

'Oh yes. And they shouldn't be too slim, either. I've been long enough with him to know from personal experience that he likes women with a little meat on their bones.'

'Oh, Mr Linton!' Reaching over, she clasped my hand. 'Thank you! This is exactly what I need. Please, go ahead and look through the images, and dispose of those you think are unsuitable.'

A smile spread across my face. 'My pleasure.'

I looked back down at the image in my hand – a slim, beautiful blonde girl with gorgeous green eyes. With a scowl, I threw it over my shoulder.

'No. Next one...No, too tall. Next one – no, too small. Next one – yikes, no! Much too beautiful.'

Lady Samantha blinked. 'That is a bad thing?'

'Umm...well, yes, of course. You don't want your son to marry for looks alone, do you?'

'Well, no of course not, I would never...'

'There, you see? We need ugly girls! Lots and lots of ugly girls.'

'But...how do you know these ones will be more intelligent?'

'We'll only pick ones with really big heads, of course. Here, like this one.' I showed her a picture – and she flinched back. 'Didn't you read of this brilliant new scientific discovery? Professor William H. Anstruther found compelling evidence that the intelligence of a person is relative to the size of their heads.' Inconspicuously, I crossed my fingers behind my back. *Please God, if you exist, forgive me.* 'It's quite simple, really. Larger heads means more space for more brains.'

'Oh.' A smile brightened her face, and she squeezed my hand. 'Thank you so much, Mr Linton! I'm so glad I have you to help me. I don't know what I would do without you.'

Throw a magnificent ball with beautiful guests, probably.

'So, let's continue, shall we?'

'By all means, do.' She watched eagerly as I continued to sort through the pictures.

'This one – God no! Just look at that devious smile of hers. She can't be trusted. That one – no! She looks far too grim. Mr Ambrose needs someone with a little humour in her. This one – blonde Next one – blonde. Next one – blonde again!'

'Um...that looks more like red to me.'

I gazed at the image critically. 'Strawberry blonde,' I decided, and it sailed over my shoulder onto the rubbish heap.

'Next one – no. And... no. And no. And no. And not that one, either. Nope, she hasn't got a chance. And that one? God, no!'

The rubbish heap grew. Lady Samantha gifted me with a radiant smile. 'It's heartwarming to see someone besides me who thinks nobody is good enough for my boy.'

Nobody? Well, that's not precisely true...

Finally, I had managed to wheedle down the competition – officially known as 'honoured guests' – from five hundred to thirty-six.

Thirty-six.

Thirty-six maybe not particularly beautiful but still much too womanly women, who, in a short while, would be invading this house and vying for the attention of Mr Rikkard Ambrose. With narrowed eyes, I surveyed the selection of harpies spread out in front of me. There were a few I could discount immediately – like Daphne Belleville, a seventeen-year-old hatchling who had just had her debut last month and, by all reports, was too shy to ask for sugar with her tea. One frosty look from Mr Rikkard Ambrose, and she would be scurrying off in the opposite direction. And as for Lady Caroline Sambridge, she had spent two thousand pounds last year on jewellery alone. Mr Ambrose wouldn't touch her with a ten-foot pole.

But the rest...

They were not actually horrific. Some didn't even have the decency to be ugly. Was it too much to ask for a hump or a wart on the nose?

Sure, they were nothing to write home about, but then, neither was I. Not in the eyes of the stupid, chauvinistic public, who badly needed a new set of standards by which to judge women. The question now was: were society's standards also those of Mr Rikkard Ambrose? Yes, we had had fun in the jungle, but if he ever seriously wanted a woman, could it really be someone like me?

The time for doubt is over, Lilly. You're at Battlewood. Time for the battle to begin!

'Oh...' Lady Samantha gazed down at the selection of ladies on the table, her eyes dreamy. 'They're wonderful! I can just feel it: we have the right girl. We have her here.'

Gazing at the images of the competition with narrowed eyes, I cracked my knuckles. 'Oh yes. We have.'

THE MANY WEAPONS OF A WOMAN

The very next morning, Lady Samantha gave orders for invitations to be made. Instead of sending orders to a printer, she handed a list of names to Hastings, who would convey it to Jeremiah Jones, an antiquary and calligraphist whose work, apparently, was praised by all the noble families in the North. Tomorrow, the marchioness would have a hundred and fifty beautiful, hand-crafted invitations.

'Including,' she whispered to me at the breakfast table while Mr Ambrose was busy oozing disapproval for the expense, 'thirty-six very, very special ones.' She winked.

I suddenly didn't feel at all like eating anymore.

'Mr Linton? Is something wrong?'

I set the fork with my bacon down. 'Everything is fine, Your Ladyship. I just need a little fresh air.'

I walked away before she could say anything else, and caught her glancing worriedly after me. It felt strange having someone older worry about me. Someone who felt almost like a...mother?

Shaking my head, I shook off the thought and marched out into the hall. No Christmas preparations for me this morning! I needed to blow off some steam. So I got my gun out of my suitcase and, wrapping myself in the warmest clothes I had brought, went down to the shooting range behind the house. The targets were nothing but little snowy hills, covered from head to toe in a thick blanket of white, but it was the work of a moment to brush away the snow and reveal the coloured circles beneath. Time to forget all my troubles for a while and have some fun! Besides, considering that many of the soon-to-come new arrivals would be ladies in pursuit of Rikkard Ambrose, sharpening my skills with the gun might not be a bad idea.

Bam!

A hole appeared in the middle ring. I grinned. So I wasn't completely out of practice.

Bam!

Nearly there...nearly there...

Bam!

Bull's eye!

Twirling my gun, I blew the smoke off the end and proceeded to the next target, imagining it looked like the serene profile of Lady Caroline Elaine Sambridge, the most aggravatingly beautiful of our thirty-six special guests.

Bam! Bam!

Bull's eye – twice! Or should I say cow's eye? My grin broadened. I was just raising my gun again when, from behind me, I heard footsteps.

'Mr Linton? Mr Linton, Mother sent me to look for you, to see if you're all right. And then I heard a racket like – oh!'

Turning, I lowered my gun and saw Lady Adaira Louise Jannet Melanie Georgette Ambrose standing behind me, her eyes widening at the sight of the gun in my hand. At that moment, with her mouth slightly open and the stern expression banished from her face, it was quite obvious how young she still was. Sixteen? Seventeen?

'You...you're shooting?' she whispered.

'Yes. Would you like to try?'

If possible, her eyes grew even wider.

'You would let me try?'

I stared back at her, taken aback – then I remembered that to her, I was Mr Victor Linton, a man, part of the chauvinistic machinery that prohibited young ladies like her from doing almost anything. Anything interesting, anyway. Time for a little progressive manliness.

'Certainly, why not?' Putting the safety on the gun, I held it out to her, grip first. She approached it as if it were a snake that could strike out at any moment.

'I...I don't know whether I should...Father would never allow...'

'Your father is currently cooped up in his study, refusing to come down to breakfast because he's too stubborn to welcome home a son who has returned after over a decade abroad. Does that sound like someone you should be taking advice from?'

'Well...if you put it like that...'

Licking her lips, she tentatively reached out, let her fingers slip around the handle – then suddenly flinched back again. I worked hard not to laugh.

'Go on, take it. It won't bite. Well, at least not while you've got the safety on.'

'Safety?'

'That little lever there. As long as it's up, the gun won't fire. Pull it down, and you're ready to unleash your wrath upon unsuspecting passers-by.'

Adaira gave a nervous little laugh. 'Mr Linton...You're unlike any man I've ever met!'

'You have no idea how right you are about that, My Lady.' Stepping behind her, I took hold of her arms. 'Now, first the stance. Face the target squarely, legs apart...'

'Mr Linton!'

The voice was like a knife of ice, cutting through the air with the threat of violence. Jumping back, I whirled around, and came face to face with Mr Rikkard Ambrose. He was striding across the snowy yard, his face set into an immovable mask, a storm of cold fury roiling in his eyes.

'What,' he whispered in a way that made me shiver even through five layers of clothes, 'do you think you're doing?'

Adaira stepped forward. 'It was my fault. I just wanted to learn–'

'Silence.'

The word wasn't loud. It wasn't even angry. But it shut Adaira up quicker than a gag in the mouth. Her eyes, though... her eyes screamed murder and rebellion.

Mr Ambrose met her gaze head-on. 'Go to your room.'

'You can't–!'

'Go. To. Your. Room. *Now*.'

The last word was like a whiplash. And once more, I witnessed the miracle of Mr Ambrose's ice cold voice, a voice that could strike terror into the hearts of kings, scatter armies, and make a little sister obey her big brother. Fuming, Adaira turned and marched off towards the house.

Which left only one target for Mr Ambrose's freezing gaze: me.

'What,' he whispered, his voice even lower and more dangerous than before, 'was that?'

I shrugged, desperately flicking through any ways I might know to disappear into thin air. None came to mind.

'Err...well...'

'I'm waiting.'

'She, um...wanted to learn how to shoot. So I thought I'd teach her.'

'You? Teach *my little sister* how to use a *firearm*?'

I raised my chin defiantly. 'Hey, I'm pretty good at it! I bet I could–'

He moved so fast I didn't even have time to blink. From one moment to the next, he was in front of me, grabbing the gun I still held half-raised, twisting it out of my grasp and around, until the muzzle pointed directly at me.

He cocked his head.

'You were saying?'

I swallowed. The safety was on. I knew that. And I told myself that over and over again. But the black hole of that muzzle, right underneath the two ice-cold orbs that were his eyes...

He dropped the gun. It landed in the snow with a soft thud.

'Listen to me.' His voice sent a renewed shiver through me – and not one of cold, nor of fear. 'My sister is a young lady. The only stance a young lady needs to learn is a graceful one. The only firearm a lady ever needs to touch is *none at all*. Especially if that young lady is my sister.'

'Indeed?' I raised an eyebrow. 'And what would you think of a girl who flouts those rules? A girl who does what she wants, when she wants?'

His mouth opened, preparing to condemn that girl, to fling curses at her and everything she did – and then his mouth closed again. And opened. And closed again. All that came out was silence.

Slowly, my defiant expression melted away, and a grin spread over my face. He couldn't. He could not condemn me. Not anymore.

With a growl that sounded as if it were ripped from his very soul, Mr Ambrose grabbed me by the shoulders. I was lifted up off the ground, flung backwards until we were in the shadow of a colonnade. Whirling me around, he pushed me up against the closest column and his mouth came crashing down on mine, demanding, devouring, devastating.

'You,' he breathed against my mouth, 'are the most infuriating female I have ever met in my entire life!'

'Thanks so much for the compliment, Sir.'

With another growl, he plunged his hands into my hair and pressed into me until he had stolen my breath and I didn't even want to try and get it back.

~~**~*~*

The invitations arrived that evening. I was tempted to burn a couple with certain female names on them, but I knew the marchioness would notice and just order new ones. At least I managed, with a bit of water, to smudge the ink on several envelopes addressed to eligible ladies. With luck, they'd get lost in the post.

'So!' Breathing a sigh, Lady Samantha gazed after the servant who was riding off on a grey mare, the invitations stashed in his saddlebags. 'It's done! Now all we can do is wait and hope.'

'Yes,' I mumbled. 'That the invitations get lost in the mail.'

'Pardon? What did you say, Mr Linton?'

'Nothing, Your Ladyship. I was just talking to myself.'

Unfortunately, the post was not obliging enough to mislay our invitations. The replies started coming in the very next day, starting with a beautifully handwritten note from Lady Dorothea Asquith saying that yes, she would be delighted to attend the festivities, and would it be agreeable to the marchioness if she brought her three cousins as well? All three were, of course, very beautiful and agreeable young ladies.

Lady Samantha nearly broke into a spontaneous dance at the reply. And that was only the beginning. Acceptance letters and notes flooded in from all sides, showering the marchioness with thanks and expressing their eager interest in seeing her son, returned to his ancestral seat after so many years abroad. Among the most vocal in their thanks were the officers of the local regiment, who, in this snowy, solitary place, had about as much entertainment as a polar bear floating on an arctic ice floe, and were ravenous for some pretty girls to dance with.

But they're not nearly enough to keep all the girls occupied! Besides, what potbellied corporal can compare with the most powerful, heartbreakingly handsome man of the British Empire?

None. Which was why acceptances from ladies kept pouring in.

Finally, I'd had enough. It was time to prepare for battle. A battle not just for Mr Ambrose, but for the approval of his mother and sister. And that was a battle I couldn't win as Mr Victor Linton. I needed to unsheathe different weapons.

Time to give Mr Ambrose and his mother a little surprise.

'Your Ladyship?'

The Marchioness looked up from the pile of acceptance letters she was studying and beamed. 'Yes, Mr Linton?'

I took a deep breath.

'There's something...'

'Yes?'

'I wonder whether I could ask...but no.' Quickly, I shook my head and took a step back. 'Forget it.'

The marchioness lowered the pile of letters. 'What is on your mind?'

'I...was going to ask a favour. But it's too big a thing to ask. I couldn't impose on you like that.'

'Please, ask!' Letting go of the letters completely, the marchioness captured my hands in hers and squeezed. 'You, young man, have been a godsend to this family. Anything that is in my power to give you will be yours.'

'Well...' I bit my lip in fake hesitation. Dear me, I was quite the accomplished little actress. 'I was wondering whether I could possibly invite my sister to your Christmas festivities. Mr Ambrose and I have been travelling around the world, and I haven't seen her in a long time. Besides, she would love the chance to attend an affair like this. But I see now it's too much. Forget I ever mentioned it.'

'Nonsense! I shall do nothing of the kind.' A broad, motherly smile spread over Lady Samantha's wrinkled face. 'Your sister shall be as welcome here as you are! But...' A frown marred her brow. 'Won't it be too late for her to attend? The festivities will start soon, and if she has to travel here all the way up from London–'

'Don't worry.' I answered her smile with one of my own. 'She'll be here. I have a feeling she's already quite close.'

SELFSAME SIBLINGS

Ding-dong...

The elderly tailor looked up from his books with a distracted little smile and nodded at me. 'Welcome, Sir.'

'Hello.' I smiled back. 'Are you the proprietor of this lovely little shop?'

'Yes. Are you a customer?' He chuckled. 'Sorry for asking, but at this time of year, practically no one comes by here. I might get an occasional order for winter gloves from Battlewood Hall, but new faces are rare.'

'I'm a guest at Battlewood. Linton is the name.'

'Ah, that explains it.' He gave a little arthritic bow. 'Welcome to my humble shop, Mr Linton. Is there anything I might show you? Tailcoats? Top hats with a warm lining for the winter weather?'

'No, thank you. I'd like to take a look at your dresses.'

The little man blinked. 'Err...dresses? For women?'

'I've yet to see ones for orang-utans. Oh, and I would also like to see your selection of bonnets, ribbons and parasols, if you have them.'

'Um...well, yes, of course, Sir. May I enquire what the measurements of the lady in question are?'

I smiled brightly at him. 'Mine.'

If the little man had been off-kilter before, this really did him in. 'Yours, um...Sir?'

'Oh yes. Hurry up a little and bring out what you have, will you? I'd like to be back at Battlewood in time for breakfast.'

Mumbling to himself, he hurried off into the back room, and not long after was back with several dresses slung over one arm and a selection of bonnets, ribbons and parasols in the other.

'I must commend you,' I said, smiling as I studied a magnificent red silk dress. 'For such a small shop out in the country, you are amazingly well stocked. Just look at the detail in the hem! I've never worn a finer dress in my life!'

'Err...worn, Sir?'

Instead of answering, I gifted him with another bright smile. 'Where is the changing room, please?'

With a trembling hand, the little man pointed to a curtained-off area at the back of the room.

'Thank you.'

I disappeared.

Twing.

Twong.

'Crap! Bloody corset!'

Twang!

'Crap, crap, crap! Fit already!'

A few moments and curses later, I pulled aside the curtain and beamed at the little tailor, who was supporting himself by holding on to the corner of his counter.

'And? How do I look?'

'Um...magnificent, err...Sir?'

I took a long, critical look at myself in the full-length mirror on the wall. 'Hm...I agree, not bad. Red is a nice colour on me. But there's a certain something missing.'

I disappeared back behind the curtain.

Snap!

51

Twong!
'Bloody stinking Hell!
Twang!
'Blast, blast, blast!'
Once more, I reappeared.
'And? What do you say?'
'Grgsfgl.'

Since that was not very constructive criticism, I stepped in front of the mirror again to give myself a once-over – and a broad smile broke over my face. The dark green-blue dress was magnificent. Every inch of the shimmering fabric seemed to hover just between the deep blue of a still pool and the green of the deep forest, making me look like some wild goddess, freshly returned from the hunt. Or, better yet, about to embark on one.

'Perfect! I'll take it, the red one, and those accessories there. How much?'
'Nnnfgdl.'
'How much is that in pounds sterling?'
'Um...err...three pounds two shillings, please, Si– um...Mada...'

I placed the money on the counter. 'Here you go. Thank you, Sir. You've been a great help.'

Whistling, I stepped outside, my purchases partly under my arm, partly fitting very comfortably on my body. The air was still cold outside, but it had stopped snowing, and the wind had calmed down to a breeze. So I set out towards Battlewood the same way I had come: on my own two feet.

I reached the hall just in time for breakfast. My first instinct was to enter the main house and direct my steps to the little pink breakfast room, where the four of us usually consumed the first meal of the day. But then I saw movements through the glass panes of one of the winter gardens and stopped, squinting through the foliage.

Yes, there they were! Adaira, Lady Samantha and Mr Ambrose sitting around a small table amidst the greenery, chatting amiably over their breakfast. Or at least the two women were chatting amiably, while Mr Ambrose was sitting in silence morosely. Well...time to liven things up a bit.

Quickly and silently, I crossed the distance to the winter garden's outside door. With cautious fingers, I gripped the doorknob, twisted and pushed. The door swung open without a noise.

'...first guests are going to start arriving soon. I've already received letters from many of our old friends and neighbours – and from ladies, oh, such charming young ladies – saying they'd all be delighted to come. Isn't that wonderful?'
'Indeed.'

'And the Pearsons say their daughter is now ready for her coming out, and they asked whether she might have her debut at our ball. Little Philomela has grown into quite a charming young lady, apparently.'
'Indeed?'

I give everyone three guesses which part of this conversation was Mr Ambrose and which his mother. Smirking at the suffering non-expression on my employer's face, I slowly crept closer in the shadow of the plants. He thought this was bad? He had no idea. Things were going to get a whole lot more interesting.

'And the Garringtons are coming, too,' Lady Samantha started a last attempt. 'They have such a lovely young daughter, and–'

'Hello there.' Stepping out from behind the bushes, I did my best imitation of a curtsey. 'Good morning everyone.'

'Mr Linton.' Mr Ambrose started to turn around. 'Where have you b–'

The remainder of the sentence got lost in a sort of gurgling noise. Lady Samantha and Lady Adaira turned, too, and when they caught sight of me their eyes went wide.

'May I?' Not waiting for a response, I pulled out a chair and settled myself down next to Mr Ambrose. He made another indistinct noise. 'What a lovely winter garden you have here. It's so nice to meet you all – well, except for Mr Ambrose, of course. The two of us are already quite well acquainted.'

'You are?' Lady Samantha's eyes lit up at the prospect of her son actually knowing a female that wasn't related to him, dead, or cleaning his room wearing a chambermaid's uniform. Reaching over, she gave Mr Ambrose's hand a decisive squeeze. 'Then why don't you introduce us to this lovely young lady, dear? Although–' her eyes wandered over my face, and warmth lit her eyes. '– to judge by her familiar features, I can already guess who she might be.'

I could nearly hear the sound of Mr Ambrose's teeth grinding.

'This,' he somehow managed to get out, 'Is Miss Lillian Linton, Mr Linton's–'

'– sister,' I finished and piled mushrooms on top of my toast. 'Twin sister, actually.'

'I thought as much!' Both women's eyes were on me, wonderingly. 'The two of you really have the most amazing resemblance.'

'Yes, I've been told so.'

'How did you get here so quickly? Your brother only asked me to invite you yesterday.'

'He did, did he?' Mr Ambrose's cold gaze speared me. I ignored it and took a bite of toast. 'I wonder why Mr Linton neglected to mention this to me.'

I smiled at him. 'How would I know? You'd better ask him.'

'Oh, rest assured, I'll do that.'

'Miss Linton?' The marchioness's eyes were gleaming with curiosity. They were flicking between Mr Ambrose and me, betraying intrigue at our little exchange. 'Well? How did you get here so quickly?'

I winked. 'I have my ways. Besides...I don't approve of tardiness.'

She clapped her hands. 'Neither does my son! How wonderful! The two of you already have things in common.'

Under the table, Mr Ambrose gave me a kick, and I kicked back, promptly. Ah, the sweet exchanges of romance...

'Why, pray,' he demanded of his mother, 'is that wonderful?'

'Oh, well, you know.' The marchioness cleared her throat. 'It's nice to have a friendly and happy atmosphere at breakfast. That's all.'

'Of course.'

She cleared her throat again and, quickly evading her son's gaze, extended her hand across the table for me to shake. 'Well, anyway, welcome to Battlewood Hall, Miss Linton. I'm sorry my husband is not down here to greet you but he is...indisposed. I hope we can make your stay an enjoyable one.'

'Oh, I'm sure of it,' I said, smiling at her and giving Mr Ambrose another kick under the table, just for the fun of it.

Adaira, who had been watching the whole discussion with dark, thoughtful eyes, now too extended her hand.

'Welcome, Miss Linton. If you're anything like your brother, I already know I'm going to like you.'

'Oh, trust me, the two of us are very much alike.'

She frowned, glancing around. 'Where is your brother, by the way?'

'Oh, he had to take care of something. Don't worry. He'll be back.'

The two ladies lapsed into silence for a while, concentrating on that ladylike art of not speaking with your mouth full which I had never entirely mastered. Mr Ambrose took the opportunity to lean over towards me and hiss, in a voice hardly audible over the clatter of knives and forks: 'What are you doing here?'

'Whatever do you mean?' I blinked up at him in the manner of the perfectly innocent little maiden. 'I've been here all along.'

Lightning flashed in his storm-coloured eyes. 'What are you doing here...like *that*?'

'Eating breakfast, you mean?'

'Mr Linton, I–!'

'Say, Miss Linton,' the marchioness said, unaware that she was interrupting, 'I didn't hear your carriage arrive. Did you arrive on horseback, in this cold weather?'

'Oh no.' I gave her a bright smile. 'I walked.'

The eyes of the two women went wide. 'Walked?'

'Oh yes.' My smile widening, I gestured out over the white wasteland, stretching as far as the eye could see beyond the windows of the winter garden. 'A nice little walk is just the thing to warm one up, isn't it?'

Under the table, Mr Ambrose stomped on my foot. Or at least he tried to. I was prepared now, evaded him easily and kicked right back. This was fun!

'Um...Miss Linton?' The marchioness regarded me with a mixture of awe and doubt. In the eyes of her young daughter, however, I could see the beginning glimmers of hero worship. 'Where exactly do you live?'

I reached for a piece of toast and started to butter it. 'London. Why?'

'Um...nothing.' She regarded me, then her son, and the way he was still leaning towards me. Immediately, Mr Ambrose jerked back into a ramrod straight position. 'Where exactly do you know my son from, Miss Linton? Through your brother?'

'No.' I glanced at Mr Ambrose out of the corner of my eyes and sent him a brief smile that made him sit even straighter. 'I was fortunate enough to be at a ball at Lady Metcalf's one evening, when your son arrived and demanded my hand for the next dance.'

'Demanded?'

'Oh yes. I declined at first, but he insisted.'

Adaira's eyes went wide. 'You said no to my brother?'

'Oh yes.'

Her eyes gleamed – definitely hero worship!

'But he simply wouldn't give up so, in the end...' I shrugged. 'I gave him a chance. It would have been a bit cruel, letting him beg.'

'He was that interested, was he?' Lady Samantha's eyes gleamed as they gazed at me. I knew that expression. It was the same my aunt had on her face every time she caught sight of an eligible bachelor. She beamed. 'You know, I'm really so very glad you came, Miss Linton! You must stay for the whole holiday season.'

'Could I really? Oh, I would be delighted.'

Under the table, Mr Ambrose's foot found mine, and pressed down, hard. Out of the corner of his mouth, he growled, too low for anybody else to hear: 'You will pay for this later.'

'Will I?' I batted my eyelashes up at him. 'In pounds sterling?'

Quick as a flash, so quick that even the eagle's eye of a mother could not detect it, his hand darted under the table and took hold of my thigh possessively. His fingers were like iron vices wrapped in velvet. 'Oh no. I had another currency in mind.'

The marchioness cleared her throat. 'You know, Adaira...I think I forgot something up in my room.'

'Really, Mother? What?'

'I can't remember what exactly, but it's something really, really important.' Rising swiftly to her feet, she started backing towards the door, her eyes never leaving me and Mr Ambrose. 'Yes, really, really important. I hope you don't mind, Miss Linton. I'll just have to leave you alone with my son here for a little bit, while I go fetch...whatever it is I have to fetch.'

'Well, you go and get it, then,' Adaira told her mother, not moving an inch. She was watching me and Mr Ambrose, too, with quite a lot of interest gleaming in her eyes. 'I'll stay here.'

'But, Adaira, my dear, I think I need you to come with me. I might need help carrying the...the...'

'...the thing that you have to fetch but can't remember at the moment?'

'Exactly! I seem to remember it is very heavy.'

'Oh, don't worry.' Adaira gave her mother a bright smile and slid closer to Mr Ambrose and me. 'I distinctly remember you telling me earlier it is very light. Very light indeed. Besides, I think I'd really like to stay here. I have a feeling the conversation is going to get interesting.'

'Still, I'll need you. I...I...might need your help remembering the thing I have to fetch that I can't remember right now.'

'Don't worry. If I remember I'll send a servant with a note.'

'Adaira Louise Jannet Melanie Georgette Ambrose, get to your feet and come with me right now!'

'All right, all right...' With a sigh of disappointment that would have melted any heart but that of a mother, Adaira got to her feet and let herself be dragged out of the room, leaving Mr Ambrose and me alone on the winter garden bench.

Silence reigned when the door had closed behind mother and daughter. Long, cold, intense silence. Dark, sea-coloured eyes bored into me, wandering up and down my figure, taking in my female attire.

'What are you playing at, Mr Linton?'

I raised an eyebrow. 'I told you before, Sir – I'm not playing. Not anymore.'

'You made it sound like...like the two of us were...'

'Yes?'

He opened his mouth – and pounced on me. One moment he was sitting there, fighting with his words, the next, he pulled me towards him and his lips claimed mine, fighting another battle and winning fast. A groan rose from his chest. For a moment, I melted into him – then my hands gripped his shoulders, and I pushed hard, sending him flying backwards. He hit the padded bench with a *thunk*.

'I'm not playing,' I repeated, my eyes ablaze as I gazed down at him. 'We've sailed the seas together, hunted outlaws in the desert, hacked our way through the South American jungle and always, always we've had each other's back! I'm not going to stand by while your mother plans your married life, and you're snatched up by some good-for-nothing ninny of a girl. Not while I still have breath in my body!'

And then I leant down to claim his mouth again and demonstrate that yes, indeed, I did still have breath in my body. Quite a lot of it. And I knew how to use it, too.

'Don't you think I know what my mother is up to?' he breathed against my mouth. 'I have won victories over kings, queens and sultans! I'm not about to succumb to the matchmaking plans of my mother.'

'I don't care!' Reaching down, I gripped his face fiercely, refusing to let go. 'I refuse to pretend anymore! There's something between us. I don't know what it is, and I don't know what will come of it, but it's there, and I want it. I want *you*.'

I saw the ripple in his eyes, like a wave in the Arctic Ocean, causing an iceberg to crack.

'Lillian, I...'

He suddenly broke off, and a moment later, I knew why. Footsteps could be heard from outside, fast approaching.

'Up!' he hissed, and moved. In a wink, we were sitting upright. A shove from him, and suddenly I was sitting at a respectable distance. I was just reaching up to try and finger-comb the wild tangles of my hair, when the door of the winter garden burst open and Adaira stormed in.

'They're here!' she crowed, dancing around, too excited to even glance at us – thank God! 'They're coming!'

'Wh-who?

'The first guests of course! Come and see!' And she was outside again, rushing down the corridor. Slowly I managed to get my trembling knees under control and rose to follow. Behind me, I could hear Mr Ambrose do the same. I didn't look back. I didn't speak. I didn't dare just yet. Unspoken words hung in the air between us, heavy with the power to crush my heart, or make it soar.

What had he been about to say before his sister had burst in?

Damn those guests! If it's pretty little Lady Caroline Elaine Sambridge, I am going to skewer her with my parasol!

Luckily, I still had the one I had purchased earlier with me. And it seemed to have a pretty sharp tip.

I caught up with Adaira just before she reached the big arched windows next to the front door. Stretching up on my tiptoes, I peeked over her shoulder. Behind me, I could feel Mr Ambrose approaching.

'Who is it?' I demanded.

All I could see was a coach rolling down the driveway. There was no coat of arms on the door, no emblem of any kind. Either whoever was in there was not of noble blood, or it was a rented coach.

Please let it be a nobody! Someone thoroughly ineligible, unmarriageable, and if possible, male, old and ugly!

'Well? Who is it? Who is coming?'

'I don't know yet! Come! Let's go and greet them!'

I took a tighter grip on my parasol. 'Yes...that might not be a bad idea.'

Behind me, Mr Ambrose's hand shot out and plucked the parasol from my fingers. I only had time for a brief glare before Adaira flung open the door. Lady Samantha appeared beside us, not tall at all, but nevertheless as regal as any queen, her blue eyes shining with warmth and welcome.

Please don't let it be the first load of ladies! The thought repeated in my head over and over, a fervent prayer. *Please! Let it be anybody, anything else!*

Which just goes to show – you should be careful what you wish for.

The coach slowed, rolling in a circle around the frozen fountain until it came to a halt in front of the portico. I could see figures shifting inside, and breathed a sigh of relief. These were not ladies – unless young ladies had, in time since I'd last checked, developed big, broad shoulders, beards and a penchant for red and golden uniforms.

We were standing on the portico steps and watched as the first of the men climbed out of the coach. The marchioness stepped forward, a broad smile on her face.

'Welcome, gentlemen. Welcome to Battlewood. I am Samantha Genevieve Ambrose, The Marchioness Ambrose.'

'A pleasure, Your Ladyship.' The foremost of the officers, whose big bulk hid most of the others, made a deep bow that nearly toppled him over. 'May I say how much I and my comrades in arms appreciate your kind invitation?'

'Oh, you're very kind, Major...?'

'Strickland, Your Ladyship. Major Anthony Strickland. May I introduce my fellow officers?'

'By all means do so.'

With a smile on his plump face, the major stepped far enough aside to allow a semi-free view of his subordinates. 'This is Lieutenant Woodard. Here we have

57

Lieutenants Hartley, Cooley, and McGraw. And...hey, come out, what are you waiting for?'

'Coming, Sir!'

The voice from inside the coach was like a bucket of ice water in the face. For an instant, I thought my heart had stopped. A moment later, a familiar head of mahogany curls appeared from the coach. My breath caught, and I felt Mr Ambrose's cool gaze bore into me.

'Here's my right hand, the golden boy of our regiment, and the ladies' favourite – Captain James Carter!'

OPPOSING ARMIES

'A pleasure to make your acquaintance,' Captain James Carter said, unfolding himself from the coach and bowing deeply to our little group. 'A true plea–'

Then he noticed me.

His mouth dropped open, and he stared at me unblinkingly.

If Mr Ambrose's eyes had been burning into me with icy cold before, it was nothing compared to what they did now. My ears started to heat. Why the heck were my ears turning red? I had done nothing wrong!

Right?

'What's the matter, Carter?' The major chuckled. 'Stunned by the ladies' charms, are you?'

'No. Well...yes, Sir. Of course. But it's not just that.' He cleared his throat. 'I just noticed that I am already acquainted with one of the ladies.' And, right there, under the icy gaze of Mr Rikkard Ambrose, he stepped forward, bent over my hand, and pressed a kiss on its back.

Now it wasn't just Rikkard Ambrose who was boring holes into me with his gaze. I could feel the stares of Lady Adaira, Major Strickland and Lieutenants Woodard, Hartley, Cooley, and McWhat's-his-name on me equally intense, if not nearly as frigid. Only Lady Samantha, I noticed, wasn't watching me. She was watching her son watching me with considerable interest.

'Delighted to see you again, Miss Linton.' Captain Carter's words tore me from my thoughts. 'I've thought of you often since last we met, and I wondered when luck would grant me the chance of renewing our acquaintance.'

Yes, I'd been wondering that, too. And wasn't it just my kind of luck that now and here, in the company of Rikkard Ambrose and his entire family, was the moment it had to happen?

'How do you do, Your Ladyship.' Captain Carter repeated the hand kiss with Mr Ambrose's mother – not a wise move. It suddenly grew even colder outside. If looks could kill, Captain James Carter would be nothing but a skeleton frozen forever in a giant cube of ice. 'Such a pleasure to make your acquaintance. And these lovely people are your family, I presume?'

'My son, Rikkard, and my daughter, Adaira Louise.'

'Charmed.' Once again, he reached for a hand to kiss – that of *Mr Rikkard Ambrose's little sister*.

Oh God. You're dead. So absolutely, one hundred per cent dead. R.I.P. Captain James Carter.

Miraculously, he was not killed on the spot. Instead, he reached out and took the hand of Rikkard Ambrose. For one horrible, horrendous moment I thought he was going to kiss it, too – then his fingers squeezed in a handshake.

'Such a pleasure to make your acquaintance, Mr Ambro–'

That was the moment when Mr Ambrose started to squeeze back.

'Nng!'

'Yes.' Mr Ambrose's voice was a soft arctic wind, promising the coming blizzard. 'Such a pleasure. I've snatched glimpses of you from afar, Captain, and have taken the liberty of following your career and interesting exploits. I look forward to our getting to know each other better.'

Never had a death-threat been worded in so gentlemanly a manner.

'Mmmh. Rrrg.' Captain Carter swallowed and squeezed back, beads of sweat appearing on his forehead. 'You...have quite a grip, Mr Ambrose.'

'Yes. On everything.'

Abruptly, he let go of Carter's hand, and the captain pulled it back, clearly working hard to resist the urge to cradle it against his chest. Mr Ambrose's gaze swept over the captain's colleagues.

'Greetings, gentlemen. Welcome to my father's home.' And he extended his hand.

The officers took an instinctive step backwards.

'This,' Adaira whispered in my ear, her eyes gleaming, 'is getting exciting! I never dreamt a Christmas ball would be this much fun.'

The marchioness intervened then, taking the major by the arm with one of those motherly smiles of hers and ushering everyone out of the cold, into the toasty warm hall. She engaged the military men in conversation, enquiring what they thought of their winter quarters, and how the reception of the country to their arrival had been so far. I tried to join the conversation. I tried to engage the captain and his friends in small talk, smile and be polite – while from behind me, Mr Rikkard Ambrose was deep-freezing the back of my head. Captain Carter, however, who was still nursing his hand with a bemused expression on his face, seemed to be blissfully ignorant of the tension in the air. He gave me a bright smile.

'I still remember the last time we danced together. At Lady Abercrombie's, wasn't it? You looked so beautiful that night.'

Ice crystals started building on my neck. I manufactured a smile. 'Really? I'm sure I didn't. You were probably thinking of someone else.'

Please say you were thinking of someone else! Please! I don't want you to end up deep-frozen.

'Oh no, I remember you distinctly.'

Crap!

'You were the most beautiful lady at the ball. Simply resplendent.' Taking my hands, he half-turned towards me and gazed down at me in a manner that could not be misinterpreted. *Crap, crap, crap!* 'There was no other who could compete with you. Why do you think I danced with you twice in a row?'

The ice crystals on my neck were quickly getting ambitious and developing into icicles. 'Oh, I don't know,' I replied with a sort of suicidal levity. 'Pity? Insanity? Lack of options?'

Suddenly looking unusually serious, he squeezed my hands.

'It was none of those things, Miss Linton,' he whispered. 'I might have thought so, once – but not any longer. I've thought a lot about you during these last few months.'

Oh dear Lord...

'Captain Carter—'

'Sh. Don't say anything now. It's not the time or the place. But I think that, when you have a moment, it is time for us to have a little private talk,' he told me, too softly for anyone else to hear.

The problem was: Mr Rikkard Ambrose wasn't just *anyone.*

Swallowing, I felt his ice-cold gaze burn into me from behind, cutting a path to my very soul.

I made myself smile up at Captain Carter. 'I...look forward to it.'

~~**~*~*

I just want to make one thing clear from the start: I was *not* afraid of Captain Carter. Not of him, and not of what he might have to say to me. Fear had nothing whatsoever to do with the fact that, having made my excuses, I ran as fast as my hoop skirt would allow back towards my room and changed into blessedly male protective gear.

It was just more comfortable, clear?

All right, all right.

I admit it.

I'm a coward.

I didn't want to have a talk with Captain Carter. At least not the one he had planned, which, I suspected, he could only have with Lillian, not with Mr Victor Linton. So I put on my shirt, peacock vest and tailcoat, and returned to the drawing room where the company had gathered, feeling like a new man. Literally.

'Hello, everyone.'

I smiled as I closed the door behind me, trying to ignore the familiar icy stare burrowing into me from the moment I entered.

'Mr Linton!' Lady Samantha beamed. 'Where have you been? The first of our guests have arrived.'

'Linton?' Captain Carter's head jerked around and he blinked at me, his mouth opening a fraction at the sight. 'Any relation of...good God! You must be. You're her spitting image.'

I gave him a broad, friendly, thank-god-I'm-wearing-trousers smile. 'You must be talking about my sister Lillian.'

'Yes. Forgive me for expressing my shock, Sir, but the resemblance really is–'

'–remarkable,' I sighed. 'I know.'

He was still staring at me. And he wasn't the only one. The whole room was curiously gazing at Miss Lillian Linton's identical twin.

Finally, the captain cleared his throat. 'I was under the impression that Miss Linton had only female siblings.'

'They don't really talk about me.' I gave a shrug. 'I'm the black sheep of the family because I decided to work for a living. I am employed by Mr Ambrose as his private secretary.'

'Ah. That explains it.' The captain looked relieved, then seemed to remember himself and bowed. 'I beg your pardon for addressing you without an introduction, Mr Linton. It was unaccountably rude of me. I was just so surprised...well, you are probably used to reactions from people who see you and your sister at the same time.'

'That,' I assured him, 'happens rarely.'

'Well, I am sorry, in any case. Now – the introduction. Marchioness, would you be so kind?'

Lady Samantha rushed in to introduce everyone to me – again – and then, when the attention was finally off me once more, and I was just readying to find a quiet corner with an iron door I could slip through to hide from Mr Ambrose, two female raptors descended on me without mercy.

'Your sister is fabulous!' Adaira gushed, grabbing me by the arm and dragging me over to a table with refreshments, away from the men. Another hand closed around my other arm, and I saw Lady Samantha, looking happier than I had ever seen her. Adaira squeezed my arm so hard it nearly fell off. 'Why didn't you tell us about her sooner? I've never seen anyone handle my brother like that! Actually, come to think of it, I've never seen anyone try to handle my brother and survive.'

Well, to be honest My Lady, the way his eyes are burning holes in my neck this very moment I'm not sure I am going to survive...

'And she's so warm and open,' Lady Samantha sighed. 'And what a lovely smile she has! Tell me, Mr Linton – is your sister engaged?'

My eyebrows shot up. The motive of her question was about as subtle as a flying brick in the face, and it...

It overwhelmed me.

Marriage?

Yes, I wanted Mr Ambrose, but...marriage?

To love? Maybe. Honour? A *big* maybe. Obey? Ha! Never in a million years!

Could I marry Mr Rikkard Ambrose? Could I marry anyone, taking into account what that institution would mean for my freedom?

Before I could find an answer to that question, a hand settled on my shoulder.

'Mr Linton?' a familiar cold, hard voice reached my ear. 'A word. We have some business matters to discuss.'

I swallowed.

'Tush!' Lady Samantha chastised. 'Can't you see Mr Linton is speaking to us?'

'Yes,' I agreed desperately. Anything was better than facing that cold fury behind me. Anything. Even a discussion about the M-word.

'I'm talking to Lady Samantha, Mr Ambrose, Sir. If you will please excuse me...'

I tried to step away. The grip of the hand on my shoulder tightened.

'Last I checked,' he breathed into my ear, 'I pay your bills, Mr Linton. Which means I get to decide when you talk and whom you talk to.'

And without waiting for an answer, he grabbed my arm, dragging me off like a caveman. We were across the room in a blink, and he shoved me into a cur-tained-off alcove, pulling the curtain closed behind us.

'What do you think you're doing?' I demanded. 'You can't manhandle me like that! I'm not-'

But exactly what I was not - A duck? A giant garden gnome? A pink-haired pygmy? - I never got to reveal. Those were the last words I got out before his lips came down on mine and silenced me.

'You know that man.' Every hard word, every harsh breath, was a punish-ment against my mouth. 'I've seen you with him, back in Alexandria.'

I didn't pretend not to know whom he was talking about. 'Yes.'

His arms slammed into the wall on either side of me, caging me in, cutting off any avenues of escape. Dark, sea-coloured eyes, churning with the rage of the ocean, bored into me.

'Who is he? And more importantly, who is he *to you*?'

'Don't you already know?' I raised a defiant eyebrow. 'After what you said to him, I supposed you had dug through every aspect of his life.'

'I have. But that still doesn't give me the necessary information to answer my latter question.' One of his hands slid away from the wall, caressing my face in a move so caring, so gentle, it almost took my breath away. Not fair! 'Who. Is. He. To. You?'

I opened my mouth to say 'no one' - and closed it again.

Captain Carter wasn't no one. He was the man who had taught me to dance the galop, who had helped me foil the plans of my devious aunt and who had risked his career to bring me safely home. He was the man who had saved my little sister Ella from a fate worse than death - marriage to his best friend. How could I call a man like that nothing?

It turned out I didn't need to. My silence was answer enough. Mr Ambrose's jaw muscles tightened, the cold sea in his eyes freezing over with ice and iron.

'I see.'

I see? What did that mean?

'Mr Ambrose?'

Silence.

'Mr Ambrose, Sir?'

More silence. I leaned forward, peeking up at him, trying to decipher the immovable mask of his face.

'Sir? Please tell me you're not going to do anything stupid, Sir!'

He cocked his head, gazing at me as if I were a bug under the microscope questioning the scientist about his methods.

'I am not going to do anything stupid.'

For a moment, I wanted to breathe a sigh of relief – until I remembered that a man who had spies in Buckingham Palace transcribe the Queen's private diary and engaged in sea battles with foreign nations that didn't appreciate his particular brand of 'free trade' policy probably had a different definition of 'something stupid' than sweet little me.

'Then what are you going to do?'

He met my eyes and his gaze was...impassive. Calm. Ruthless.

'I am going to my room and do some paperwork. There is a file I've suddenly remembered I need to take care of.'

'A...file?'

'Yes.'

Relief flooded through me. 'Oh, very well, if that's all...'

'Mr Linton! Rick! Come and see! More guests are arriving!' Suddenly, rapid footsteps were approaching us. In an instant, Mr Ambrose was at the other end of the alcove, assuming a perfectly innocent pose, as if he hadn't just been ravishing my mouth. A moment later, the curtain was pulled back, and Adaira's face was framed in bright light.

'There you are! What are you two doing in here?'

'Um...we–'

'Oh, forget it! What do I care about boring business stuff?'

'Err...yes. Boring. Very boring. Wouldn't interest you at all.'

'Come and see! The next coach is rolling up in front of the house right this moment.'

She latched onto me, and reluctantly I let myself be dragged outside, Mr Ambrose following in my wake, colder and more silent than ever. We followed her out into the yard where, indeed, several more carriages were pulling up.

I had to admit, after the earlier surprise with Captain Carter, meeting the ladies was something of an anti-climax. Yes, some of them were – in spite of my best efforts – quite beautiful, and all of them eyed the silent figure of Mr Ambrose as if it was already Christmas and he was the present they wanted to unwrap first. But their arrival had lost the bite of shock. After all, how could anything be more shocking than the captain's sudden arrival on the scene?

I found out how soon enough.

'Oh, look!'

Adaira's excited words made me glance up – and my eyes widened. A coach was rolling across the courtyard – a coach so monumental, so luxurious, so perfect it practically breathed wealth and power. It looked like you'd imagine Cinderella's coach would have looked like if her fairy godmother hadn't just been an amateur, but had come with a PhD in fairygodmothering. Only...I was fairly sure that, unfortunately, this coach wouldn't turn into a pumpkin at midnight.

'Who is that?' Lady Samantha breathed.

'Don't you see the crest on the door, mother? It's Lady Caroline!'

'Caroline...no. That can't be her. I heard her father had recently made some good investments, but *this–*'

I swallowed. To judge by the amount of gold on that coach, those had to have been some really good investments. This girl had money. A lot of money.

Unable to look at Mr Ambrose, I stood there like a statue while the most magnificent of coaches rolled to a halt, the door swung open, and out of the interior emerged the ice queen herself. Or at least that's what she looked like. Blonde hair, brilliant blue eyes, and clad in a breathtakingly bejewelled fur coat under which the hem of a blue-white dress peeked out just enough to showcase the gold on the hem.

This girl, in her current attire, was worth at least five thousand pounds. And the worst thing was: she looked as if she were worth twice as much. I hardly recognised her as the shy-looking girl I had seen in Lady Samantha's engraving collection. And apparently I wasn't alone in that feeling.

'Caroline?' Adaira's incredulous whisper from beside me was barely audible.

I guess it was right what they said. Clothes do make the man – *and* the woman.

'Hello, everyone. It's so good to see you again!' Lady Caroline smiled a brilliant smile, whiter even than the snow around her. 'Adaira, you look lovelier each day. Lady Samantha! I can't wait to see your Christmas decorations. I'm sure they're even more beautiful than last year. And–'

Her eyes widened as they caught on Mr Ambrose.

'Oh my! Is that...'

And Mr Ambrose, Mr Rikkard Ambrose, stepped forward, grasped her hand, and pulled it to his lips.

'Lady Caroline. What a pleasure to see you again after all this time.'

DELICIOUS SLUSH

'Rick' she whispered.

I stiffened. *Rick?*

'Rick? Is that you? Oh God, I...' An unarguably flattering blush rose to her cheeks. 'I probably shouldn't have called you that. We aren't small children anymore.'

'By all means, continue as we were before.' Giving her a long, long look from under dark lashes, Mr Ambrose straightened out of his bow. 'There's no need for ceremony among old friends.'

Old friends? What the heck–

My heart froze in my chest – but unlike Lady Caroline, *I* wasn't an ice queen. A moment later, the ice splintered, broke apart, and my heart exploded into fire. Hot, red, angry fire!

I stepped on Mr Ambrose's foot.

'Ng!'

'Pardon?' Lady Caroline enquired. 'Did you say something?'

My dear employer, the treacherous weasel, cleared his throat. 'No, it's nothing.'

Oh? I was 'nothing' now, was I?

I pressed down harder on his foot. Somehow, damn him, he managed to maintain an absolutely impassive expression. I might as well have been standing on the foot of an elephant, for all the difference it made.

Time for a switch in tactics.

'Won't you introduce us?' I asked with enough sweetness to fill a dozen pots of honey and still have enough left to sweeten tea.

'Certainly.' With a jerk, Mr Ambrose removed his foot from under mine. 'Mr Linton, may I introduce you to Lady Caroline Elaine Sambridge, an old friend of the family's. Caroline, please meet Mr Victor Linton, my–'

'–his private secretary,' I cut in, bowing to Lady Caroline just about an inch or two. 'I manage his appointments. Which means that if you should wish to see him, you will have to make an appointment with me.'

This time, it was Mr Ambrose who stepped on *my* foot, and I wasn't quite as successful as he had been in keeping my face expressionless.

Lady Caroline gave me a genuinely happy smile, completely unaware of the marvellous multitude of tortures I was devising for her in my head at this very moment.

'Delighted to meet you, Mr Linton.'

Likewise – not!

Adaira stepped forward hesitantly. It was pretty clear that she knew the other girl but was somewhat intimidated by her extravagant attire. I made a mental note to have a little talk with Adaira about confidence. If she could manage her brother, she sure as heck shouldn't have any trouble with this lady.

'Won't you come inside and have a cup of tea, Caroline? I'm sure you could use something to warm up after the journey.'

'Thank you, I'm quite warm and comfortable thanks to this.' She stroked an admiring hand over her fur coat. 'Isn't it wonderful? The finest quality, all the way from Russia.'

'Um...yes. Quite.'

'But a cup of tea is always welcome.'

'As you wish. Willie? Reginald?' Adaira clapped her hand to call the footmen. 'Take care of Lady Caroline's baggage and–'

'Oh, don't trouble yourself.' Caroline waved Adaira's words away, gesturing at two men in lavish uniforms who had been riding on the back of the coach and now jumped off to hurry and get the luggage. 'My own servants will take care of it.'

'Oh. Well, I see.'

With what I thought was admirable restraint, Adaira refrained from kicking the arrogant little witch. This Caroline was altogether too fond of herself and her money.

Money which Mr Ambrose might find very attractive.

'Ladies and gentlemen?' Hastings the Butler had appeared out of nowhere in the typical manner of perfect butlers and bowed deeply to the new arrival. 'If you would please follow me? Tea is served in the small green parlour.'

'Yes.' Mr Ambrose nodded, his eyes on Lady Caroline. My fingers itched to close around his neck, and not for the purpose of gentle caresses. 'Let's go.'

Oh yes, Sir. We'll go all right - but not where you think!

I did just as the others did and followed Hastings inside. But the moment the company stepped into the entrance hall and redirected its steps towards the small green parlour, my hand fell on the shoulder of Mr Rikkard Ambrose.

'Excuse me, Sir?'

He stopped in his tracks. The others halted and glanced back, wondering what was the matter. I gave them the bright, professional smile I usually re-served for charitable organisations coming to call at Mr Ambrose's office - the official 'sod off' smile.

'I'm so sorry, ladies, but I'm afraid I'm going to have to steal Mr Ambrose away for a bit. He and I have a very important business matter to discuss.'

And before any of them could say a word, I tightened my grip on Mr Ambrose and dragged him off.

Neither of us spoke until we had reached his room. Tugging open the door, I shoved him inside and followed, slamming the door behind me.

'Well?' He stood there, arms crossed, back straight as a rod, ice glittering in his eyes. The arrogance in every inch of his stance...it was unbelievable! It prac-tically screamed *Do you think you could have dragged me here if I didn't want to be dragged? I could have stopped you at any time. I was in control. I still am. And no matter what I say to or do with Lady Caroline, it is none of your business.*

He cocked his head. 'Tell me, Mr Linton - what was this important business matter that you - mmmph!'

The rest of his sentence was cut off by my mouth slamming against his. In a flash, his arms unfolded, taking hold of me, crushing me closer - until he re-membered that this wasn't exactly a business discussion and pulled away, his eyes glittering.

'Mr Linton...what in Mammon's name...?'

I didn't let him finish.

'You know her?' My voice was rough from the kiss, demanding.

'Who?'

'Don't play dumb with me, Sir!'

'If you are referring to Lady Caroline–'

'You bet I am!'

'–then yes, I know her.'

My fingers, clenched around the lapels of his tailcoat, curled into tight fists. 'How?'

And more importantly: how intimately?

'I do not appreciate being cross-examined in this manner, Mr Linton.'

'Too bad. Get used to it! Now tell me: how do you know her?'

His left little finger twitched. 'Her family's estate is not far from here. We, err...crossed paths occasionally.'

'Crossed paths?' That sounded suspicious.

His little finger twitched again. 'If you must know, Mr Linton, I used to throw things at her. Snowballs in the winter, mud balls in the summer.'

Well, well...that was a nice surprise. Much better than the kind of interactions I had been imagining. For a moment, I indulged myself gazing at the mental image of Lady Caroline Sambridge covered in slush – but then I shook myself. I refused to let myself be side-tracked! There was too much at stake.

'You didn't throw mud at her today!'

'How observant of you, Mr Linton.'

'You...' I had to swallow before being able to get out the words. 'You *kissed her hand*!'

'Yes. And?'

'*And?*' I gaped at him. He sounded perfectly casual. 'You didn't do that with any of the others!'

'Quite true.'

'You never even kissed my hand!'

'Of course not.'

'Why not?'

'Because,' he told me in a tone of someone explaining the elementary mathematics of one plus one equals two to a very slow pupil. 'Unlike you or any of the other ladies, Mr Linton, she is immensely rich.'

My mouth dropped open. I had suspected that he wanted her for her money – I really had. But I also had never expected him to just admit it to my face.

'You...you...'

'You seem to have some speech problems, Mr Linton. Is something the matter?'

'You...I hate you!'

'Indeed?'

'I'm going to kill you!'

'Is that so?' He cocked his head, regarding me for a moment. His eyes narrowed, infinitesimally. 'Mr Linton...you aren't labouring under the delusion that simply because she is one of the wealthiest heiresses in the north, I intend to *marry* this girl, are you?'

I opened my mouth to scream some quite inventive obscenities at him – and then my brain registered what he had said.

'Wait...you aren't?'

'Of course not.' Cool eyes bored into mine, driving their way into my very soul. 'I have varied methods for enlarging my fortune – but marrying is not among them. I do not relish the thought of a business model that, barring murder, can only be implemented once. Besides...' His eyes took on a whole other kind of intensity. '...if I ever planned to claim a woman as my own, I would not waste my time with kissing her hand. I would pursue a very different strategy.'

'Such as?'

I had just time to utter the last syllable of that sentence before strong hands closed around my wrists and I was shoved against the wall, trapped between hard wood and even harder Ambrose. The breath was knocked out of me, and I stared up at the most powerful man in the British Empire, utterly lost to the mesmerising power of his eyes.

'Well, to begin with,' he growled against my ear, 'I would lure her into my room under some pretence, like, for instance...a business discussion.'

'W-would you?'

His lips graced my earlobe, sending a firework through my flaming body. 'Oh yes.'

I managed a weak smile. 'What woman would be stupid enough to fall for that?'

Chuckling, he moved down from my ear, over my neck, caressing my skin with his lips all the way. 'You'd be surprised. Once I have her in my clutches, I would press her up against the nearest wall so she can't escape–'

In flash, his arms shoved my wrists together over my head until he could keep me pinned with one single hand. His free hand began to travel down my side, eliciting a dangerous shiver.

'–then, I would drive her wild.'

'Y-you would?'

'Oh yes.' His mouth had reached my collarbone now and followed the curve until it reached that most sensitive little spot right at the centre. 'If I ever want a woman to be truly mine, I will stoke the fire inside her until she thinks about nothing but me and her, and she will submit. There will be no going back. All that she has, all that she is, all that she dreams will be mine, forever and ever.'

'Oh...'

'So you see,' he said, stepping abruptly away and letting go, nearly causing me to topple over, 'it's absolutely ridiculous to think that I would be interested in Lady Caroline. Shall we go?'

I stood there, panting and gaping at him. 'G-go?'

'Yes, go. To join the others. Or do you wish to waste more time leaning idly against that wall? If so, be advised that that time shall be deducted from your pay cheque. Knowledge is power is time is money, Mr Linton.'

And without another word, he turned and marched out of the room.

~~**~*~*

Suffice it to say that Mr Rikkard Ambrose's version of reassurance was not particularly reassuring. I mean, think about it. The man of your dreams kisses you to convince you he cares – then suddenly stops, glances at his watch, and says it's time to stop wasting time and join the lady you're jealous of. That just makes you feel great, right?

Clearly, this battle wasn't over. It might be for Mr Ambrose – but I would be damned if I let that ice queen sink her cold claws into him! He was mine! And anyone who disagreed had better watch their back.

I entered the small green parlour hot on the heels of my employer. Immediately, my eyes zeroed in on him standing in a small group with Lady Caroline and his mother. Ordinarily, that would have reassured me – there was no better buffer against romantic atmosphere than the presence of a mother. But in this case, the eager glow in Lady Samantha's eyes made me suspect she wasn't so much a buffer as a screw compressor clamp.

I was just about to start towards them when, from beside me, I heard a familiar voice.

'Mr Linton! There you are. How fortunate. I've been wanting to have a word with you.'

Dread roiling in my stomach, I turned and came face to face with a smiling Captain James Carter.

'Um...right now isn't really the right time...' My eyes strayed towards Mr Ambrose again. Had he just *smiled*? At one of *her* comments? No, surely that was a trick of the light!

'Please. It is important.'

'I'm sorry, but I'll have to–'

'It's about your sister.'

That stopped me in the middle of my sentence. My eyes snapped back to the captain.

'My *what*?'

'Your sister? Miss Lillian Linton?'

'Oh. Haha. Of course. My sister. Yes.' The dread in my stomach had a growth spurt and prepared to develop into full-blown, adult panic. 'What about her?'

The captain glanced around. 'This is not the best spot for this discussion. I wonder if we could go somewhere more private?'

Any hope I'd still had that he wanted to ask me about a suitable Christmas present for my female alter ego disappeared into thin air.

'Of course,' I groaned. 'Lead the way.'

Beaming, he opened a door to a small side room and stepped inside. I followed, wondering how the bloody stinking hell I was going to get out of this!

ALTAR EGO

The room was a small, plush space with flowery curtains and – could it get any worse? – *pink* wallpaper. The late afternoon sunlight sparkled on the snow outside, adding a romantic glow. The whole scene looked as if it had been taken straight out of the pages of a romance novel. The only problem with that was: both of the people in the room were wearing trousers.

With an earnest expression on his face, Captain Carter turned towards me. Never before had I seen him looking so serious before.

Crap, crap, crap! What am I going to do?

He cleared his throat.

'Mr Linton–'

'No!'

He blinked.

'Pardon?'

I crossed my arms in front of my chest. 'No. Whatever it is you want, no. On principal.'

That roguish grin I knew and loved flitted across his face. 'I suppose that is the standard response taught to you by your employer? He seems to be a...formidable man. Don't worry! I'm not going to ask you for his money or the clothes off your back. In fact, I don't want anything from him or you.'

Wrong. So wrong.

He took a step towards me, his face returning to that serious expression that was so very unusual for Captain James Carter.

'This isn't about you, Mr Linton.'

Oh boy! You have no idea...!

'This is about your sister.'

Here we go.

He took a deep breath. 'May I have the great honour of asking your sister to become my–'

'No!'

The captain blinked at me. 'But...you haven't even heard what I want to ask her yet.'

'Err...well...that doesn't matter!' I raised my chin, the image of the protective big brother. 'I, um...don't allow my sister to be asked things on principal. Especially if the asker feels honoured by it. That, err...would be bad for her. Very, very bad. It would, err...ruin her character. Yes, that's it!'

'Mr Linton, I do not propose anything immoral or unreasonable. I have great regard for your sister – in fact, I feel more than that, much more. Which is why I want to ask her to–'

'No!' I took a step back, waving both hands in the air. 'No asking. No asking of any kind.'

'But I want her to be my wife!'

The words were out. I felt my heart make a leap, and my mouth go dry. Had he really just said that?

Wife...

Wife...

Wife...

Oh yes, he had. I was still hearing the echoes in my empty, numb mind.

'Of course,' he continued with a reassuring smile that did not at all reassure me, 'I will understand if she declines. It is always her choice. But I feel deeply for your sister. I could see us spending the rest of our lives together happily. I am not a wealthy man, but my prospects in the military are good. I would be able to support your sister in the style to which she is accustomed–'

Oh really? Would that be her peacock vest, tailcoat or bowler hat?

'–and I would always respect her and give her the freedom she desires.'

You would, would you? Be careful what you promise...

'If you permit, I will begin to court your sister here, at Battlewood, and after a suitable period I shall make my intentions known.'

'And...' I cleared my throat to dislodge the hedgehog who had apparently taken up residence there. 'Just out of curiosity...what if I don't permit it?'

The captain stared at me. He seemed too taken aback to be angry or even annoyed. 'Is there any reason why you would? Anything you find objectionable about me as a suitor for your sister?'

I gave him a quick once-over.

Please! Please let there be some good excuse!

My eyes roamed across the tall figure of the officer in his immaculate red coat, staying for a moment on his strong face, roguish, intelligent eyes, long mahogany hair and broad, chiselled chest.

'Err...you have a speck of dirt about three inches below the knee on your left trouser leg?' I offered.

The captain stared at me, probably trying to figure out whether I was being serious or making a joke. To be honest, I was trying to figure out the very same thing. This whole situation was a bad joke! For a moment, I considered simply switching alter egos and shouting 'Surprise, Surprise!' Should I? Did I dare trust Captain Carter with that part of myself?

Better question, Lilly: what would it change? You know him. Do you really think that the fact you occasionally dress up as a man is going to deter him?

Even better question: did I want him to be deterred?

Swallowing, I opened my mouth. 'Captain Carter, I...'

The door behind me swung open. Without even glancing back, I knew who it was. I could feel him.

'Mr Linton? Am I interrupting something?'

'No!' Damn! Why did my voice sound like a squeaky hamster. 'No, not at all!'

'Actually, you are.' Before I could I could stop him, Captain Carter, the dear suicidal fool, stepped past me to block Mr Ambrose's path. 'Your secretary and I have some private business to discuss.'

'Indeed?'

Never in my life had I heard such an ice-cold death-threat vibrating in one single little harmless word. Mr Ambrose locked eyes with Captain Carter, and the air between them crackled with tension. Cautiously, I took a step back, my eyes flicking from one to the other.

Technically, Mr Ambrose should have been the one shirking from a confrontation. Captain Carter was a soldier, a trained fighter armed with a military sabre. But there was something in Mr Ambrose's eyes that told anyone it would be unwise to bet against him. I had no idea what kinds of things he'd done in his years in the colonies, but I knew what kind of world it was out there. A world ruled by the principle 'might makes right'. A world where he'd fought his way to the very top with tooth and claw. 'Come here,' his eyes seemed to say as they bored into the captain. 'Come at me, and I'll shred you to pieces.'

Almost involuntarily, Captain Carter took a step back.

'Your "private business" is at an end,' Mr Ambrose announced in the same tone a god would use to proclaim his commandments. 'Mr Linton and I have matters of importance to attend to.'

'Very well. We were finished anyway.'

We were?

Apparently so. The captain turned towards me with a resolute expression on his face. 'I'm sorry to hear that you disapprove, Mr Linton. I would have preferred to have your blessing, but in the end, it will not change my mind. Even if it did, it's not my mind I have to listen to. In this case, I have to follow my heart.'

'*Your heart?*' The words came from Mr Ambrose in a low whisper. Too low for Captain Carter to hear, probably, because he completely ignored them.

'If you wish, Mr Linton, you are free to try and prevent me from courting Miss Linton. But whatever you choose to do or say, I shall not be deterred. I shall be declaring my intentions to your sister very soon. Goodbye.'

And with a curt nod, he left the room.

There was moment of very, very silent silence.

'What intentions,' Mr Ambrose enquired, his voice almost eerily calm, 'was he talking about?'

'Um...his intention to dance with me at the Christmas ball. Which I disapproved of, because, um... of course I, um, despise dancing. Yes.'

'Is that so?' His eyes bored into me like drills of frost-coated diamond.

'Um...Yes, Sir.'

'Mr Linton?'

'Yes, Sir?'

'You do know what I would do if you ever lied to me, don't you?'

'Err...no?'

'Good. Keep wondering.'

And, with that ominous statement hanging in the air, he turned on his heel and marched out of the room.

~~*~**~*~*

With the way things were going, I would have preferred to bury my lady clothes in the closest ditch and forget my femininity until I was a hundred miles away from Battlewood Hall and Captain James Carter. But I couldn't. Every second I watched Mr Ambrose, surrounded by a gaggle of greedy-eyed ladies, Lady Caroline at the front, I felt the urge to shove them back, to get into their faces and tell them to sod off. But I couldn't. At least not as a man.

Gentlemen, for all their manifold freedoms, I was discovering, were deplorably limited when it came to telling ladies to go bugger themselves. Ladies, on the other hand – trust me on this – exchanged all kinds of spiteful, spiky comments with each other, hidden behind perfect smiles. But men? If a man was even suspected of being impolite to a lady in public, he was decried as being a rake and a barbarian. It was really abominable! Someone should really do something about this unfair treatment.

The moment I realised part of me was seriously considering setting up a men's rights movement, I knew it was time to get out of my male clothes in a hurry.

'Will you excuse me, please?' I bowed to Lady Samantha, who had just been gushing to me about how wonderfully things were working out because of all the ladies who were flocking around her son. Wonderfully? Ha! 'I just remembered that Mr Ambrose gave me a task to finish up before tonight. I'd love to stay, but...'

I let my words trail off meaningfully. Lady Samantha shook her head in disapproval.

'That boy is working you too hard, Mr Linton. You work hard enough for two people.'

If only you knew how right you are...

'If you come by your sister's room, please look in on her and see if she is all right, will you? I had a footman knock earlier, but he received no reply.'

'I'll go and check. It's probably just delayed travel exhaustion.'

'You think so?'

'Oh yes. I have a feeling she'll be up and about in no time.'

With a last glance at Mr Ambrose and his pack of admiring hyenas, I raced out of the room.

You know the saying 'out of sight, out of mind'?

Well, it's true. I was hardly out of the door when Mr Ambrose dwindled into insignificance in comparison to the dreadful doom that awaited me if I went back in there in female clothing. A doom by the name of Captain James Carter.

He was honestly going to court me. Court me and, one day, go down on one knee and make a you-know-what. The very thought set my heart racing, and I wasn't even completely sure why. It wasn't as if this was the first you-know-what of my career as an independent woman. I had fended off many a man with speed, sass and a spiky parasol. But this time...

This time it was different.

This time it was Captain James Carter.

What would he do if I said no?

And, even more terrifying...what would happen if I said yes?

Because a tiny little part of me was actually considering it. It wasn't that I was confused about my feelings. I didn't love Captain Carter. Not in that way. But when I thought back on everything we'd been through together, I thought that one day I possibly might. He was the only man I'd ever met who had instantly, without question, accepted me for who I truly was. He had laughed with me and danced with me, had helped me when I needed help and let me be when I needed freedom. If I had to pick one man who would be easiest to live with for the rest of my life, and would never get boring, it would be him.

But...this wasn't about ease. It wasn't about boredom. It was about me and what I longed for deep inside.

Did I want him?

The answer rang clear and true in my heart. And it wasn't a yes. It wasn't even a no. Because when I asked myself 'do you want him', it wasn't a word that came back as an answer. It wasn't even a thought. It was an image of a face. The face of Rikkard Ambrose.

Gah!

What was wrong with me? Wanting a man? Fine! That might possibly be squared with my feminist principles, if I managed to put a leash on him and

73

make sure he was house-trained. But wanting a cold, arrogant bastard when a perfectly amiable man was there for the taking – that wasn't just not feminist. It was insane!

And yet...

And yet...

Growling, I pulled open the door to my female version's room and grabbed the dress. Time to put on my uniform and march into battle!

WHERE THE SUN DOESN'T SHINE

The doors to the small green parlour swung open and, as if by magic, all gazes slid to the door. Captain Carter straightened. Mr Ambrose stiffened (which was impressive, considering how stiff he already was). The ladies all around the room narrowed their eyes.

I smiled, meeting all their gazes, and let my fan snap open. May the battle begin! 'Oh dear. I hope I'm not too late?'

'Miss Linton!'

Lady Samantha rushed forward, the relieved look on her face making me almost forgive her for the way she had been shoving girls at a certain someone the entire evening. Heck! Who could stay angry at a face like that?

'We were so worried! Are you ill? Should I send someone to town for the doctor?'

'Please don't trouble yourself.' Taking her small hands, I gave them a gentle squeeze. 'It's nothing serious. I was just feeling a little faint. The cold weather has that effect on me, sometimes.'

'Oh dear! Really?'

'Yes.' A cool voice caressed my ears from behind. I didn't need to look around to see who had circled the room to stand behind me. 'Miss Linton is such a delicate flower. A regular damsel in distress.'

Resisting the urge to elbow him in the gut, I gave Lady Samantha a smile. 'Don't worry. I'll be fine.'

Unlike your son, once I'm through with him!

'Lady Samantha?'

That sickly-sweet voice announced the arrival of the enemy. They circled us like a pack of hyenas, their ball gowns swishing, their eyes focused on the single, weak little victim they were planning to devour: me.

I smiled. These ladies were about to get a big surprise.

'I don't believe I've had the pleasure of meeting this young lady before.' One of the hyenas stepped forward, a perfect smile on her polished face. 'Would you be so kind as to introduce her to us?'

My eyes narrowed. *Introduce her to us...* It was always the social inferior who was introduced to his or her superior.

So, you think you're better than me, do you?

I was just about to open my mouth and tell this witch where she could stick her opinions, when Lady Samantha smiled her most grandmotherly innocent smile and said, 'Of course I'll introduce *you* to *her*! Miss Linton, may I introduce Lady Eveline Maria Westwood?'

Instantly, the smile disappeared from the newcomer's face.

Three cheers for Lady Samantha!

Showing her all my sparkly teeth, I curtsied. 'Maria? How charming. I have a sister of that name.'

'Is that so?'

'Yes. For some reason, you remind me of her.'

'And Lady Eveline, this is Miss Lillian Linton. Her brother works as a secretary for my son.'

'Oh.' Lady Eveline's smile reappeared in a flash. 'You invited the help for Christmas, Lady Samantha? How very charitable of you.'

Snickers came from all around.

Strangulation is against the law! Strangulation is against the law!

I repeated the words again and again – but that didn't make them any more palatable.

Still, I refrained from putting my hands around her scrawny neck. There were so much more sophisticated ways of destroying her, along with the rest of those hyenas.

'Oh, I don't think I was invited because of my brother's connection to Mr Ambrose,' I told them all with a genteel smile. 'Didn't you know? Mr Ambrose and I have known each other for a while now.'

'You have?' Lady Eveline's voice dripped with disgusted disbelief.

'You have?' Lady Samantha, on the other hand, sounded as if she had just received an early Christmas present. Behind me, I could feel Mr Ambrose freeze into a block of ice, and my fake smile turned into a real one. This might be more fun than I had expected.

'Oh yes. We met over a year ago at a ball at Lady Metcalf's. Since then, we've spent quite a lot of time in each other's company.' *I just happened to be wearing trousers during most of that time.*

'Why, Rick!' Lady Samantha's eyes, gleaming with undisguised plans for the future, fastened on her son. 'You never said!'

Mr Ambrose made an indistinct noise in the back of his throat. It sounded a little bit like a Siberian tiger choking.

'Well, he wouldn't.' Sidling up to my dear employer, I gazed up at him from under my lashes. 'He can be a little shy. I remember, when we were at the Royal Wedding–'

'The *Royal Wedding*?'

I didn't know who had spoken. The voice had been an unfamiliar squeak – one of the hyenas, presumably. When I glanced at them, they were all staring at me, mouths hanging open. Lady Samantha was not in much better shape.

'N-not *the* Royal Wedding, as...as in...'

'...as in Queen Victoria and Prince Albert? Yes, that one.' I gave Mr Ambrose a gentle nudge. 'Have you been holding out on your dear mother? Dear me, why would that be? Come on, tell them all about it. I know you want to.'

Mr Ambrose's jaw worked. Out of the corner of my eyes, I saw his little finger tapping a furious staccato against the palm of his hand. Finally, he parted his lips and, taking a deep breath, said:

'We were there.'

His lips shut again.

The circle of ladies gazed at him, waiting avidly for the story. Inconspicuously, I glanced at the clock on the mantelpiece to see how long it would take them to realise that was all they were going to get out of him. Thirty seconds...forty-five...

'That was it?' Lady Eveline demanded.

Under one minute. Impressive.

Mr Ambrose cocked his head. The silent gesture was as clear a 'What more do you expect?' as ever I heard spoken out loud.

'The Royal Wedding?' Lady Samantha breathed. Her eyes were practically shining with motherly glee, and I could have sworn she suddenly had wedding rings and little hearts for pupils. 'You truly were there? Together?'

Mr Ambrose engaged in a manly battle against his vocal cords, but finally he had to pry his lips apart and push out a cool, curt 'Yes!'

'Oh dear. Oh my goodness...'

Reaching out, Lady Samantha supported herself against the mantelpiece. She pulled her feather out of her pocket and began fanning herself.

The eyes of the hyenas became as big as saucers. They stared at Mr Ambrose, then a few of their gazes flickered to me, with an entirely new appreciation. I smiled at them, and placed one hand on Mr Ambrose's arm.

~~*~**~*~*

It was late in the evening. Lady Samantha and her daughter had been busy. Mr Ambrose had been forced, under pain of embarrassing baby pictures, to recount every single little detail of the Royal Wedding. The hyenas stood by, turning progressively greener and greener with envy. Lady Samantha, on the other hand, was in seventh heaven, and her daughter's eyes sparkled with nefarious plans.

Even under such pressure, however, Mr Ambrose did not reveal all. He did not reveal my double identity, for instance. And...

And he didn't reveal we had held hands almost throughout the entire ceremony.

When his lips closed tight on the subject, and his gaze met mine, I felt warmth rush up inside me. Somehow, even though I was the one who had brought up the subject, I was intensely glad that he hadn't mentioned that part. That was something private. Something just between the two of us.

'Miss Linton?'

My head jerked around. I had been so lost in Mr Ambrose sea-coloured eyes that I hadn't even noticed someone approaching – which was a problem, considering that the someone in question was my soon-to-be suitor.

'Oh, hello Captain Carter.'

'Good evening, Miss Linton.' Smiling, he performed a magnificent bow. 'Lost in thought?'

'Something of the sort.'

'I'm sure all this must be quite something after the quiet life you've led at your aunt and uncle's.'

'Ehem. Yes. Quiet life. Very quiet.'

'And, of course, in certain bloodstained caves in the Egyptian desert.'

I looked up, sharply. Captain Carter's eyes were sparkling. Damn, that man was sharp! How much about my secret escapades did he know? How much did he suspect?

'I haven't seen much of you since that trip to Egypt,' he said, softly. 'I'd like to change that.'

Here it comes.

'Would you like to go riding with me tomorrow?'

Oh. I had not expected that. I had reckoned on something more mushy-gushy, like reading poetry or singing love ballads. Glancing down, I wasn't sure how to answer for a moment. Finally, I managed: 'I don't know how to ride.'

Bloody hell, did I ever hate to admit that there were things I couldn't do!

A finger entered my field of vision, then a hand. I glanced up just in time to see Captain Carter reach out. His fingers gently clasped my chin and lifted it.

'Let me teach you.'

Learn how to ride?

Excitement rushed through me. To most ladies, it might have been not been important – just another silly sport, like tennis or croquet. But I knew differently. Riding was freedom. If a rider had a good, steady horse, he could go anywhere, escape from anything, be wherever and whoever he wanted to be.

Or in this case: she.

'Really?' I demanded, trying to keep the excitement out of my voice and miserably failing.

'Yes, really.' The captain smirked. 'Let me guess...you like the idea?'

'I'll see you tomorrow morning at six!'

I was so excited about the prospect of tomorrow's lessons that I hardly took in anything from the rest of the evening. I was going to learn to ride! To ride! To fly across the country on the back of a horse and be free! How could I think about anything else but that? I couldn't! Nothing could catch my attention! Nothing, except...

A strong, hard hand landed on my shoulder

'So, Miss Linton,' a familiar cool voice drifted to my ear. 'I hear you'll be taking riding lessons on the morrow?'

Crap.

'Um, well...'

'I had no idea you were so interested in horses. You seem less than enthusiastic about most animals.'

My back stiffened. I didn't have to explain myself to him! I didn't have to apologise for what I wanted. Turning, I fixed him with a fiery glare.

'That's because they persist in not doing what I tell them to.'

'I know the feeling.'

'Riding will be different. I'll be in control. I'll be learning something useful. Something I might very well need.'

'Need?' Cold eyes boring into me, he cocked his head. 'When would you need to ride, Miss Linton?'

Not evading his icy stare, I lifted my chin. 'You know very well what I am referring to. Certain...expeditions might require certain...skills.'

Silence.

Not because he didn't want to say anything, but because, in this instance, not even Mr Ambrose could find a reason to object. His jaw tightened.

'I hope you enjoy your "lesson", Miss Linton.'

And he was gone.

Just in time. A moment later, Lady Samantha appeared, little hearts still blinking in her baby blue eyes.

'Lillian, my dear!'

Holy...! I had been promoted from 'Miss Linton' to 'Lillian my dear' in one evening? I had to say, I was thoroughly impressed with myself. My tactics really had to be working their magic.

'Oh, Lillian, my dear! I'm so glad your brother asked to invite you. It must have been fate.'

Only if you count a trip to the local tailor as fate.

'I had no idea my son and you knew each other this well.'

Trust me – you still have no idea.

'Do you think it's possible that...' Blushing, she sidled up to me. I felt my body stiffen. I had wanted this, hadn't I? I had wanted to win!

Well...yes. I had wanted to chase the hyenas away, and impress Mr Ambrose's mother. But impress her this much? The look she was giving me made me slightly nervous. Like I was an incredible treasure from the bottom of a bottomless gorge of despair.

'Do you think it's possible that you...you and my son...' More colour rushed to her cheeks, and she lowered her eyes. 'No, forget it. Forget I said anything. I'm just babbling aloud the dreams of a silly old woman. And...Oh God! I called you Lillian, didn't I?'

If it was at all possible, the colour in her cheeks deepened even more.

'Please forgive me, Miss Linton! I didn't mean to insult you. I was just so...so...'

'I know.' Impulsively I reached out, taking hold of her hand. Her skin was papery and wrinkly, but in that moment, I wouldn't have exchanged it for the hand of the most beautiful angel in heaven. 'Lady Samantha?'

Cautiously, she glanced up at me. 'Yes?'

I squeezed her hand. 'Dream your dreams. Sometimes, dreams come true.'

˷˷**˷*˷*

What an evening! Yawning, I slowly made my way through the candle-lit corridors of Battlewood towards my room. Tomorrow would be a big day, and it was already late. If I wanted to be awake for my riding lesson tomorrow, I had better get a good night's slee–

A hand shot out from a bedroom door and closed around my arm.

'Hey! What the–?'

Before I could utter another word, I was jerked into the dark room and pushed up against the wall. My hoopskirt groaned and protested as it was flattened against the wood. A dark figure loomed above me, and in the little moonlight filtering in through the windows I could just make out a pair of eyes boring into me. Cold eyes. Sea-coloured eyes.

I slapped a hand against his chest.

'Has anyone ever told you that your manners leave a lot to be desired?'

'Yes. You. On multiple occasions.'

'Well, aren't I observant? You should give me a raise.'

He lifted one hand. Slowly, torturously slowly, he dragged a single finger down the side of my face. I couldn't help a shiver running down my spine. 'Indeed, Miss Linton?'

'Oh yes, indeed, Sir.'

'I don't give raises.' With deadly dangerous gentleness, his hand cupped my face. 'Especially not to people who fraternise with the enemy.'

'Enemy?' I gave him an innocent look – which dissolved under the icy glare he shot at me in return. I scowled. 'Captain Carter is not the enemy.'

'To me he is.'

'Since when?'

'Since now!'

'Why?'

His hand on my cheek tightened its grip, and he bent down, bruising my lips with a fierce kiss. 'You're a semi-intelligent female. Try to guess.'

I didn't need to. I already knew.

'I'm going to say this only once.' His words were barely audible. But still, they echoed in the dark room like the peals of an iron bell. 'Don't go!'

I lifted an eyebrow. 'I'm not going anywhere, Sir.' Lifting a hand to touch his face, I gently caressed that hard, immovable jaw of his. 'Strange as it may seem, I feel very comfortable here and now.'

Swooping down, he claimed my mouth with another hard kiss. After only a moment, he broke away and once more speared me with his icy eyes. 'You and I both know I am not talking about here and now. Don't go riding tomorrow!'

It wasn't a request. It was an order.

I sighed. Really, he should have known me better by now.

'Mr Ambrose, Sir?'

'Yes?'

'You can take your order and stick it where the sun doesn't shine.'

His eyes burned with cold fire. 'Oh, I can, can I?'

'Yes, Sir.'

'And where exactly does the sun not shine, Mr Linton?'

'Well, a few places come to mind.'

Strong hands grabbed my arms, lifting me bodily off the ground. A moment later I felt a soft mattress at my back, and then a hard Ambrose at my front.

'Why don't you show me some of them?' he whispered.

'Ha! In your dreams.'

'Indeed.'

A shiver ran down my back. Did that really mean what I thought it meant? Did he dream about me... about him and me...?

My thoughts were cut off by his mouth claiming mine. And, as the sun sank beyond the horizon, we found quite a few interesting places where the sun did not shine. At least not at this hour of the night.

THE STRANGER

'All right,' Captain Carter said, trying very hard to suppress a smirk. 'Maybe this was not such a good idea.

'This bloody thing might be a bit bloody easier if I could actually look in the bloody direction I'm supposed to ride in! I – *no! Hold still, you creature of hell! No, not in a circle! Straight! Do you hear me? You're supposed to walk straight ahead, you bloody beast!*'

'I think it understands the reins better than insults,' the captain suggested.

'You can take your reins and stuff them up your–'

By the time I was finished explaining to the good captain where exactly he could stick the reins, he was laughing hysterically.

'Merciful God! Miss Linton, where did you learn such inventive language?'

I shrugged, and nearly fell off my horse. 'I guess one picks things up in London society.'

'London society? Some of the words you've used I last heard from a Portuguese pirate three years ago, while he was busy cursing me to hell in his native tongue before being executed!'

'Um...well, I attend some very interesting balls. Besides – *Don't move! Don't move, you beast, understood? I'm in charge here!*'

'I'm not quite so sure the shouting method is working,' the captain dared to suggest. 'May I show you how to use the reins again?'

'I have everything under control!' I informed the captain firmly.

'Yes, certainly.'

'But...I wouldn't mind you showing me an alternative method.'

'Thank you. Here, you hold them like this...'

Two hours later, we had made real progress: I had acquired over a dozen bruises from falling off my horse, and was now cursing in Arabic instead of Portuguese.

'This is impossible!' I swiped my riding crop through the air, just barely missing Captain Carter's head. 'I'm sure I could do it if not for this infernal sidesaddle! I'm sitting on this thing like an oyster on a serving tray! How am I supposed to ride while staring off to the side? I have to see what's coming ahead, don't I?'

'Yes of course, and you can. Just slip your one leg over the pommel, and–'

'But then I'll be sitting all twisted up! I'll have a back ache the size of Yorkshire when I get off this thing. And besides, it's unnecessary! Why should I twist myself up when I could just be sitting straight and looking ahead?'

The captain blinked at me, confused. 'Well...because that's not possible on a sidesaddle.'

And that really was the crux of the problem, I realised later as I trudged back through the snow towards the stable. I wanted to learn to ride, yes, but...like this? Arranged like a pretty bouquet of flowers, hardly able to see where I was going, unable to ride faster than a brisk trot?

No! A hundred, a thousand times no!

Snow began to fall as I approached the stable, obliterating my tracks. My mouth quirked up in a smile that didn't really have much humour in it. How fitting. All traces of my brief foray into the equestrian world would soon be gone. As if I'd never been there in the first place.

'Well, maybe it's better this way,' I sighed, patting my horse on the neck. 'After all, I wouldn't want to have to bother with a beast like you for the rest of my life, would I?'

In response, the nice little horsey tried to bite my fingers off.

'Yes, that's right. You're a sweet, bloodthirsty monster. Should I see if I have an apple and a lump of arsenic for you?'

I reached the stable without loss of limb. Looking back, I sighed. The light snow falling outside had turned the world into a glittery wonderland. The thought of rushing through that beautiful place, uphill and down across the valleys...

'Welcome back, Mr Linton.'

I didn't even have to turn to know who it was. Even if it hadn't been for that familiar, icy tone, only one man in the entire world would address me as 'Mister' while I was dressed in a lady's riding costume.

'Come here to gloat, did you?' I asked, reaching up to unfasten the saddle. 'Go ahead.'

'Gloat? I do not waste precious seconds on such a senseless activity. It is enough to know I was right. I don't need to indulge in frivolous pleasure by reminding others of the fact. Knowledge is power is time is money. Remember?'

'I do.' Huffing, I pulled down the heavy sidesaddle and wiped sweat off my forehead. 'Which is why I'm sure you have some place to be. Aren't there any important memos for you to read or contracts to review?'

I reached for straw to rub the beast down.

'Stop.'

I froze. I didn't mean to. There was just something about Mr Ambrose's voice that said: first instinct = obey!

'Let's make a deal,' I sighed, tightening my grip on the straw. 'You leave me to my business, and I'll leave you to yours.'

Soft footsteps approached from behind me.

'This *is* my business. Drop the straw. The horse isn't yet done for the day. It has work to do.'

I didn't want to feel it. I really didn't. But I couldn't help it: a sting of jealousy swept through me.

'Are you going riding with someone, Sir?'

With one of the hyenas?

The footsteps came even closer. Mr Ambrose appeared in my field of vision, looking impossibly perfect, self-possessed and powerful in black boots, a black tailcoat and grey riding breeches. How did he do it? The clothes looked well past their prime. They were probably just as old and moth-eaten as anything else he owned. And despite that – no, *because* of it – he looked more of a man than any I had clapped eye upon before.

'Yes, as it happens I am going riding with someone,' he told me.

Who? Bloody Hell, who?

'Put a normal saddle on, will you?'

Relief flooded through me. It was a man!

But the question still remained – who?

His eyes met mine, and there was icy fire in them.

'When you're finished with the saddle – go get your trousers, Mr Linton.'

It took a moment for the meaning of his words to sink in. When it finally did, a slow but radiant smile spread across my face.

'You...you don't mean you're going to...?'

'Trousers, Mr Linton. *Now*.'

My grin blossoming into a full-blown beaming smile, I saluted and scurried off. For once, I was happy to let myself be bossed around. In a matter of minutes, I was back in the stable. Two horses stood ready and waiting at the open doors. Mr Ambrose was already in the saddle of the white stallion that made a startling contrast to his austere dark wardrobe. My charming horsey was prancing around beside him, waiting for its next dish of bitten-off fingers.

I shut the door behind me. Mr Ambrose looked around. 'Ah, Mr Linton. You are here.'

Our eyes met.

There was no need for words. No need for a please or thank you, or anything else. In that one look, we told each other more than other people did in a lifetime. He was here for me. He knew what I wanted. What I needed. And he was willing to give it to me. Despite this meaning he would have to give up the most precious thing he possessed: his time.

Oh dear.

I was in deep. Terrifyingly deep.

'Quit standing there like a spare lemon, Mr Linton. Let's go!'

'Yes, Si–'

Before I could even finish the word, he'd given his mount the spurs, and it dashed out into the white wonderland, spraying up diamond dust with its hooves. The snowy stallion nearly disappeared into the sparkling white whirl, making it seem as if Mr Rikkard Ambrose flew across the land by his own power alone. Swallowing at the sight, I took my own horse by the reins.

'Come on, beastie. We'd better go join him.'

And I stepped outside.

'What are you waiting for?' In a whirl of white. Mr Ambrose circled me and came to a stop beside me. 'Up into the saddle!'

'Yes, Sir!'

I was up in the saddle before the horse know what hit it. When it realised what had just been dumped onto its back, the beast pranced, whinnying in protest.

'Hey! I'm not that heavy!'

'The horse is intelligent, Mr Linton. It realises that you're nervous.' Mr Ambrose appeared beside me, grabbing the reins. Instantly, the beast calmed. 'Show some confidence! Sit up straight.'

My first instinct was to give a biting reply. But I guessed that, as long as I wanted him to teach me, I more or less had to do what he said. Clamping my legs around the horse to get a tighter hold on it, I straightened my back.

'No! Not like this. You're stiff as a board, Mr Linton. Relax your back and your legs. If you clamp on like a limpet, the horse won't be able to move freely. Relax.'

'Oh wonder of wonders! God be praised! I'd never thought I'd live to see the day when you tell me to relax.'

'Wipe that smirk off your face and concentrate, Mr Linton.'

'Yes, Sir! Right away, Sir!'

'Now, make sure your grip on the reins is not too tight and not too loose. Your arms and the reins should form one straight line. No! Not your whole arms, just your forearms. And loosen your hips. You have to move with the horse, and under no circumstances should you–'

As I sat there and listened, a strange feeling came over me. It was almost a premonition. Was I turning psychic? I suddenly had a firm feeling that Rikkard Ambrose was going to be a lot less patient a teacher than Captain James Carter.

So what, as long as he teaches me what I want to learn?

I smiled.

~~*~**~*~*

Time passed in a blur. After only a few lessons, I had passed from trotting around the yard to galloping across the snowclad meadows, hair flying in the icy air. During the next few days, Mr Ambrose and I raced each other around the manor house, rode into town, and every so often made trips into the solitary forest, watching the birds that had decided to stay and tough out the winter – all of course under the guise of helping me learn to ride. But now and again, when he would ride close to me or correct my position, his eyes and his hands would linger, and unspoken words would dance in the air with the snowflakes.

But the riding itself wasn't even the best part: no, what I particularly enjoyed was watching the hyenas from a distance as they desperately (and fruitlessly) searched for their new, mysterious rival Miss Lillian Linton, all the while wondering why the heck Mr Rikkard Ambrose would spend all his priceless time riding around with his little bumpkin of a secretary when he had a covey of beautiful women at his beck and call.

Poor dears! Life was frustrating sometimes, wasn't it?

Lady Samantha was a little more problematic. Apparently, the grandmotherly old lady had decided to take Miss Lillian Linton under her wing. And when she couldn't find her for hours on end, she became nearly hysterical. I – that is, the male I – had to stop her several times from sending Captain Carter off to his regiment, to gather a search party and turn the whole county upside down.

As for the good captain himself – he didn't make any more overt attempts to capture my attention, like the riding lesson. It made me hope, for just a moment, that he'd given up. But then I would walk past him in my lady clothes, and his eyes would follow me intently, and I realised I'd been wrong.

He hadn't given up. And, for the first time in my life, I found myself wondering how to let down a man gently. Up until now, I had been more interested in ramming them head-first into the ground. How did one do it? Was it possible?

Note to self: think about this in greater detail when you aren't having this much fun.

I was on another morning ride with Mr Ambrose when it happened. We had just passed a little hunting cottage that looked charming with its roof and chimney all covered in sparkling snow, and were about to turn back, when Mr Ambrose pulled on the reins and brought his stallion to an abrupt halt.

'What is it?' I asked. 'Do you–'

His hand shot up, silencing me in one single, swift motion. And then I heard it: soft thuds in the distance. Hoof beats. Hoof beats that were approaching fast.

'What's the trouble?' I whispered. 'It's probably just one of the other guests.'

A minute shake of the head. 'No. None of the others were out when we left. We rode hard, and in a straight line. No one could have overtaken us. Whoever it is, it's a stranger.'

In a flash, his hand darted into his tailcoat. When it came out again, it was holding a gleaming gun, cocked and ready for action. With enviable ease, he turned around his horse one-handed and, cantering off the path, hid behind a clump of trees. Following, I hissed: 'Don't you think you're being a little over-cautious? We're on your own family's land. Why wouldn't you be safe with your family?'

'As Brutus said to Caesar on the Ides of March.'

I stared at the back of Mr Ambrose's head. Brutus stabbed Caesar to death. He couldn't honestly mean that...No, that wasn't...

Was it?

Good Lord, what had happened between him and his father? What could possibly cut any family in half like this?

The question was driven from my mind a moment later when the hoof beats came around a bend, and a figure appeared in front of us that more than justified Mr Ambrose's precaution. I gasped.

The man was a wreck. His clothes might have been good quality once, but that was before a factory chimney had vomited all over them. That's what it looked like, anyway. He was covered from head to toe in soot. Several places were charred and bloody – and not from a fall or other accidents. I'd been with Mr Ambrose long enough to recognise the signs of punches and knife cuts. A slash went down all the way over the left side of his face to his chin, narrowly missing his eye.

In his left hand, the man clutched a rifle.

Maybe – just maybe – Mr Ambrose hadn't been overreacting after all. I supposed we were about to find out.

'Stay here,' Mr Ambrose commanded in an icy whisper. Raising his revolver, he took a firm grip on the reins.

'Gee-up!'

In a swirl of white, he darted out onto the forest path, gun already aimed and ready to fire. The stranger's horse shied and nearly hurled him to the ground. With a yelp, he grabbed onto his horse's neck, desperately holding on. The rifle in his hand came up.

'Drop that. *Now.*'

There was no room for debate in Mr Ambrose's icy voice – and no room for doubt about what would happen if he wasn't obeyed. The man's hand froze, rifle half-raised.

'I don't like to repeat myself. Drop. Now.'

The rifle clattered to the ground.

His revolver aimed directly at the man's heart, Mr Ambrose slowly directed his horse forward, until he was only a few yards away from the stranger. 'Who are you, and what is your business here?'

The stranger licked his dry, dirt-encrusted lips. Wild eyes flickered from Mr Ambrose to me, and back to Mr Ambrose.

'I'm looking for someone.'

'Indeed?' Mr Ambrose cocked his head. 'And who might that be?'

'A Mr Rikkard Ambrose. I'm looking for Rikkard Ambrose. Where can I find him?'

TAKING ICE TO NEWCASTLE

'I need to see Mr Ambrose immediately,' the wounded man demanded. 'Please, do you know where I can find him?'

'I might.' Mr Ambrose didn't lower the gun. 'What do you want with him?'

'I haven't got time for this!' His hands clenching into fists, the stranger moved to dismount – until Mr Ambrose's revolver swivelled to point directly at his head.

'Make time.'

The man swallowed.

'M-my name is Godfrey Baker. I am an assistant manager at one of Mr Ambrose's mines at Newcastle.[5] I have to see him! One of his mines–'

'There was an explosion.'

Mr Baker blinked. 'How did you know?'

Eyeing the soot-stained clothes of the other man, Mr Ambrose slowly lowered his gun. 'Let's just say I am perceptive. But if there was an explosion, what do you need Mr Ambrose for? The manager should be able to manage the situation. That is why he is called manager.'

'Um...yes, Sir. Except, the late Mr Gibbons isn't managing much of anything anymore, unless you are talking about lying very, very still in a wooden box. And, um...there's also this slight other problem...'

'The workers.'

'Yes, Sir.'

'They're striking.'

'Yes, indeed. You are very perceptive, Sir.'

Nudging my horse forward, I approached Mr Baker and eyed the cuts and bruises on his face. 'From the looks of it, they've been striking pretty hard.'

He gave me an exhausted smile. 'Indeed, Mr...?'

'Linton. Victor Linton. Private secretary to Mr Rikkard Ambrose.'

'*What?* Please, tell me, where can I find him? Where...?'

The man's voice trailed off, and his eyes slid back to Mr Ambrose, widening in a silent question. Mr Ambrose gave a curt nod.

Baker groaned. 'Forgive me, Sir. I've never had the pleasure of making your acquaintance, but still, I should have realised. I'm not at my best today. I rode all night and all day to reach this place, and haven't had a decent meal in...well, I don't even want to think about it.'

'Then don't. We don't have time to waste in any case. Your credentials?'

The man pulled a singed piece of paper from his pocket and handed it over to Mr Ambrose, who studied it briefly and returned it.

'Adequate. What happened?'

'Well, as you guessed, Sir, there was an explosion at one of the mines. You know the rumours that have been going around among the workers, about you cutting funding for safety precautions?'

'Yes. Like I told the manager, completely ridiculous. As if I would ever spend money on something like that in the first place.'

---

[5] In the 19th century, Newcastle (or Newcastle upon Tyne, which is the town's full name) was one of Great Britain's biggest mining centres, exporting huge amounts of coal. In fact, the city became so well known for its main export that the expression 'taking coals to Newcastle' became proverbial for doing something utterly superfluous and senseless. The expression is still used today with some justification, for although the British Newcastle ceased being a big name in the coal industry years ago, Newcastle in Australia, named for its famous predecessor, is today's biggest exporter of coal.

For a few moments, Mr Baker unsuccessfully searched for a polite reply. When he had opened and closed his mouth three times without anything coming out, I decided to help the poor fellow out.

'You were talking about rumours...?' I prompted.

'Ah, yes. The rumours. Of course.' He cleared his throat. 'Well, after the explosion, the rumours, well, um...exploded. People believe what happened is your fault, Sir. And quite a few people died in this incident.'

'Indeed?'

'Yes, indeed, Sir. And now the miners are rioting, and–'

Mr Ambrose held up one hand. Baker shut up and closed his mouth.

'Mr Linton?'

I snapped to attention. Not an easy thing to do while sitting on a horse, but I managed. 'Yes, Sir?'

'Return to the house. Pack our things, and a few supplies. Meet me back here in ten minutes.'

'Yes, Sir. Um...should I give our apologies to your mother?'

'You can give her yours, if you wish. I'm keeping mine.'

With that, Mr Ambrose removed me from his cognition, and turned his intense, sea-coloured eyes on Baker, unleashing a barrage of questions. As I turned my horse and galloped away, their voices faded behind me. It didn't take long until the house came into view in front of me. A small figure in a pink dress was standing at a downstairs window.

Poor Lady Samantha. I'm sure a miner's rebellion wasn't exactly part of her Christmas plans.

True. But right now I had other, much more pressing concerns. With his usual effortless, elegant callousness, Mr Rikkard Ambrose had dropped a nice, big problem into my lap: Mr Linton could make his excuses and ride off with Mr Ambrose. But what about *Miss* Linton? I had a feeling that, if a smiling Miss Linton were to approach Lady Samantha and say: 'Hello? I'm sorry to be rushing off in such a hurry. It's just, there's a violent uprising in a mining town a few dozen miles away, and I have to go with your son to expose myself to deadly danger and potentially get my head bashed in', the response might not be very positive.

What to do?

Well, you can always leave without saying anything.

Yep. I could – if I wanted her to send Captain Carter and half the British Army after me and her beloved son. Not good.

Well...that leaves only one option. The tried and trusted last resort of magnificent misfits: lying like a rug.

'Lady Samantha? Lady Samantha?' Pushing open the door, I strode inside. Something in my tone must have alerted her, because she was already rushing towards me.

'Yes, Mr Linton? What's the matter? Is everything all right? Is my son–'

'He's fine,' I hurried to reassure her. 'Nothing has happened to him. But we met someone out in the woods – a messenger from Newcastle. He told us that, um...one of Mr Ambrose's friends there is sick.'

'Oh dear!' Covering her mouth with one dainty hand, Lady Samantha took an involuntary step towards the door, as if she wanted to reach out and comfort her far-off son. 'That's terrible! I'm so sorry to hear that someone is ill. But...' She glanced at me, guiltily. 'Does it make me a horrible person when I say that, in a way, I'm almost relieved? I didn't know my son had any friends.'

Oh yes, he has made lots of friends. And they're all shiny and golden, with the face of King George III embossed on one side.[6]

So, in a way, what I was telling her was even true. For Mr Rikkard Ambrose, any enterprise that could potentially make money but currently didn't was probably the closest thing to a sick friend he was ever likely to have. Great justification, right? I had always been brilliant at justifying fibs. Still, the next one was a bit, well...

I cleared my throat.

'His friend might die.'

Any hint of gladness disappeared from Lady Samantha's face.

'Goodness gracious!'

'And he would like to see Mr Ambrose one last time. So you see—'

'Yes, yes, of course!'

Stepping forward, she clasped both my hands in hers, her eyes shimmering with tears of sympathy. It was almost enough to make me feel bad for lying – which was saying something. I didn't normally apologise for my favourite hobbies.

'Of course you must go, but...oh dear.' Shaking her head, she through a regretful glance down the hall into the house, from where the sound of music and merry laughter came. The sounds of approaching Christmas. 'I had so hoped that Rick would...well, it can't be helped. Will you tell your sister, or would you like me to deliver the news?'

'My sister? Oh, she will be coming with us.'

Lady Samantha's face lit up in a manner that was not entirely appropriate for a lady who had just been told one of her son's friends was about to take a trip to the hereafter.

'She will?'

'Yes, My Lady.'

'And...how long do you think you will be gone?'

'A few days, certainly.'

'And...you will all be staying in the same house?'

'I imagine so.'

'And...will Miss Linton be spending a lot of time with my son?'

'Oh yes. Definitely. Why?'

'Oh, nothing, nothing.' Hurriedly, she waved my question away. 'By all means, go. Of course you must, it's the right thing to do. I shall have Hastings get the coach ready for you.'

---

[6] Refers to the British gold sovereign, a gold coin worth one pound sterling. It was called 'sovereign' because it had the head of the current sovereign (or a past one, if the coins were older) embossed on one side.

Woah! I had not seen that coming. Wracking my mind, I desperately searched for an excuse why it would be difficult for a coachman to take me, Mr Ambrose and my non-existent sister to Newcastle.

'That...um...that won't be necessary. Mr Ambrose has already procured transportation.'

'Oh.' She appeared positively surprised. 'And is it appropriate for a lady such as your sister?'

If you consider a saddle-bruised butt to be appropriate... 'Yes, absolutely.'

Lady Samantha smiled. 'He really has changed for the better. Could it be that you and your sister are having a mellowing influence?'

Ha! In my most outlandish dreams!

'Thank you for the compliment, Your Ladyship.' I bowed. 'I'm afraid I will have to take my leave. I still have to prepare things for the journey, and–'

'Of course, of course! Go attend to your duties, Mr Linton. If you need any supplies, let the cook know that I said to let you have anything you want. The sky is the limit.'

'Thank you so much, Your Ladyship.' *Although, actually, the size of my saddle bag is the limit.* 'We'll be back as soon as we can.'

'Oh, don't you worry.' She smiled at me reassuringly. 'And do give your sister my warmest regards, will you?'

~~*~**~*~*

We were on the road to Newcastle within half an hour. It was just the four of us – Mr Ambrose and me, Mr Baker and Karim, whom I had fetched from his room back at Battlewood. While we rode, Mr Coal-Blackened Assistant Manager laid out the details for us. The farther we got, the blacker things seemed. And that wasn't just because of the thick black smoke we saw, rising up from the horizon.

'They're completely out of control,' Baker panted. Underneath his coating of coal dust, he looked pale, and he was hardly able to keep himself on his horse. Naturally, Mr Ambrose hadn't suggested we stop and rest yet. 'They're rioting all around the mine, seizing anyone who even looks as though he might be management. Some have even gotten pickaxes, and are roaming through the town, smashing shop windows and plundering.'

'Indeed.'

'Yes, Sir! They absolutely refuse to go back to work. After all the accidents we've had recently, that explosion was simply the last straw. They–'

'There were more accidents?'

'Yes, Sir. As I was saying–'

Mr Ambrose didn't particularly seem to care what Baker had been saying. 'What kind of accidents?'

'Oh, well...ropes snapping, brakes on mine cars giving out, that sort of thing.'

'Did those kind of things always happen that frequently at your mine?'

'No. We had a stroke of really bad luck, recently.'

'Indeed? How interesting.'

There was something in the tone of his voice...

Ice.

Lots of it. Much more than usual.

Spurring on my horse, I caught up to him. 'What are you thinking, Mr Ambrose, Sir?'

'I am thinking, Mr Linton, that we should ride faster.'

And he spurred his horse to a brisk canter, almost a gallop.

Soon, we came to the bottom of a hill. Mr Ambrose didn't slow when we started upwards, and the horses began to pant, sweat running down their flanks even in the bitter cold. He didn't pay any attention, and didn't let up even a bit until we reached the crest of the hill and looked down onto the town beyond.

On our way south, we had come past several towns and villages – delightful little places with busy markets, fresh snow sparkling on the rooftops and carol singers going from door to door.

Newcastle was not such a town.

Oh, there was snow – coloured various shades of grey, sometimes leaning towards black. And there were plenty of markets, to judge by the stench of tar and old fish drifting up towards us. There was even singing of a sort – though these singers had probably consumed a little more alcohol than the average caroller. Still, this was no happy little country town.

Cheap brick houses stretched as far as the eye could see. Black smoke rose from nearly every chimney, attesting to the city's one and only abundance: coal. The spires of several churches rose above the rooftops, competing for dominion over the town with the massive towers of the castle keep. Beyond it stretched the river Tyne, sparkling in the light of the sinking sun. And beyond that...

'Oh my God,' I breathed.

Thick columns of smoke were rising from an area beyond the river, more than could ever be produced by any factory. Flames were licking at the sky, mingling with the red glow of the sinking sun. It looked like a scene straight from Dante's *Inferno*.

'The mine is still burning?' I turned to Baker. 'I thought you said it was only an explosion.'

'An explosion in a coal mine.' He looked grim. 'Coal burns well.'

Between the flames and the smoke, figures were moving. I could hear distant shouts of 'Get them! Get them,' punctuated by screams of pain.

'Looks like we arrived just at the right time,' Mr Ambrose stated coolly. 'Let's go.' And he spurred his horse into a gallop, down the hillside, straight towards the city.

PANDEMONIUM

Unlike I expected, we didn't go directly to the mines. I soon realised why. If Mr Ambrose was anything, he was a cool-headed tactician. And appearing amidst a blood-thirsty mob in a rush, alone and on exhausted horses would not be a good move.

Instead, he led the way to a small two-storey town house on the safe side of the river. It was painted a dark brown colour that made soot stains hard to see, and ivy was climbing up one side of it. The door stood half open, and I could hear the voices of people whispering accompanied by soft crying.

'What is this place?' I asked.

'The mine manager's house,' came Mr Ambrose's curt reply. 'Since he won't need it anymore, we shall be using is as base of operations while we are in Newcastle.'

'Um...will his family let us stay?'

'They don't have any say in the matter. The house doesn't belong to them, but is on loan from the mining company.'

I opened my mouth to suggest whether we maybe shouldn't intrude on them in a time of mourning – but then I remembered whom I was talking to, and shut my mouth again.

Riding up straight to the front porch, Mr Ambrose slid of his stallion.

'Karim, Mr Linton – with me!'

We followed wordlessly as he strode up the stairs towards the open door. The whispers and crying from inside continued. We stepped into the house, Mr Ambrose in the lead, and through the first open door into a room where a sort of impromptu pre-funeral seemed to be going on. There were lots of people in black, and a sniffling woman wearing a veil. Mr Ambrose marched right up to her and placed himself before her, giving her a look as if she were a soldier whose bravery was in doubt, not a woman who had just lost her husband.

'Stop crying. Now!'

Everyone turned to stare. A hush fell over the room, and – *voilà* – the woman stopped sniffling. She blinked up at Mr Ambrose. 'W-what...who...'

Mr Ambrose didn't let her finish. 'Where are your guestrooms?'

'P-pardon?'

'I said, where are your guestrooms?'

'Why would you want to know? Who in heaven's name are you?'

'I'm the man who's going to avenge your husband and see to it that the people responsible dangle from the gallows by the end of the week. Now, for the last time, madam – *where are your guestrooms?*'

Slowly, the woman reached up and pulled her veil aside. Tears were still glittering on her cheeks. But there was a look in her eyes that I bet hadn't been there a moment before.

'Y-you can do that? You can get justice for my Jack?'

'Not justice. Vengeance. And yes, I can.'

'Who are you?'

He leaned forward just an inch or two. The woman seemed incredibly small and breakable in his shadow. 'Rikkard Ambrose.'

If it had been quiet in the room before, that was nothing compared to the absolute nothingness of silence that suddenly fell over the gloomy space. You could have heard a pin thinking of maybe dropping in a couple of hundred years. A ferocious gleam entered the woman's eyes, making one thing a hundred per cent clear: she knew the name. And she wasn't the only one.

'*The* Rikkard Ambrose?'

'Yes.'

The woman's face hardened, and she said something that made my respect rise for her a hundred miles. 'How do I know that it wasn't you who was responsible for my husband's death? It was chaos down there! Nobody knows who or what killed him. Maybe it wasn't one of the miners but the explosion. Your mine, your explosion. Maybe it is you I should want to see dangling from the gallows.'

Well now, that was a brave woman. A woman to admire. Sure, she had just basically accused the man I loved of murder and threatened to see him hang, but between kindred spirits such small faults can be easily overlooked, right?

Mr Ambrose didn't retreat an inch. He gave the woman his iciest stare. 'All my miners are equipped with Stephenson safety lamps, the latest models of CGDIs, and–'

'CGDIs?'

Mr Ambrose half-turned, throwing me an icy look for my interruption. 'Canary Gas Detection Implements. If the canary dies, there's gas in the mine and you had better get out.'[7]

'Oh. I see. Pray continue.'

'As I was saying, there are extensive security measures in place. The miners are checked for flammable material before entering the mine, and if any is caught with a dangerous object, he is dismissed immediately. So how could this explosion have been a simple accident? There is more to this than meets the eye, and I can find out what. The only question is – will you work with me, or against me?'

Silence. Mrs. Gibbons stood there, looking up at Mr Rikkard Ambrose. Really looking at him, deep into his hard, dark, unfathomable eyes. I knew what she saw there. It was the same thing I had seen there the first day I had crossed paths with this man. The message that was written in stone there for all the world to see.

You want to take me on? Try it, if you enjoy suicide.

'Vengeance?' she asked.

He nodded. 'Vengeance.'

There was another moment of silence – then, taking a deep breath, Mrs. Gibbons lowered her head and curtsied. 'We have an agreement. How may I be of assistance, Mr Ambrose?'

'First of all, I need you to stop feeling sorry for yourself. Stop this nonsense.' With a dismissive gesture, he waved at the people in black. Eyes widened all around. Gentlemen murmured. Ladies gasped. 'Get these people out of here.

---

[7] This is not a joke. The Victorians' method for detecting gas in a mine was indeed sticking a canary in there and seeing if it came out alive again. However, they were not commonly referred to as CGDIs. That lovely term is my own invention.

First comes revenge – then you can waste as much of your time crying as you want.'

'Well, you heard him. Out!'

Outraged whispers rose all around as the lady began herding her guests out of the room. One gentleman's voice rose over the others: '...outrageous! Is there no respect left in the world?'

'I have plenty of respect, Mr Bingham!' Mrs Gibbons retorted, sharply. 'Particularly for my dead husband. Which is why I am going to find out who the hell is responsible for this, and I'm going to grind them into dust! Outside, now!'

Well, well...the two of us really were going to get along well.

In minutes, the salon was empty. For the first time, Mrs Gibbons noticed the rest of our little party: Mr. Baker, sweet little me, and the not-so-sweet-or-little Karim. For a moment, her eyes lingered apprehensively on the latter before returning to Mr Ambrose.

'What now?'

'Now we need something to eat and fresh horses. We've been on the road since early morning to get here, and the mounts we arrived on can't go another step. Who has good horses here in the city?

'There's Albright's stables, and there's Bell's, and Blenkinsopp's. Blenkinsopp's is closest, but–'

'It's Blenkinsopp's, then.'

'But his stable is to the south, quite near the river! If someone were to go there, he might come across those...those...'

She shuddered and glanced out of the window at the flames in the distance. The faraway echo of men chanting and shouting drifted into the room.

'That won't be a problem.' Mr Ambrose snapped his fingers. 'Karim?'

'Yes, *Sahib*?'

'Get us horses.'

'Yes, *Sahib*.'

'And, Karim?'

'Yes?'

'If anybody should happen to get in your way...' Mr Ambrose gave the big Mohammedan a long, long look.

'I understand, *Sahib*.'

So did I. Those poor little striking miners. There were only a few hundred of them. This was so unfair.

'Mr Linton?'

At hearing my name – well, sort of, anyway – I snapped to attention. 'Yes, Sir?'

'Get Mrs Gibbons to show you the kitchen. You and Mr Baker can eat there before we leave.'

'Yes, Sir. And you?'

His face was stark. Looking away, he said, 'I don't need anything.'

'Sir, you should–'

'I said I do not need anything, Mr Linton!'

'Yes, Sir. Sorry, Sir.'

'Let me know when Karim returns. I shall be in Mr Gibbons's office, reviewing his records. Maybe I shall find a clue there as to what happened here.'

'Yes, Si–'

Before I could finish, he had marched out of the room.

'–r.'

'Dear Lord.' Shaking her head, Mrs Gibbons looked after him. 'I pity the girl who that man sets his sights on.'

'So do I,' I sighed. 'So do I.'

~~**~*~*

It was about an hour later when I knocked at the dark wooden door of the late Mr Gibbons's office. There were footsteps, and a moment later, the door swung open, revealing the figure of Rikkard Ambrose looking just as indomitable and hard as ever, and not in the least as if he hadn't eaten or rested for over eight hours.

'It's time,' I told him.

'Did Karim get horses for all of us?'

'What do you think?'

If I were a stable owner and Karim showed up at my door demanding mounts, I would resort to begging my imaginary fairy godmother to turn rats into horses just to get him what he wanted.

'So...we're ready to go.'

'Yes.'

I stood there, waiting. Waiting for Mr Ambrose to say: 'Well, let's go then! Knowledge is power is time is money, Mr Linton.'

But he didn't.

Instead he took a step towards me and said, 'I suppose there's no way I can talk you out of this?'

I shook my head. 'No.'

'I didn't think so.'

He moved so fast I didn't have time to blink. In a flash, he had grabbed me by the arms and pulled me into the empty office. The door slammed shut behind us, and the next moment my back slammed up against it, and he was kissing me. Hard. Fast. Heedless of the consequences. And I was heedless, too. Headless. Mind completely blown. Everything around us vanished, and there was just him, fighting for control of my mouth, and me, fighting back with everything I had.

And then it was over.

Panting, I stared up at him, still pinned to the door. He stared back at me, sea-coloured eyes fierce and cold as ice. 'Stay!'

My answer was just as determined. 'No!'

He was on me again in an instant, his lips reclaiming mine – and mine reclaiming his! The kiss was like an explosion. Fire sizzled through my veins. I could almost feel the ground rocking beneath my feet, so hard did he–

No, wait.

That *was* the ground rocking beneath my feet. Crap!

'Mmmh!'

I pushed against Mr Ambrose – to no effect whatsoever. There was a rumble, and the earth trembled once again.

'Nnn! Mmmh!'

My fists thudded into his chest – and still not the slightest reaction. Apparently, an earthquake was not important enough for Mr Rikkard Ambrose to interrupt his kissing schedule. And some part of me had to agree. After all, we were in a pretty important meeting right now, conducting significant business...

No! Bad Lilly! Bad Lilly! Think 'Feminist'! Think 'Strong, independent woman'!

Crap, crap, crap. Oh well, if I had to...

How to get Mr Rikkard Ambrose's attention?

Well, there was always one way.

I slipped one hand into his tailcoat. Down it went, and farther down. Beneath my lips, Mr Ambrose uttered a groan. My hand wandered even further down, slipped between two layers of cloth, and –

He stiffened.

'Mr Linton?' His whisper against my lips was hardly audible. But it was cold enough to give a polar bear hypothermia.

'Yes, Sir?'

'Let go of my wallet.'

Slipping my hand out of his tailcoat pocket, I held up the slim leather container and gazed innocently up at him from under my lashes. 'What, this wallet?'

He made a grab for it. Ducking under his arm, I danced out of the way.

'Mr Linton?'

'Yes, Mr Ambrose, Sir?'

'Give that ba–'

He was interrupted by the sound of the world exploding outside. Red-gold light illuminated the room in a flare worthy of Armageddon.

Our eyes met.

'I think, perhaps, we had better leave.'

'Indeed.'

Taking a deep breath, I tossed him his wallet. He nodded.

'Let's go! Knowledge is power is time is money, Mr Linton.'

Oh, how wonderful that some things never changed.

And how wonderful that some other things do, my tingling lips whispered in silence.

Karim was waiting for us outside. Without a word, we got on our horses and started down the street. Not far ahead, beyond the river, we could see the red glow of the fires. As the darkness of night began to fall around us, it seemed as if we were riding straight into hell.

'Halt! Who goes there?'

And here was Cerberus.

This guard dog, however, didn't have three heads. He had just one, and two arms and legs, and a bright red uniform.

'Sergeant.' Mr Ambrose nodded to the man. 'We'll be crossing the bridge.'

'I'm sorry, Sir.' Stepping sideways so he was right in the middle of the street, the sergeant blocked our way. 'I cannot let ye do that. I've got orders from Corporal Hicks to not let nobody through.'

'I suppose it would be superfluous to point out that if you have orders to not let nobody through that would be a double negative, meaning that, in fact, you had orders to let everybody through?'

The sergeant's honest forehead furrowed. 'Sir?'

'Forget it! Step aside, man. Now!'

'Sorry, Sir. Cannot do that. I've got orders from Corporal Hicks to not let–'

'–nobody through, yes. I heard you the first time.'

'There's miners rioting on the other side of the river, Sir,' the sergeant added, helpfully, clearly hoping that this additional information would finally make the tall gentleman in black see sense.

Mr Ambrose's eyes narrowed infinitesimally. 'Yes. *My* miners.'

The good sergeant needed a moment or two to process this information. When he had fully understood, his face paled. In the red firelight it looked like cream with strawberries, only a lot less appetising.

'You mean...you are...'

'Yes. Now step aside.'

'Yes, Mr Ambrose, Sir! Of course, Mr Ambrose, Sir!'

I raised my eyebrows as we rode past. 'Pretty impressive.'

'Things can be quite easy when you own half the town, Mr Linton.'

'I'm sure they can, Sir. Just one question...'

'Yes?'

'Is it the half that's burning?'

'Shut up and ride, Mr Linton.'

It didn't take long until the stench of smoke invaded my nostrils. The crackle of flames became louder and louder. Not for the first time, I asked myself whether it would be wise to continue. But whether wise or not – Mr Ambrose was not turning back. So I'd be damned if I chickened out!

Dark shapes shifted in the blackness ahead. Slowly, five men, three armed with pickaxes, the other two with clubs, emerged from the shadows.

'Piss off,' one of the men growled. 'We're on a strike. There ain't no place for fancy tossers like ye here!'

Mr Ambrose gazed down at them from his horse like a king at vermin beneath his feet.

'I am Rikkard Ambrose. Take me to the leader of your rabble.'

The men stiffened. They exchanged long, hard looks – then started towards us, their weapons raised to strike.

Crap!

NORTHERN CHIVALRY

The men had not even taken half a step when something long and shiny suddenly appeared in Mr Ambrose's hand. Firelight glinted off the revolver's barrel.

'This gun,' Mr Ambrose said in a tone as cool and composed as if he were discussing tomorrow's weather prospects, 'can fire seven rounds in quick succession. There are five of you. I am an excellent marksmen, and my associate,' he nodded at Karim, 'is also armed. I'll leave it to you to make the calculations.'

The men stopped.

One of the ones in the background frowned. 'What's a calcalashion?'

'Maybe leaving the math to them was not such a good idea,' I whispered.

But then my eyes landed on the fellow at the head of the little group. He had definitely got the message. His fists clenched around his pickaxe – but he didn't move an inch.

'Bloody hell! All right, let's go! But you I'm warning ye, if ye shoot...!'

Mr Ambrose's only answer was a silent nod.

The men turned and started down the street and, at another nod from Mr Ambrose, we gently nudged our horses and followed at a slow trot. As we went, more men appeared out of the darkness, staring at us. Grim, coal-covered faces with hard eyes and even harder pickaxes. As casually as possible, I leaned across to Mr Ambrose.

'Just out of curiosity... What was your plan again?'

'I am going to tell these people to end the strike.'

'Oh, I see. And...then?'

'Then they'll end the strike. That is the plan.'

'Ah. I see. And, just in case, let's say, it didn't work – I mean I'm sure it will. It's a great plan, just ordering people to do what you want. Really great – but imagine for a moment that, hypothetically, it won't work. What's plan B?'

'There isn't one.'

'Oh. I see.'

Why me? Why oh why do I have to be in love with a maniac?

'Brilliant, Sir. Absolutely brilliant.'

'Silence!' one of the men who led the way shouted.

He was lucky that this was about the only command in the world that Mr Rikkard Ambrose had no problems complying with.

Apart from the crackle of flames and the occasional whisper out of the darkness around us, we rode through the gloomy street without hearing a thing. The stench of smoke became more intense with every step our horses took. So did the red glow in the distance. The houses around us were replaced first by warehouses, then by ramshackle wooden huts. Finally, they disappeared altogether. Red flames enveloped us. But not because we were standing in front of a burning mine. Oh no. That was a long way off yet. I could see the black-red column of flame and smoke rising ahead of us, reaching for the sky. No, we were surrounded by hundreds upon hundreds of dirty, dark-faced, angry miners standing in the cold winter night, grouped around dozens of coal fires. As we rode past them, the heat was almost intense enough to scorch my skin.

'Murderer!'

The shout came from the left. My head whirled around just in time to see the dark object whizz past, and–

Thud!

Karim's hand shot out, catching the thing in mid-air, before it could hit Mr Ambrose in the head. My dear employer hadn't even flinched. Glancing at Karim, he gave a small nod.

The mountainous bodyguard clenched his fist. There was a grinding sound, and black coal dust drifted from between his fingers. A moment later, the impromptu projectile had disintegrated into nothingness.

'Anyone tries that again,' Mr Ambrose said, in a very calm, very controlled voice, 'and the accusation will become true.'

Fire glinted off his gun.

The crowd was silent.

'Very well, then. Now that I have your attention...' His gaze swept over the assembled miners, fastening on a tall, emaciated man with a scar on his left cheek. 'You! Yes, you there. You're the leader.'

The man exchanged unsettled glances with his compatriots. 'How did ye–'

Mr Ambrose didn't let him finish.

'Tell your men to get out of my way.'

The man's jaw tightened. 'Ye ain't in no place to give orders! People died! We want justice!'

'Strange.' Mr Ambrose cocked his head. 'The widow of the manager said the very same thing to me not half an hour ago.'

Uncomfortable glances were exchanged.

'I've not got nothing to do with that!' the man growled.

'I'm sure you don't. But someone here has.'

'The manager died in the explosion!'

'Did he? A manager's job is to do paperwork. To write reports and sign cheques. You think he was doing that down in the mine shaft before it exploded?'

The men shifted. Again there was whispering.

Mr Ambrose fixed his most arctic stare on them. 'If he was down there, there must have been something wrong. Something happened that shouldn't have happened. Let me pass. Let me find out what was behind that explosion.'

'Why should we believe anything ye say?' one of the men spat. 'We don't mean nothing to ye!'

Mr Ambrose met the man's glare with a gaze of frost-coated iron. 'You're right. You don't. But the coal down that mine does. That is a fortune burning down there. *My* fortune. So if you think that I am stupid enough to let my own mine catch fire and kill several people in the process – then by all means, try and kill me. Get your "justice". But if you don't – then you will get out of my way and let me do what I came here to do!'

98

The mob hesitated. Our fate hung in the air, suspended by a thread. I had never trusted threads. The darn things always refused to go through the eye of the needle.

Almost against my will, I glanced at Mr Ambrose.

Would we die tonight?

Would the two of us never get a chance to–

'All right!' Growling, the scarred man stepped aside. 'Go through! Do whatever it is ye wanna do, and find out who did this. But I'm warning ye: if ye dunno have names for me in half an hour, I'm coming in there after ye!'

And, with a barked command, the crowd parted, opening the path to the mine's office building. It was a stark brick structure, one side scorched by the heat of the fire, but as yet completely intact. Nodding to the scarred man, Mr Ambrose nudged his horse forward, and we rode through the gap in the muttering crowd.

We still weren't completely through when I leaned over to Mr Ambrose, whispering: 'How exactly are you going to find out in half an hour how an explosion was caused in a mine that you can't enter, because it's still burning?'

'I'm not.'

'Y-you're not?'

'No.'

'And you are not even slightly worried about the heavily armed mob who said they'd kill you if you don't do what you just told me you have no intention of doing?'

'No.'

I wanted to scream at him. I wanted to grab him by the throat and shake him, and kiss him, and–

No. No kissing! Forget about the kissing!

And I had better forget about the yelling, too. At least while we were still in hearing distance of the mob. So I seethed quietly instead, following Mr Ambrose and Karim up to the smoke-blackened office building. Sliding down from his horse, Mr Ambrose strode up to the main door and straight inside. I rushed after him, fire blazing in my eyes.

'What the bloody hell do you think you're doing?' I demanded as soon as Karim had closed the door behind us.

Ignoring me completely, Mr Ambrose grabbed a nearby desk and with an ease that betrayed the hard muscles under that unassuming old black tailcoat, shoved it towards the door.

'I said *what are you doing*?'

'Barricading the door, Mr Linton.'

'I can see that!'

'Then why ask?'

'Gah! You're impossible!'

'Karim?'

That one word was enough. With a muttered 'As you wish, *Sahib*,' the big Mohammedan grabbed a huge shelf full of files and shoved it against the desk.

'Can someone tell me what is going on?' I demanded. 'I thought we were supposed to be investigating, not redecorating!'

Mr Ambrose threw me a look.

'We're waiting and preparing. We have to hold out until the reinforcements arrive.'

I blinked. 'Reinforcements?'

'Well, of course, Mr Linton. You did not think I was insane enough to go into this alone, do you? A squadron of hired men is approaching from the south to disarm the miners and put the fire out. We are merely the distraction.'

'Oh.'

'I knew that if I myself appeared at the miners' flank, they would focus all of their anger and attention on me and leave the other flank unguarded. Now we only have to wait it out until my men arrive.'

'Your men?'

'Which I sent for from Mrs Gibbons' house.'

'Ah. Of course. I knew that.'

'Indeed?'

'Of course! I'm not stupid! I knew all along that you weren't just barging into this and leading us all into deadly danger.'

'Indeed.'

That was the moment when something huge and hard slammed against the door, making it shudder and creak.

'Ambrose, you bloody swine!' The voice of the scarred men was a roar in the night outside. 'Ye lied to us! Ye aren't alone!'

'I never said I was.' Mr Ambrose's voice was icy calm. How did he do it? 'Surrender. End this, and nothing will happen to you.'

'Surrender? To ye? You bloody capitalist maggot, we ain't surrendering to nobody! We want justice!'

'And you'll have it. *My* justice.'

'Ye... I'm gonna kill ye! Yer goons might get me, but before they do, I'm gonna get to ye! I'm going to rip your liver out!'

There was another shuddering crash against the door.

I swallowed.

'What was that I just said about being safe from deadly danger, Mr Ambrose?'

My dear employer threw me a cool look. That didn't worry me half as much, however, as the voices outside the door yelling 'Get that beam! Battering ram, against the door! Now!'

'I think we had better procure more material for our barricade,' Karim suggested.

'Oh, you think, do you?' Repressing my urge to give the man who had probably known about this inane plan from the start a good kick in the butt, I grabbed the closest shelf full of files and pulled.

It didn't move an inch.

I pulled again. 'Nnnnnng!'

Still nothing.

'Nnn – aah!'

The shelf made a sudden jolt forward and began to tip, threatening to squash me – then suddenly stopped. Glancing up, I saw Mr Ambrose standing beside me, his hand tightly gripping the shelf. I expected him to make a remark about how weak and helpless we little women were – but he didn't. Instead, all he did was nod at me. Our eyes met.

'Together?'

All right. Maybe I wasn't going to strangle him after all.

I nodded back. 'Together.'

It didn't take long until we had a solid wall of desks, shelves, and several sacks full of coal piled up against the door. But even so, the wood of the door groaned under the repeated onslaught, and our barrier slowly shifted. From outside, I heard shouts of encouragement mixed with the noise of fighting.

'So,' I panted, leaning with all my weight against the end of the barrier and for the first time glad about my generous behind, 'is this an average day in the life of a coal mine manager?'

'Not quite.' Somehow, Mr Ambrose's voice was still as calm and collected as ever. He wasn't even out of breath. 'This is somewhat extreme.'

Another strike hit the door, nearly toppling the shelf and squashing me. 'I'll say!'

Another strike. And another. Again, the shelf wobbled dangerously. I pressed myself against it with all my strength.

'Mr Linton, get away from there!'

'Don't worry, I've got this. I–'

Grabbing my wrist, Mr Ambrose yanked me back, just as another hit smashed into the door, and the shelf toppled over. For a moment, I was wrapped in Mr Ambrose's arms as dust, wood splinters and stray pieces of paper whirled around us in a cloud of debris. For a moment, I felt safe. Then, the door gave a tortured groan, and a crack appeared down the middle.

'Upstairs!' Mr Ambrose commanded. 'Now!'

And for once, I didn't argue.

We dashed up the stairs to the upper floor. It was built above only half of the house, with a big landing, almost a platform at the top of the stairs – probably for speaking to miners at meetings. Well – there certainly would be lots of miners in here, soon. But they probably wouldn't be in the mood to listen.

Tearing open the door, I rushed inside and slammed it shut behind me. The glass pane in the door clattered.

'Really?' I panted, glaring at Mr Ambrose. 'A *glass door*?'

'It is very useful to keep an eye on your employees, Mr Linton.'

'Not so useful to survive a siege, though, Mr Ambrose!'

'Mr Linton?'

'Yes, Sir?'

'Silence!'

Promptly, a stone smashed through the glass door, and shouting flooded in from outside. Apparently, the dear miners didn't care much for Ambrosian commands. They were coming up the stairs, their footfalls making the whole building tremble. But then shots suddenly rang out, and the footfalls ceased.

'The reinforcements!' Karim shouted. 'They're here!'

The door shuddered under an onslaught of blows. Fists slammed through the glass.

'I don't think that's going to make much difference!' Backing away, I glanced around for a weapon, a way out, anything! But there was nothing.

'There's only one thing to do.' Mr Ambrose's voice was cool and firm.

'What?'

'Speak to them. They know my men are coming. They can't hope to win this. Any logical human being will be forced to concede defeat.'

And he stepped towards the door before I could point out that people who punch through glass with their bare hands weren't my idea of logical human beings.

'Mr Ambrose, don't–'

'Stay here!'

And, ripping the door open, he stepped outside, and slammed it shut again behind him.

From one moment to the next, it went deathly quiet outside.

It stayed like that for about two seconds – then the mayhem started. Men bellowed in rage. There was no sense to it, no meaning. Here and there, I caught words like 'kill' and 'skinflint' or 'murderer' – but beyond that, it was just rage erupting from a thousand throats.

'Blast! We have to get out there! We have to help him!'

Karim stood unmoving as a mountain, both hands resting on his sabre stiffly.

'The *Sahib* said to stay.'

'But–' I started towards the door. Moving quicker than I would have believed him capable of, Karim grabbed my arm, holding me in place. Wait...was he actually *concerned* for me?

'The *Sahib* said to stay. We must obey.'

Of course not. He was just following orders.

'Let go of me!'

'No!'

Outside, I heard Mr Ambrose's cool voice speaking, audible even over the angry shouts of the crowd. And then, the first stones started flying. One of them crashed through a glass pane, and through the new opening, I saw the glint of metal. They had knives!

Another rock crashed through a window.

'Let go, you big-bearded buffoon!'

'The *Sahib* said to stay. The *Sahib* has given us an order.'

'Well, the *Sahib* can take his order and stick it where the sun doesn't shine!'

Tearing free of Karim's grip, I rushed towards the door. I couldn't stay here! I couldn't! They would kill him out there – and I was the only one who might prevent it. If I ran out there, if I shielded him with my body... Surely, not even these animals would be so vile as to attack an unarmed woman?

Ripping open the door, I was momentarily blinded by the light of torches and the glint of weapons. But I still heard him, heard his voice trying to rise above the din – and failing. Another rock slammed into the door behind me. Without hesitation, I hurled myself forward, shielding his body with mine.

'Stop,' I shouted. 'Don't!'

A cold growl erupted from behind me. 'Mr Linton–!'

'Don't worry!' I panted. 'I've got this! They won't attack a woman!'

'Mr Linton! Right now you aren't–'

It was when the first stone slammed into my stomach that I remembered the thing that the little voice at my mind had been trying to tell me for the last two minutes. The thing that Mr Ambrose had probably wanted to remind me of just then: I was wearing men's clothes.

'Oh, blast!' I said, just before a shower of stones came raining down upon me.

PROP WITHOUT THE OSAL

The first thing I noticed on waking up was that I wanted to die. Probably because of the intense pain that was burning in every inch of my body.

'Nnnnraaaarg,' I said.

Or at least something like that. You know, one of those lovely death-groans that murder victims utter just before they're given the gentle shove into the hereafter?

'Are you awake?'

That cool, distant voice... It sounded familiar. With all my might I tried to open my eyelids, but the stupid things wouldn't budge an inch! Who did that voice belong to? For some reason I had a feeling it was important to remember. Who? Who?

'Yes, you are awake.' A hand grabbed mine, pressing gently, almost lovingly. 'If you think that, because of the stupid stunt you pulled, I will give you paid sick leave, you are very much mistaken, Mr Linton. You will get better *right now*. That is an order. Open your eyes!'

Ah, yes. Mr Ambrose. Mr Rikkard Ambrose, the only person in the world who could phrase get well wishes as a command. How could I have forgotten?

'Eyes, Mr Linton. *Now.*'

Was that worry in his voice?

Surely not.

Still, just in case...

With another monumental effort, I heaved. Slowly, incredibly slowly, my eyelids began to lift. Spears of searing hot light stabbed into me.

'L-light!' I croaked.

His hand was torn from mine. A second later, I heard the rustle of curtains, and blessed darkness spread across the room. I parted my parched lips to thank him – but then I closed them again. The silence and dark was just so nice, so comfortable, so...very...

'Mr Linton? Mr Linton, stay awake!'

'Hmmm?'

'Stay awake. That is an order!"

Oh. An order from Rikkard Ambrose. Well *of course* that had to be obeyed. A painful smile tugging at one corner of my mouth, I lifted one eyelid a bit higher, squinting up at his tall, dark form.

'Hello, Sir.'

'Mr Linton.'

So much lay in those two little words. So much hidden meaning. So much not-so-hidden wrath.

'Where are we?' I croaked.

'In the town house formerly inhabited by the late Mr Gibbons. You are occupying one of the guest bedrooms. Karim and I are sharing the other.'

'How charming. How are you two lovebirds getting along?'

'Mr Linton?'

'Yes, Sir?'

'I will make allowances for the severe head trauma you most likely suffered and pretend not to have heard that remark.'

'What a shame. I was so looking forward to your cold glare.'

Kind as he was, he promptly gave it to me. Wasn't Mr Ambrose a wonderful man? No wonder I had fallen in love with him.

Hm...with thoughts like that running through your mind, Lilly, maybe you really did get knocked on the head too hard.

'So,' I rasped, thinking it was time to change the subject, 'what happened after I, well, um...'

'...made yourself into the target at the Newcastle rock-throwing contest?'

'Well, that's one way to put it.'

'I grabbed you and shoved you back inside. And then...' His voice trailed off. Glancing up at him, I saw him staring at his hands. Both of them were covered in scratches and stains of dried blood. Straightening, he met my gaze with one of his own that made a shiver run down my back. 'Suffice it to say that I held them off from the door until reinforcements arrived. My men dispersed the strike, established a secure perimeter around the mine, and allowed a team of specialists to start working on putting out the fire.'

'And you?'

His gaze did not waver from mine. 'I made sure that you were safe.'

I swallowed. Warmth started to spread through my chest. With the way he looked at me right now, I did not for a moment doubt his sincerity. He'd had a fortune in coal going up in flames and a million things to do. And the first thing he had done was make sure that I was safe.

Mr Rikkard Ambrose never did anything without a reason. He analysed and judged all things according to their value. And he always took care of the most valuable thing first.

I didn't smile. I didn't say thank you. I just held his gaze, and gave him a small nod, signalling that I understood. He nodded back. For several more long, heart-pounding seconds, our gazes held – then I glanced away.

'And the mine?' I enquired.

'It was sabotage. There's no doubt about it. Once the fire was out, we found the body of the late Mr Gibbons at the bottom of a shaft. He was charred by fire and explosions, but not enough to conceal the giant hole in the back of his head. He was struck down from behind with a pickaxe.'

'A pickaxe? How can you be so sure?'

'Because we found the pickaxe, still with some remnants of bloodstains on it, under the bunk of the miner who killed him.'

My eyes flew back to him. 'You...you've found the man responsible?'

'Oh yes.' Mr Ambrose was standing at the window now, gazing out over the city of Newcastle through a gap in the dark curtains. I watched him flex and steeple his fingers. 'Oh yes, we have him. Or to be more precise – Karim does. He has not yet been able to discover who paid the man, but it is only a matter of time. Besides, even if he does not, I suspect I already know.'

A shadow seemed to fall over the room, blocking out even what little light streamed in through the gaps in the curtains.

I felt my mouth go dry. 'Dalgliesh?'

'Indeed, Mr Linton.'

Well, well...that was nice news to wake up to. If Mr Ambrose's nemesis had indeed returned from whatever dark corner he had been hiding in the last couple of months, we were in for interesting times. Lord Daniel Eugene Dalgliesh was not to be trifled with.

But...could it really be him?

He couldn't possibly know that Mr Ambrose was up here in the north. Mr Ambrose had postponed all the arrangements until the very last minute, and I had been the only one to know about them in the first place. No. He couldn't possibly have known. It must have been someone else. Or maybe the discontented miner had just acted out of hatred. Yes. That had to be it.

'I must leave.' Mr Ambrose's cool voice tore me out of my contemplations. 'There are many things I still have to take care of. But I will make sure that you have the best medical care available.'

'Thank you, Sir.'

'The medical bill shall be deducted from your wages, of course.'

'How kind of you, Sir.'

'And...'

'Yes?'

In a flash, he was beside the bed and leaning over me. His stunningly perfect, granite-hard face was only inches away from mine, his fathomless, sea-coloured eyes boring into mine.

'Don't you dare do something like this ever again! Trying to shield me with your body, betting your life on the chivalry of a mob of northern mine workers? That is the single most foolish idea in the history of the world, and anyone who thinks of it should sell his brain for soup! If you ever try something like this again, you can consider yourself fired, do you understand? Fired!'

A muscle in his jaw twitched.

I simply lay there, gazing up at him for a long, long moment. Then, with a herculean effort, I lifted one aching hand and gently touched his cheek.

'Yes, I understand.' A smile tugged at the corners of my mouth. 'Maybe even better than you, Sir.'

His eyes flashed – then, without another word, he whirled around and stalked out of the room.

~~**~*~*

The day drifted by in a haze of sleep and pain, with occasional spurts of normality. The doctor came to see me and was very solicitous for my health – until he learned that I, the humble secretary, and not the mega-super-ultra-rich Mr Rikkard Ambrose would be footing the bill for his efforts. He left in a huff, recommending leech therapy. The 'Why don't you stay then?' I shouted after him presumably didn't help.

Oh well, it was probably better if he didn't examine me too closely. If I lifted my shirt so he could check for broken ribs, it would have been rather difficult to explain what he found there. Not much, true, but enough to unequivocally disqualify me for trousers.

I was just poking experimentally at my ribs, trying to decide whether there was anything cracked, or whether it was the wobbly stuff that was hurting like hell, when I heard shouting from outside the house. Shouting, hoof beats and...trumpet signals?

Maybe I was becoming delirious.

Or maybe not, I decided a minute later, when heavy footsteps came thundering down the corridor.

'Sir, Sir you can't go in there! Sir, Mr Linton is recuperating, and–'

'I don't bloody care! Out of my way, woman!'

Hey, wait a minute! I knew that voice. That was–

Something – or someone – hit the door. It slammed open, and there he stood: Captain James Carter in his bright red regimentals, his hat still on his head and an expression on his face the like of which I had never seen before.

'Ah,' I croaked. 'Captain Carter, it's you. Do come in, make yourself comfortable. Such a pleasure to see you again.'

'I'm not here for pleasantries, Mr Linton!'

'Aren't you? Dear me, I would never have guessed from the courteous way you beat my door down.'

'Where is she?'

'Who?'

'You know perfectly well who! Lady Samantha told me you had taken her to Newcastle – then, not two hours later, Major Strickland receives a message that riots have broken out all over town, people are being lynched and houses are being plundered! Where is she, Mr Linton? Where is your sister?'

'Ah, ehem...well...' How best to answer this question? After a moment's consideration, I decided on, 'I'm afraid Lilly can't see you right now. She is too badly hurt to see anyone at the moment.'

To judge by the look on his face, it had been the wrong thing to say. '*Hurt?* She was injured? Mr Linton, so help me God, if you don't act the man you are, get up off that damned sickbed and lead me to her right now, I will pull you up on your feet and strangle you!'

'Dear me. Well, if you put it like that...how can I refuse? I'm sure Lilly will really, really appreciate your concern. Please wait here while I see whether she is awake.'

Somehow, with the help of a bedpost, a curtain, a bedside table and a helpless nightshirt misused as a rope, I managed to manoeuvre myself to my feet. Groaning, I hobbled towards the connecting door leading to the next room.

'And you're sure you absolutely – ouch! – must see – ow! – Lillian, Captain Carter?'

'I will not rest till I've seen that she is safe and well. I won't trust her to you, Mr Linton. Not after today. From what I've seen of you so far, you are a highly reprehensible young man, and the sooner she is away from you, the better!'

'Really? Ouch! Good luck with that.'

Shutting the connecting door behind me, I quickly hobbled to the empty four-poster bed in the corner and sank down onto the sheets. Giving the curtains a hasty tug, I pulled them closed until there was only a slim sliver of myself visible, and pulled the covers up to my chin.

'Come in,' I called in a tremulous, pain-wrecked voice. Funnily enough, it wasn't very hard to fake.

With a squeak, the door swung open. Quick, lithe footsteps crossed the room, and, a moment later, the curtains began to move back.

'Please, no!' I called. 'The light hurts my eyes.'

'Miss Linton?'

'Captain Carter? Is that truly you? My brother said you were outside, but I–'

'–didn't believe it?'

'Well, not quite, no. I mean...why would you be here, in Newcastle?'

Cautiously pulling the curtains aside just a few inches at a time, he made a broad enough gap to peer in, and, kneeling beside the bed, gazed at my face. Thankfully not at the rest of me, though.

Please don't let him notice my tailcoat. Please don't let him notice my tailcoat.

I could only hope it was all hidden under the covers.

'My regiment was called in to disperse the strikers and rioters.'

'Oh?'

'But, for some reason, by the time we arrived here, they had already disbanded.'

'Fancy that.'

'Still...' Reaching out, he gently took my hand and pulled it towards him – far enough that the sleeve of my tailcoat slipped out from under the covers a few inches. *Please don't let him see! Please!* 'Still, Miss Linton – orders or no orders, I would have come. If I'd known what you were walking into, I would never have let you leave! I would have convinced you to stay safe at Battlewood. This would never have happened.'

'Don't be so sure.' Even though my face hurt from doing it, I gave him a smile. 'Convincing me of anything can be rather difficult.'

He smiled back at me – but then, his face suddenly turned unusually serious. He knelt at my bedside and, tightening his grip on my hand, he told me, 'I mean to try, nevertheless. Miss Linton, I... I wanted to ask–'

He hesitated.

I looked into his eyes – and instantly I knew what he was going to ask. It wasn't that I had suddenly turned psychic. It just so happened that I had considerable experience with this particular question, and even more experience in answering it with a resounding 'Hell, no!'

Only...

Was this the right answer here and now?

Screwing his courage to the sticking place, Captain Carter squared his shoulders and met my gaze.

'Miss Lillian Linton, will you do me the very great honour of becoming my–'

Shoeblack?

Pinworm?

Chicken soup?

I never found out whether this was what he would have said next, because right in that moment, quick footsteps approached from outside, and a second later, the door burst open, revealing the tall, dark form of Mr Rikkard Ambrose.

WRAP THE CAPTAIN

Silence.

It was utter. Complete. Unbreakable. And yet...it was louder than any silence I had ever heard before in my life. I had a sudden urge to clamp my hands over my ears to protect them from the sudden lack of noise. The temperature in the room dropped by a hundred degrees. Not wishing to be frozen into an ice sculpture, I said nothing and didn't move. Especially not in the direction of Mr Rikkard Ambrose. In fact, I avoided looking at him altogether. After all, there was no particular reason why I should be looking at him, right? He hadn't walked in on anything bad. It was all perfectly innocent, and I was blameless, and if I just kept my mouth shut and avoided looking into his icy eyes I might, possibly, survive this.

Captain Carter had no such compunctions.

'Excuse me, Sir!' Rising to his feet, he sent Mr Ambrose a glare that would have made most men retreat with their tail between their legs. 'Didn't your mother teach you how to knock?'

Most men. Not this one.

Mr Ambrose regarded Captain Carter as if he were something he had found stuck to the sole of his ten-year-old mint-condition shoes.

'She did – just like she taught me that a gentleman has no business being alone in a lady's room. Leave.'

'Miss Linton and I–'

'–can speak later. Miss Linton is recovering from injuries. Leave. *Now*.'

Captain Carter opened his mouth to protest again – and closed it. What could he do? This house belonged to Mr Ambrose. In fact, the captain would probably have to walk for a good, long while to reach a portion of the city that didn't belong to Mr Ambrose. His gaze bored into my employer, then slowly moved from Mr Ambrose to me, and back to Mr Ambrose. His eyes narrowed infinitesimally.

'Very well.' Rising to his feet, he marched to the door. He very nearly shoved Mr Ambrose as he strode past. Nearly, but not quite. Just as he reached the door, he turned and looked back straight at me. 'I shall return. Very, very soon.'

And he was gone.

Silence reigned.

Earth-shattering, ice-cold, terror-inducing silence.

Silence that promised death and destruction.

'Well, well.' Turning towards Mr Ambrose, I gifted him with one of my best fake smiles. 'Nice weather today, isn't it?'

'Which part? The snow storm or the thick fog?'

'Well...'

Taking a step into the room, Mr Ambrose let the door slide shut behind him. Never in the history of carpentry had anyone been able to make the soft click of a door sound so terrifyingly threatening.

'What,' my dear employer enquired in a tone that tickled my spine with icy fingers, 'was he doing here?'

I waved dismissively, then stopped when the motion hurt like hell. 'Oh, just the usual. Stopping by, asking how I'm doing...'

...proposing marriage...

For some reason I didn't mention that last point to Mr Ambrose, though.

He gave me a long, hard look. One of those looks that could make accountants quake in their boots and confess embezzlement on the spot. I was preparing for an inquisition including thumbscrews and Chinese water torture – after all, why not? I was prone and helpless. But it didn't come. Instead, he gave a curt nod.

'I see.'

I blinked. 'You... you do?'

'Oh yes, Mr Linton.' His cold, sea-coloured gaze bored into me, making me shiver. 'I see everything.'

~~**~*~*

The days passed slowly and torturously. As I lay there, waiting for my ribs to stop poking me with red hot irons, I reflected that this probably was what marriage to an eligible bachelor would be like: nothing to do all day but be idle until you were bored out of your skull.

So I was determined to approach my injuries with the same brilliant strategy with which I had always approached the prospect of marriage: ignore it and hope it goes away.

'Ah! Ouch! Argh!'

'Um...Miss? I'm not entirely sure you should up on your feet. Your poor ribs–'

'Blast, blast, blast! Ow! Ouch! Bloody hell!'

'Miss, please! Mr Ambrose said you weren't to overexert yourself.'

'Really? He said that?'

Nellie, the maid Mr Ambrose had assigned to me as my personal whipping boy and dogsbody during our stay at this lovely house, blushed. 'Well... he said "Get her up on her feet by the day after tomorrow, or you'll be out of a job." But I'm sure he *meant* for you to not overexert yourself.'

I patted her head. 'Bless you. Of course he did. Now help me hobble over there, will you? I think I can manage another round across the room before I collapse.'

'Yes, Miss.'

My get-well-or-die-trying approach showed definite results. After only a week, I could hobble across the room without help, and after only a few days more, I managed to get back to my bed without falling on my face. Captain Carter visited me quite often, providing moral support, and Mr Ambrose also dropped by, providing icy glares and threats of cutting my wages. It was hardly a surprise that with such loving support, matters steadily improved. It wasn't long before, finally, I was able to go outside again.

'Aaah!' Stretching, I breathed in the fresh stench of coal mines and factories. 'It's so good to be out again. And will you look at that? Most of the city *isn't* burned to the ground. How wonderful.'

'Indeed.'

'I always try to look on the bright side of things.'

'I've noticed.' Stepping to the edge of the balcony, Mr Ambrose gazed out over the city of Newcastle. 'Speaking of a bright side...'

'Yes, Sir?'

'The army made some enquiries into the miners who were suspected of assaulting you in front of the manager's office.'

'And?'

'And those men seem to have disappeared.'

'Is that so, Sir?'

'Yes, Mr Linton.'

'Ah.'

Out of the corner of my eye, I glanced at him. He was still looking out over the city. His face was completely impassive, giving nothing away, and demanding a refund of two hundred pounds and thirty-seven shillings into the bargain. Surely he wouldn't...

Would he?

Time to change the subject. And, fortunately, I had just the right thing ready at hand. Drawing a folded piece of paper from my pocket, I cleared my throat.

'I received another letter from your mother this morning, Sir.'

'Indeed, Mr Linton?'

'Yes, Sir.'

Silence.

And a bit more silence.

'Um...well, Sir?'

'Well what, Mr Linton?'

'What should I answer her?'

'That the strike is still continuing and our return will be delayed for at least another week.'

Silence.

This time, it was a diplomatic silence, maintained by me. But I couldn't keep it up for long.

'Err...but the last remnants of the strike were crushed five days ago, Sir.'

'Correct, Mr Linton. Your point is?'

'Um...never mind, Sir.'

I didn't broach the subject again. Although I did wonder why exactly Mr Ambrose wanted to stay in Newcastle at this point. Captain Carter had to stay for now to help maintain order in the city, but Mr Ambrose? His business was concluded. What was he waiting for? What was he doing?

I got an answer to that question all too soon.

~~**~*~*

It was around five p.m. and the sun had just begun to set when the pounding on the door started. By the time I reached the hallway, the maids were gathered in a frightened gaggle, clutching each other as if squeezing the blood out of each other's fingers was somehow a magical protection.

'What in God's name is going on here?' I demanded.

'Th-there's someone at the door, Miss,' Nellie mumbled.

'I had surmised as much,' I shot back as the door reverberated under another thunderous blow. 'Why don't you welcome our visitor?'

'Well, um...' Nellie's nervous glance strayed to the door. She flinched when there was yet another loud thud.

'Where's Mrs Gibbons?'

'Out, Miss.'

'And Mr Ambrose?'

'Out as well, Miss.'

'Well, then we'll have to take care of this. Open the door!'

'But, err...Miss...'

Boom! Boom! Boom!

Nellie shrank back.

'Oh, for God's sake!' Rolling my eyes, I marched down the stairs, and grabbed a solid-looking walking stick from the umbrella stand, likely the property of the late Mr Gibbons. My motto: Better wreckful than reckless. 'Out of the way! I'll do it myself.'

111

Very happy to hear the news, the maids dutifully retreated to a safe distance. I for my part got a good grip on the walking stick, grabbed the doorknob, twisted and pulled.

'Now listen here, Mister,' I began. 'Whoever you think you are, you can't go around–'

The rest of the sentence stuck in my throat. In front of me stood Captain James Carter. His uniform was torn, and he had a bloody great gash on one side of his head.

'Holy...!'

The captain staggered inside. Grabbing his arm, I half led, half dragged him towards a chair and dumped him into it.

'What happened?' I demanded. 'Who did this to you?'

'Close the door!'

'Not before–'

'Close the door! Now! They might still be after me.'

At that little comment, the maids moved quicker than a debtor running from Mr Rikkard Ambrose. In a flash, the door was closed, locked and bolted. I turned back to Captain Carter.

'*They*? There was more than one?'

'I don't know, really.' Raising his hand, he cautiously felt the back of his head and groaned. Only then did I realise that he had an impressive bump back there. 'It might have been only one. But if it was, hell, he must have been Goliath's grandson. By George, was that brute strong!'

Bloody hell! Someone had really gone after him. This wasn't just some stupid prank. This was real.

But...Captain Carter? He was the sweetest man I had ever met! In fact, he was about the only man I had met who deserved that adjective! What kind of despicable scum would go after him? Oh, if I ever got my hands on them...!

Trying my best to contain my rage (and my raging curiosity), I dashed into the kitchen and returned with a bottle of brandy and a cloth. At the sight of the bottle, the Captain's face brightened considerably, and he held out his hand.

'You're a lifesaver, Miss Linton.'

'Let's wait and see if you still think that in a minute.' Evading his hand, I opened the bottle and emptied a good part of the brandy onto the cloth. Without any ceremony I slapped it onto the Captain's head and began to vigorously dab at the bloody gash.

'Ouch! Ow! What are you doing?'

'Cleaning your wound. We have to make sure it doesn't get inflamed.'

'Well – ow! – it feels pretty inflamed right now. That burns!'

'It's supposed to. Hold still.'

'And then I'll get to drink the rest of the bottle?'

I felt relieved. If he could still make comments like that, his head couldn't have been too severely damaged. He was still the same Captain James Carter.

He waited – not patiently, but he did wait – until I had cleaned and wrapped his wound, and fetched a cold wet cloth for the bump on his head. Then, finally,

I settled myself down in a chair across from him and fixed him with my best Ambrose-imitation stare.

'Talk! What happened? Start from the beginning.'

'The beginning...' Uttering another groan, he pressed the cold cloth more firmly to his head. 'Well, I suppose that would be when I went out for a drink with a few of my friends in the Bull's Head Inn. It's just down the road from here. I stepped out and was thinking, since I was in the area, I might come to visit you – when suddenly, someone grabbed me from behind.'

Instinctively, my fingers twitched, itching to reach out for a sharpened parasol. 'Who was the son of a bachelor?'

'I only wish I knew. Whoever it was, they pushed me into a dark alley, and I was just about to turn and show them that they'd picked the wrong man for a fight when they whacked me over the head, hard.' Another groan. 'Good Lord, he was fast! And strong as Atlas! But I could have lived with the blow to my head. The blow to my ego that came a second later when they pulled a sack over my head was more difficult to digest.'

I stared at him. 'A sack? Over your *head*?'

'Yes.'

'Why would a thief or a robber–'

He grimaced. 'Oh, this was no thief, Miss Linton. They were only after one thing: my pretty head on a platter. I don't know why they didn't just ram a knife between my ribs. As quick as they were, they could have managed. I suppose they had something more interesting planned for me than a simple, quick death.'

'But you got away. You escaped.'

'Barely.' He pulled another face. 'Somehow, I managed to twist around, even with those giant arms around me squeezing me half to death. I lashed out, and by pure dumb luck, hit the fellow in the face. I tore off the sack and ran down the alley without even looking back.'

'Blast and double blast!' Shaking my head, I stared at the marks on him, wondering what kind of beast would be able to inflict that kind of damage on a professional soldier. 'So you have no idea who it was?'

For the first time since he had staggered into the house, the impish grin I knew and loved spread over the face of Captain James Carter.

'Well...not entirely.'

My eyes narrowed. 'What aren't you telling me? Out with it!'

Slipping one hand into his pocket, the Captain pulled out something from his pocket. Metal and wood glinted in the candlelight. A moment later, he held something up between us.

'I got hold of this while I was trying to land a blow,' the Captain explained. I heard his voice as if from very, very far away. 'Well, what do you say, Miss Linton? There can't be very many of those in Newcastle.'

I swallowed, my eyes fixed on the object in his hand. 'No, there can't.'

'As soon as I find out who it belongs to, I'll have my man!'

'Yes. Yes, I suppose you will.'

In front of me, in the faint light of the candles, glinted a beautiful curved dagger in an intricately worked mahogany and metal sheath. It was very oriental in design, and, what was more important, very, very familiar.

'Do you see there, the strap, where it's been torn loose? It could be easily matched if the owner were to be found.'

'Oh. Yes, indeed.'

'The only question is where I'll keep it while I make enquiries. I don't want to take it back to headquarters. There's just a chance that one of the local officers did this as payback for our role in the suppression of the strike.'

'Why don't you leave it with me,' I offered, reaching for the dagger as if to check whether it was truly real. It was. 'I'll...look after it.'

'Would you? Thank you, Miss Linton. That's very kind of you.'

'Oh no,' I whispered, my fingers closing around the dagger. 'I think I'll have a use for it.'

~~**~*~*

Quite a long time later, when the sun had set and Captain Carter had long departed, I still sat in the hallway, the dagger in one hand, the brandy bottle in the other. Whatever happened tonight, I would probably murder someone or need a drink, so it was best to be prepared.

I had to wait quite a long while. When finally the door opened, and a large, turban-wearing figure entered the house muttering low curses, I rose. With a flick of a finger, I lit a match and held it to the candle on the chair next to me. In the sudden light, Karim stood frozen in the door.

Smiling like a shark, I raised the dagger. 'Looking for this?'

PATRIOTISM À LA AMBROSE

I marched down the corridor like a train at full steam. All my energy, all my focus, all my considerable wrath was concentrated on the door at the end of that corridor - or, more precisely, on the man behind it.

'Miss?' a servant dared to step in my way. Bad idea. 'Mr Ambrose does not wish to be disturbed at the mo-'

He met my gaze and broke off instantly, swallowing.

I raised an eyebrow. 'You were saying?'

'I, um...well, Miss...'

'Out of my way!'

'Yes, Miss! Right away, Miss!'

He jumped aside just in time to not get flattened to the floor. I marched past and slammed my foot against the door, kicking it open.

Mr Ambrose was sitting behind his desk, studying an open file in front of him with impeccable concentration. He didn't even bother to look up when I stormed into the room, the son of a bachelor! Seething with righteous rage, I marched up to his desk and, gritting my teeth, bit out: 'Tell me you didn't do it!'

'I didn't do it,' he said, then turned over a page in the file and proceeded to ignore me.

'Liar! It *was* you! I know it was!'

'Indeed?'

'Who else could it have been? Oh, you...you're going to pay for this! You...you...!'

Slowly, very slowly, Mr Ambrose raised his eyes from the document resting on the desk in front of him and met my gaze.

'What are we talking of, precisely?'

That bloody son of a...!

'Captain Carter, of course!'

'Indeed, Mr Linton?'

'Oh yes, indeed, Sir!'

'And what has happened to the good captain that warrants your barging into my office at this hour of the night?'

'Don't you play the innocent! You know exactly what happened! You were the one who sicced that bearded brute on him!'

'Bearded brute?'

Just then, the door behind me creaked open, and I saw the reflection of Karim appearing in the dark windows behind Mr Ambrose. What little was visible of his face behind that beard of his was a grimace of discomfort that would have made me laugh at any other time. Never in my life had I seen the huge Mohammedan looking so much like a naughty schoolboy who had just been caught with his hand in the cookie jar. But right now wasn't any other time. Right now was right now. And right now, I just wanted to chop his bloody head off!

'Karim.' Just one word. That was all. Mr Ambrose gave his bodyguard a look, and the huge man grimaced, ducking his head.

'I am sorry, *Sahib*.'

'I'm so glad to hear that, Karim.' Half-turning, I gifted him with a smile you could have cut iron with. 'What are you sorry about, exactly? Walloping Captain Carter over the head and trying to stuff him into a sack, or getting caught in the act?'

Wisely, the big man did not answer.

I whirled back to Mr Ambrose, my eyes flashing. 'It *was* you! It really *was* you who ordered this!'

Silence.

'Why, damn you? Bloody hell, why?'

More silence. Clenching my fists, I strode forward until I stood right in front of his desk. Slamming my fists down on the hardwood, I leaned forward until our faces were only inches apart.

'Why would you do this? Captain Carter was here to help suppress the riots! He was helping you!'

'Oh yes.' Mr Ambrose's eyes were two dark oceans of ice. His words were only a whisper – and yet I understood every cold, hard word. 'I'm sure the good captain was *very* desirous of helping me. I could tell from the way he was kneeling beside your bed, clutching your hand in his!'

I blinked. What in the...

Out of all the possible things for him to say, I had not expected this.

'You had a man knocked over the head and stuffed into a sack because he visited while I was ill?'

There was a noise from behind me. It almost sounded...no. That couldn't be. It had almost sounded as if Karim had choked on a laugh. But that couldn't be true. There was about as much humour in Karim as in a grumpy old camel.

'No.' Mr Ambrose's cold voice drew my attention back to him. He was sitting even stiffer than usual, as if someone had injected steel into his spine. His dark, sea-coloured eyes were swirling, focused on me with an intensity I did not understand, and that made me slightly uneasy. 'I didn't do it just because he paid you a visit.'

'Why then? Why would you go after a perfectly nice man like Captain Carter?'

His hands shot out, grabbing my face. Before I could even think of resisting, he had pulled me across the desk and kissed me once, hard, on the mouth.

Then he released me.

Stunned, I stumbled back, staring at him.

'Try to guess,' he growled.

Silence.

Icy silence on the part of Mr Ambrose. Diplomatic silence from Karim. And from me – stunned silence. Absolutely steamrollered, gobsmacked, speechless silence.

Had that really just happened?

I tried to look at Mr Ambrose, tried to read his face – but I found I couldn't. I could not look into those deep, dark, sea-coloured eyes, or I would lose myself in them. And even if I did...that would not help me decipher his words. His face would be a mask, unreadable as stone.

What was he talking about? Why had he done this to Captain Carter? He couldn't possibly mean that because he had seen Captain Carter on one knee beside me, he had assumed...that he was feeling...that he had done all this because he was...

No.

That wasn't possible.

I tried to look up again, but still found I could not meet his gaze. Instead, my eyes flitted across his desk, searching desperately for anything innocent to cling to.

And they found something.

At first sight, the slim black folder looked quite innocent. It was just a folded piece of cardboard, after all, not even in a very interesting colour. But then my eyes snagged on the letters printed on it: *J.C. from L.L. Waste Disposal.*

Strange, I wondered, staring at the letters. *JC. What a funny coincidence. Those are the initials of Captain Carter. James Carter. What a funny coincidence indeed to find that on Mr Ambrose's desk and–*

116

My thoughts screeched to a halt.

Coincidence?

How likely was it that the words 'coincidence' and 'Ambrose' would appear in the same sentence?

Suddenly, something made *click* in my head, and I remembered. I remembered it all, and for the first time, I understood.

Slowly, very slowly, I raised my gaze to meet the arctic eyes of Mr Rikkard Ambrose.

'No,' I whispered. 'Tell me you didn't.'

'I didn't,' he told me without the slightest hesitation. 'Now, what exactly is it that you are referring to this time, Mr Linton?'

'That file!' I slammed my hand onto the desk. 'I've seen others like it before!'

He cocked his head, as if he had no idea what I was talking about, the cheeky bastard! 'Indeed?'

'I saw one on your desk the day before Lieutenant Ellingham disappeared!'

'Is that so?'

'You remember Lieutenant Ellingham, don't you Sir? My *suitor*?'

His face was perfectly impassive. It didn't give away a thing, and had upped its refund demands to six hundred pounds sixty-seven shillings.

'Now that you mention it, Mr Linton, I do seem to remember something of the kind.'

'And then I saw one like it again!'

'Indeed?'

'Oh yes, indeed! The very day before Morty vanished from the face of the earth!'

'Morty who?'

'Morton Marmeduke Fitzgerald – my *other suitor*.'

'My, my, Mr Linton. You do seem to be in high demand.'

'Apparently.' Breathing hard, I clenched my fists. One of them curled around the black folder on the desk. 'Yet somehow, my suitors always seem to disappear into thin air at the very last moment.'

Mr Ambrose's face had upped its refund demands to at least a thousand pounds, plus interest.

'Indeed?'

'Don't you indeed me! You...you...' I took a deep breath, preparing to speak the incredible truth. All this time...and I had no idea, and he...he...

'You were behind it,' I whispered. 'Every single time. Every single man. It was always you. You and your sabre-swinging thug!'

From behind me, Karim made a noise that sounded as if he were about to protest against his newest nickname. Whirling around, I shot him one single glare and raised a warning finger. That was more than enough to shut him up. I whirled back to Mr Ambrose, who was sitting in his armchair, regarding me over steepled fingers, cool as a cucumber in the supply hold of a sunken arctic exploration ship.

'It was you!' I stabbed an accusing finger at the fiend. 'Don't you try to deny it!'

'Deny it?' He cocked his head, still regarding me so infernally unperturbed over his steepled fingers. 'Why would I wish to deny it?'

I opened my mouth – and closed it again.

'Because...because...well, how about because it's illegal, for a start!'

'I'm not in the habit of begging, but still, I beg to differ, Mr Linton.'

I stared at him. The nerve of the man...! 'Making people disappear *isn't* illegal?'

'No. Not if you get the men you wish to disappear drunk, and you then leave them conveniently in the path of a press gang looking for new brave recruits for our great nation's Royal Navy. I have a little arrangement with a certain captain that...well, let's just say that, over the past few years, I have contributed considerably to the growth of our country's proud fleet.'

'That's...that's...'

'Patriotic?'

'Despicable! Immoral! Horrifying!'

'I didn't hear you complaining at the time. In fact, I seem to remember a certain person whose name I won't mention singing and dancing through my office, overwhelmed with joy that her suitor was no longer–'

My ears suddenly burned. 'That's beside the point!'

'On the contrary.' His dark, stormy eyes bored into me. 'I'd say it *is* the point.'

'What about Lieutenant Ellingham and Captain Carter?' I demanded. 'Are you going to try and pass that off as patriotism, too? They already were in the military! They were both British Army officers!'

'Well, then I suppose it was time for a career change to the Navy. I hear sea air is healthy.'

'You...you...! I...I'm going to–'

'–thank me?' He gave a magnanimous wave. An absolute monarch couldn't have done better. 'No need. A bit of free overtime will do. You can stay an hour longer in the office for six months. That will do.' And, with another little wave, he dismissed me and picked up his file again.

Thank him?

Thank him?

Oh, I was going to...

'What. About. Captain. Carter?' I repeated, every word leaving my mouth as if pushed out between grinding millstones. 'What about today? Do you see me dancing with joy today? Do you think I'd want to thank you for today?'

The file froze in mid-air.

'No.' Those dark, sea-coloured eyes of his fixed on me again, turning even stormier, a hurricane forming in their depths. 'Which leads me to wonder...why is that? What is so special about the captain?'

My breath caught. I tried, tried desperately to think of something to say, but under that intense gaze, my mind froze and my heart melted away.

Pull yourself together Lilly! You're a strong, independent woman! Even if every bone in your body doesn't feel like being one, you are!

'Why?' I whispered. 'Why did you hurt him?'

'You know why.' In an instant, he was up and around the desk, crowding me, pushing me back against the wall. His face was only inches away from me, his dark gaze burning into me.

'You can't possibly think that he...that he and I...'

'Can't I, Mr Linton?'

'That's ridiculous!'

'Indeed?'

'You won't lay another finger on him, do you hear? Not another finger!'

Casually, confidently, he raised his hand and stroked one finger down my cheek. 'I lay my finger wherever I please, Mr Linton.'

Grabbing his hand, I pulled it away – but in an instant, he had turned the tables on me, grabbing my wrists and slamming them against the wall, trapping me.

'Ehem.' Somewhere in the background, Karim cleared his throat. 'I think I'd better go now, *Sahib*.'

We both ignored him.

'Arrogant, chauvinistic pig!' I growled.

'Stubborn, unreasonable female,' he hissed.

The door closed behind Karim with a discreet click. We ignored that, too. We were too busy glaring at each other.

'I think someone here needs a little lesson about who exactly is in charge,' he whispered, his breath tickling my skin.

'I couldn't agree more,' I shot back, glaring pointedly straight at him. He glared right back.

'Stay away from that man, Mr Linton,' he ordered in a voice that put the lie to the male address.

'Don't be ridiculous!'

'Stay away or I will *take* him away! I'm sure Captain Carter would enjoy a little journey to China. I hear the Royal Navy is having a nice time there right now.'

'You wouldn't dare!'

'Look into my eyes, Mr Linton, and then tell me there's anything I wouldn't dare where you are concerned!'

I looked.

And I couldn't speak.

He would dare. He absolutely would. This was Mr Rikkard Ambrose, a man who would grind someone into the dust just for pinching a few pennies. My throat suddenly felt dry. What would a man like that be capable of if he thought someone was threatening to take away something that was really important to him? Something he cared about. Something like...me?

The realisation settled cold and heavy in my stomach.

Captain Carter was a dead man.

Unless I could do something about it.

Conducting Business

Cautiously, I crooked a finger. His iron hands were still pinning my wrists to the wall. I could hardly move an inch. Still, I managed to just reach the tips of his fingers and stroke, gently, once.

He twitched under my touch.

Careful, Lilly. Careful. One wrong move, and Captain Carter will find himself chained in the hold of a frigate bound for Beijing.

'You don't really want to do that,' I said softly, continuing to stroke his hand. With every touch, his grip loosened infinitesimally. 'You don't really want to do something that callous and heartless.'

He returned my gaze with a stare so icy it nearly broke my resolve. Leaning forward, he brought his face near enough that I could feel his breath on my cheek. 'Do you know what happened to the last man who tried to manipulate me, Mr Linton?'

'Something unpleasant, I'd guess. But you forget something, Sir.'

'Indeed?'

'Yes, Sir,' I said, my eyes sparking with fire, 'I am not a man!'

And, throwing myself forward, I kissed him.

If he had taken me by surprise with his earlier attack, it was nothing to what I did to him. His grip around my wrists instinctively tightened, until it was almost painful. His whole body jerked as my lips took his, claiming what was rightfully mine. But the shock didn't last long. After only a few seconds, his hands released my wrists, coming up around me to pull me against him. Hard muscle pressed into me, caging me in just as securely as the wall had a moment before.

And what did I do?

I kissed him. I kissed and kissed and kissed for all I was worth, utilising every trick I knew, and a few I didn't. Inwardly, I sent a thousand thanks to Amy, to whom I owed ninety per cent of my expertise. God bless prostitutes! Unless, of course, one of them ever got it into her head to come too close to the man currently clutching me in his arms and kissing the life out of me...

'Lillian...' His voice was a rough whisper against my lips, unused to saying my name out loud. 'Lillian, I...'

'Shh.' I silenced him with another kiss. And another. And another. Slowly, my fingers trailed down to the front of his shirt, popping open the top button, and I spoke words to Mr Rikkard Ambrose that I would never have thought necessary: 'No need for talking now.'

He groaned his agreement. Another searing cold hot hard soft kiss. Another button popping open. Tightening his grip, he pulled me off my feet. I saw the room fly by, and then there was softness, and warmth against my back. A sofa? He settled us down, deepening his kiss. I popped another button, revealing taut, hard muscles. Gently, my fingers began stroking along his collarbone, eliciting a shiver. He was nearly there. Nearly at the edge. Just where I wanted him.

Drawing back my fingers, I broke the kiss.

He stared down at me, blinking.

'*Now* is the time for talking,' I informed him. 'What do you think of a little business negotiation?'

'Business...negotiation?'

'Yes. It's simple, really. Just a tiny little thing.'

His eyes narrowed infinitesimally. 'What do you want?'

'No need to be so suspicious.' Playfully, I trailed my lips along his neck. He didn't even flinch. Impressive. But I could see it in eyes: he was burning. Burning with cold, ice-blue fire. 'It's really not much.'

'What. Do. You. Want?'

You could have frozen lava with his voice. Ignoring old frosty's mood, I smiled up at him. 'Simple. You leave Captain Carter alone for one day – and in return, you get this.'

Grabbing him by the back of the head, I pulled him down into a hard, hot, merciless kiss.

When I released him, I wasn't the only one who was breathing heavily.

Victory!

'Just...' His voice sounded rough. Clearing his throat, he tightened his grip on me. 'Just one day?'

'Yep. For every kiss, of course.'

'*What?*'

'And anything else that goes beyond a handshake.'

Cold fury blazed in his eyes. The kind the frost giants feel just before Ragnarök.

'Are you,' he said, his voice no more than a whisper, 'going to use your body as a weapon to *keep another man safe?*'

'Pretty much, yes,' I agreed cheerily. 'Don't let it bother you.'

'I should *not let it bother me?*'

'Yep.'

His arms tightening around me, Mr Ambrose leaned forward, pressing me harder into the sofa. His face above me was a mask of granite. 'I should just sit back and relax, letting that red-coated fool go free to gallivant around you and pant at your feet, and for what? A kiss each day?'

I met his cold gaze without blinking. 'Not *a* kiss.' Grabbing his face in my hand, I pulled him down on top of me. '*This* kiss!'

And I kissed him.

And kissed him.

And kissed him.

When, a long, long time later, I finally released him and gazed into his eyes, I saw everything that was burning in me reflected there.

'Well, what do you say, Sir?' I whispered. 'Do we have a deal?'

~~**~*~*

I had to admit, I reflected as I sat in the coach back to Battlewood, gazing out over the white landscape rushing by, I was quite pleased with myself. Not only was I now a private secretary, but also a businesswoman in my own right, who had just brokered her first major deal with one of Britain's richest financiers. Granted, the deal was a tad unconventional, but still, it was something to be proud of, right?

Particularly at night, when I was going to enjoy the dividends and benefits.

Pulling my gaze from the endless white outside, I glanced around the coach from one of the two men to the other, and only with a lot of effort managed to suppress a smirk. Dear Lord...! This would have been funny if it weren't so deadly serious.

Who was I kidding – it still was funny!

Captain Carter cleared his throat. 'So kind of you to let me travel in your coach, Mr Ambrose,' he said.

Silence.

The captain cleared his throat again. 'Riding all this way on horseback again would not have been comfortable.'

More silence. Utter, complete, ear-killing silence.

'I suppose what I wanted to say was...I really appreciate the gesture. You're a true gentleman.'

At that, Mr Ambrose made a sound somewhere between the grumble of a volcano and the grunt of a polar bear. His hand tightened around the handle of his cane with a force that...

Well, 'poor cane' was really all that needed to be said.

'But where is Mr Linton?' the captain enquired, glancing around in the coach, seeing only two other occupants. 'Isn't he coming back with us?'

'He,' my dear employer said with frostbite in his voice, 'had to ride. I thought he deserved a lesson. His performance has been less than pleasing, lately.'

'Indeed?' I raised an eyebrow. 'You sang a different tune yesterday night when–'

A kick from Mr Ambrose silenced me. Probably better that way. The ending of that sentence would likely have given the good captain a rather nasty shock.

With three passengers, plus luggage, and a coachman and gigantic body-guard on the box of the carriage, we travelled more slowly than we had done on our way to Newcastle. Still, only once did we stop at an inn. The sun was just rising high enough to peek over the trees when we continued our journey to-wards Mr Ambrose's ancestral home.

'Do you think anyone will be expecting us?' I enquired as I caught the first glances of the huge manor house through the trees. 'Did you send word ahead?'

'And waste perfectly good money on a message that will only arrive a day earlier than us?' Mr Ambrose gave me a cool look. 'Don't be absurd, Miss Linton.'

'Oh. Well, I suppose we can knock and see...'

'There! There they are!'

The last words didn't come from me. They didn't come from Captain Carter either, and they most certainly did not come from Mr Rikkard Ambrose. No, they came from two figures on the steps of the manor house, waving and calling as if we were a whole boatload full of prodigal sons returning.

'Seems like your dear mama has been missing you.' I gifted Mr Ambrose with a brilliant smile. 'Isn't that sweet?'

The look I got in return didn't contain much sugar.

'Well, let's not keep her waiting!' The coach rolled to a stop and, grabbing Mr Ambrose by the hand, I towed him out of the coach and towards the waiting women. They started to rush down the steps towards us. 'I'm sure your mother will be ecstatic to see you agai–'

'Lillian!' Throwing her arms around me, Lady Samantha engulfed me in an ocean of pink fluff. 'Lillian, dear, oh we were so worried! Are you all right? Are your injuries better? Oh, we were so terrified when we heard! We're so happy that you're back on your feet again!'

'Yes,' Mr Ambrose's voice came from somewhere beyond the fluffy pink vice that engulfed me. 'I can see that my mother is clearly ecstatic to see me again.'

'You...' Letting go of me, Lady Samantha marched up to her son, glared up at him and poked him in the chest. I am not joking. She actually and truly extended her forefinger and poked Mr Rikkard Ambrose in the chest. And her finger didn't freeze and drop or anything like that. 'How could you! How could you take Miss Linton into such terrible danger? Rick, I don't know what to do with you! I really don't...'

Her words drained away, and she simply stood there, gazing up at her son. She didn't look angry. She didn't even look mildly annoyed. No, it was much worse than that. She looked *disappointed.* Her big blue eyes gazed up at her son with a look that said: *You did this? I thought you were better than that. I thought I could rely on you,*

Mr Ambrose shifted.

'Miss Linton insisted on accompanying me. She–'

'Well, of course she did!' Lady Samantha glanced over at me, and her gaze held so much warmth and love and tenderness, I felt the instinctive urge to duck behind a bush to shield myself from the onslaught. 'I wouldn't have expected anything less.'

'You shouldn't have listened to her!' That was Adaira, jumping into the conversation and glaring at her brother. 'It obviously was a stupid idea!'

Then she turned to me and threw her arms around me. 'I'm so happy you're back! You're the only sensible female hereabouts!'

I could have pointed out that those two statements were a tiny little bit contradictory, but instead simply hugged her back and grinned at Mr Ambrose over her shoulder. The look he shot back at me was less than pleased. My grin widened.

'Lady Samantha?' Bowing, Captain Carter approached the lady of the house. 'I see that you have quite a lot to discuss with Miss Linton and your son. I shall return to my room and see you at dinner.'

'Of course, Captain. Of course. Thank you for ensuring that this county is secure again, and we can all sleep safely in our beds tonight.'

'Only doing my duty, Your Ladyship.'

And, with another bow, he marched off towards the house, where a footman was already waiting for him.

'I will leave as well,' Mr Ambrose stated coolly. 'I have some urgent business matters to take care of that cannot–'

'You stay right where you are!' Letting go of me, Adaira marched up to her brother, blocking his way. 'Mother and I have a few things to say to you, brother dear.'

'But first,' Lady Samantha added, turning back to me with that expression that simultaneously made me feel warm inside and made me want to run for the hills, 'we'll take care of you, my dear. You must be exhausted! After all the things that excuse for a son of mine put you through–'

'I'm fine,' I protested. 'Really, my injuries weren't as bad as you might have heard. A few scrapes, a black eye, a couple of bruised ribs – nothing much.'

'*Black eye? Bruised ribs?*'

Oh. Hadn't I mentioned those in my letters yet? Oops.

'Rikkard Ambrose!' Blue eyes wide with horror, Lady Samantha turned on her son. I judged this might be the right opportunity to sneak away – but no such luck. She immediately turned back and engulfed me in another hug, as if trying to shield me from the whole big, bad world. A second later, she was joined by Lady Adaira. Unfair! Two against one!

'Oh, you poor, poor dear...'

'We'll keep you safe here, don't worry.'

'Come. Let's find you a quiet place to rest, and you can tell us all about it.'

Can I? Does that include my crossdressing and my recent 'business deal', My Lady?

But I didn't even get a chance to ask that question. Instead, I was dragged away, well aware that something was going to happen to me that I hadn't experienced for nearly fifteen years. I was going to be intensely, thoroughly, and lengthily mothered.

May God have mercy on me.

~~**~*~*

I was sitting in the small pink drawing room – a rather great honour, probably, for from the decor I deduced this was the favourite room of the lady of the house – when a knock sounded from the door. Lady Samantha ceased plying me with tea and biscuits for a moment, and glanced over her shoulder.

'Come in.'

The door opened, and Rikkard Ambrose appeared in the doorway.

'Not you! You stay out. You've caused enough damage as it is.'

'Mother, I–'

'Not another word!'

Hurriedly, I swallowed a mouthful of biscuit, clearing the way. 'It's all right, Lady Samantha. I don't mind if he comes in.'

'Of course *you* don't, child.' She gave me a smile that was more motherly than a pregnant midwife expecting her thirteenth child. I almost could read her thoughts stamped on her forehead: *He's let you get hurt so badly, and still you want to be near him. Oh dear, you can't help yourself, can you?*

Well, as a matter of fact, I couldn't. But there was also the small fact that he was the one who signed my monthly pay cheque. I could hardly order him from the room, especially one that wasn't mine.

Mr Ambrose's jaw tightened. 'I am coming in.'

'Rikkard Ambrose, don't you dare! I forbid–'

Ignoring his mother, Mr Ambrose strode into the room, followed by the hulking figure of Karim.

'I will speak to Miss Linton alone, Mother.'

'You will do no such thing!'

It sounded brave, and Lady Samantha even tried to put her hands on her hips and look properly outraged, but next to the towering form of Karim and the black-clad menace that was her own son, she appeared distinctly unscary. There was simply no way you could look as sweet and harmless as Lady Samantha and order someone like Mr Rikkard Ambrose around. It was a physical impossibility. I wondered how she had gotten him to eat his spinach when he was little.

'Please, Your Ladyship.' Just as she was about to gather her courage and attempt to move mountains and icebergs for me, I placed a restraining hand over hers. 'I'd like to have a word with him.'

'Oh dear...are you sure?' Her eyes wandered from me to Mr Ambrose, and back to me and the faint remnants of bruising still visible on my face.

'Yes,' I told her. 'I'm sure.' *Sure that I don't want him to pick you up and throw you out of the room. Which he will do, if you don't move.*

'Very well. You may speak with him, and I will go. But I will not leave you alone with him. A gentleman alone–' She interrupted herself, glanced at Karim, and after some clearly painful deliberation, corrected herself: '*Two* gentlemen alone with a lady in her room – that isn't seemly. I won't allow it.'

Reaching for a little bell on the table next to the chaise longue where she had wrapped me up in blankets and started stuffing me with home-made biscuits, she rang. Immediately, a maid scurried into the room and curtsied.

'Yes, My Lady?'

'I shall leave for a little while. Remain here and keep Miss Linton, my son and Mr...', again, she glanced at Karim, '...and his associate company. If Miss Linton needs anything, or there is anything else amiss, fetch me immediately, understood?'

The maid's eyes flickered from me to Mr Ambrose and back. She blushed, and her eyes widened.

'Oh. Um, yes My Lady.'

'Good. I shall take my leave, then.'

And giving her son a last meant-to-be-stern-but-really-loving look, she strode out of the room.

Silence descended.

For a long, long moment, Mr Ambrose simply stood there, staring at me with those icy, sea-coloured eyes of his. Then, finally:

'I am sorry you were hurt, Miss Linton.'

I raised an eyebrow. 'Indeed?' *An apology from Mr Rikkard Ambrose? A rare thing indeed. But why is he telling me this? I already know this.*

'Yes. I can think of people who deserve it much more than you do. One in particular comes to mind.'

Ah. So that's it.

This wasn't about what had happened to me. This was about what might happen to someone else if I wasn't careful.

'I trust you remember our agreement?' Mr Ambrose enquired, his voice soft as the snow before the avalanche.

'Indeed I do.'

'Adequate.'

In the corner of the room, the maid was practically panting with the effort to appear as if she weren't listening.

'And you shall keep up your end of the bargain?'

'Certainly I shall.'

'And you are, I presume, aware that it is an exclusive agreement?'

'It is?'

'Oh yes, Miss Linton. In fact, I insist on exclusively receiving the benefits from this particular contract.'

'I see.'

In the corner, the maid was blinking fast, trying to decipher Ambrose's speech – to no avail.

'Is that all?' I enquired.

'Yes, Miss Linton. That was all.' Turning, he strode towards the door. Only when he had reached the door did he turn around once more, and for the first time I noticed that Karim hadn't moved.

'One more thing, Miss Linton...after the terrible ordeal you've lived through, I feel concern about your safety.'

'You do?'

'Oh yes. You must allow me to extend my protection to you. Karim here, my trusted bodyguard, will remain with you for the foreseeable future. He has sharp eyes and will make sure that nothing untoward happens in my absence.'

My eyes went wide with shock. He couldn't be serious! He couldn't be planning to–

In the corner I heard the maid sigh. 'How romantic...'

Romantic? Romantic my feminist foot!

'Till we meet again, Miss Linton.'

And he strode out of the room, closing the door behind him.

A COMPANION FOR A LADY

I had a chaperone. A *chaperone.*

And not just that.

I had a turban-wearing, sabre-swinging, seven-foot-tall chaperone with a figure like a whole team of wrestlers and a beard the size of Lincolnshire. A chaperone who would use hard fists instead of soft reprimands to make sure nothing 'improper' would be going on.

Concerned about my safety?

Ha!

Mr Rikkard Ambrose was about as concerned about my safety as a turtle was concerned about forgetting its shell at home. It was just a ruse! A ruse to make sure that a certain captain of the British Army didn't come within a hundred feet of me.

Lady Samantha, unfortunately, wasn't quite perceptive enough to see through her son's diabolical plans. Instead, she was delighted at the interest her dear Ricky seemed to take in my 'safety', and immediately forgave him everything for which she had been blaming him, the scheming son of a bachelor!

'Isn't it sweet of him that he's being so thoughtful?' she whispered, pressing my hand and glancing over at Karim, who stood in the corner of the room, arms crossed, stiff as a piece of furniture. (If furniture could scowl and carry heavy weaponry.)

'Oh yes. Very sweet.'

'He must really care for you.'

My heart made a leap, and I glanced over at Karim again. Had he heard? He shouldn't be able to. We were speaking very low, and he was across the room from us. But I wouldn't put it past that big bearded brute to have the ears of an Egyptian fruit bat hidden away somewhere under that turban of his.

So I simply gave Lady Samantha's hand a gentle squeeze in return and winked. Her face broke into a dreamy smile. Never in my life had a wink been received with so much delight.

'Oh, my dear! So there is something between the two of you! I knew it! I simply knew it! Has he...has he said anything yet?'

'Hm, let me think...' Considering, I tapped my chin. 'I think I do remember him speaking a word or two...'

'Really?' Her eyes went wide.

'Yes. I think it was last year. The words were "work" and "faster". If I remember, he used them quite a bit on his employees.'

'Oh, Miss Linton! Don't jest with me!'

'You called me Lillian before,' I pointed out.

'Did I?' Her ears turned pink. 'Oh, I'm so sorry, my dear. I must have been overcome, seeing you safe and sound again after I heard you were injured.'

'I don't mind.'

Our gazes met and held for a long, long moment. There was understanding in the air between us. 'Neither did I,' Her Ladyship said, softly. 'I shall look forward to the day when I can call you Lillian, my dear.'

With a smile, she rose and turned away. Perhaps it was my imagination, but just before she left the room, I thought I heard the whispered words '...and maybe even call you daughter.'

Blood rose to my cheeks, and I hoped against hope that Karim had not heard that.

~~**~*~*

Thud!

'Ow! What, by the beard of the–!'

'He! What is this?' Shoving forward, I pushed against the door.

Thud! 'Ouch! Stop that, you accursed woman!'

'Karim? Karim, is that you?'

'Who else?'

'I don't know,' I shot through the gap. 'Offhand, I can think of about fifty people who would be more likely to stand in front of my bedroom door in the morning. What in God's name are you doing out there?'

'Standing guard.'

'*Standing guard?*'

'Yes. On Ambrose *Sahib*'s orders.'

'What for?'

'To protect you from anyone who might wish to come inside to do you harm.' A snort came from beyond the door. 'Although I must wonder whether the reverse would not be more practical.'

'Get out of my way or I'll brain you with my parasol!'

'My point exactly.'

Feet shuffled outside. The way was clear. Buttoning up the last few buttons of my dress, I pushed open the door – and there he was: big, bearded and beastly as ever. Karim was just missing a bonnet, a fan and a plain brown dress to make the perfect young lady's chaperone. I refrained from mentioning that to him, however.

'Why exactly are you here?' I demanded. 'Don't tell me that Mr Ambrose is afraid Captain Carter would sneak to my room at night to sing love ballads to me and ensnare me in a web of passion?'

Karim's face remained as impassive as a block of wood with a big beard.

'It is not for me to question the *Sahib*'s instructions.'

'No, of course it isn't. So, you are going to follow me around everywhere from now on?'

'Yes.'

'Is there any way I can get rid of you?'

'No.'

'What if I bribe you?'

'No.'

'What if I knock you over the head?'

'No.'

'What about if I start taking my clothes off?'

A slightly unusual tactic, I admit, but one I had actually employed with success in the past. Only...that had been in the wilderness of the Amazonian jungle, not in the hallway of the most lavish British manor house north of the River

Trent. I had a feeling that Lady Samantha would be less understanding of my semi-naked state than the nice Indian tribe we had visited back then. I wouldn't do it. Not here.

Still...Karim didn't need to know that, did he?

His eyes widened. 'You would not! Not even you would dare...not here, no!'

'Are you sure?' Suggestively, I played with the top button of my dress. 'You'd better run, if you want to preserve the innocence of your eyes.'

For one long moment, he wavered, torn between his duty and escaping the clutches of yours truly – then his face set into even grimmer lines, and he crossed his arms in front of his chest.

'Do your worst, woman who is worse than *ifrit*. I have orders from Ambrose *Sahib*. I shall not go.'

Damn!

Uttering some very unladylike curses – in Portuguese, just in case someone was listening in – I started marching down the hall, followed by my new, bearded, sabre-swinging shadow. This was intolerable! I was going to make someone pay. And I knew just who had the deepest pockets around here...

Mr Rikkard Ambrose was sitting at breakfast with his mother, sister, and a gaggle of admiring young ladies who were plying him with questions about the mine strike, ooh-ing and aaah-ing, fluttering their eyelashes and compliment-ing him on his bravery. Needless to say that when I stormed into the breakfast parlour, this sight didn't exactly improve my mood.

'And then, Mr Ambrose?' Lady Caroline whispered, leaning closer in a way that displayed certain assets of hers to their best advantage. However, since the assets were neither inventory, cash nor receivables, Mr Rikkard Ambrose didn't appear particularly interested. That mollified me somewhat – until I heard him say, 'Well, Lady Caroline, after my secretary had let himself be knocked down, I grabbed the stupid boy and dragged him into the manager's office. My body-guard covered the door, while I pulled him out of danger.'

What?

'Oh, Mr Ambrose!' sighed Lady Caroline. 'You're so brave.'

'Yes,' sighed Lady Dorothea, not to be outdone by a little competition. 'So terribly brave!'

'Yes,' Mr Ambrose concurred succinctly, and took a succinct sip of tea.

Excuse me? Who was it who jumped in front of whom to save him from being stoned alive?

'Tell us more,' pleaded Lady Caroline. 'What did you do next? How did you save the day?'

I cleared my throat.

Everyone looked up. A broad smile spread over Lady Samantha's face.

'Ah, Miss Linton. I'm so glad you felt up to joining us. How are you this fine morning, after the exhausting journey yesterday?'

Everyone *except* Mr Ambrose. His eyes didn't move an inch. He took another sip of tea.

'Very well, thank you,' I told her, staring at him. 'Although I sometimes feel a little bit uneasy after that terrible ordeal. For some reason, I feel watched, as if someone were following me everywhere I go.'

'Oh, my dear.' Reaching out, Lady Samantha patted my hand. 'That's perfectly natural, after all that you've been through. All those brutes attacking you... If I'd had an experience like that, I'd be checking for strangers around corners, too. But it's just an irrational feeling. In time it will fade.'

'Really?' I asked, taking a seat. A shadow fell onto my plate as Karim took up his post behind me. I heard the scrape of metal against metal as he took a tight hold of his sabre. 'I'm so relieved to hear that.'

'So it is true?' Lady Caroline demanded. 'You were really caught up in the strike? The miners attacked you?'

Ladling my toast with liberal amounts of beans, I considered how best to answer that. Finally, I decided on: 'Yes.'

'Dear Lord!' she gave a fake little gasp and fanned herself, as if the mere thought of mine workers caused acute lack of oxygen. Her eyes, however, stayed hard and sharp as shards of flint. 'That's dreadful! You poor thing! And to live through that at your age, when you're hardly a woman yet, nearly a child...how horrific. I'm so sorry that you were hurt.'

And not killed instead, her eyes completed the sentence she could not finish out loud.

'So am I,' I agreed with a smile. *I'd rather it had been you.*

Then the men started in, propounding their theories about the declining morality of the lower classes and the need to take them into a firm hand to save Britain's economy. We ladies contented ourselves with throwing poisonous looks at each other, and occasionally at each other's breakfast, in the hope the looks would be literally effective. But just because I was silent, that didn't mean I no longer intended to haul Mr Ambrose over the coals. Oh no. I simply waited. I bided my time. As soon as there was a lull in the conversation, I leaned forward, and with a sweet smile said, 'Mr Ambrose, Sir?'

Everyone hushed. His name alone was enough to cast silence over a table.

Meticulously, Mr Ambrose speared a piece of bacon with his fork, deposited it in his mouth, chewed, and swallowed. Only then did he look at me.

'Yes, Miss Linton?'

'I wanted to thank you for your generosity in lending your personal bodyguard to me.'

'Indeed?'

'Oh yes, indeed. I feel so much safer since I have a dangerous, armed man lurking in front of my bedroom door every night.'

'I see.'

'Although...'

'Yes?'

'I have noticed that such security measures tend to get in the way of private conversations, or privacy in general.'

'Do they?'

'Oh yes.'

'Well, you needn't concern yourself, Miss Linton. Karim is confidentiality it-self.'

'He is?'

'Oh yes. No matter what he hears, he takes me into his confidence.'

Gripping my fork, I stabbed at a piece of scrambled egg, imagining it to be Mr Ambrose's head. 'That's what I thought. Thank you again, Mr Ambrose. Words simply cannot express how grateful I am.'

'And thank you from me, too, Sir.' I glanced up to see who had spoken. It was Captain Carter. He was looking at Mr Ambrose with an earnest expression of thanks on his face, the poor deluded man. 'It means a great deal to me to know that Miss Linton will be safe at all times. I truly appreciate what you have done.'

Oh boy...let's wait and see if you still feel that way after the first time you try coming within ten yards of me.

Behind me, Karim shifted and rattled his sabre.

~~**~*~*

Oh, Lord, please let this torture end! Please give me back Mrs. Ponsemby!

A few years ago, a distant relation had invited Gertrude, Lisbeth, Ella and me on a seaside holiday to Bath. Though 'holiday' had probably not been the right expression for it. Mrs Ponsemby had been our hired chaperone for the occasion – a fat old bird who was allergic to sun, sea water, music, sweets, all other kinds of fun and, to judge by the looks she gave us, adolescent girls as well. She could read children's minds and blister a conscience at fifty paces. The most treasured memory I had of Mrs Ponsemby was the scream she uttered when she found the frog I had put into her shoe. Under normal circumstances, it would have taken huge bribes or horrifying torture to even make me think of Mrs Ponsemby. But now...

Now I wished her back with all my heart.

If only I had her back.

If only I had her back.

If only I had her, instead of–

'Ow!' Whirling, I grabbed the spot on my delicate derriere that had just been poked by a sabre sheath. 'Will you watch where you stick that thing? Don't walk so closely behind me!'

'The *Sahib* instructed me to remain close to you at all times.'

'Then put that bloody pigsticker away!'

'I cannot discard my weapons. The *Sahib* instructed me that your safety is of the utmost–'

'Oh, stop gabbling gobbledygook, you big, bearded block of basalt! You know as well as I do this has nothing to do with my safety.'

'The *Sahib* assigned me to protect you. The *Sahib* instructed me that your safety is of the utmost importance. I shall protect you with my life.'

Just then, a voice called out from behind us. 'Miss Linton? Miss Linton, wait.'

I turned to see who it was. Then, seeing only massive amounts of beard, I stepped to the side and peeked around a big shoulder to see who it was.

Captain James Carter was hurrying down the corridor. He mustn't have had much more appetite than I if he had ended his breakfast this early.

'Oh, hello Captain,' I began. 'I was just–'

That was about as far as I got before Karim kicked open a door right beside us, shoved me into the room, stepped in behind me, slammed shut the door and jammed it with a chair. All this happened so fast I didn't even have time to blink. When I finally did have time again, I was already three rooms farther away, being pulled along without a hope of resistance by the mountainous bodyguard.

Bodyguard?

Ha! Walking chastity belt, more like!

'So,' I enquired sweetly. 'You are here to protect me from danger?'

'Yes.'

'And what kind of danger did Captain Carter present just now? Pray tell, I'm dying to hear.'

'The dangerous kind.'

'Of course. Why did I even ask? It's so obvious.'

We didn't stop until we reached the winter garden. The sun sparkled on the frosted windows, and the plants glinted with morning dew. Throwing a very deliberate look around the empty green space, I turned to raise an eyebrow at Karim.

'What exactly am I supposed to do here?'

'I do not know.' He waved an imperious paw. 'Do what women do in gardens.'

'Tend roses?'

'Yes.'

'Play croquet?'

'Yes.'

'Go on romantic walks with lovers?'

'Ye– no! No, not that!'

'I could think of someone who would be only too happy to go on walks with me, if–'

Faster than I would have believed it possible, Karim moved and positioned himself in front of the only exit.

'Roses!' he commanded, with a scowl that was probably supposed to look fierce. 'Croquet!'

I gave him another sweet smile. 'I don't have a croquet mallet. I suppose you wouldn't be so kind as to lend me your sabre as a replacement?'

'No.'

'I thought not. A pity. I could think of a very good use for it, right now.'

That's how it went on, and on, and on. During the next few days, every time a male dared to step too close to me, Karim was there, placing himself between the 'danger' and sweet little unprotected me, or simply growling at the newcomer. That sent most scurrying off in the opposite direction. And whenever we met a certain red-coated captain on whom a growl wasn't likely to have the same effect...well, let's just say his tactics got a little bit more inventive.

'Thff fff rdffffcffff!'

No answer.

'Lttt mmm ggg!'

No answer. Over Karim's shoulder, I could just see the puzzled face of Captain Carter. His thoughts were as clear as if they had been painted on his forehead: *I thought I saw her here just a moment ago. Where could she be?*

Then he shrugged, and marched away down the corridor.

Removing his paw from my mouth – not without wincing at the bite marks I had left, I noted to my satisfaction – Karim let go of me. I strode out from behind the potted plant where he had dragged me.

'This,' I told him, taking deep calming breaths, 'is getting ridiculous.'

He did his best to keep his face serene and dutiful. 'My orders from the *Sahib* are to keep you safe. Your safety is of paramount–'

'Oh, put a sock in it! Enough is enough!'

I was pissed off. Really pissed off. And do you know why? Officially, of course, I was pissed off because Mr Ambrose, that chauvinistic son of a bachelor, was trying to control who I could and could not speak to. That was outrageous! Unspeakable! As a strong, independent woman, I simply could not allow it.

But really, deep down inside, I was pissed off because I could have used a suitor-deflecting shield like Karim years ago. He would have come in so damn handy during my adolescent years, when my dear aunt's goal in life was to marry me off before I was sixteen. But had he shown up then? Oh no, he and his megalomaniac master had to wait till I was grown up and able to fend for myself before they appeared in my life. Thanks, but no thanks!

Finally, the exhausting day drifted to a close. With a sigh, I slammed the door of my room behind me and leaned against it. At least here I was safe from persecution. At least here I would be blessedly, blissfully alone.

'Well?' came a cool voice from right beside me, nearly making me jump out of my skin. 'Ready to hold up your end of our deal?'

I whirled.

It was dark inside the room. Too dark to see, really. But even if I hadn't recognised the tall, dark, figure in the shadows in an instant, that cool voice would have removed any doubts about its identity.

'You!' Breathing heavily, I stabbed an accusing look at the dark silhouette. 'What are you doing here?'

'Collecting my dividends,' Mr Rikkard Ambrose said in a voice that betrayed not a hint of remorse.

'You dare show your face here after what your goon has put me through today?'

He took a step forward. 'I gather you are referring to Karim?'

'You bet I'm referring to Karim! I didn't ask for you to set him on my tracks like some overeager guard-dog! I didn't–'

In that moment, my voice cut off.

Why?

Because Mr Rikkard Ambrose had taken a step forward, gripped my face in both hands and claimed my mouth with a kiss. It was a long kiss. A hard kiss. A kiss he worked for all it was worth, until he'd tripled every single penny of his investment, and made me melt into the bargain. When he finally released me, my breath was gone and my brain was on holiday.

'Karim stays,' he told me, his voice as hard and cold as a frost giant's sword. 'Your safety comes first.'

Gathering what tattered remnants of sanity I could recover, I glared up at him. It wasn't easy, after such a kiss. 'My safety? Bollocks! This isn't about my safety.'

'It is.' His eyes bored into me, deep, dark, sea-coloured pools of danger. 'Because if I catch that army captain anywhere near you, Mr Linton, you won't be safe. And neither will he.'

And with that, he tore open the door and marched out of my room.

Well, well...

Mr Rikkard Ambrose's version of a gentle good-night kiss, threats and tyranny inclusive. Wasn't I a lucky girl?

As I touched two fingers to my throbbing lips, I had to fight hard against a persistent little voice in the back of my head that told me, over and over again, that yes, indeed, I was.

I wouldn't listen! I wouldn't lie down and let him trample all over me! Safety? Protection? Ha! He could take his protection and stuff it where the sun didn't shine!

Later that night, as I lay in bed, slowly drifting to sleep, I determined that there was no way around it. I had to assert my independence. And there was only one way to do that, only one way to show Mr Rikkard Ambrose once and for all that he couldn't order me around as he pleased: I had to go on a rendezvous with Captain James Carter.

PRINCIFIED

I woke up next morning with a plan formed ready in my mind. And, oh, what a beautifully diabolical plan it was. Lying in my warm bed, gazing up at the portraits of fat little cherubs on the ceiling, I smiled. Poor Karim... He had no idea what I had in store for him.

Rising, I slipped into my female guise and, whistling merrily, stepped out of the room. Karim was already awaiting me and followed on my heels as I made my way down to breakfast. And when I say 'on my heels', that was less of a metaphor than I would have liked it to be. More than once I had to suppress a yelp of pain as the tips of his shoes stabbed into my ankles.

Patience, Lilly. Patience. Vengeance shall be thine.

When I entered the breakfast parlour still whistling and smiling, Mr Ambrose threw me a suspicious glance. But what could he say? *You look suspiciously happy this morning. What are you up to?*

Not the kind of thing you ask a lady in front of your mother and two dozen guests.

'You look suspiciously happy this morning. What are you up to?'

134

Unless your name is Rikkard Ambrose, of course.

'Rick!' From across the table Lady Samantha sent her son a reproachful look, which he completely ignored. I gave him a friendly smile.

'Oh, nothing. I guess I'm just in a good mood this fine morning. Good as in "positive" or "buoyant". In case you'd like to find out the meaning of those words, you'll find them under *p* and *b* in the dictionary.'

Several of the gentlemen at the table chuckled. The ladies didn't, but then again, you can't really expect hyenas to laugh at an antelope's joke. Unless maybe it starts with 'A lame antelope came into a bar full of hyenas waiting for their dinner, and...'

Breakfast passed without any major events. Now and then, Mr Rikkard Ambrose threw me a suspicious look or two, but since he did the same with the lady next to him, who was trying to get his attention through giggling and eyelash-batting, I wasn't particularly worried he was suspecting something. Oh no, he felt secure in the knowledge that his big, bearded bulldog would follow me wherever I went.

Big mistake.

After breakfast, the gentlemen departed. Most to go shooting or riding, a few, like Mr Ambrose, to burrow into their happy world of paperwork and business correspondence, from which this inconvenient Christmas invitation had so cruelly torn them. Only we ladies remained behind. Soon, most were engaged in activities traditionally associated with the fair sex – needlework, mindless little musicales, and general undermining of the feminist cause. Only one little detail didn't quite fit into the homely idyll...

'Um...what is *he* doing here?' Adaira whispered, leaning over to me and, as inconspicuously as possible, pointing at Karim. The giant Mohammedan was standing in one corner of the room, arms crossed, spearing a young lady doing her needlework with a glare so fierce, you'd think he suspected her of planning an assassination by needle-stabbing, or maybe yarn-garrotting.

I pulled a face. 'Haven't you heard? Since my little adventure in Newcastle, I have my own personal bodyguard. He follows me everywhere.'

'*Everywhere*? Even to the–'

'Yes.'

'*Inside*?'

'If he tries that, I'll stab him with my parasol.'

'Good for you!'

I sighed. 'But it's bad enough as it is. I stumble over him everywhere I go. I hardly have a moment's peace anymore. And it's all so unreasonable! I'm perfectly safe here. I don't know why he insists on it! Your brother–'

The two little magic words worked like a charm.

Your brother.

Slumping back in her armchair, Adaira covered her face with a pillow. 'Don't get me started on him! He's the most stubborn–'

'–unreasonable–'

'–cold, calculating–'

'–block of ice you could find–'

135

'–south of the North Pole.'

Slowly, Adaira pulled the cushion from her face, just far enough for me to see the smile that was tugging at the corners of her mouth. 'You know...it really is wonderful to be talking with a sensible girl for a change. I have a feeling that the two of us could become friends. We seem to understand each other on such a deep, basic level.'

I grinned back. 'My thoughts exactly.'

Adaira's eyes slid back to Karim. 'You know...in the spirit of friendship...'

'Yes?'

'If there's something I could do to help...'

This was what I had been waiting for.

'Yes,' I told her. 'Actually, there is.'

~~**~*~*

Giggling like little girls, Adaira and I sank onto a sofa only a few feet away from a pack of the most vicious hyenas, Lady Eveline, Caroline and Dorothea among them. They ignored us – or at least me – with disdain worthy of three grand duchesses. But as we kept giggling, whispering, and every now and again throwing glances over our shoulders at Karim, standing in the corner, you could practically feel curiosity beginning to gnaw at them.

Finally, they snapped. Literally.

'Pardon me!' Lady Caroline snapped at me. 'We are engaged in serious pursuits. Please quiet your stupid antics, or at least share what it is that you find so highly entertaining.'

We looked at her, then looked at Karim, and burst into another excited fit of giggles. Eyebrows raised – they never would have gone so far as to actually frown and put wrinkles onto those perfect faces of theirs – the ladies followed our glances and took in the huge, turban-wearing stranger in the corner.

'Unbelievable.' Lady Eveline shook her head. 'What can there possibly be that could be so fascinating to a proper lady about a savage like that?'

I had to admit, I was impressed. Twice now, she had fished for information, both times without posing a direct question to either me or Adaira.

But she wouldn't need to.

'Well...' Adaira began, just as we had discussed.

'Don't tell them!' I hissed at her, sending her a quite impressive glare, if I do say so myself. 'They don't deserve to know!'

'*What* don't we deserve to know?' Eveline's voice was sharp as a knife. Her eyes narrowed into slits.

'That–'

'Don't!' I interrupted Adaira again, shaking my head. But the three hyenas glared at me, and I shut up. How could I not be intimidated by three pampered society beauties? It was such a terror to behold.

'Tell us,' Lady Caroline commanded – never mind that she was a guest in Adaira's house.

136

Adaira's eyes flashed for a moment, betraying her real feelings – but just for a moment. The next she was smiling an impressively genuine 'oh, I'm just a silly little girl' smile, and leaned forward conspiratorially.

'You know, I shouldn't tell you this, but...'

'Adaira, no!' Jumping up, I took a few dramatic steps back. 'How could you? I thought you were my friend!'

And, whirling around, I marched away.

But not all the way away. Instead, I slid behind a screen, still within comfortable hearing distance.

'What is the matter with her?' Lady Caroline asked.

'Oh, she is just worried she'll get some competition.' Another silly girlish giggle from Adaira. Dear me, that girl was good. She should try getting a job as an actress.

'Competition?' Now, Lady Caroline sounded truly interested. 'For Lord Ambrose?'

'What, my brother?' Adaira gave a dismissive snort. Somehow I had a feeling that this time, she wasn't acting. 'No, he's old news.'

'Old news?'

'Yes. Who cares about a little lordling–' conspiratorially, she lowered her voice, '–when there's a prince to catch?'

Stunned silence filled the room. Absolute, complete silence. The talent must lie in the Ambrose family.

'A...a prince?'

Lady Dorothea sounded only slightly breathless. Impressive. One might almost think that she wasn't salivating.

'You didn't know?'

Adaira's voice contained just the right amount of surprise and delight. 'Well, I suppose you wouldn't. He is remaining incognito for very good reasons, after all. Even I found out only yesterday.'

'Who?' Caroline demanded, sounding as if she were ready to tear the secret out of Adaira if she didn't give it willingly. 'Who is a prince? Where is he?'

'Why, right over there.'

Cautiously, I leaned forward just enough to peek around the screen – just in time to see Adaira raise a hand and point one delicate finger straight at Karim, who was still grimly contemplating needle and thread as a possible murder weapon and didn't notice a thing.

'Him?'

'You must be joking!'

'I...I thought he was supposed to be your brother's bodyguard!'

Smiling the smile of the all-knowing, Adaira leaned back. 'That's what he would like everyone to believe. He's running around, posing as my brother's bodyguard under the name of Karim. But honestly! Look at him. Don't you see the nobility in his eyes? Haven't you noticed his commanding posture? A bodyguard? Honestly, I ask you!'

'Well...' Caroline murmured, 'now that you mention it, I have to admit...'

'His true name is Utairah Jafri fi al Qurram Qumrah III,[8] heir to the principality of Bakavāsa[9] in India. He is here to negotiate a business agreement with my brother.'

'Is that so?'

'Oh yes. British goods in exchange for tons of Bakavāsian gold and ivory.'

The ladies' eyes went big. 'Tons, you say?'

'Yes. The prince is quite eager to have all the most modern conveniences in his five palaces, and that does not come cheap.'

'I would imagine so. *Five* palaces?'

'Five.'

'I say! And that little vixen wanted him all for herself. Well...' Rising to her feet, Caroline let her fan snap open. 'That ends here and now.'

'What do you mean?' Lady Dorothea sprang to her feet.

'I mean, of course, that I am going to make the acquaintance of His Highness the Prince.'

'I saw him first!'

'No, I did!'

A brief struggle ensued. By the time it was over, five other ladies had already noticed what was going on. The news spread through the room like the plague, only much, much more dangerous: a prince! There was a prince in the room!

'Your Royal Highness?'

Karim stood there, staring grimly ahead, arms folded, unaware of the approaching doom in silk and satin.

'Your Royal Highness?'

'Prince Utairah?'

Finally, after the third time that a female right next to him addressed the air with royal titles, it began to dawn on the Mohammedan that maybe, just maybe, they were not addressing the air. Maybe they were talking to him. Slowly, he turned his head and surveyed the two females before him.

'Hrm?'

That was what the noise he made sounded like. A bit like the noise a tiger would make when he means to enquire 'Should I eat you now?'

The ladies giggled.

Two more joined them. One put a hand on his arm. Karim looked down at it as if it were a slimy snail, which didn't seem to put the lady off.

'Prince Utairah, we know we're not supposed to know who you are, but I just have to know...how is life in Bakavāsa?'

Karim's mighty brow furrowed. 'What are you speaking of, woman?'

The ladies giggled as if he had made a hilarious joke.

'So mysterious,' one whispered.

'So strong,' another added.

Five more ladies joined the group, whispering and giggling. Karim's eyes swivelled from right to left, looking for a way to escape. There was none.

---

[8] Fragrant Yellow Flower in the Happy Moonlight

[9] Nonsense

'What is this?' he demanded.

'Oh, Prince Utairah,' sighed a girl right next to him. 'I knew there was something special about you from the first moment I saw you.'

'So did I,' whispered another one who had somehow managed to squeeze into the corner and sneak up on the bodyguard from behind. He jumped when her hair brushed his face. 'Your disguise didn't fool me for a moment. You're such a powerful man, so strong, so commanding...'

'What is this? Leave! Avaunt!'

The ladies giggled again, and moved closer.

'Isn't he wonderful?' sighed one.

'Simply incredible,' murmured another, reaching up to stroke his beard.

'Ah! Stop! Don't you–'

'Why don't you come with me for a little stroll in the winter garden, Prince Utairah? It is so beautiful this time of day.'

'I don't think–' Karim began, but he didn't get any further.

'Don't listen to her, Your Royal Highness!' another one cut him off. 'Come with me. I'm Lady Francine, Daughter of the Duke of Northumberland. What does she matter? She's just a baronet's niece!'

'You...you...! Don't you listen, to her, Prince Utairah! Her father is a gambler and has lost his entire fortune!'

'And yours never had one to begin with! Come with me, Prince. I promise you won't regret it!'

'Cease touching me! Step back, women! It is not proper–'

But what exactly was not proper, I never found out. The rest of the women had heard the word 'prince'. The moment they realised what prospects were hiding behind that rough, hairy, weaponised exterior, things really started to get interesting.

'Prince? Did I hear someone say prince?'

'How big is your palace, Prince?'

'Are you still unmarried?'

'Should we play some music, Prince? Would you like to dance?'

'Come dance with me!'

'No, me!'

'Me!'

Slowly but surely, Karim was swallowed up by a jungle of hoop skirts, waving fans and dance cards. When the noise level had reached ear-damaging proportions, I snuck to the door and slipped out of the room. Nobody noticed. Nobody, that is, except for Adaira, who joined me a few moments later.

I raised an eyebrow at her.

'Prince Utairah Jafri fi al Qurram Qumrah III,[10] heir to the principality of Bakavāsa?'

She shrugged. 'My governess was very thorough. Besides French and German, she insisted on oriental language training.'

---

[10] Fragrant Yellow Flower in the Happy Moonlight

Her voice was very nonchalant, but there was a little devil dancing in her eyes.

'Adaira?'

'Yes?'

'What does that name mean, exactly?'

She managed to keep up her nonchalant front for about two more seconds – then burst into laughter and ducked back into the room to avoid the barrage of questions I was about to fire at her.

Oh dear.

That couldn't be a good sign. What exactly had she cooked up in that brain of hers?

Well, I'd get to the bottom of it later. Now it was time for a little rebellion!

I made my way back towards my room to fetch a cloak, just in case my search for Captain Carter led me outside the house. But, as it turned out, a search wasn't necessary. The captain was standing in front of my door, just raising his hand to knock as I approached.

'Miss Linton? Miss Linton, are you in there?'

'No,' I told him, and he jumped, whirling around.

'Shouldn't a soldier be a little more on guard?' I teased. 'I could have been a Frenchman, preparing to stab you in the back.'

'We currently are at peace with France, I believe, Miss Linton. I met with their ambassador only a few weeks ago. He invited me to have dinner with him, sometime soon.'

'Even more reason to be on your guard, Captain. Just one word: snails.'

That got a small smile out of him, but it was gone almost immediately. He was still in the same unusually serious mood I remembered from our last meeting. And in his eyes I could see that the subject he wanted to discuss hadn't changed, either.

'Can we have a talk, Miss Linton?' he enquired, his voice soft. 'In private? There's something I have to discuss with you.'

'Certainly.' I extended an arm. 'Shall we take a little walk together?'

ROMANCE IN THE AIR

It was cold outside. I told myself it was *not* because Mr Ambrose was staring at me. He wasn't even here. It was just the winter. Cold is perfectly normal in winter. Still...it felt as if two dark, sea-coloured eyes were burning into my neck with permanent frostbite.

Relax, Lilly. You are doing nothing wrong. You are an independent girl, and can go on romantic walks with whomever you choose. Even if it's not the one you'd actually like to be walking with.

Mr Ambrose had to learn a lesson. He had to understand that even if I didn't want anyone but him, I was, theoretically, perfectly within my rights to choose anyone else, whether it be the King of England, the shoeblack in the local tavern, or Captain James Carter. Only once I had managed to hammer this fundamental principle into his thick head would it be possible for us to have a future.

Really, Lilly? So you have to go on a romantic walk with one man to secure your future with another?

All right, maybe my logic was a little bit unconventional, but then again, so was Rikkard Ambrose.

And besides...

Out of the corner of my eye, I glanced up at Captain Carter. Poor man... The way he was gazing at me, with that gleam in his eyes...

He had the words 'love confession incoming' practically tattooed on his forehead. He was full to bursting with romance! If I didn't let him vent it soon, it would explode. What might he do then? Start painting the walls of Battlewood pink? Dance through the halls, writing valentines across all the ancient portraits? There was no way to tell.

We walked through the silent winter day, the noise of our footsteps muffled by the soft flakes underfoot. His hands nervously worked at his lapels, tugging and readjusting every other second. Every time he threw a nervous glance my way, I could have sworn he was going to say something. But he didn't. He waited until we reached a small grove of trees. Frost sparkled on the branches, and a bird or two hopped from twig to twig high above. They weren't songbirds singing a beautiful melody, but still...

My heart started to beat faster.

Captain Carter halted, opened his mouth, and–

–closed it again.

Bloody hell, what was taking him so long? One measly little love confession couldn't be that difficult, could it? *I love you, do you love me, too? No, thanks. Oh well, too bad.* That was pretty much it, right?

Taking a deep breath, the captain turned towards me, gazing deep into my eyes.

'Miss Linton, I...um...'

That was it.

Miss Linton I um?

That was his best effort? If that was all he could manage, he shouldn't be surprised when I told him no. What was the matter with him? His eyes were boring into me with an unnatural intensity, his cheeks were flushed, and the muscles in his jaw were working overtime. Was he having a seizure? None of my other suitors had looked like this when asking for my hand. But then...they probably hadn't been in love.

Did I look like this when I looked at Mr Rikkard Ambrose?

What a horrifying thought. I would have to take a mirror with me next time and check.

Captain Carter was still chewing on air. I decided to throw the poor man a bone and start the conversation.

'What happened with the man who attacked you?' I asked. 'Did you ever find out who it was?'

He snatched the harmless topic of kidnapping attempts as if it were a lifeline.

'No. No, I have no idea who is after me.' Gazing into the distance, he shook his head. 'I can't think of a single reason why anyone would want to harm me. Oh, sure, there are some officers I've disagreed with over the last few years, and the locals in Newcastle probably weren't too thrilled about my involvement in putting down the strike, but my fellow officers are gentlemen. If they wanted satisfaction from me, they would call me out. And the locals...there were hundreds of other soldiers there. Why single me out? It doesn't make sense. No, there's something there I don't see yet. Some dark plot is afoot.'

You bet a plot is afoot! Especially regarding a certain foot of a certain man who would like nothing better than to crush you beneath his heel.

'But the thing I'm worried about most,' he continued, abruptly returning his gaze to my face, 'is that they might be after you.'

'Me?'

'Yes. After all, I was on the way to visit you when this happened, wasn't I? What if it's somehow connected with you and your family? That man your brother works for, that Mr Ambrose...he seems like a man who has a lot of enemies.'

Yes, including you, I'm afraid.

'No. No, I don't think so.'

'Miss Linton, please.' Reaching out, he took hold of my hands. My heart made a jump. His warm brown eyes suddenly seemed hot enough to melt the snow around us. He was staring at me with an unsettling intensity. 'Please take this seriously. If something happened to you...'

'Believe me.' I gave his hands a gentle squeeze. 'Whoever it was that pulled a sack over your head that day, they were not after me.'

Though they might be, if they find out who invented Prince Utairah Jafri fi al Qurram Qumrah III.

'I wish I could be so sure,' the captain murmured, still not letting my hands go. 'I wish....'

His voice drifted off into nothingness.

'What?'

'I wish I could always be there to protect you. Always at your side.'

Ah. It was coming. Well, it was about time!

'Miss Linton, I have something to ask you. Something very important.'

Finally!

I gave him an encouraging smile. 'Shoot.'

Taking a deep breath, he stood straight and took a firmer hold of my hands. 'I have long thought about this, long searched my feelings. I can't deny it any longer. Since the moment we first met, I knew–'

'–that I was someone special? Someone who would have a place in your heart?' I suggested.

'Well, um...yes. But I never would have guessed how special a place, how important. Every time we danced together, every time you smiled at me, every time I held you in my arms, I felt-'

'-our connection growing stronger and stronger, until you couldn't resist any longer?' Holy moly, I was on a roll.

He blinked. 'Err...yes. That's pretty much it. I simply couldn't deny it any longer. I am completely and utterly-'

'-in love with me?'

I grinned up at him. He tried to look stern, he really tried. But he was Captain James Carter. After about two seconds, he grinned back at me (in a really stern sort of way).

'Miss Linton! I appreciate your assistance, but I'm supposed to be the one doing the talking here!'

'I do apologise. Pray continue.'

'As I said - well, you said, actually - I am completely and utterly in love with you and...'

He trailed off, looking down at me with an almost wistful smile on his face. 'This isn't going the way I hoped, is it?'

'Don't let me discourage you. You're doing a very good job so far.'

'Good enough to get a "yes"?'

Gently, I freed one hand from his grip and placed it on his arm. 'Maybe not quite.'

Raising his chin, he took a step towards me. 'I'll try anyway.'

'I thought you might.'

'Miss Lillian Linton, I love you. I love your fiery spirit. I love the way you dance and laugh and live to the full, and always fight for what you believe in. Will you-'

'-marry me?' I guessed.

'Bloody hell, that was supposed to be my proposal!'

I smiled up at him apologetically. 'Sorry.'

Silence stretched between us. I gazed up into his face, the face of one of my best friends in all the world, and wondered how things had come to this? How had I not seen this in him before that day in Newcastle? How could I have missed it?

'Well?' he asked, his voice hardly more than a whisper. 'Will you?'

Oh, right. Blast! I hadn't answered yet.

'Captain...James, I...'

There must have been something in my expression (or maybe in the way I didn't throw my arms around his neck, crying 'Yes, darling, Yes, God bless you! I'll be yours forever and ever and ever!'), because his eyes narrowed, and he sucked in a breath.

'There's someone else!'

I blinked. 'Wait? What? I didn't say that!'

'You don't have to.'

'Will you at least let me give you my answer?'

'Why?' His lips twitched into a smile – one of the old Captain Carter smiles, the ones I recognised as belonging to my friend. 'You wouldn't let me finish my proposal, either.'

I punched his arm. 'Be serious!'

'I am being serious.' And he was. No matter that he was still smiling, his face somehow was the most serious I had ever seen. 'There's someone else, isn't there?'

I hesitated for a moment. Never, ever had I admitted to anyone I knew that there was someone. Someone special. Someone my heart belonged to. But if there ever was a time to be brave, it was now.

'Yes.' The word was a whisper, carried away on a cold winter breeze. 'Yes, there is.'

'Is he good to you?'

I considered the question. I considered it for a quite a long time. And finally, a smile tugging at the corners of my lips, I gave the only possible answer. 'I wouldn't say "good". I'd rather say... "adequate".'

His grip on my hand tightened. 'Has he done something to hurt you? Lilly...Miss Linton, I will–'

'No, no!' Raising my free hand, I gently touched a finger to his lips, silencing him. 'It's not like that at all. He is what I want. What I need.'

'You could do so much better,' he whispered.

I smiled. 'You don't even know who it is I am talking about.'

'It doesn't matter. You are you. You can always do better.'

'Even better than you?'

'Of course.'

'You're silly!'

One corner of his mouth curved up in a smile. Still incredibly full of sadness but, yes, it was a smile. 'That's part of my charm.'

'Yes. Yes, it is.'

'But...I'm not charming enough?'

I tried to sound gentle when I answered. Gentle when talking to a man...what a novel experience.

'No.'

Just as gently, I slipped my hands from his grasp and took a small step back. He looked after me as if he were Menelaus, and I was Helena, disappearing in the distance.

'If you change your mind...'

'I'm sorry. I won't.'

'I thought not. Well, then...'

He fell silent. For a while, we just stood there, gazing at each other. Reflected in his eyes I saw flashes of a future, a life that might have been – and maybe it would have been a happy one. But for me?

No.

There was only one man for me. And his name was–

'I hope,' said a cold voice from the shadow of the trees, 'I am not interrupting anything?'

FRAGRANT YELLOW FLOWER IN THE HAPPY MOONLIGHT

Mr Rikkard Ambrose stepped from the shadows of the trees like a wraith from the bowels of the underworld – only that wraiths from the underworld probably were a lot more warm and friendly. The way he was looking at me...

I was in trouble.

Big trouble.

'Interrupting?' I smiled a smile so bright it nearly hurt my face. 'Good heavens, no! Why would you be interrupting anything? There's nothing here to interrupt. I'm totally uninterruptable.'

'Pleased to hear it, Miss Linton. Captain.' He gave the captain a nod so sharp I was surprised it didn't cut the poor man's head off. 'Miss Linton, do you perchance know where your brother is?' His cold eyes pierced me. 'I need to talk to him about a certain business matter.'

I swallowed. 'I'll help you find him. You don't mind that I leave you to yourself, Captain, do you?'

'No, by all means go look for your brother.' He gave me a nod, his eyes darting back and forth between Mr Rikkard Ambrose and me. 'We'll talk later.'

I felt *his* cold gaze burning into me.

Don't be too sure about that. First, I have to survive the next half hour.

'Yes. We'll talk later.'

And Captain Carter – the bloody brave, foolish man – reached out and gave my hand a gentle squeeze goodbye. I could practically feel the air freeze around me. The good captain, however, noticed nothing whatsoever, and with a last '*Au revoir*, Miss Linton,' strode off towards the house.

There were a few long, long moments of silence.

'*Au revoir?*' enquired an icy voice from beside me. I didn't dare to look at him. What if he –

Before I could finish the thoughts, hard hands grabbed me and whirled me through the air. In a flash, we were among the trees, hidden from view. My back slammed up against the trunk of the tree, my front against him. I was caged in, unable to escape. Breathing hard, I gazed up into his deep, dark, dangerous eyes.

'Now, Mr Ambrose, Sir...don't go jumping to any conclusions.' I cleared my throat. 'I don't know how long you were watching us. You might have seen us, um...standing rather close–'

'I did.'

Oh crap.

'–and holding hands–'

'I did.'

Double crap.

'–but that doesn't mean that he and I...you know...'

He cocked his head like snow leopard contemplating the best way to tear out a throat. He was so close to me. So terribly close. 'Pretend for moment I am very ignorant and do *not* know, Miss Linton. Why don't you explain it to me?'

Bloody son of a bachelor!

Heat rose to my cheeks. Why, dammit? I had done nothing wrong!

'He...Captain Carter had something to ask me. Something private.'

'Indeed?'

'It's not what you think! I didn't say yes! I couldn't, I–'

'I know.'

I blinked up at him, thrown off track. 'You...you do?'

'Certainly.' Leaning closer, he nailed me to the tree with his stare. 'I heard every word.'

'You did?'

'Of course.'

'Then...why are you so...' I looked at him. The word 'angry' was on the tip of my tongue. But it wasn't the right word. For the look in his eyes, I needed a different word. A word that was a thousand times more terrible. A word that made me shiver inside, that caused my heart to melt and my bones to freeze. '...displeased?'

A muscle in his jaw ticked.

'He put his hands on you.'

'That's all? You can't be serious! You–'

His lips came crashing down on mine, silencing me. It was a hard kiss. A kiss of ice and fire that made my brain freeze and my blood boil. I felt the cold, hard bark of the tree digging into my back. I felt snow trickling down from above, decorating my hair with a coating of powdered sugar. And I didn't care, because I was in his arms, and he was kissing me.

'I,' he breathed against my lips, his hot, misty breath tickling my skin in the winter air, 'am always serious, Miss Linton.'

'But–'

'No buts!' Breaking the kiss, he stared down at me with arctic ferocity. 'He put his hands on you. He put his hands on what is *mine*.'

Whoa there! Hold your horses. What did he just say?

'I'll have you know that I am an independent woman!' I told him, tapping on his chest. 'I belong to nobody but myself, and you can't treat me as if I'm a piece of luggage to be guarded and carted around, because–'

He pounced. His lips covered mine once more, and suddenly, I couldn't remember exactly why he couldn't cart me around like a piece of luggage. It must have been a pretty important reason, but...oh...his lips...

Maybe life as a suitcase would be rather interesting. Or maybe I could be a hatbox?

Bad Lilly! Bad! Remember why you did this! Remember who you are.

It wasn't easy. With the way he was devouring my mouth, my soul, my heart, it was difficult to remember I existed at all and hadn't yet died and gone to heaven. But heaven wouldn't be this cold. And St Peter could never make me this angry. Only one man could do that.

Wrenching away from his kiss, I pushed against his chest – to no avail. He was as rock-solid as Mount Ararat, and probably just as difficult to move. Where was a divine flood when you needed one?

'You can't do this,' I told him, my eyes blazing.

'I can do anything I want.'

'Not this. You can order me around during working hours, you can send me to fetch files and paperclips and pens – but you cannot put me under guard and build a wall between me and the rest of the world. I'm free! I go where I wish, when I wish, with whomever I wish!'

His eyes narrowed infinitesimally. 'So you want to spend time with *him*?'

'That's not the point!'

'Then, pray, explain the point to me, Miss Linton. I confess, I fail to see it so far.'

'The point is,' I told him, my voice suddenly gentle for some reason, 'that if I want to spend time with Captain Carter, I can. If I want to spend time with any other man or woman, I can. If I want to leave and never see you again, I can do that, too.'

I had never seen Mr Rikkard Ambrose flinch before. But he did so now. His whole body jerked as if he had been electrocuted. On either side of my head, his hands, pressed against the thick trunk of the tree, curled into fists.

'No!'

'Yes,' I told him, softly. 'I can leave any time I wish. That's the only way.'

'The only way?'

Raising one hand, I gently cupped his cheek. The muscles underneath were tense as cords of iron, yet the moment my fingers touched him, he began to relax. 'The only way for me to be with you. Let me have freedom. The freedom to choose you.'

He stared into my eyes for one immeasurable second of time. I could see his throat move as he swallowed once, hard. There was a moment of silence. A very long moment of silence. Then...

'Very well.'

I had to work hard to keep my mouth from dropping open. 'You...agree?'

'Yes.'

'You will stop Karim from following me around everywhere?'

'Yes.'

'And you won't mind if I have a chat with Captain Carter now and again?'

'Oh, I will most certainly mind.' His eyes glittered darkly. 'But I shall not stand in your way.'

I narrowed my eyes. 'You promise?'

'I swear. Whenever the two of you cross paths, I shall not interfere.'

I tried to read his face to see if he was being honest with me – and it did me absolutely no good. I might as well have tried to read coded mathematical formulas written in Chinese with invisible ink. Still...he was a gentleman. He would keep his word.

Standing up on my tiptoes, I brushed a gentle kiss against his lips.

'Thank you.'

Maybe, just maybe, we were moving forward. Maybe, Mr Ambrose could be reasonable and understanding. Suddenly, the future looked hopeful.

I guess I should have known better.

~~**~*~*

We had hardly re-entered the house when I noticed him. Grim and mountainous as ever, Karim stood tall, arms crossed and a look on his face that had to be illegal in at least twenty-one countries. Rouge was smeared over his cheek, and part of a lady's fan had gotten entangled in his turban.

Oh dear.

I tried to take cover behind Mr Ambrose, but too late. He had already spotted me. Murder and mayhem in his eyes, the Mohammedan strode towards me. Cautiously, I peeked out from behind Mr Ambrose's shoulder. Hey, I might be a strong, independent female, but it's common sense to duck behind a rock when a bomb is in the vicinity, about to go off.

Karim's gaze burrowed into me.

'*Prince Utairah Jafri fi al Qurram Qumrah III, heir to the principality of Bakavāsa?*' The words were a tiger's growl.

Mr Ambrose coughed. 'Pardon, Karim?'

'That, *Sahib*, is the name she invented to introduce me to a few of the female guests at the house, so she could slip away in the mayhem that followed.'

Mr Ambrose stared into space. 'Oh. I see.'

Silence.

A quite long bit of silence.

I tried to appear nonchalant. Tried.

'What does it mean, anyway?' I enquired.

Karim's eyes flared with hellfire. '*You. Don't. Know?*'

'Not really, no.'

Silence.

An even longer one.

'It is a rather peculiar mix of oriental languages,' Mr Ambrose offered in a tone he somehow managed to keep cool and unaffected, 'But, roughly translated, it means something like Prince Fragrant Yellow Flower in the Happy Moonlight, heir to the Principality of Rubbish.'

'Oh.'

Privately, I had to applaud Adaira's ingenuity. I hadn't thought she had it in her. The two of us really should get to know each other better.

Karim, however, did not seem to share my appreciation for creative name-giving. He started cursing in his native tongue.

'*Sahib*, may I remove that dissembling female's tongue with hot irons?'

Thoughtful silence. Mr Ambrose stroked his chin, apparently contemplating the merits of the idea.

'Hey!' I jabbed a finger into his ribs, and nearly broke my finger. Damn! Why did every inch of him have to be so hard? 'Answer! A simple "no" will do!'

'I am simply doing what you requested, Mr Linton – not being overprotective, leaving you the freedom to deal with things on your own.'

'You're allowed to be protective when your own bodyguard threatens to remove my tongue!'

'May I? How fortunate.' Turning to Karim, he gave a small shake of the head. 'Not today, Karim.'

The bodyguard uttered an oath and, turning, marched outside – probably to vent his wrath on some poor, unsuspecting apple tree. I, for my part, stepped close to Mr Ambrose and, rising to my tiptoes, whispered into his ear: 'That was not exactly the indignant refusal I was hoping for.'

'Indeed, Miss Linton?'

'Yes indeed, Sir!'

'Well...' Whirling, he caught my shoulders in his hands. Before I could resist he had pushed me back into an alcove, behind the statue of a Greek god who looked almost handsome enough to be Mr Ambrose's ugly little brother. 'Maybe I'll rephrase my order, then.' His cold gaze speared, making a shiver run down my spine. 'If you prove generous in keeping our deal today.'

Breathless, I swallowed. 'Our...our deal?'

'Yes.' Leaning forward, he brushed his lips against mine, and the shiver became a slow burn of need. 'Our deal.'

Oh. *That* deal.

'Well, Sir,' I breathed, taking in the delicious scent of him – the scent of man, money and power. 'I shall be most happy to fulfil my side of the bargain.'

'Adequate.'

He pushed me deeper into the shadows, and began taking his payment for the day. And it was so very, very adequate.

~~**~*~*

The days that followed were probably some of the happiest of my life. The sun was shining, the birds were singing, and Captain Carter was still breathing. Even more astonishing, Mr Ambrose had shown he was capable of bending, allowing the aforementioned activity of the captain to continue, and thereby giving me true hope for the future. And – best of all – Karim was still being ambushed by females at regular intervals, who were so eager to meet Prince Utairah Jafri fi al Qurram Qumrah III. And if you think I should have listed my blossoming romance with Rikkard Ambrose under 'best of all', you have never seen Karim trying to defend himself against a pack of husband-hunting young ladies. Ah, the joys of love...

Plus, in addition the immense entertainment value, the continuing rumours about the noble heir to the mighty and ancient Principality of Rubbish had the added benefit of redirecting the hyenas' attention away from Mr Ambrose. Lady Caroline and her cohorts were a lot less persistent in their pursuit now that a 'prince' was available. I had no doubt that eventually they would figure out the truth. In the meantime, however, it was highly amusing to watch them make complete fools of themselves.

Mr Ambrose, however, was less pleased by Karim's sudden popularity with the ladies. A bodyguard could not do very effective bodyguarding while he was being chased across the grounds by a pack of young females. I decided to neglect mentioning to my dear employer that his little sister had been the one who originally come up with the idea. The poor girl had enough to deal with as it was. Besides, the more Karim was occupied, the more time Mr Ambrose and I could spend alone to...discuss business.

Personal business.

As I said, those days were some of the happiest of my life.

Up until *that* day when all went wrong.

THE DAVIDIAN METHOD

The day started out so nice. I woke up at a reasonable hour and knew immediately that I didn't have to go to work. Even Mr Ambrose could not force me to work while I was a lady guest in the house of his parents over the Christmas season. (Not that he didn't try, but sometimes Lady Samantha could be admirably firm.)

So I just lay there in bed that fine morning and listened to the birds sing for a while. When the maid arrived to help me dress I was well awake and eager for breakfast.

Breakfast, too, was nice. I was seated next to Mr Ambrose (Lady Samantha, besides being firm, could sometimes also be very lacking in subtlety) and together, we enjoyed the first meal of the day in semi-companionable silence. Everyone was smiling. Everyone except Mr Ambrose, of course, but even he seemed to be not quite as stony as usual. There was a light in his eyes that, with any other man, might have produced a smile. Captain Carter was smiling, too – positively beaming, actually, for some reason! It was all so nice. Which made what happened next even more of a shock.

The moment breakfast was over, Captain Carter strode over to me. 'Might I have a brief word with you, Miss Linton? There's something I'd like to tell you.'

He was smiling so broadly, it was hard for me not to smile back. My fear that yesterday would lead to awkwardness between us instantly evaporated. He was still the same wonderfully strange Captain James Carter. Something really amazing had to have happened to put him in such a good mood.

I held up my half-finished glass of hot chocolate. 'I'll be with you directly. Wait for me in the small green drawing room, will you?'

'Certainly, Miss Linton.'

When he was gone, I threw a sly sideways glance at Mr Ambrose. I wasn't going to do anything like asking his permission, of course. That would be absolutely unfeminist. But there was nothing to say against checking to see his reaction, right? Just to see if I would have to deal with full-blown arctic rage, or only mild frostbite.

Apparently, however, my sly glance wasn't sly enough.

He nodded. 'Go.'

I raised an eyebrow. 'Really?'

Again, a nod. 'As I said – whenever the two of you cross paths, I shall not interfere.'

Odd...those were the exact same words he had used yesterday. Only now it occurred to me how strangely that sentence was phrased. My eyes narrowed. I opened my mouth to demand answers – but then, out of the corner of my eyes, I saw Captain Carter disappear into the small green drawing room.

Mr Ambrose could wait. Whatever devious plan he was pursuing would surely take at least a few hours to be ready. More than enough time to have my little chat with Captain Carter, go back and squeeze all the necessary information out of Mr Stone Face. So I gulped down the last bit of hot chocolate, put down my cup, rose and followed the good captain into the next room.

We weren't alone – a few older ladies, friends of Lady Samantha, were sitting in a corner chatting over their needlework – but the other occupants of the room didn't bother us, and besides, Captain Carter looked excited enough to have blurted out his news even if French and Russian spies had been in the room with us. And so he did, promptly and without ceremony.

'I've been promoted!'

I blinked. 'What?'

Out of all the possibilities, this was not what I had expected. Not that I didn't think Captain Carter a very capable officer – on the contrary. But why now? Why here? After all, the English countryside around Christmas does not offer very many opportunities for rapid military advancement. Unless...

'I got a letter from General Graham this morning, telling me how pleased he was with my performance during the strike in Newcastle. So they're making me a major–'

'Oh, Captain – I mean, Major! That's wonderful!'

'–if I take the mission to Uruguay.'

The broad smile that had been about to spread over my face decided it preferred to be thin and went on a strict diet instead.

'What?'

The captain beamed. 'They're making me a major!'

'I heard that. What was that about Uruguay? For that matter, what is Uruguay?'

'Oh, it's a country down in South America that recently declared its independence. The leaders of the independence movement seem to have a little disagreement.'

'What kind of disagreement?'

'One tried to assassinate the other.'[11]

---

[11] This refers to two leaders of the Uruguayan independence movement, Juan Lavalleja and Fructuoso Rivera. Lavalleja's supporters were unsatisfied with Rivera

'Oh. *That* kind.'

'And now, it appears, Britain is getting involved. Army headquarters has decided to send a detachment to South America to help defeat the Biancos. And they want me to head a task force to spy out enemy positions and attack key targets behind the lines. Isn't that wonderful?'

I considered my answer for a moment. 'Um...to be honest, it sounds rather dangerous to me.'

'Yes!' He clapped his hands, like an excited schoolboy who had just found out he was going on a trip abroad with his favourite uncle. 'Plenty of adventure, lots of opportunities to fight for Queen and country and prove myself. With any luck, this could make my career.'

'Or break your neck.'

But Captain Carter wasn't listening to me. He was much too busy tugging on the speck of beard on his chin, going aloud through a mental list of things he'd need for a lengthy journey into the jungle.

'Captain? Captain Carter, are you in there? Anyone at home?'

'...rope, twine, wax-coated matches, a good horse used to uneven ground...'

Men! I snorted. Even the best of them had a little loony spot in their brains stamped 'Caution! Masculinity! Do not enter!' How could anyone be excited about going to war? I had seen enough bloodshed myself to know that I never wanted to see what real war looked like. Skimming by its edges during my adventures with Mr Ambrose had been more than enough.

I froze.

Mr Ambrose?

No. No, it couldn't be.

'...I'll ask Her Ladyship to lend me a horse. If I change horses regularly, I can be in Dover in a week, and–'

'Captain?'

'–should be no problem getting all necessary supplies there. Plenty of shops with–'

'Captain!'

Blinking, the captain resurfaced from his planning. 'Yes, Miss Linton?'

'Tell me, is it usual for officers to be called in from so far away when, surely, there are troops stationed closer at hand?'

'No. It's quite out of the ordinary. But General Graham apparently wanted me specifically for this mission.' He grinned broadly. 'Do you know what that means?'

Oh, I have an idea...

'Someone high up is pulling strings. Whoever it is, he must really be impressed with me.'

You can say that again. Oh, when I get my hands on him...!

---

being chosen as president, whereupon they decided to retire him into an early grave. This sparked the conflict that is known as the Uruguayan Civil War, and which lasted from 1839 until 1851. The British and the French eventually got involved, strangely enough on the same side.

But no. He wouldn't, would he? No one could be that cold and calculating? *Really? Think about that sentence again, and then think about Mr Rikkard Ambrose.* Blast.

'Tell me,' I said to the captain, trying to keep my voice light and only mildly interested, 'did you expect this promotion?'

He shook his head, grinning a broad, boyish grin. 'No. I had no idea. Then, this morning, suddenly this letter arrives, not even a day old. Whoever pulled the strings to get it done must want me down there badly, and he has to be pretty powerful.'

Oh yes, he is.

How had he done this? *How?* It was the *British Army*, for God's sake! The bloody British Army! He didn't have command over that, too, did he?

Maybe not command. But influence? Certainly.

Suddenly, I felt a hand grasping mine. Looking up, I saw Captain Carter's eyes had lost their excited gleam. Instead, he was looking at me now, if possible even more intently than when he had been dreaming of adventure in far-off lands. As if the real adventure were standing right in front of him.

'This doesn't change a thing between us, Miss Linton. Queen and country call, and I must go – but I stand by what I said. I want you. If you ever change your mind...'

He let the end of the sentence hang in the air, full of possibilities. I tried to part my lips and answer, tried my very best – but couldn't.

'Think about it.' Gently, he squeezed my fingers. 'You'll have plenty of time to think, now. Whoever the other man is – he's not your only choice.'

Yes, he is, blast him! Because I love the cold-hearted son of a bachelor!

Which wouldn't prevent me from tanning his hide when next I got my hands on him.

The captain gave me a roguish grin. 'Will you wish me luck?'

The words hit me in the stomach like a fist. I looked up into his cheerful face – the face of a friend who had been there whenever I needed him. And now he was going off adventuring a thousand miles away, and there was nothing I could do about it. What could I possibly say?

'Good luck.' The words were a whisper, but he heard. A smile spread across his face.

'Thank you, Miss Linton.' Lifting my hand to his lips he pressed a gentle kiss on the back of it. 'I shall be thinking of you every time someone in Uruguay steps on my feet during a waltz.'

I swallowed, somehow managing to smile. 'How romantic.'

He flashed me a boyish grin. 'I know. I'm a regular Casanova, aren't I?'

'Yes, you are. Do me a favour?'

'What?'

'Don't get yourself killed.'

That smile flashed again. 'Anything to oblige a lady. Goodbye.'

And, with a last gentle squeeze of my hand, he turned and strode out of the room.

I was not an enthusiastic reader of romance novels, but even I knew how this kind of scene was supposed to go:

- Girl discovers that romantic interest A has sent romantic B to what will probably be a painful and violent death.
- Girl becomes ballistic.
- Girl marches to romantic interest A and proclaims him a vile villain, black-hearted beast and dastardly devil.
- Romantic interest A falls to his knees begging for forgiveness.
- Girl leaves him hanging a little bit for the fun of it.
- Girl grants forgiveness on condition that there will be an immediate marriage, the diamond on her ring will have at least twenty carats, and love interest B be rescued (if possible).

Needless to say that, with Mr Rikkard Ambrose, things did not go quite like that.

I marched into the breakfast parlour under full steam, smoke practically curling out of my ears. No Mr Ambrose. But Adaira was sitting at a window, a cup of hot chocolate in her hand, gazing out over the snowy landscape.

'Where is he?' I demanded.

She cocked her head. 'What has my brother done now?'

I told her.

She nearly dropped the cup of chocolate.

'He didn't!'

'He did.'

'That poor man!'

'Poor?'

I had some words in mind to describe Mr Rikkard Ambrose – but that was certainly not one of them. Seeing my face, Adaira waved a hand.

'Not my brother! The captain!'

'Oh.'

'He seemed like such a nice man.'

'He is.'

'And now he'll be crawling through the South American jungle, hunted by wild animals and bloodthirsty soldiers!' She shuddered. 'Can you imagine living like that?'

I kept diplomatically silent. Because if I had answered truthfully and said 'Yes, I did it a few weeks ago', that would probably have led to a few questions I did not have the patience to answer right now. Instead, I took a step forward and repeated the question that was still hammering against the inside of my skull. 'Where. Is. He?'

Adaira raised an eyebrow. 'Where do you think?'

Five minutes later, I kicked open the door to Mr Ambrose's room. The space had been transformed into an impromptu office. Files decorated the bed in orderly piles, a table had been pushed away from the wall to serve as a desk, and behind the desk sat a familiar figure, busily going through page after page after page of documents.

'You...!'

My whispered accusation got his attention. Slowly, he looked up.

'I am working, Miss Linton.'

'I wouldn't care if you were dancing tango with a monkey on the moon! I'm going to have a word with you!'

'Indeed?'

Stepping inside, I slammed the door shut behind me. 'Oh yes indeed, Sir!'

'What, pray, is it that you wish to discuss?'

'You broke your word!'

His eyes glittered dangerously. 'Never.'

'You said you wouldn't have Captain Carter killed or kidnapped!'

'Yes. And?'

'And? What do you mean, and? You...'

My mouth worked as I searched for the right words – but they would not come. Damn and blast! I had been so busy being enraged that I had completely overlooked the fact that, technically, he hadn't broken his word. Technically, he had done nothing but exert a little bit of influence so Captain Carter would get a job he was trained to do, and would most likely have been doing sooner or later anyway. He had managed to keep his word, get rid of his rival, and achieve the satisfaction of knowing that the aforementioned rival was probably going to return bullet-riddled and mosquito-bitten – all in one swoop.

I raised a trembling finger. 'You're a despicable, sneaky son of a bachelor!'

He cocked his head. 'Indeed. Was that all, Mr Linton?'

'I hate you!'

And I love you, too!

'Indeed.'

'Go to hell!'

And before he could say 'indeed' again and give me reason to strangle him, I stormed out of the room.

~~**~*~*

The days that followed were definitely *not* the happiest of my life. The tension crackling between Mr Ambrose and me was nearly unbearable. Every time I looked at him, I couldn't help thinking about Captain Carter hacking through the South American jungle. Mr Ambrose might have sent him to his death!

And, whispered a treacherous little voice in a hidden corner of my heart, *he did it for you.*

And then I felt warm inside.

Warm!

That damnable son of a bachelor actually managed to make me feel good about having sent someone into deadly danger because of me! If that wasn't a sign that he was dangerous for my sanity, I didn't know what else it could be.

I avoided him as much as possible. When we did have to enter the same room, I avoided his eyes, his voice, his touch and any other part of him I could evade. It didn't go unnoticed. The hyenas sent smug smiles my way, and Lady Samantha and Adaira exchanged anxious glances. I couldn't bring myself to care about either.

It got progressively worse as Christmas drew nearer. With everybody coming together to put up more decorations, practice carols, and generally be merry to a mind-numbingly maddening degree, I seemed hardly able to look at Mr Ambrose anymore. The season of love and good cheer? Ha! Not where we were concerned.

More than once, Lady Samantha threw me questioning glances, as if burning to ask what was wrong, but not daring to. Then, slowly, her intent looks changed to sad ones. Even she thought things between Mr Ambrose and me were heading downhill fast – and I couldn't blame her. In my desperation, I switched from female to male costume. Miss Linton had several bad migraines during those days, and Mr Victor Linton sat in her place, blessedly unmolested by the sad looks of the lady of the house and the scathing stares of her guests.

Only...*he* didn't look at me either. He was silent and cold as the grave.

At least there was one positive aspect to the whole disastrous situation: things couldn't possibly get worse.

'Pardon, Your Ladyship?'

It was a few days later. The whole company was sitting at lunch, discussing such marvellously interesting subjects as whether to put a star or a golden-winged angel on top of the Christmas tree, when the butler entered and alerted everyone to his presence with those words.

Lady Samantha cocked her head. 'Yes, Hastings?'

'A coach is approaching, Your Ladyship?'

'Now?' Lady Samantha's eyebrows rose. 'So late?'

'Are we expecting any more guests?' Adaira asked with a little frown.

'No. No, I'm quite sure of it.'

The butler cleared his throat in that dry, delicate manner that only butlers know to perfection. 'Begging your pardon, My Lady, but it appears that the approaching carriage bears the coat of arms of the Howard family.'

'The Howards?' A broad smile spread over Lady Samantha's face. 'They said they couldn't come because Sir Howard was sick. But maybe he has recuperated enough to join our festivities.'

'Let's welcome them.' A jolly gentleman in pinstriped trousers and a too-tight tailcoat rose to his feet with a smile, holding the door open for Lady Samantha and her daughter. 'Shall we?'

'Oh yes.' Getting up, Lady Samantha stepped outside, and the rest of the company followed, eagerly chattering about the newcomers, with two glaring exceptions. The first was me, and the second...

Well, you can probably guess.

I trudged after the rest of them, not really interested in any Lady Holland or Howler or whatever her name was, but too indifferent to my meal to want to continue. Hastings hurried ahead and opened the front door as the ladies and gentlemen stepped into the entrance hall. Cold air rushed into the house, and through the open doorway, I saw a beautiful coach approach in the late afternoon light, drawn by a team of fine white horses.

'It's really them!' Lady Samantha smiled. 'Oh, I've been so looking forward to seeing Lady Howard again.'

She moved down the steps, Adaira beside her. And, I noticed, they weren't the only ones. Mr Ambrose stepped up beside them, almost instinctively, it seemed. The son of the house, greeting guests. I felt a tug at my feet, wanting to follow him. Clenching my teeth, I suppressed the urge and stayed right where I was. My place was not beside that man.

With a crunch of gravel, the coach rolled to a stop in front of the steps. The footmen jumped down, extending the steps for the lady passengers and opening the door.

'Ah, Lady Howard!' Stepping forward, the duchess smiled fondly and curtsied in front of the other middle-aged lady, who was just descending out of the coach. 'Such a pleasure to see you again – especially since this must mean your husband has recovered.'

'Alas, no.' The lady gave a sad smile. 'Rupert is still languishing in bed. But he was so sad to see my daughter sitting alone at home with Christmas approaching, and when an old friend dropped by and offered to escort us, he insisted that we come without him.'

'Oh, that's just like him. He was always such a generous soul. And there is little Rebecca! My, my, how you've grown!'

'And here's our escort, who was kind enough to offer us his noble company,' Lady Howard beamed, gesturing at a shadowy figure in the carriage. Suddenly, I felt a prickling sense of unease. But why? 'I hope you do not mind an additional guest?'

'Not at all, not at all. Come out and be welcome, Sir.'

'Sir?' Lady Howard giggled. 'Pardon me, Marchioness, but I have to correct you.' At that moment, the door of the coach swung open, and in the sinking winter sun, golden light shimmered on golden hair. Behind me, I could feel Mr Ambrose go stiff as a rod of iron. I sucked in a sharp breath. 'It is "my Lord". May I introduce our friend, Lord Daniel Eugene Dalgliesh?'

Blast!

SILENT WARFARE

In an instant, everything changed. From one moment to the next, the peaceful winter wonderland around us transformed into a warzone, swords waiting to be drawn, the hounds of death salivating to be unleashed. Mr Ambrose's hand instinctively jerked to the place where he kept his revolver hidden – only to freeze when Dalgliesh leisurely brushed his tailcoat aside, revealing a holster, and glanced at Lady Samantha.

'By all means,' his steel-blue gaze was saying. 'Go ahead.'

Mr Ambrose's hand moved back to hang at his side, clenching and unclenching. Instinctively, I reached out, squeezing his hand from behind. He squeezed back, and suddenly everything between us was all right again.

Now if we only survived to enjoy it...

Mr Ambrose's stare bored into his enemy with a force that would have made any normal man freeze to death. 'Lord Dalgliesh...What a surprise to see you here.'

'Oh, I couldn't stay away.' A broad smile spread over His Lordship's face. The kind of smile unfortunate swimmers in southern waters might see, topped with a grey fin and rapidly approaching. His eyes wandered over the assembled Ambrose family. 'I had heard that the son of the house had returned to the fold. How could I miss such a unique event?'

For the first time, I dared to take my eyes off him and glance over at everyone else. Lady Samantha's face was white as a sheet. Adaira's lips were pressed into a thin line. The rest of the company, however, didn't seem to have picked up on the subtle threat of murder and mayhem under the polite, polished words that were being exchanged. Whatever had happened between Lord Dalgliesh and Mr Ambrose in their mysterious past, the secret had been locked away more tightly than an ancient Pharaoh's tomb.

And Lord Dalgliesh was playing on that exact fact.

'Well?' His smile hardened the tiniest bit. 'Won't you invite us inside?'

I glanced around. Nearly everyone was smiling, waiting, expecting to go back inside. The eyes of the world were watching. Mr Ambrose knew it, and he had to act accordingly.

'Certainly.' The word was steel and ice. 'Only let me call the servants to take care of your luggage. Mr Linton?'

His hand shot out, taking hold of my wrist in a grip that was almost painful.

'Mr Linton, please fetch the servants – especially my *trusted servant Karim*. I think I might have need of him ere long.'

'Yes, Sir.'

'And then stay inside. There are a few things His Lordship and I need to discuss in private.'

I opened my mouth to object – but the look in his eyes stopped me. Besides – there was no time for objections. I had work to do!

Whirling around, I marched back up the steps. The moment I was out of sight, I started running. My feet slapping hard on the cold stone floor, I passed several startled servants before I reached the room somewhere between the servant and guest quarters in which Lady Samantha had situated Karim. When I skidded to a halt in front of the open door, the huge Mohammedan was just cleaning his sabre. Never had I been so happy to see so scary a sight.

His head snapped up the moment he heard my footfalls. 'What is it?'

Panting, I got out only one word – but it was enough. 'Dalgliesh!'

Instantly, Karim was on his feet. In whirl of steel, the sabre disappeared into its sheath, and from under his mattress, the bodyguard pulled two revolvers, fully loaded. I wondered what the chambermaid would say if she came across those while making his bed. But if today went the wrong way, I wouldn't have to bother about that. I would never find out.

'Where?' Karim demanded, already out the door.

'Entrance.'

Holy moly! I was becoming as taciturn as Mr Ambrose.

Mr Ambrose...!

Tightly, I clamped down on the surge of fear in my chest. For just a moment, I stood and watched Karim dashing off down the hallway – then I turned and ran. I had my own task to accomplish. And it wasn't staying nice and safe in my room, as Mr Ambrose had not-so-subtly suggested. Instead, I ran – up two flights of stairs, down another corridor, and into the first room facing to the courtyard that I knew would be empty. Gasping for breath, I dashed to the window and pulled it open. Cold air flooded in, slapping me in the face. Gritting my teeth against the icy cold, I plunged my hand inside my tailcoat and pulled out the one item that, since Newcastle, I always carried with me, no matter whether dressed as a man or as a woman. A moment later, the barrel of the revolver settled on the windowsill.

It swivelled, searching, searching for...there! There they were!

My hand froze.

Right there underneath me, out in the courtyard, were Mr Ambrose and Lord Daniel Eugene Dalgliesh. I zeroed in on the latter, noticing that the guests and ladies were gone now, and once more, His Lordship had his hand at his belt, close to where I knew his gun would be.

Do it, bastard! Go on, do it! One wrong move towards my man, one twitch of your finger and I'll...

With a click, I pulled back the cock of my weapon.

Neither of the two men down in the courtyard noticed. They were too busy trying to kill each other with the pure force of their eyes.

Mr Ambrose's voice cut through the air like a whip.

'What are you doing here?'

Lord Dalgliesh's voice was lower – the whisper of a snake in the grass. I could hardly hear it over the wind whistling around the manor house.

'To celebrate Christmas, of course. Isn't Christmas the season of hope, love, and forgiveness?'

There was a moment of silence.

'There are some things,' Mr Ambrose said, vivisecting Dalgliesh with cold eyes, 'that cannot be forgiven.'

'Is that so?'

'Yes!'

'Well, well...if that is the case...'

Dalgliesh's hand slid to his belt again. Up in my bird's nest, I tensed, my forefinger curling around the trigger–

–and suddenly, the front door burst open, and there he stood: Karim, in full battle regalia, ready to reign down wrath upon anyone who would dare to touch a hair on Mr Ambrose's hard head. In that moment, I loved the turban-wearing, sabre-swinging son of a bachelor.

'Ah.' Lord Dalgliesh's hand froze, his eyes narrowing. 'The lapdog has arrived.'

'No.' Mr Ambrose took a step forward, and Karim marched down the stairs, taking a place beside him. 'When my dogs arrive, you'll know, because they'll be biting your hand off. Now leave.'

'What?' Dalgliesh raised his eyebrows in mock shock. 'You are denying entry to a guest? And at Christmas to boot? That is not exactly following the rules of polite society.'

'I don't care. Leave. Now.'

Karim and Mr Ambrose started moving forward, circling Dalgliesh, pushing him backwards. The muzzle of my revolver shifted with their movement, not deviating a fraction of an inch from its target. The coachman on the box of Lady Howard's coach watched all this with eyes as big as saucers. This probably wasn't the kind of welcome he'd expected at the Christmas party of the Marquess of Ambrose.

Suddenly, two men appeared from behind the coach, where up until now they had been hiding. They were dressed in the liveries of servants, but the hard set of their faces and the way they had their hands rested at their belts spoke a different language.

'Ah.' Lord Dalgliesh's smile widened. 'Gentlemen, may I introduce Harold and Thomas, my two manservants? They shall carry my luggage inside, and also assist me with any little...additional problems that might arise.'

My heart leapt. For a moment, my revolver did, too, jumping from Harold to Thomas and back again – before I remembered that, no matter how good they were with their weapons, there was only one man who would give the orders. The man who was the real danger here. Instantly, the muzzle of my gun swung back aim directly at the heart of Lord Daniel Eugene Dalgliesh.

His Lordship swept an imaginary speck of dust from his bespoke tailcoat. 'Now, if you will excuse me, gentlemen... It has been a long trip, and I would like to settle in.'

He made to step forward, but Karim blocked his way.

'I don't think so,' he growled. 'I shall–'

I would dearly have loved to hear what Karim had thought up in that bloodthirsty, bristly brain of his. But at that very moment, the front door was flung open, and noise echoed through the courtyard. I was so focused on my aim, that it took me a moment to recognise the sound: the laughter of happy people looking forward to Christmas.

'There you all are!' someone called. 'What are you standing out in the cold for? Come in, come in!'

'Excellent idea.' Smirking, Lord Dalgliesh stepped passed Karim, and neither the bodyguard nor Mr Ambrose did anything to stop him. They watched in silent fury, as Dalgliesh strode up the steps of the portico and disappeared inside, into the ancient home of the Ambrose family.

~~**~*~*

I reached the entrance hall just in time to catch Mr Ambrose striding in. Or maybe 'striding' wasn't the right word. How about...devastating? Killing? Destroying?

At least that's what he wanted to do. I could read every one of those words in his eyes.

'Mr Linton!' Those very same eyes flashed with something undefinable the moment he caught sight of me. 'I told you to stay upstairs! I told you to–'

His words were cut off by my lips.

It was just a moment. A fraction of a second, incredibly risky, and incredibly foolish. But the moment I broke away and felt him trembling against me, I knew it had been worth it. Stepping back, I met his eyes.

'What now, Sir? What is Dalgliesh planning?'

'If I knew that, Mr Linton, he wouldn't be here.' His left little finger twitched, and twitched, punching a staccato rhythm against his palm. 'According to my spies, he is supposed to be in South Africa right now. Heads are going to roll for this.'

I didn't dare ask whether he was being metaphorical.

Behind Mr Ambrose, Karim entered the hall, swiftly barring the doors behind him.

'That'll only hold them for so long,' he growled, and I realised he had locked the charming Thomas and his fellow crony, Harold, outside in the cold. 'One of the servants will let them in eventually, unless we can get rid of their master.'

'I still can't believe he's here!' Shaking my head, I gazed down the corridor. From the other end drifted the sound of merry laughter. 'How could the Marchioness let him breathe the same air as Adaira? Doesn't she know the things he's done?'

Not that I knew much myself, of course—but what I'd seen was more than enough.

'She knows enough to hate him,' Mr Ambrose spit out. 'But not enough to fear him.'

A shudder went down my back, and I had to resist the urge to run down that corridor drag Adaira and her mother away from that man.

'How could they not know?'

'The better question is why would they? I haven't talked to my family in years, haven't told them of any of my dealings with Dalgliesh over the last few years. What they know doesn't scratch the surface of what he's done. If they knew...' That muscle in his jaw twitched. 'I have to talk to my father. If mother and Adaira... I...I have to get that man out of here!'

I could see the struggle under the perfect façade of his impassive face. If this had been his house, he would have just thrown Dalgliesh out, social niceties be damned. But it wasn't. And the fact that he had to go up there to his father, the man he hadn't spoken to in over a decade and *ask...*

I watched with trepidation as he stomped off, down the hallway and towards the stairs leading up to the first floor and to the rooms of The Most Honourable The Marquess Ambrose.

~~**~*~*

I sat in my room, straining my ears, trying to hear anything – anything at all – from upstairs. But there was nothing. Absolutely nothing, until–

Bam!

I jumped. Either...either Mr Ambrose had just shot his father, or someone had slammed a door, really, really hard.

When, a few moments later, Mr Ambrose marched into the room, no gun in his hand and no blood spatters on his ten-year-old mint-condition tailcoat, I breathed a sigh of relief. Then, when I saw the non-expression on his face, I realised that had been too soon.

'What's the matter?'

Mr Ambrose's jaw worked, hard. 'He stays.'

I blinked. 'What?'

'I said he *stays*.' Reaching out, Mr Ambrose grabbed the poker and rammed it into the fireplace, making the flames of the fire shoot upwards. A fire he would not, or could not, allow to burn within himself. 'Dalgliesh will remain. Apparently, since he came as an escort to one of our guests, he now, too, is a guest, and that cannot be undone. Apparently, my dear father tells me, it would be ill breeding to get rid of him.'

Once again, the poker stabbed into the flames.

Getting to my feet, I slowly, tentatively approached. I had never seen him in...was this a mood? Dear me! I was actually witnessing Mr Ambrose being in a real life mood! That was halfway to emotion. I had to hand it to him, he hid it well – every movement still methodical, his face still as impassive as a block of granite – but I had been with this man for over a year. I had seen him bloody, bare and lost to the world. I knew how to read the signs.

Slowly, carefully, my arms came around him from behind, my hands coming to rest on his clenched, trembling fingers.

'Did you tell him the things we've seen Dalgliesh do?' I asked, my voice quiet.

'Of course I did!'

'And?'

One corner of Mr Ambrose's mouth twitched for just an instant. But it was most definitely not a smile. 'He didn't believe me. A peer of the realm smuggling, stealing, committing murder? That doesn't happen in my father's world.' His hands clenched into fists. The next words were spoken so low I wasn't even sure he said them. 'Sometimes I wish I could live in the same deluded dream.'

'So...' I swallowed hard, gathering strength to say the words. 'Dalgliesh is staying.'

'Yes.' His whole body was tensing now, as if preparing for a battle. 'I want to kill something, Mr Linton! The thought of being under the same roof as him, of my mother and my sister sleeping just a few rooms down the hall...' He finished the sentence by tearing one of his hands from my grasp and slamming a fist into the wall. That was the moment when I realised that Mr Rikkard Ambrose, Mr Cold-hearted Miserable Miser Ambrose, loved his family. He might have died rather than admit it, might not even know it himself, but he would fight for them to the death. For his mother and sister, at least. As for his father – in that case, I thought fighting *with* him to the death was the more likely option. But still, he cared. He cared a lot.

I did the only thing I could. I tightened my grip around him and pulled him against me, willing all my warmth to flow into him and heat his icy heart from the inside. I didn't expect to get to get a response. I most certainly didn't expect him to turn around, grab me tightly and lift me up to crush against him.

'And you...' His voice was a threat of death in a desert of ice. But not to me. No, the threat was to anyone who dared to harm me. 'How can I stay here, knowing he'll be under the same roof as you?'

'Don't worry.' I smirked up at him. 'I'm just Mr Victor Linton to him, just one among thousands of your downtrodden serfs. He doesn't care about me.'

And he won't know that you do, either.

He met my eyes, and the darkness that flashed in them sent a forbidden shiver down my back. 'Why do you think I'm still standing here and not calling in my men to break through the window of his room and dispatch Dalgliesh with a bullet through his head?'

It took a few moments for the meaning of his words to penetrate.

'You brought *armed men* to a family reunion?'

The look he gave me looked almost insulted. 'Of course, Mr Linton! Did you think I'd come unprepared?'

I didn't quite know how to answer that, to be honest. I had never considered an armed escort as one of the necessary preparations for a family Christmas. But then I remembered Aunt Brank, and Anne and Maria. When you thought about it like that...

'Where are they?' I demanded. 'I've seen no one except Karim.'

'Some are camped out in the forest all around the hall. A few are permanent members of the staff here.'

'Permanent members of the–'

A look from him cut me off. 'I like to keep an eye on my father's activities.'

And an eye on how your little sister is doing, I thought, but didn't say a word aloud. I was too busy gazing up the man in front of me, at his hard, perfectly chiselled face, his beautiful cold eyes, wondering how I ever thought an enemy could take him by surprise.

'These men...they had their guns trained on Dalgliesh during that whole little confrontation out in the courtyard, didn't they?'

'Certainly. What do you think I pay them for?'

Take *him* by surprise? Ha! He was Mr Rikkard Ambrose. Slowly, a grin began to tug at the corners of my mouth. We were on more even footing than I had thought.

And besides...even if those men hadn't been there, there had been one more gun trained on Dalgliesh in that moment. One that nobody, not even Mr Ambrose, had known about.

You want war, Dalgliesh? All right, you can have it!

'What do you think he's planning?' I whispered, right into Mr Ambrose's chest.

'I have no idea. But whatever it is, it'll have to wait for tomorrow.'

Only then I noticed how dark it had gotten around us. The fire in the hearth was the only source of light in the room now. Not even the moon, hidden behind thick clouds as it was, sent a sliver of light in through the windows. Exhaustion flooded over me. Captain Carter, all those ladies, Lord Dalgliesh...it all suddenly became too much. I could see it in Mr Ambrose, too. In the light of the flames his face was still an impassively perfect mask, but that tension in his shoulders...

He was just as exhausted as I was.

But how could one sleep in a house that held the world's worst enemy?

Mr Ambrose, apparently, had an answer to that ready. A determined hand grasped me by the shoulder, pushing me forward. Before I knew what was happening, I found myself stumbling through the connecting door into his room, where Karim was waiting, a silent sentinel in the corner.

'What...what are you doing?'

'You are going to share my bed tonight, Mr Linton.'

'I'm going to *what*? But I-'

His eyes flashed in the darkness. 'No buts! Do you think I would dare letting you out of my sight while Dalgliesh is within ten miles of this place?'

It was the tremor in his voice that did it. It was so, so slight...hardly detectable with the human ear. But I heard it. He wasn't simply being dictatorial. He was scared. Scared for me.

I nodded. 'All right.'

I felt his arms tighten around me. Looking up, Mr Ambrose met the eyes of his bodyguard, and in that one look conveyed a command as unshakable as any of the Ten Commandments.

Karim nodded. 'I shall stand guard before your door.'

Then, to my utter shock, he turned to me and, in a voice that almost sounded...kind? He said, 'Do not fear, *Sahiba*. I shall defend this door with my last breath. No one will cross this threshold as long as I have life in my body.'

And before I could reply, he stepped outside and turned, taking up his guard position in front of the door, from which I knew he would not move unless hell broke loose. The door slid shut with a click, and the tension in my body that up until this point I hadn't realised was there, eased the tiniest bit.

'Come.' Strong arms slid around me, pulling me towards the bed. I was so tired, I didn't even care that I was still in my trousers and tailcoat. I just let myself be pulled into bed, snuggling close against the hardest and most wonderfully uncomfortable cushion I had ever encountered in my life. Long, smooth fingers stroked through my hair, tucking a strand behind my ear.

'My little *ifrit*...'

'Mmmm...'

'Sleep safe. Nothing and no one is going to get to you.'

I believed him. Slowly, peacefully, I sank into velvety darkness–

–and was rudely awakened by voices arguing outside. Blinking, I tried to shield my eyes against the sudden sunlight. Sunlight? Yes, it was morning again. But if this wasn't a nocturnal attack of Dalgliesh's, who was trying to get in?

That very moment, Karim's terrifying growl came from outside.

'I warn you. Not one step farther! Ambrose *Sahib* gave strict orders–'

'Oh, shut up!'

No. No, that can't be...

'Ambrose *Sahib* authorised me to use deadly force, if necessary!'

'I said shut up, you big oaf!'

...her?

'Adaira *Sahiba*, I cannot allow you–'

'Out of my way!'

My eyes went wide and flew to meet those of Mr Ambrose. For once, his weren't full of icy determination. If they were cold as usual, that was only because he was frozen in shock.

'What do we do?' I hissed, pulling the blanket over me, instinctively.

Silence.

At least from Mr Ambrose. Karim was rather desperately loquacious.

'For the last time, these are the *Sahib*'s private chambers. I cannot allow a young lady to enter–'

'Oh for God's sake, bushy beard! He's my brother! I've seen him with his trousers down more times than I care to remember. Get out of my way, will you?'

'No, *Sahiba*! Don't– ouch!'

'I said get out of the way!'

And before I could move another muscle, the door swung open and Adaira strode into the room. 'Rick, I have to talk to you! I demand to know what this–'

Then her eyes landed on the bed. The bed in which Mr Ambrose and I lay huddled together under the blankets. Her eyes went big as saucers, and she stopped in her tracks. 'Miss Linton!'

Bloody hell! It was over.

Well, not quite. The worst was yet to come.

Slowly, I dropped the sheet. At the sight of my tailcoat and trousers, Adaira's eyes decided saucers weren't nearly big enough and tried for a career as dinner plates. '*Mister* Linton?'

I raised my hand and gave her a little wave. 'Err...Hello there.'

BUGGER!

Adaira was still staring. She simply didn't seem able to wrap her pretty little head around what she was seeing. Slowly, she took a step back and sat down, unaware that she had sat on a dresser instead of a chair. Still staring, she pointed a trembling finger at me.

'Mr Linton. Mr Victor Linton.'

'Well...yes. And no.'

'Mr Victor Linton. In bed with my brother.'

'Um...yes.'

'Oh well....that's...that's just...Bugger it all!'

'Adaira!' Mr Ambrose snapped, sitting up abruptly to glare at his little sister. 'Mind your language.'

Her eyes flew to him and suddenly flashed with fire. 'I'll say whatever I bloody well want, thank you very much. Besides, it wasn't a curse. It was a description! The two of you were...oh my God! I can't even...!'

I cleared my throat demurely. 'It's not as bad as it looks.'

She raised an eyebrow at me.

'All right, all right, it probably is. But still–'

I didn't get to finish. Springing to her feet, Adaira started pacing up and down gesticulating wildly.

'Hell! Bloody, stinking hell! Rick, do you have any idea what will happen if people....Oh God, I don't even want to think about it! And if mother hears about this...no, no, no! She's going to have a coronary. She'll think it's her fault. She will! She'll tell herself she should never have let you play with those dolls when you were a toddler, and–'

My head whipped around to stare at Mr Ambrose. 'You *played with dolls?*'

He gave me an arctic look. 'Mr Linton! Would you please focus on the most important subject of the current discussion?'

A grin spread across my face. 'I am! What kind of dolls? Were they nice and cuddly?'

'Be quiet! The both of you!' Pulling out her folded fan, Adaira waved it in our direction like a sword. 'You've done enough damage for one day – or should I say night? Good God! The thought of what the two of you have been up to...'

'Actually, we just–'

'Don't! I don't want to know!' Pressing a hand hard over each ear, Adaira retreated, grabbing the doorknob of the connecting door. 'I have to think! I have to get out of here! And...heck.' Her eyes darted to me. 'I have to warn your sister! She doesn't have any idea what's going on here, does she, Mr Linton? You have been making the beast with two backs with my brother all this time, and have dragged that poor, innocent girl into this house of sin you've created, this Sodom and Gomorrah? What kind of man are you? Oh, I don't even want to know! Where is her room? Tell me! Where can I find her?'

I pondered how best to answer that question. 'Um...well, you see...'

'Never mind! I'll find her myself!'

And she dashed through the connecting door, into my room, on the search for clues.

There followed a few moments of silence.

Then, slowly, she backed out of the room again, clutching an empty dress in her hand.

'Why,' she asked in a very calm, very collected voice, 'is there a lady's dress on your dresser, Mr Linton? The same dress I saw your sister wear the first time I met her?'

I didn't answer. Instead, I simply rose to my feet, took the dress out of her unresisting hand, and held it up against myself, raising my chin and meeting her gaze. Adaira's eyes went wide with comprehension. Wider than saucers. Wider than dinner plates. Wider than wagon wheels, actually.

'Oh my,' she breathed.

'Yes.' I nodded. 'Let's just say...I'm versatile.'

~~**~*~*

'So...you're really a girl under that tailcoat?'

It was about a quarter of an hour later. Adaira and I were alone in Mr Ambrose's room. My dear employer had departed to establish new security parameters with his men, and to avoid more questions on the subject of dolls. No matter. I would get my hands on him sooner or later. For now, it was more important to acquaint his little sister with my alter ego.

I smiled at Adaira.

'Yes. Yes, I am.'

'Really? You're sure?' Cautiously, Adaira poked a finger in my side – then yelped and pulled it back when she felt something hard.

'Relax! That's just my corset.'

'R-really?'

'Yes!' I grinned. 'I'm one hundred per cent certified female. Here, see?' Taking her fan, I snapped it open and waved air at myself and batted my eyelashes in a way no self-respecting man could have imitated without choking to death. Well, except Sir Philip Wilkins, maybe.

'Heaven be praised! You're a girl. A real, honest to God girl!' Placing a hand over her heart, she sank back into an armchair. 'Thank God! My brother is a ruthless womaniser!'

'That's one sentence I'd never thought to hear out of a sister's mouth,' I commented.

'Well, considering the alternative...' Adaira shook her head, dazed – then suddenly started to laugh. 'Heck...I only just realised! You have been his secretary for *over a year* haven't you? How long has this been going on? How long has my dear brother, the patron saint of miserdom and abstention, been carrying on an illicit office affair behind the backs of London's high society?'

'Well, I wouldn't exactly call it an illicit–'

'How long?'

I felt my face heat. I was blushing! Why was I blushing? I was a feminist! A strong, independent woman, who happened to believe that a woman's body was her own and that she could do with it whatever she liked, thank you very much. I didn't care about social norms or other people's opinions.

So why are your ears getting red from the nosy questions of a pesky young girl?

'Ha!' She pointed at me, grinning as if she had won the grand prize in a lottery. 'I knew it! You've been at it this whole time!'

'What? No, we–'

'Ooooh, this is sweet! So sweet.' She rubbed her hands, her eyes dancing in ecstasy. 'I'm never going to let him forget about this. My dear brother had better not dare be difficult next time I want to go dancing with Thomas Ecclestone. If he is – oh, the things I'll do...' She sighed in bliss, fully in devious little-sibling mode.

I decided this would be the best time – maybe the only time – for me to escape. Cautiously, I shifted towards the door. But the moment I tried to slide away, she abruptly returned from big brother torture paradise and grabbed my arm.

'Where do you think you're going? You're not getting out of this room until you've told me every single little detail about the two of you. I want to know how you managed to convince the king of chauvinists to take on a girl! You've been with him on his travels, right? Was it dangerous? Did you see pirates? Indians? Pyramids?'

'Err...well, pirates and Indians, yes. Pyramids, no, not unless you count the South American kind.'

'Oh my God, oh my God, oh my God.' She was jumping up and down like an overexcited baby kangaroo. 'Do you think he'll take me along one day, too? I've always wanted to see America, and Paris, and Rome and the African jungle, and India and...oh, we'll talk about that later! Tell me about yourself? How did you manage to talk him around? What did you do? Did you seduce him with your feminine wiles? Did you work your irresistible charm on him until finally he succumbed to you and–'

Clearly, I decided, someone had to check up on Adaira's reading material. Her mother obviously wasn't paying close enough attention.

'I most certainly did not,' I told her. 'I was accepted for the job solely for my intelligence and diligence as a working woman.'

'You were?' Now an expression of awe was spreading across the girl's face. 'By *my brother*?'

'Yes. The seducing with feminine wiles came later.'

'I knew it! How did you do it? How?'

I smiled.

'Come,' I told her. Gently grasping her arm, I led her to the bed and settled us both down, relaxing for the first time since she had burst in through the door. 'Now that you know, it's probably best if I tell you everything. It all started on a misty, cold morning in London, on the day of the general election...'

~~**~*~*

168

My wide-eyed audience went through several stages while I told my story: incredulity, awe, admiration and voracious curiosity, finally settling on hilarity. By the time I had ended my story, Adaira was sprawled on the floor, laughing hysterically. Bottom line: she was so relieved that her brother wasn't going to be executed for buggery, and so happy she'd gained a major piece of leverage for the sibling wars, that she didn't care a bit about the fact she had caught him in bed with a girl he was not married to. Perhaps not the ideal positive impression a girl could hope to make on her man's sister, but you couldn't have everything, right?

As for my alter ego, Mr Linton – Adaira was so eager to hear about all of my adventures that she wasn't really bothered by the fact I was a crossdresser. By the time we were finished talking, Lady Adaira Ambrose and I were the best of friends. Somehow, I felt as if I'd known this fiery girl with the eerily familiar sea-coloured eyes all my life.

Which was the reason why I felt comfortable enough to take a deep breath and ask, 'Adaira?'

'Yes?'

Somehow, during our little chat, we had switched to first names.

'I was wondering...Lord Dalgliesh–'

The mere mention of the name caused the smile to vanish from her face. A storm started brewing in her eyes. 'That man doesn't belong under this roof!'

'No, he doesn't,' I agreed. 'But what I want to know is: why? What did he do to all of you? To your brother in particular?'

She shook her head, a frown marring her lovely brow. 'I wish I knew. But I was only five years old back then, and when that night came...' She shuddered. 'All I know is that Dalgliesh and my brother had been friends. Dalgliesh was a sort of mentor or elder brother to him. Rick followed him around everywhere. Then, that night came...that terrible night. Someone from Dalgliesh's staff came to visit, and the next thing I know, wild shouts are coming from downstairs. Father bellowing, Rick yelling back – things were being thrown around! I was afraid they'd kill each other. The next morning, my brother was gone. That was the last I saw of him for over a decade.'

She glanced at me. 'In a way, I never saw him again. Because the happy, carefree big brother I knew never came back from America. That cold, calculating man who came back...' She swallowed, moisture glinting at the corner of her eyes. 'He's a stranger. I don't know if I know him.'

I felt a tug at my heart. Instinctively, I wanted to fold the girl in my arms and hug her close – but, just as instinctively, I knew that would be the completely wrong thing to do. She was an Ambrose. She had pride. Lots of it.

Her eyes suddenly became hard again. 'But one thing I know: just like Dalgliesh was the man my brother most admired when he was young, he's now the man my brother hates more than any other in the world. If Rick decides it's time to have it out with Dalgliesh here and now, we are in deep, deep trouble.'

~~**~*~*

169

We sat there for a few minutes in silence. Finally, I elbowed her gently in the ribs. 'Hey – isn't it time for breakfast? I'm hungry.'

Immediately, she brightened. 'Of course! And...oh my!' She covered her mouth with a hand, hiding her sudden grin. 'I only just realised! I get to parade you in front of the whole household in trousers and a tailcoat, and only I will know that there's a girl under there! Please let me take you to breakfast as a man! Please!'

'Certainly.' Rising, I gave a mock bow. 'I wouldn't be a proper gentleman if I didn't offer to escort a young lady to the table, now, would I?' And I offered her my arm.

She nearly keeled over from laughing.

'You wound my manly pride,' I chastised.

Gasping for breath, she managed to scramble to her feet, and grabbed me by the arm. 'Come on! Come on! Oh God, this is going to be brilliant!'

When we stepped outside, Karim was still standing guard next to the door, his hand on the pommel of his sabre. I glanced at the girl beside me, then raised an eyebrow at him. '*I shall defend this door with my last breath? No one will cross this threshold as long as I have life in my body?*'

The bodyguard tried his best to hide behind his beard. Giggling, the two of us escaped down the corridor. Only when we approached the breakfast parlour did I take care to assume a more gentlemanly demeanour and once again offered Adaira my arm.

'Why, thank you, Sir.' She smiled and accepted with a gracious curtsey.

A footman awaited us in front of the breakfast room, bowing deeply as we approached.

'Lady Adaira, Mr Linton – the Marchioness desired me to let you know that the company will be taking breakfast in the east-wing winter garden today. She thought the scenery might, ehem...lighten the mood of her guests.'

With Lord Dalgliesh still among the guests? Adaira and I exchanged doubtful looks.

'Come on.' Gripping my arm more tightly, Adaira pulled me off in the direction of the east wing. 'We'd better go.'

It didn't take us long to reach the winter garden, and we didn't waste a minute before stepping inside. The sight that met our eyes would have been comical – if it hadn't been so deadly serious.

In the centre of the garden, amidst beautiful flowers beyond which lay the sparkling glory of the wintery landscape, a table had been erected and ornate chairs placed all around it. No one had taken their seat yet. They were standing around admiring the beautiful scenery. Or at least most of them were.

The more intelligent people present had caught on to what was happening in their midst and had retreated to the corners of the garden, leaving a space in the middle for the two contestants. On the left, Lord Daniel Eugene Dalgliesh, steel-blue eyes as hard as a bank-vault door, his golden hair glinting like an angel's halo in the morning sunlight. On the right, Mr Rikkard Ambrose, his eyes dark as the fathomless depths of the sea, and just as warm and inviting. Every single line of his perfect face was etched in stone.

The air between the two men was like the Antarctic before a thunderstorm. The air crackled. The The hairs on the back of my neck stood up just from watching.

'Ah, Lady Adaira. There you are.' A plump young lady stepped towards us, a bright smile on her face, completely unaware of what was happening. I hardly spared her a glance. 'We've all been waiting for you. Won't you introduce your companion to me?'

Adaira, unlike me, managed to scrounge up enough presence of mind for a reply. 'Certainly. Mr Victor Linton, may I have the pleasure of introducing you to Miss Violet Bardley?'

'If you really think it's a pleasure,' I replied absent-mindedly, my whole attention still focused on the pair of men staring each other down in the centre of the room. Adaira coughed. The plump girl beamed as if I had given her a huge compliment.

'Um...Mr Linton is my brother's private secretary, Miss Bardley.'

'Really? That must be such an interesting occupation.' Miss Bardley smiled even more brightly. It seemed to be her aim in life to outshine the sun. 'It's a pleasure to meet you as well, Mr Linton.'

'Charmed,' I murmured to a potted plant about half a yard to the left of Miss Bardley's ear. People had started milling about, obscuring my view of Mr Ambrose and Lord Dalgliesh. Had they drawn weapons yet? God, if that bastard Dalgliesh harmed him...!

'I'm really glad I accepted Lady Samantha's invitation to come here to celebrate Christmas. It's so wonderful up here in the north.' That was Miss Bardley again. She gave a sigh, no doubt meant to encourage my agreement. 'So serene and peaceful.'

Craning my neck, I managed to peek through the crowd – just in time to see Mr Ambrose clench one hand around the back of a chair, as if tempted to throw it. 'Um...well, yes. Serene. Peaceful. Absolutely.'

'I have a feeling we're going to have a memorable Christmas.'

'Err...well...'

That was the moment when Lord Dalgliesh moved forward.

'Excuse me!' Shoving Miss Bardley aside, I darted forward. Without paying any attention to the startled yelp behind me, I began to work my way through the crowd. How fortunate I had well-practised elbows. 'Sorry, sorry, excuse me, pardon me, secretary coming through! Sorry sir, I'm in a hurry! I have to–'

Despairing of coming up with a convincing excuse, I just shoved the startled gentleman aside and dashed forward, one hand sliding into my tailcoat, gripping my gun. If push came to shove, I wouldn't hesitate. Not an instant!

Lord Dalgliesh took a step towards Lady Samantha. The hand around my gun tightened. He opened his mouth.

'What a beautiful home you have, Your Ladyship. I must congratulate you. It must have been quite a bit of work to restore it to its former glory after...certain unfortunate events.'

I almost collapsed with relief. Panting, I came to a stop. My hand relaxed – but then tensed again. The words were perfectly harmless. Perfectly normal. But Lady Samantha paled as if he had slapped her across the face. And Mr Ambrose...

The chair he was clutching groaned as Mr Ambrose's hand tightened like a vice around the back. In a flash, I realised what Dalgliesh was doing.

He's trying to provoke Mr Ambrose. He's trying to make Mr Rikkard Ambrose angry.

And what was really disturbing: it seemed to be working. Mr Ambrose's perfect granite mask was still in place, still unbroken, but it had grown thin. Through his eyes, I could see the emotions roiling underneath. And suddenly, I was terrified of what would happen if that mask would shatter.

'Thank you, My Lord.' Lady Samantha's voice was so cold it could almost have rivalled her son's. 'That means so much, coming from you.'

'I'm glad to hear that.' Lord Dalgliesh's smile widened. 'I might be coming to visit your delightful home more often in the future. Now that you have such beautiful blossoms decorating these halls...'

His eyes slid over the flowers all around – and then landed on Adaira.

There was the crack of wood, as something snapped under Mr Ambrose's hand.

Adaira groaned behind me. 'Now we're in deep crap.'

Mr Ambrose was just about to take a step forward and plunge the whole room into war when the door behind us opened. Glancing around instinctively, I jumped when I saw an unfamiliar, liveried servant with a long staff in hand enter the winter garden.

'Attention please, ladies and gentlemen.' The servant cleared his throat, and struck his staff against the ground in an ominous manner. He certainly had my attention – and that of every other person in the room. 'Please rise for your illustrious host. It is my pleasure to announce–'

Oh no. Don't say it. Not now.

'–His Lordship The Most Honourable The Marquess Ambrose.'[12]

And, as the servant stepped aside, a dark figure marched into room, clad in a pristine black tailcoat and searching the room with piercing, cold, sea-coloured eyes I had only ever seen on one other person. They found what they were looking for, halting on Mr Ambrose and hardening into stone.

Adaira had been wrong. Things had been rosy before. *Now* we were in deep crap.

A PROMISING START

Breakfast. So significant for a healthy life. The most important meal of the day, they said.

---

[12] This is not a typo. One really has to use 'the' twice to announce such a nobleman correctly.

Or maybe the most deadly?

The Marquess Ambrose stepped into the room, accompanied by utter silence. He was a tall man – nearly as tall as his son – and might, long ago, have been as perfectly beautiful. But long years had eaten furrows into his face, and his waistcoat bulged over an impressive paunch. Still, his eyes...

His eyes were exactly the same as those of Mr Ambrose.

The same ice.

The same darkness.

The same iron will.

All innocents duck. Let the battle of the titans begin.

Adaira seemed to share my thoughts. Beside me, she took a tentative step back.

'Pardon my delay in joining you, my dear guests,' the Marquess said in a voice as warm and welcoming as an arctic blizzard. 'Important matters kept me detained. However, now that I have been able to join you, let me personally welcome you to Battlewood Hall. Consider my house yours for the duration of your stay. Breakfast will be served in a moment. Please be patient while I greet a...very special guest.' His gaze returned from his guests to Mr Ambrose. 'Someone I haven't seen in a very, very long time.'

No one dared object as the Marquess stepped towards Mr Ambrose, lowering his head about half an inch.

'Son.'

Mr Ambrose lowered his head as well – no more than a quarter of an inch, at most.

'Father.'

Silence.

And more silence.

It stretched out like an insurmountable precipice between the two great men, becoming wider, deeper and more deadly with every passing second – while Lord Dalgliesh stood a little way away, watching. The corners of his mouth were twitching.

'William!' Trying to force a brave smile onto her lips, Lady Samantha stepped right into the middle of the deadly crevice, gazing up at her husband. 'You're here! It was most inconsiderate of you to remain absent and leave it to me to greet all our guests.'

'My apologies, my dear.' The Marquess didn't sound particularly apologetic. He didn't even glance at her. His eyes were still riveted to those of his son, fighting a silent battle of wills. 'As I said – I had some important matters to attend to over the last few days. Besides...' His eyes bored into Mr Ambrose with renewed force. 'I had hoped that certain guests of mine would not object to climbing a few insignificant stairs to see me again after so many years.'

'That is the problem with hopes one has of relatives,' Mr Ambrose shot back, his eyes narrowing infinitesimally. 'They are so often disappointed.'

'Marquess! Such a pleasure to see you again, after such a long time.'

Two pairs of sea-coloured eyes broke contact and flicked to the speaker who had dared to interrupt. Lord Dalgliesh didn't flinch under the double onslaught of ice. He didn't even shiver. One brilliant, shark-like smile deflected everything.

'Lord Dalgliesh.' The Marquess inclined his head. It did not escape my notice that he bowed significantly lower than he had for his own son. My hand suddenly itched to reach out and slap the old man across the face. But since I was not suicidal, I refrained. It would have been madness enough to get involved before, when there were only two people wanting to kill each other. But now? By the looks of it, there were three people, each of which wanted to kill the two others – the only reason all were still alive being that no one could decide on whom to murder first.

'Ah, those family reunions...' I jumped, nearly breaking my neck whirling around to see that Miss Bardley had joined Adaira and me. She had – surprise, surprise – a smile on her face. I'm not kidding. A *smile.* 'Aren't they wonderful? Family and friends finding each other again after such a long time always makes me feel warm inside.'

'Yes, um. Very warm indeed.'

Mr Ambrose took a step forward. Instantly, my attention jumped back to the threatening battle in the room. 'Lord Dalgliesh was just complimenting Mother on your beautiful home,' my dear employer informed his father. *Your* home. Not *ours.* He really knew how to wield every word like a blade. And between the words, there was another meaning, one able to do much more damage. I could feel it slamming into his father.

'Was he?' The Marquess pierced Lord Dalgliesh with a look, then gave the same treatment to his beloved son. 'I would have thought you might have learned to be cautious about paying attention to idle words from certain sources by now, son.'

'Oh, I have.' Mr Ambrose's gaze was ten times as cold as his father's. 'Independence is a useful trait, particularly when dealing with stubborn old men who–'

'Shouldn't we sit down for breakfast?' Lady Samantha broke in with an insanely hopeful smile. 'Our guests are surely getting hungry!'

'Oh, do not hurry on my account, My Lady.' Lord Dalgliesh gifted her with a bright smile. 'I'm enjoying myself immensely.'

She glared at him, and he closed his mouth.

'*Now*, William,' she insisted. 'We are keeping our guests waiting.'

The Marquess exchanged one last, long, lethal look with his son, then turned to offer his wife an arm.

'Of course, my dear. Let me escort you to your seat.'

~~**~*~*

I had to admire Lady Samantha. With superhuman skills of diplomacy, she managed to scatter her husband, her son and Lord Dalgliesh around the table, with plenty of military men and talkative young ladies as buffers between them. By the time she was finished, I couldn't even see Lord Dalgliesh, and neither could Mr Ambrose, from where he was positioned. As for his father – he was so far away, safely placed at the host's rightful position at the foot of the table, that he and his son could do nothing but shoot each other icy glares – which they did. Apparently, a little ceasefire had been declared. I started to breathe a little more easily.

At least until Lady Samantha appeared beside me with Lady Adaira.

'Mr Linton, may I entrust her to you?' she gazed up at me with big, hopeful eyes. 'I have those three men to contend with and if I have to keep an eye on my little girl...I simply can't. Please.'

I stared at her. 'B-but...'

'Please?'

Crap! Why did she have to have such big, blue grandmotherly eyes? How was I supposed to be able to say no?

'Very well.'

'Oh, thank you! Thank you, Mr Linton. You are a true gentleman.'

And she dashed off, leaving behind a stunned me and an Adaira convulsing with giggles.

'It's not funny!' I snapped.

'Oh yes it is, *Mr Linton!*'

'What am I supposed to do now?' Panicked I glanced around. All of the other men – crap, had I just thought 'other men'? – were standing beside their chairs like stuffed penguins. 'I have no idea how a gentleman behaves towards a lady at the breakfast table!'

'I'm sure you'll do fine,' Adaira said, watching Mr Ambrose who grabbed his dinner partner, dumped the lady onto a chair and shoved it forward before taking his own seat. 'As long as you do the exact opposite of my dear brother.'

Grimacing, I pulled out a chair for her.

'Why, thank you, Sir.' Batting her eyelashes up at me, she sank onto her seat. 'My mother was right. You are a true gentle*man.*'

'Shut up! This is not funny!'

'On the contrary. Three men who would like to kill each other but are forced to be civil because of table manners? A lady in trousers as my dinner partner? This is first-class comedy. It's a wonder I'm not rolling around on the floor with laughter.'

I had to admit, she had a point. The situation was funny – in the same way that an assassin being pecked to death by a murder of crows was funny. Lady Adaira seemed to have an admirable talent for looking at the bright side of life.

Her poor mother, though...

'Toast, Sir? Mushrooms? Kipper?'

Torn from my thoughts I looked up to see a footman standing beside me, balancing a huge platter with food on one hand and wielding a scary-looking serving fork with the other. I prayed Mr Ambrose wouldn't get his hands on that while his father and Lord Dalgliesh still were in the room. Otherwise, things at the breakfast table might get rough.

I opened my mouth – and underneath the table felt the pressure of a foot against mine. Ah yes. Manners.

'Ladies first.' I gave Adaira a strained smile.

'Thank you, Mr Linton.' The little minx beamed at me. 'It's so heartwarming to see that there are still men with manners out there in these uncouth, modern days.'

She really was enjoying this a little too much.

'A selection of everything for me, please, Oscar.'

'Certainly, Your Ladyship. And the gentleman?'

It took a gentle kick from Adaira to make me realise he was talking to me.

'I, err...I'd just like a few mushrooms on toast, please. I'm not feeling very well. I, um...didn't get a lot of sleep last night.'

'Oh, really?' Adaira's eyes lit up with ravenous curiosity. 'Why was that? Do tell. Were you very...busy?'

Crap, crap, crap! Why can't I keep my big mouth shut?

I sent her a censorious look. 'No, My Lady.'

'Are you sure?'

'Yes. If you must know...' My eyes flicked to Mr Ambrose and his father. 'I was worried.'

It wasn't a lie.

'Oh, well...' Adaire cocked her head, thoughtfully. 'I think I know what we can do about that.'

That took me by surprise. 'You do?'

Had she suddenly become a miracle worker?

A cheeky grin spread over her face. 'Oh yes. We only have to catch my brother's attention.'

'And how do you propose we do that, my Lady?'

'Simple. All we have to do is make him think about something that he is even more obsessed with than money, power, or his feud with our father.'

'Such a thing exists?'

She gave me a very odd, very long look. 'I think it does.' And without waiting for a response, she turned towards her brother, leaning over towards him and asking sweetly: 'Tell me, brother – where did you find this charming secretary of yours? I've never met such a pleasant man in all my life.'

Conversation all around us halted. All the guests' eyes focused on me. And then, a moment later came the eyes that mattered. Cold eyes. Hard eyes. Eyes that sent a tingle down my spine.

'Indeed?'

'Oh yes, indeed.' Adaira gifted her brother with a smile. 'It was most unkind of you to hide such a handsome young fellow away in your dusty office all this time.' And she gave me a flirtatious smile. Mr Ambrose nearly choked on a fish bone.

'I have not been "hiding away" anybody,' he ground out. 'Mr Linton has been busy with work, as have I.'

'I bet.' Eyes twinkling, Adaira winked at her brother. 'I can just imagine all the boring work the two of you get up to behind closed doors.'

This time it was I who nearly choked. Bloody hell! Was she insane? Had she completely lost her mind?

But when I glanced around, the only reaction I could see were pitying glances – most likely from people who had heard of Mr Ambrose's reputation as an employer. Nobody understood the true meaning of her words. Nobody but her brother, that is, whose left little finger was now tapping a furious prestissimo on the table. His father tried to shoot him an icy glare and re-initiate the duel of eyes, but Mr Ambrose didn't seem to give a flying fig.

'We are indeed very busy,' he ground out. 'With *work*. Lots of work. Knowledge is power is time is money, Adaira.'

'Is it?' With a cheeky grin, she glanced sideways at me. 'I definitely have to agree that the *knowledge* of certain secrets can give you a certain amount of *power*. On that note...what will you be giving me for Christmas this year, my dear brother?'

I nearly swallowed my spoon.

She wouldn't! She couldn't really...

No. She wouldn't. But to judge by the look in Mr Ambrose's eyes, he wasn't as sure about it as I was.

'I shall have to see,' he managed to get past his clenched teeth.

She gave him a bright, brilliant I've-got-you-by-the-balls smile. 'Do that. I really hope it's something nice and sparkly. And expensive.'

I tore my handkerchief out of my pocket just in time to bury my face in it and disguise my snort of laughter as a sneeze – or at least so I thought.

'Something wrong, Mr Linton?'

'N-no, Mr Ambrose, Sir. Nothing at all.'

'Linton?' The voice that cut in was chillingly familiar. I looked up to see Lord Dalgliesh lean out from between the row of guests to study me. 'Any relation to Miss Lillian Linton?'

From one moment to the next, my urge to laugh evaporated.

'Yes,' I answered hesitantly. 'I am her brother.'

'Her brother....?' His Lordship stroked his chin, studying me through narrowed eyes. 'Hm...most interesting. Most interesting indeed.'

'Who is this Miss Linton we're talking about?' one of the other guests asked.

'Oh, a most charming young lady,' Lady Samantha answered before I could even open my mouth. 'As Mr Linton said, she's the sister of my son's secretary, and a smarter, sweeter girl you couldn't wish to meet.' Glancing around the table, she frowned. 'I wonder where she is. I've been so preoccupied I only just realised she isn't at the table.'

'What – Miss Linton is a guest here? At Battlewood Hall?' Now Lord Dalgliesh's eyes seemed to be positively gleaming. They flicked from Mr Ambrose to me, then back to Mr Ambrose, filled with a malicious understanding I didn't like. Not at all. 'How fascinating. I am very much looking forward to renewing our acquaintance.'

Ruffling my Feathers

That night, someone broke into my room to kill me. Luckily, I wasn't at home. I was slumbering peacefully about three dozen yards away in the room of Mr Victor Linton, my door firmly locked and a grouchy, bearded bodyguard standing guard in front of my male alter-ego's door.

'Dear me...' Whistling, I reached down and picked up a couple of loose feathers. 'Either someone wants me dead, or someone in this place really hates down pillows.'

'Neither, Mr Linton.' Picking up one of the pillows, Mr Ambrose examined it with icy eyes. 'If someone wanted you dead, there would be much easier ways to accomplish it than breaking into your room at night. The first time you – or in this case, your female alter ego – set a foot outside, a marksman could take you out with his rifle. Swift. Easy. No risk of discovery.' He straightened, pinning me with his gaze. 'This wasn't an attempt at murder. They wanted to abduct you. This-' he gestured at the slashed covers and cushions '-is merely a warning.'

'Abduct?' I blinked. 'But why would anybody want to abduct me? I haven't got a penny! And as for my uncle Bufford, the only thing he would give a kidnapper is a bill for the inconvenience. Why would anyone-'

It was only then that I noticed the intense expression in Mr Ambrose's eyes. It wasn't the gaze of an employer looking at his subordinate. He was devouring me with his gaze, raking it over me from top to bottom, assuring himself that I was still there, still alive, still in one piece. If I didn't know better I would almost have said it was the gaze of a lover. The gaze of someone who cared.

Oh.

He seemed to read the dawning understanding in my eyes.

'Yes, Mr Linton. Exactly.'

Oh. Oh my goodness...

Feeling my ears heat, I glanced away.

'So...it was Dalgliesh?'

'Who else?'

'What do we do?'

'We? Nothing.'

'But-'

'*I* will do a great many things, Mr Linton. But as for you – your primary task will be to keep yourself safe.' Marching to the wardrobe in the corner, Mr Ambrose tore open the doors and began pulling out dress after dress after dress. Then he started opening drawers and pulling out ladies' underwear.

'Mr Ambrose!' I started forward. 'I don't know what your idea of safety is, but I doubt those will be of any great help as body armour!'

Unperturbed, he continued rummaging through my underwear. Then, when he had pulled out everything he could find, he turned, and unloaded it onto Karim.

'*Sahib?*'

'Pack these.'

'*Sahib!* I...I cannot...I could not possibly...'

Mr Ambrose met the bodyguard's eyes, and the protests ceased instantly.

'Miss Linton will take a little trip away from this place.'

'I will?' My eyebrows rose.

'No. Not you. You are *Mr* Linton. It is *Miss* Linton who will be going.'

It took me a moment to understand.

'Ooh...'

'Yes.' Grabbing a suitcase from a corner, Mr Ambrose also pushed it into Karim's arms. 'Let me know when you have packed all of Miss Linton's things. I shall arrange for a coach to take her away.'

A coach driven by his own men no doubt. A coach that would only take me a few miles before depositing me in the snow as my male alter ego, ready to double back to the house.

'Mr Ambrose, Sir?'

'Yes, Mr Linton?'

'Have I ever told you that I love that devious mind of yours?'

'Restrain yourself, Mr Linton. Such strong feelings between gentlemen are inappropriate.'

Grinning, I snatched up another suitcase and started to help them pack. Only the underwear did I leave to Karim.

~~**~*~*

Everything went smoothly. I drove off in a coach only half an hour later – under the eyes of plenty of servants and a few surprised guests, who had stepped outside to see what was going on – only to return to the back of the house half an hour later as Mr Victor Linton, riding atop a speckled mount that didn't resemble either of the carriage horses.

'How long can we keep up this ruse?' I asked as I slid from the saddle.

A muscle in Mr Ambrose's jaw twitched in infinitesimal irritation. 'Only a day or two, I'm afraid. Christmas is approaching. My mother would be...displeased if you were not present for the festivities. For some inexplicable reason, she has taken quite a liking to you.'

I grinned, looking past him towards a fast approaching figure he could not yet see. 'You don't say...'

'Rikkard Ambrose!' He turned, just in time to see a pastel-coloured harbinger of doom descend upon him. 'What is the meaning of this? What is this I hear about Miss Linton leaving?'

Lady Samantha was not pleased, it appeared.

'Miss Linton has received urgent news.' Mr Ambrose met his mother's gaze head-on. 'She's had to leave on a family matter.'

'A family matter? Then why is Mr Linton still here?'

'The fact that his relative has had the impudence to fall sick at an inconvenient time is no reason for me to relieve my secretary of his duties. Miss Linton will have to fend for herself on her journey.'

179

'Rikkard Ambrose! You churl! You blaggard! You cannot send that sweet girl off on her own, out there where anything might happen! I can't believe...I can't...'

'I share your astonishment, Lady Samantha,' came a familiar voice from beyond the marchioness. Looking up, I felt a shiver travel down my back as I saw the new arrival: Lord Daniel Eugene Dalgliesh, flanked by his two 'footmen', Thomas and Harold. For footmen, both looked extraordinarily tall, extraordinarily strong, and extraordinarily deadly.

'I, too, am somewhat concerned for Miss Linton.' Lord Dalgliesh smiled. 'I'll send Thomas after her. We wouldn't want anything to happen to her, now, would we?'

Lady Samantha looked hesitant. But there was hardly a way she could politely refuse. 'Really, Lord Dalgliesh, I don't think...'

'I insist.' His Lordship took a step forward. 'After all, what kind of gentleman would I be if I didn't offer a lonely lady my...protection.'

Lady Samantha was just about to open her mouth again, when I merrily interrupted. 'I agree.'

She blinked. 'You do?'

'Certainly.' I gave His Lordship my most brilliant go-kiss-my-generous-derriere smile. 'By all means, send your man after my sister. I'm sure she will be glad for the company.'

Lord Dalgliesh raised one golden eyebrow. 'Is that so...? Well, you heard the gentleman, Thomas. Move.'

Thomas gave a curt bow and, without a word, dashed off towards the stables. He seemed to be quite eager to catch up with my 'sister'. Quite eager indeed.

Shuddering, I tried to push aside images of what might have happened if I were still inside that coach, or worse, right here at Battlewood in female garb.

'Shall we go inside?' I offered Lord Dalgliesh another smile. 'Don't worry. My sister will be perfectly safe now.'

Lord Dalgliesh returned my smile, and even though he didn't say a word, his reply was clear: *We shall see.*

And we did indeed see. Or at least I did, from the window up in my room. Grinning, I perched on the windowsill, gazing down at the rumpled figure of Thomas trudging through the thickly falling snow. He looked like a man who had just spent two hours combing a blizzard for a girl that currently did not exist. I might almost have pitied him, if his employer hadn't been a murderous madman with delusions of grandeur.

'Enjoying yourself?' enquired Adaira from behind me.

'Very much so.'

'Well, I hope it lasts.' Smirking, she settled down on the windowsill beside me. 'Mother is looking for you. She is quite disappointed with you because you let your "dear sister" leave the estate. Apparently, she had begun to harbour certain hopes...'

She trailed off. But she didn't need to say anything more. Her wickedly dancing eyes spoke more than a thousand soppy romance novels. My ears started to burn, and I glanced away. So I didn't see her face when she added in a soft voice: 'She's not the only one, you know.'

My breath caught.

Had she really just...

No. No, she couldn't just have given me her approval to... no. It simply wasn't possible. I mean, we liked each other, but she knew who I really was and what I had been up to with her brother. What kind of little sister wanted a girl like that for her brother?

A soft hand took mine and gave it a firm squeeze. 'As far as I'm concerned – welcome to the family.'

This one, apparently.

I looked up, opening my mouth – but she was already slipping out of the room, closing the door behind her. My heart pounding like a poltergeist's kettledrum collection, I turned back to the window and the marvellous sight of Lord Dalgliesh's henchman cursing and shaking snow out of his boots.

It wasn't the only such sight that helped to amuse and distract me over the following days. My – that is to say, Miss Lillian Linton's – remaining luggage was stolen, the gardens were patrolled, the attics and cellars were secretly searched – all to no avail. Lord Dalgliesh looked more and more sour every day and, I had to admit, I would have found it extraordinarily amusing, if I hadn't missed my copies of *Frankenstein* and *Ivanhoe*. I had paid good money for those books! What right did that hook-nosed nasty of a lord have to pinch them, simply because he was looking for information on how best to kidnap me?

Still, every time I saw Lord Dalgliesh's fists clench in aggravation at the sight of me, I had to suppress a smile.

Here I am, Your Lordship. Right here in front of you – a girl hiding in plain sight. Only, you are too narrow-minded to even suspect it.

Unlike Lord Dalgliesh, however, the lady guests at Battlewood Hall didn't seem particularly upset by Miss Lillian Linton's sudden departure.

'She's such a greedy little witch, that one,' Lady Caroline whispered in a voice that she thought was low enough not to carry over the room to where I was standing. 'A real fortune hunter. I've asked around, and, apparently, her father's estate was entailed on the male line. She and her pack of sisters are living off the charity of some relative until they can catch themselves an unfortunate man.'

The other ladies giggled, and I had to suppress my urge to march across the room and slap the little witch across the face. That would not have been the kind of gentlemanly behaviour befitting Mr Victor Linton. Damn and blast good manners!

We were all gathered in one of the drawing rooms. When I say 'all', I mean all of those who had stayed behind. Most of the gentlemen had decided to go out hunting that morning, Mr Ambrose among them. Not that he would normally spend time on such frivolous activities as hunting. But ever since Lord Dalgliesh's arrival, I had seen it glinting in his eyes: the fervent need to kill something. Better he take it out on forest animals than on his mother's Christmas guests. So I had persuaded him to go, while I myself stayed behind. As for me, I could shoot with a revolver, but hunting rifles remained, for the moment, beyond me. So I had stayed behind. A decision that I was, right now, thoroughly regretting. Shooting something seemed like a very good idea.

'How did she ever even meet someone like Lord Ambrose?' another one of the hyenas whispered, scathingly. 'He's so far above her, she shouldn't even be able to reach up to his toes.'

Bravo, lady. Such a good job at advancing the feminist cause there.

'Her brother is Mr Ambrose's secretary.'

'What? Well, that explains everything. What incredible luck that little witch must have.'

'Not anymore.' Lady Caroline sounded smug. 'She's not the only one who can use one man to get to another.'

'You mean...'

'Yes. I'm going to have a little chat with this Mr Linton.'

'You really think he'd help you? Why would he?'

She smiled. 'The better question is: how could he say no? Have you met any man so far who's been able to resist me?' Out of the corner of my eye, I saw her adjusting her dress, pulling her neckline a little bit farther down. 'Watch and learn, ladies.'

Oh, I'll be watching this. I'll most definitely be watching. This should be interesting.

Tasty Sheep's Feet

I was standing at the window overlooking the courtyard. A lady's footsteps approached, yet I pretended not to pay attention. Then a gentle feminine cough sounded from behind me. I struggled valiantly to morph my face into a serene, disinterested expression and turned around. Lady Caroline was beaming at me in a way that would probably have melted most men like butter in the sun. But for some reason it did not work quite so well on Mr Victor Linton. Strange. Can you imagine why?

She took a sensuous step closer, taking care to waggle her hips. I nearly burst out laughing.

'Mr Linton?'

'Yes, Lady Caroline?'

'I was just wondering...I heard...'

She paused and gave a shy giggle that was probably supposed to demonstrate how demure and innocent she was. Personally, I was tempted to ask if she had the laughing sickness, and how long it would be before she entered the third, terminal, stage – but on the whole, that would probably not have been very gentlemanly.

'You were wondering?' I prompted.

'A few of my friends and I were discussing London society and its great men. And one of them said something that I...no, I can't really believe it. It sounds too improbable.'

'What?'

'She said that you...that you are the private secretary of *the* Rikkard Ambrose?'

You could have filled a cathedral with the reverent awe in her voice.

'True.'

'What? You are? You really, really are?' She made big eyes and batted her eyelashes at me. I was tempted to bat her over the head with a bat in return, but I didn't have one handy. Darn! Where's a heavy wooden club when you need one?

'Oh, Mr Linton! Working for such an important man, that must be so terribly exciting!'

You have no idea.

'Oh, not so very exciting.' I waved a dismissive hand. 'Mostly it's boring paperwork.'

She batted her eyelashes again and swayed a few steps closer, offering me a good view of her cleavage. I had seen far more interesting sights in my life. 'Boring paperwork? Now, Mr Linton...I'm sure that's not true.'

No, it isn't. Would you like to know about the bandit hunts, secret infiltrations, deadly fights and the half-naked fun times in the jungle?

However, being a well-mannered pretend gentleman, I didn't say that aloud. I really was getting the hang of this manners thing.

'Of course, there are interesting moments,' I admitted instead, sighing with nostalgia.

'Such as?' she enquired, doing some more eyelash-batting.

'Well, there was the day we were checking the accounts and discovered a miscalculation of three shillings seven pence for the month of June. Mr Ambrose was so terribly excited about the additional revenue. It was one of the best days of the year.'

She blinked at me. I could almost see the question flicker in her mind: *Is this fellow pulling my delectably formed leg?*

It took her only a moment to decide. Of course I couldn't be pulling her leg. I was a man – nothing but helpless putty in her seductive hands. Just in case, though, she smiled at me broadly and once again pulled down her neckline.

If she does that again, things might get embarrassing for all concerned...

'Surely, there must be more to Mr Ambrose than accounting. He is such an intriguing man. I would be most grateful if you could tell me more...'

Just at that moment, far below, a man stepped out into the courtyard below. He was followed by another, and another. The guests were setting out to hunt. More and more of them emerged from the house until, finally, he came. Mr Rikkard Ambrose stepped out into the courtyard, as dark and menacing upon the snow as a raven among a flock of sparrows.

'Yes,' I murmured, unable to help myself. 'He certainly is intriguing.'

Lady Caroline sidled closer, gazing down at him. Below, Mr Ambrose pulled his rifle from his back, checked it in one swift, sharp move and grabbed the nearest horse by the reins, swinging himself onto the animal's back.

'Tell me, Mr Linton,' Lady Caroline purred, letting her fingers slide down my arm in a way that made me want to douse the appendage in vinegar, 'what is Mr Ambrose like? What is his favourite food? What are his tastes in art and music? What kind of woman do you think he would prefer to have at his side? If you give me your insights, I can prove very...generous.'

Ah, so this was her game, was it? Inwardly, I smiled. I'd say 'two can play that game' – but that wouldn't be entirely correct. Only one could play this game: me. Because I was the only one who knew all the rules.

Let's have a little fun...

And let's hope Mr Ambrose never finds out about it.

'Oh, well, Lady Caroline, if you ask so nicely...' I did my best to make my voice sound breathy and seduced. It wasn't easy. 'Mr Ambrose's favourite food...'

'Yes?'

'Mr Ambrose's favourite food are sheep's trotters.'

'*What?*'

'Sheep's trotters.' I made walking movements in the air with my fingers. 'You know, boiled sheep's feet? I hear they are sold by street vendors in London on every corner.'

'Boiled...sheep's feet?'

'Oh yes.' I smiled at her brightly. 'He eats at least a dozen a day. Can't have enough of them.'[13]

'Ng.'

'What's wrong, Lady Caroline? Don't you feel well?'

'No, no. I'm perfectly all right.'

'I'm glad to hear that.'

'So...what about his literary tastes?' She gifted me with another charming, seductive smile, though it looked a little more forced this time. Or should I say sheepish? 'What books does he enjoy?'

'Hm...' I thought for a moment. To be honest, I had never seen Mr Ambrose with a book other than his account and date book. But whoever said I was planning to be honest? 'If I remember correctly, he is a great admirer of the The *Ripley Scrolls*.'

Lady Caroline's perfectly arched eyebrows drew together in a ladylike frown. '*The...Ripley Scrolls?*'

'Oh yes, they are very dear to his heart.'

I wondered how long it would take her to find out that *The Ripley Scrolls* were an obscure medieval manuscript describing how to turn lead into gold. Probably very, very long.

'I see. Thank you, Mr Linton. Anything else?'

'Well, he has always been a big admirer of the *Rohonc Codex*.'

She smiled, trying to pretend as if she had the slightest idea what I was talking about. 'Really? I've always been interested in that work myself. I must read it immediately.'

---

[13] This might sound like a marvellous joke, but these delicacies did indeed exist. They were a common snack among the lower and middle classes.

I smiled back. 'Good luck with that.'

Especially considering that it's written in an as-yet-undeciphered alphabet consisting of over two hundred unknown letters, and the only existing copy was donated to the Hungarian Academy of Sciences a few years ago.

I would never have guessed reading that article about old books in the Times literary supplement would prove this useful.

Lady Caroline threw a look down at Mr Ambrose, who was currently galloping off into the woods at the head of the hunting party. It was an evaluating look. An is-he-worth-the-sheep's-feet kind of look.

Apparently, she decided he was. I couldn't blame her.

'What about his preferences where ladies are concerned?' Lady Caroline asked, cautiously. 'What would be Mr Ambrose's idea of the perfect woman?'

Me, you slimy, slithering snake in the grass.

But I didn't say that out loud. Instead, I pasted a bright smile on my face and said: 'Oh, I can tell you all about that, in detail!'

Her expression brightened. 'You can?'

'Yes. I clearly remember him expressing his views on the matter when the two of us went to this East End brothel together, and these three prostitutes came up to us– Lady Caroline? Lady Caroline, are you all right? Oh dear! Someone fetch smelling salts! I think Lady Caroline is feeling a little faint for some reason.'

~~*~**~*~*

After that nice little chat, Lady Caroline and her compatriots kept their distance from Mr Victor Linton for some reason.

All the better. I couldn't waste a minute's thought on them. Only two days were left before Christmas Eve. Soon, my true self would have to return to Battlewood for Lady Samantha's big celebration, and, from the way Lord Dalgliesh's eyes gleamed whenever I caught sight of him, he knew it. I had briefly considered just staying away – but if I did, Lord Dalgliesh might dispatch his agents to London. And if they got hold of my family...

I shuddered, cutting off the thought right there and then.

Miss Lillian Linton would have to reappear at Battlewood. But I would be safe, right? Mr Ambrose's men would stand guard in front of my door day and night. Karim would accompany me wherever I went, and this time, I certainly wouldn't try to object. But still...

This was Lord Daniel Eugene Dalgliesh we were talking about. A man who owned a subcontinent could do scary things.

'Mr Linton?'

I looked up. I had been sitting at the desk in my room, aimlessly doodling nooses, knives and bullets on a scrap of paper when the familiar voice came from behind me. Mr Ambrose had stepped into the room, and I hadn't even noticed.

Bloody hell, Lilly, you need to be more careful! What if it had been someone else?

'Yes, Sir?' Swiftly, I rose. I could tell from the look in his eyes that he was here for business.

'Your sister will soon return.'

My sister? Hm...is someone in hearing distance?

Deciding it was best to be cautious, I gave the answer with which you could never go wrong with Mr Ambrose. 'Yes, Sir.'

'You and I are both aware of the danger she will be in. Of course, Karim will be on guard. But even he has to rest sometimes. During that time, someone else will have to watch her. I have sent word to the next big town to hire reinforcements, but for now, we will have to content ourselves with one of the four people among the staff who are in my employ. The men, preferably, since they are trained fighters.'

My inner feminist wanted instantly to make a comment – but, blast him, he was right. It was unlikely that a housemaid would be of much use against one of Lord Dalgliesh's men.

'I understand, Sir.'

He nodded briskly, and stepped to the door. 'Come in.'

The door opened, and two men and two women stepped in. The women were housemaids, inconspicuous creatures who looked rather nervous to suddenly be embroiled in a cloak-and-dagger intrigue of this sort. As for the men, one was a young footman, who seemed to share the nervousness of his female counterparts, and the other –

I stared.

'Hastings?'

The venerable butler bowed as far as his paunch would allow. 'Indeed, Sir.'

'You have fighting experience?'

'Before entering domestic service I had the honour of serving with Her Majesty's 7th Royal Fusiliers, Sir.'

'Which means?'

'We were tasked with safeguarding the Royal Artillery while on the move through enemy territory, Sir.'

'What do you say, Mr Linton?' Mr Ambrose's voice was cool, almost disinterested, but there was something in there that caught my attention and held it tightly. 'Will these people suffice to guard your sister? It is your decision.'

My decision.

Our eyes met.

He wants to reassure me, I realised. The clock is ticking. Soon, I'll have to be myself again, and risk the danger. He wants to make sure that I'm not afraid.

Warmth blossomed in my chest. Another man might have given me a hug. Mr Rikkard Ambrose gave me a heavily armed escort.

Well, why not?

I directed my gaze to the younger man, who immediately stood straighter and met my eyes. He didn't look quite so nervous anymore.

'What about you?'

He snapped to attention. 'Three years in the 1st King's Dragoon Guards, Sir.'

Hm. Well, I supposed what was good enough for a king was good enough for me. My gaze slid to the house maids. 'I suppose it's too much to hope that you two served in the army?'

One of the maids gave a nervous giggle. The other looked as if she were about ready to faint. I felt a sudden, violent surge of desire to see my best friend Patsy. She would have made a better bodyguard than anyone else.

Still... my eyes drifted back to the solid, dependable form of Hastings. There was something in his eyes, a hardness I hadn't noticed before. Oh yes, no doubt: this man had been a soldier. And he was still ready to kill, if necessary.

I gave Mr Ambrose a nod.

'They'll do. And...'

'Yes, Mr Linton?'

'Thank you.'

Our eyes met again, and that brief look said more than a thousand words. That night I slept easily, secure in the knowledge that I would have someone reliable to watch my back.

I should have known it wouldn't be so easy.

EARLY CHRISTMAS PRESENT

'She's coming back! She's coming back!'

I could hear Adaira's excited cries even though the coach was still pretty far away from the manor house. When I had explained our little ruse to her, the youngest member of the Ambrose family had happily agreed to participate in a little playacting. By the sound of it, she was doing an excellent job.

Next to me, Karim scowled and gripped his sabre more tightly.

'Relax,' I told him. 'As long as I'm guarded around the clock, what can Dalgliesh do?'

He gave me a stare that could have made any man quake in his boots.

How lucky for me that I'm not a man, then.

'Dalgliesh is one man,' he told me. 'India is millions upon millions upon millions. And yet he rules with an iron fist. He is dangerous. He is ruthless. Do not let down your guard.'

I blinked. Was that...concern I had just heard in his voice? Surely not.

'I won't.'

Was that my voice, sounding so uncharacteristically soft? Christmas must be having a bad influence on me.

When the coach rolled to a stop in front of Battlewood Hall, Adaira wasn't the only one waiting for me. Mr Ambrose was there, as was his mother, smiling brightly, and–

Oh dear.

His father.

Who was *not* smiling brightly.

Before I could come up with an excuse to stay inside the coach, Karim jumped out, unfolded the steps and held the door open for me. Taking a deep breath, I started to descend.

'Miss Linton! I'm so glad you're back!' Adaira was the first to greet me – with a bone-crushing hug instead of a curtsy, which earned her an icy stare of disapproval from her father. He was altogether looking not very approving of the situation.

'Miss Linton?' Stepping forward, he sketched a brief bow. The kind of bow Alexander the Great might have given a lady. It said clearly *I'm showing you respect, but only because I feel like it. If I wanted to, I could crush you in an instant.*

I curtsied. It wasn't a very deep curtsy. 'Your Lordship.'

Icy, sea-coloured eyes raked me from top to bottom. If I had been unprepared, I might have been intimidated. But I'd had over a year of training. I didn't flinch, even when his gaze bored into mine. 'My wife has spoken very fondly of you, Miss Linton.'

'She has?'

'Oh yes, indeed. She has spoken of you *a lot*. So has my daughter.'

Oh? Did she mention the time she caught your son and me in bed together?

'How nice.'

'Interestingly enough, even Lord Dalgliesh speaks of you.'

'Oh?'

Less nice! A lot less nice!

Though right now I thought I might even prefer Lord Dalgliesh's company over that of this polished marble monolith of aristocracy. At least in Lord Dalgliesh's case I knew which kind of evil villain I was dealing with.

'So I thought it was time,' the marquess continued, 'for me to come out and personally meet this young lady who seems to have caught everyone's attention.'

I waited for more – in vain. He didn't say anything. He just stood there, scrutinising me in silence. It felt like being laid open with a fillet knife. Only instead of a knife, he was using his gaze. And instead of being prepared for roasting, I was being frozen.

To hell with him! I had survived much, much worse than this old man. Raising my chin, I met his gaze head-on and didn't blink. Not once. Finally, he narrowed his eyes and, whirling, marched off towards the house. I thought he would leave without a word. But then he stopped next to Mr Ambrose. Without touching or looking at his son, he said:

'Be careful whom you associate with. Even after what you've done in the last ten years, the Ambrose name still means something. Be very careful.'

And he swept off into the house.

'Oh, my dear!' Before I could even think of moving, Lady Samantha rushed forward, enveloping me in a fluffy hug. 'I'm so sorry about that! Sometimes he can be a bit...'

...of an arse?

'...grumpy.'

Well, that was certainly one way to put it. Sliding my arms around her, I gently patted the little lady's back.

'Don't worry. It would take a lot more than that to scare me away.'

Maybe it was just coincidence – but just at that moment, I happened to look up and, through one of the windows facing the courtyard, high up on the second floor, caught the glimpse of a figure standing half-hidden behind the curtains. A tall, blond figure with aquiline features.

Lord Dalgliesh smiled at me.

Quickly, I lowered my gaze and let go of Lady Samantha. Karim, I saw to my intense relief, was already beside me, looking dependably massive and dangerous.

As soon as her mother let go, Adaira decided that, apparently, she hadn't had quite enough of hugging yet and came back for seconds.

'He's watching you,' she whispered in my ear. 'Dalgliesh, I mean.'

'I know. Are you sure we shouldn't tell your parents–'

'No!' Her grip tightened. 'All those things you've told me about him...' I felt her give a light shudder. I had not spared her the nasty details of mine and Mr Ambrose's encounters with Lord Dalgliesh. At least one member of the household needed to know how dangerous he was. 'They'd never believe it! They've had a falling out, true, but still...He's a peer of the realm!'

I knew she spoke the truth. Lady Samantha was far too innocent to comprehend the truth. And her husband – he was one of those men who thought being 'nobility' really meant that you were noble, in the true sense of the word. There was no convincing him.

'Don't worry.' I patted her back before I let go. 'I'm well-protected, and so are you.' There were enough people in Mr Ambrose's employ on the estate to keep an eye on us both. Everything was going to be fine.

'Miss Linton?'

I would have known that voice anywhere. So cold, so hard – and yet there was no way I could ever confuse it with his father's. Smiling, I looked up at Mr Rikkard Ambrose. With the grace of a gazelle, I dipped into a curtsy.

'Mr Ambrose, Sir?'

Unfortunately, most gazelles weren't particularly good at curtsying. But that didn't seem to bother him. His icy gaze was devouring me from top to bottom.

'Why don't you come walk with me, Miss Linton? There is something I would like to discuss with you.'

In the background, I could see Lady Samantha stumble, and nearly swoon with happiness.

'Certainly, Mr Ambrose. Lead the way.'

He marched me off, and Adaira trailed behind, the dutiful chaperone (or nosy little minx, depending on your perspective). We were hardly out of hearing range before Mr Ambrose hissed: 'We have a problem!'

~~**~*~*

189

'When did this happen?' I whispered, aghast, as I stared down at the bandaged, bruised, unconscious figures of Hastings and the footman.

'Hardly an hour after Karim left to "fetch you",' Mr Ambrose retorted, the words like cold shards of ice. That muscle in his jaw was ticking like a time bomb. 'Dalgliesh must have known all along which of the servants are in my employ.'

'What about the maids?' I demanded, desperately trying to remember their names. Had I even bothered to ask?

'They're fine. But what use are they?' He glanced at me, and I knew what he really meant: *How will they be able to protect you?*

'They have two pairs of eyes, and two healthy sets of lungs on them. They can watch and, if necessary, bring the house down with their screams.'

Again, that ticking muscle. 'Better than nothing, I suppose, but...'

He glanced at me again. I knew exactly what he was thinking.

But it would be risky.

But I wouldn't be safe.

But Lord Dalgliesh might get me.

Or, worse, he might get Mr Ambrose. We held each other's gaze for a long, long moment.

'Holy hell!' Suddenly overcome with rage, I slammed a fist into the wall. Rage for him. Rage for me. But, most of all, rage for the two unfortunate souls lying bruised and bandaged in front of us. 'How was he able to do this? I don't understand...!'

'An "accident".' Mr Ambrose's voice was dispassionate, but still, used as I was to trying to read him, I could sense a touch of bitterness in it. 'A Christmas tree fell on top of them, or something like that. It always is with him.'

'And he gets away with it?'

'He's a peer of the realm,' Mr Ambrose answered simply.

'But surely your parents suspect...'

'Ha!' That muscle in Mr Ambrose's jaw twitched. 'You've met my mother, Mr Linton. She wouldn't be able to think badly of a rabid berserker, let alone a "respectable gentleman". And my father...well, as I said, Lord Dalgliesh is a peer of the realm. In my father's eyes, he can do no wrong.'

The bitterness in his voice made me burn with the desire to ask what had happened between them all those years ago. But I didn't. That was a discussion for another day. A day when no sword was hanging over our heads.

That night I slept in Mr Ambrose's arms, with Karim standing guard outside the door. Knowing that the huge bodyguard was alert outside was a relief – yet, somehow, it didn't bring half the comfort of the hard arms wrapped around me. Even in his deepest sleep, Mr Rikkard Ambrose felt like a rock. My rock, which I could always depend on.

'I should have stayed away.'

At the sound of his voice, I almost jumped out of my skin. Bloody hell!

'I thought you were sleeping!'

Ignoring my words, he repeated: 'I should have stayed away from here.'

I hesitated. 'Why?'

His arms tightened around me. 'If I had stayed away, none of this would be happening.'

'You're right.' Turning in his arms, I placed a gentle kiss on his cheek. 'None of this would be happening.' Another featherlight kiss, this time on the lips. *'None* of it.'

'Mr Linton?'

'Oh, I am "Mister" Linton right now?'

'Yes.'

'Why, Sir?' Another kiss, this one a little less gentle.

'Because you are misbehaving. Stop it!'

'Stop what?' I trailed kisses from the edge of his mouth, over his jaw and down his neck, until I was cuddling comfortably under his chin, against his chest. 'This?'

A rumble rose from his chest, threatening retribution. I smiled into him, ignoring the warning. Instead of retreating, I cuddled closer. In his arms, I felt safe beyond any rationally explicable manner.

Still, would it be enough? Step by step, Lord Dalgliesh was invading Mr Ambrose's ancestral home, taking control without its owners even realising it. There was real danger. To the both of us, and his family.

Maybe we should just leave! Run away and...

But no.

As soon as I thought that, I saw an image of the hopeful face of Mr Ambrose's mother before my inner eye. A mother who hadn't seen her son in over ten years. This was their first family Christmas in over a decade. If we left now, without being able to give any explanation...

I shuddered. I didn't even want to think about it.

We had to get through this. And we would. And then...

'Mr Ambrose?'

'Yes, Mr Linton?'

'Once this is all over...'

A moment of silence.

'Yes?'

'We're going to make Dalgliesh pay.'

Strong, smooth lips brushed against my cheek. It was pitch-black and I couldn't see a thing, but I thought I felt those lips curve into the tiniest smile against my skin.

'That sounds...acceptable.'

~~**~*~*

Next morning at breakfast, the threat from Lord Dalgliesh somehow seemed like nothing but a dark and distant dream. His Lordship was absent from the table. In fact, quite a lot of people, including Mr Ambrose's father and some of the guests, did not see fit to grace us with their presence that morning. It was just Mr Ambrose, his mother, his sister, me, and a few of the hyenas. And I didn't mind their presence as much as usual.

Why, you ask?

Well...

'A sheep's *what*?' Mr Ambrose slowly turned his head to direct his icy gaze at Lady Caroline and the dish she was holding out to him. 'Pardon, My Lady, *what* did you say?'

'Would you like a sheep's trotter, Mr Ambrose?' She pointed to the dish and gave an encouraging smile. 'I had them brought especially from Newcastle.'

Mr Ambrose's eyes glittered with ice. 'You don't say.'

'Yes. And they're so tasty...' Taking one of the sheep's feet, Lady Caroline raised it to her delicate lips and nibbled on it – then coughed and hurriedly reached for a handkerchief. I had to dive behind a vase of flowers to hide the expression on my face.

'Since they are such a delicacy,' Mr Ambrose told her, his face a mask of stone, 'I would hate to deprive you of them.' He shifted the plate towards her. '*Bon appétit.*'

I ducked behind the vase again, stifling helpless giggles.

After that episode, I was almost in something resembling a good mood. Karim was getting a well-deserved day's rest after a long night of door-guarding, so Mr Ambrose, one of 'his' maids and I retired to a sitting room on the second floor that had only one entrance – just about the securest location that was available. We sat there, not speaking, not doing much of anything, really, just sitting there and being there for each other. Which, for Mr Ambrose, truly was something special. When had he last taken the time to quietly sit down with someone, doing nothing?

Probably not for over a decade.

Downstairs, the busy Christmas preparations continued. I could hear bells jingling, and Adaira yelling orders with a voice any sergeant major would have been proud of. It almost left one feeling...merry.

'Sir?'

I glanced up before I remembered that, due to my current lack of trousers, I was probably not the one being addressed. Drat! With all this clothes-changing, I was starting to lose track of who I was currently supposed to be.

'Yes?' Raising his gaze, Mr Ambrose turned to the servant who was standing in the doorway. The young man bowed.

'Your mother was wondering where you are, Sir. She asked me to fe– um, to enquire whether you could spare her a few moments.'

There was a moment of silence. Mr Ambrose glanced at me.

'Go!' Smiling, I waved him away. 'I'll be perfectly safe! Mabel – it is Mabel, right?'

'Yes, Miss,' the housemaid murmured.

'Mabel is going to keep me company. If anything happens, I'll scream the house down.'

Mr Ambrose's left little finger twitched. 'It's a large house.'

'And I'm good at screaming, as you should know from experience. Go!'

For another long moment, he hesitated – and then rose to his feet. 'I shall be only a minute. In the meantime...' He fixed a look on the housemaid that made the poor girl quiver. 'You are personally responsible for Miss Linton's safety. If anything happens to her in my absence, you will have me to answer to.'

The girl jumped to her feet as if stung by a swarm of bees and hurried to take up position behind me. All she was missing was a red uniform and a big pelt hat, and she would not have been out of place in front of Buckingham Palace.

With a last cold look at the maid, Mr Ambrose marched out of the room. The door closed behind him with a click. Shaking my head, I picked up the book I had been reading and smiled to myself. 'Don't worry about him.'

'No, Miss?'

'No. His bark is worse than his bite.'

'I'm glad to hear that, Miss.'

That was the last thing I heard before her arm slipped around me and the sweet smelling cloth pressed down over my face.

'Merry Christmas,' said a voice behind me as dark spots started appearing in front of my eyes.

Really? How nice of you. Ho, ho, ho...

Then the darkness took me.

DALGLIESH

Light sparkled. Tiny little points of light, getting bigger, then smaller, then bigger again. I wouldn't have minded – it might even have looked nice – if every single one of them hadn't stabbed me in the head like a red hot needle.

'Aaargh...Ouww...'

'Ah. I believe our guest is ready to join us in the land of the conscious.'

That voice... that cultural, slightly amused, deadly voice...

I knew it.

If only I could remember...if only someone would help me...

A bucket of water splashed into my face.

Ah. Thanks for the help.

'Pppft!'

Spewing water in all directions, I shook my head.

'Now, really, Brewer,' came that cultured, sleek voice again. 'Is that any way to treat a lady?'

'She's a lady, Sir?'

'Most assuredly. And, though this might not be apparent at first sight, a very important one. Isn't that right, Miss Linton?'

Pushing my wet hair out of my eyes, I raised my head and gazed up at the smiling face of Lord Daniel Eugene Dalgliesh.

'I guess that depends on your definition of "important".'

My gaze wandered to Mabel, who was standing behind his Lordship, looking by no means as cowed as she had in the presence of Rikkard Ambrose. I stared at her, my eyes narrowing to slits.

'Why?' I demanded.

She shrugged. 'Dalgliesh pays better.'

Of course.

I loved Mr Rikkard Ambrose. I truly did. But right then and there, I could have strangled him until every last drop of stinginess was squeezed out of his miserably marvellous body!

'Ah, yes.' Turning, His Lordship pulled a pouch out of his pocket. It clinked in a very valuable way as it dropped into the maid's open hand. 'Your last payment. That should be enough to get you established in the colonies and make a very nice dowry.'

'Judas,' I muttered.

Half-turning to me, Lord Dalgliesh lifted an eyebrow. 'Hardly. That's gold, not silver.'

Mabel, the traitor, made a deep curtsy and hurried towards the door. Just before she stepped outside, I spoke.

'Mabel?'

She stopped in the doorway. 'Yes?'

'What I told you...'

'Yes?'

'It was a lie.' I fixed her with my coldest imitation-Ambrose stare. 'His bite is worse than his bark. Far, far worse.'

Hurriedly, she swept out of the room. But just before she did, I could see a flash of fear spark in her eyes.

Good! She should be afraid. She should be terrified.

Because at least then I won't be the only one.

Slowly, Lord Daniel Eugene Dalgliesh turned towards me and gave me his most brilliant, charming, shiny smile. It didn't make me feel any better. Apart from me, there was only one other person in his room: Thomas Brewer, his 'footman', who was standing at the door in a pose that looked suspiciously soldierly. No one else was in sight. Not a soul could help me. My hands tensed, curling into fists around the edges of the cot I was sitting on.

'Well, Miss Linton...let's have a little chat, shall we?'

'I have a better idea,' I told him, while my eyes flicked around the bare, rough wooden room, searching for a way to escape. One door – blocked. One window – but too small to fit through. Damn! 'Let's let me go, shall we?'

'Ha! You're quite amusing. I begin to see why Mr Ambrose keeps you around.' In a flash, he was in front of me, gripping my chin between two long, aristocratic fingers. His steel-blue eyes bored into mine. 'Listen here, Miss Linton. I took you, I have you, and I can do anything I want with you. You had better get used to that fact. And as long as you are in my power, you had better not do or say anything to displease me or the consequences will be...grave. Do we understand each other?'

Ah. He was one of *those* men. He enjoyed this.

'Yes.' I met his gaze head-on. 'I understand perfectly.'

'Very well.' Letting go, Lord Dalgliesh turned away and marched to the window. It was covered by a few hastily sewn-together hides nailed to the wall.

Whatever this place was, Buckingham Palace it was not. Lifting the hides a few inches, Lord Dalgliesh peered outside.

'Good,' he murmured. 'The snow is falling fast. By the time that fool Ambrose notices she's gone, our tracks will long be covered. You laid a false trail, like I ordered, Brewer?'

The footman nodded. 'Yes, My Lord.'

'And Whittock? Has he left the message?'

'Yes, My Lord.'

'Very good. Very good indeed.'

Message? I felt a cold fist clamp down around my heart. There was only man they would have left a message for.

'What do you want with Mr Ambrose?' I demanded, sitting up straight and glaring at Dalgliesh's back.

Letting go of the window's leather covering, he turned to face me. 'Will you look at that? Our resident damsel has brains between her ears. I wonder...does she have enough to answer her own question, the answer to which, I must admit, should be rather obvious?'

Suppressing my intense desire to slap him across the face, I cocked my head. They had sent a message to Mr Ambrose, after kidnapping me. He was right. It was rather obvious.

'You plan to blackmail him.'

'Blackmail is such an ugly word,' he said, waving a hand. But then a smile spread over his face that sent a shiver down my back. 'On the other hand, I *like* ugly words. Particularly when applied to my enemies.'

I did my best to laugh haughtily. 'It won't work! Blackmail Mr Rikkard Ambrose? It's impossible! He doesn't care about anything or anyone, pounds sterling excepted.'

'You know...' Thoughtfully, Lord Dalgliesh tapped his chin. 'I thought the same thing only a short while ago. But then you came along. I had my initial suspicions when I first saw the two of you dancing together at Lady Metcalf's ball. Still, I thought to myself "No, this is Rikkard Ambrose. It can't be." Of course, I had you investigated nonetheless, and I discovered that Mr Ambrose's secretary had the same name as you do – but from what I could find out, neither he nor Mr Ambrose were connected to you in any other way. And then, when you made no other appearance in his life, I began to think it was nothing. I began to forget – until I received a very interesting letter from my agent in Newcastle.'

His Lordship slid a hand into his pocket and pulled out a letter on thin, rumpled paper. It looked so insignificant. Hard to believe that such a thing could spell my doom.

'Urgent!' Lord Dalgliesh read in that sleek, aristocratic voice. 'Ambrose spotted with male and female companions in Newcastle. Last known location: London. Companions: Bodyguard, deputy manager, secretary Linton, and...' He looked up, meeting my eyes. '...and *unknown female*.'

I swallowed.

'Imagine my surprise, Miss Linton, when I discovered that "unknown female" was in fact you. The only woman whom Mr Ambrose was ever known to dance with without an ulterior motive. The only woman who'd brave danger for him. The only woman he ever invited to meet his family.'

Flipping the letter shut, he gave me a look.

I answered it by raising an eyebrow. 'What, you think meeting the The Most Honourable The Marquess Ambrose is a mark of distinction Mr Ambrose bestows on a lady? I would rather see it as a threat, or a method to efficiently make her lose interest.'

His Lordship chuckled. 'Ah, yes. The marquess has some less than pleasing qualities. But then...so has his son.'

Shut up! Shut up! You slimeball, you don't know what you are talking about! There's only one person who's allowed to insult Rikkard Ambrose, and that's me!

'If you're willing to put up with one, I very much doubt you'd balk at the other. In any case, this isn't about the marquess's likability. This is about Mr Rikkard Ambrose, after ten years, suddenly returning to his family. A month ago, I would have said he cared about them as much as he does about a rock in the Kalahari Desert – one *without* gold ore inside. He let them stew for over a decade. I would have said he never wanted anything to do with them again. And then you somehow managed to get him up here.' He gave three long, slow claps. 'Impressive. Quite impressive. Too bad you will not be reaping the rewards of your labours.'

'What happened?' I demanded, teeth gritted. 'What the hell did you do to the Ambroses? What could anyone do to sow so much hatred between father and son?'

'What? He didn't tell you?' A mocking aristocratic eyebrow rose. 'Dear me. You must not have him as tightly wrapped around your finger as I thought.'

'Right now, I'd like to wrap something around your neck!'

'Tut, tut. Such unladylike language.'

'Tell me!'

'Hm...' He started walking, circling me like a predator would a prospective victim. 'I wonder what would be more amusing...to tell you, or to leave you wondering...'

'Tell me! What did you do?'

'Hm...interesting how you automatically assume it was me.'

My head snapped around. 'It wasn't?'

He smirked. 'Oh, don't misunderstand me, I was, shall we say...the catalyst for the happy event? But it needn't have ended in their family breaking apart. Oh no, that the Ambroses managed all on their own.' Passing out of my sight, he moved behind me, his voice making the hairs on the back of my neck stand up. 'You see, thanks to my help, it came to a little disagreement between the marquess and his son. Not being quite so cool and composed back then, he went into battle with a vengeance. The old man responded in kind and...well, things took their course. From what I've been able to learn, they shouted at each other loud enough to make the walls rattle, until finally the marquess told his son to get out.'

One of his fingers touched my cheek, and I shuddered.

'And he did,' Lord Dalgliesh whispered. 'And didn't return for over ten years.'

Oh God...

I didn't want to believe it – but I could see. Two proud men, father and son, raging at each other, unwilling to give in...and then the fatal words.

Get out.

Any ordinary young man would storm out of the room, and that would be that. But Rikkard Ambrose was not and had never been an ordinary man.

'He left the country?' I whispered. 'Because of *that*?'

'Indeed he did.'

My eyes flashed up to His Lordship's. 'What did you do?'

Whatever it was, it must have been...dear Lord, I didn't even want to think about it. Something bad enough for a father to throw his own son out of the house...bad enough for the son to want to go, and never come back...

I shuddered.

'That, Miss Linton, is none of your concern.' Lord Dalgliesh gave me a smile. It was the kind of smile I was very used to seeing on the faces of gentlemen – an 'oh you are only a weak-minded female, you could not possibly understand' smile. 'Don't bother your pretty head with the details.'

I narrowed my eyes at him. Time to shoot back. 'Details like the fact that he returned?'

His Lordship stiffened.

'After you left, after you had ruined his life... You forgot about him, didn't you?' I guessed. 'You thought he was insignificant. A lowly, penniless insect not worth your exalted attention. Then he began to rise in the world. And when you finally noticed, it was too late. He was already too powerful for you.'

A muscle in his face twitched.

'He never was too powerful for me.'

'Indeed?' I raised an eyebrow. 'What about the bandits in Egypt he destroyed? The assassination attempts he survived? You desperately want to get rid of him, because you know that step by step, stone by stone, he is dismantling your empire. But you can't. He's stronger than you.'

His fists slammed into the wall on either side of me. I had to fight hard not to flinch, but somehow, I managed it.

'Have a care, Miss Linton,' he breathed, his aquiline face only inches away from mine, steel-blue eyes alight with menace. 'I need you alive. I do not necessarily need you intact.' He dragged in a deep breath, struggling to bring himself back under control. Finally, a shadow of his former arrogant smile reappeared on his face. 'We'll see how powerful Rikkard Ambrose really is very soon – when I send him your little finger on a platter.'

My mouth suddenly felt very dry.

'What are you hoping to accomplish? To lure him into a trap and kill him? He won't be that stupid!'

'Kill him?' The smile on his Lordship's face grew broader, and a look entered his eyes that I did not like. I did not like it at all. 'Why would I want to kill him?

It was only then that the full horror of the situation sank in. If Lord Dalgliesh didn't want Mr Ambrose dead, that could only mean...

'He'll be much more useful to me alive,' his Lordship continued, his breath tickling my face in a way that made me want to jump out of my own skin. 'With him under my thumb...can you imagine the things I could accomplish? It's not just the combined resources, it's the fact of my worst enemy suddenly working for me. All the people who have dared to cross me over the years – the Americans with their silly notions of freedom, the Chinese fighting against the opium trade, those pesky peasants and reformers in India – will be swept aside. No more flocking to the banner of Rikkard Ambrose! From now on, there will be order and rule within the British Empire!'

'And I'm guessing it won't have much to do with its Queen?'

'Ha!' His Lordship let out a bark of laughter. 'That green girl? As if she could ever accomplish anything!'

You'd be surprised what girls can accomplish.

However, I didn't say that out loud. I had a feeling that His Lordship wasn't the kind of man to listen. Besides...deeds spoke far better than words.

My hand crept into the folds of my skirts, searching until it felt something hard. I had to work to suppress a smile.

'Well, it's been lovely chatting with you, Miss Linton.' Straightening, Lord Dalgliesh pulled on his gloves, and picked up his hat from where he'd hung it on a nail protruding from the wall. 'But I'm afraid I have to go now. I have to meet a few of my men and lead them to this place. They will be escorting you to your new, permanent lodgings, and aiding in the removal of a digit to send to Mr Ambrose.'

'How very kind of them.'

'Yes, they are true gentlemen.' He gave me a smile that chilled my bones. 'Brewer, stay here and keep an eye on her, will you? We don't want her to take a walk and get lost in the woods.'

'Yes, My Lord. Should I bind her, My Lord?'

'Good God, no!' Lord Dalgliesh gave a short, sharp laugh. 'She's not one of those vicious street rats you're used to dealing with, Brewer! She's a lady. She can't tie her own shoes without a man's help.' Throwing me a last, mocking look, he lifted his head. '*Au revoir*, Miss Linton.'

And he strode out of the hut.

What a pity. I had hoped he'd stay for the fun.

I wonder...what would it take to convince Lord Dalgliesh that I'm not quite the conventional lady?

Under my skirts, my hand closed around the aforementioned hard object. A smile curved my lips.

Yes, that would probably do it.

How convenient that I was a helpless little damsel in distress who didn't need to be searched by her captors. Very convenient indeed.

My eyes slid to Brewer, who had stepped towards the window to watch his master depart. Hoof beats, dampened by the snow, sounded outside. Slowly, they faded into the distance, and still he stood at the window, his back to me.

How did the old saying go? You don't look a gift horse in the mouth.

I rose.

'Brewer?'

He turned – just in time to come face-to-face with the muzzle of my revolver. The click of the hammer being pulled back echoed loudly in the little room.

I smiled at the wide-eyed man over the length of gleaming metal. 'I'd like to leave now. Would you be a kind gentleman and help me tie my shoelaces, helpless little damsel that I am?'

Damsel Under Stress

For a moment, the man just stared into the muzzle of the gun. His mouth dropped open.

'You...how...I don't...'

'It's not that difficult to understand,' I told him. 'First, you in charge. Girl pulls out gun. Girl points gun at you. You in charge no more. End of story. Well, of yours, anyway.'

'I...how...you...'

Dear me. This fellow was really slow. When would he start begging for his life, or would I have to do that for him?

'I wonder, should I kill you?' I mused. 'I must admit, I really feel like it. You're a bastard who works for a bastard. You helped kidnap me and were probably planning to be involved in some finger-cutting later. So...why not?'

'I...no! I, um...well...'

'On the other hand – people might hear a shot. The wrong kind of people.' I pondered the conundrum for a moment, then brightened. 'Ah! I'll know what I'll do.'

'What?' he asked, wide-eyed.

'This.'

Swift as a fiery *ifrit*, I raised my gun and brought down the butt against his temple, hard.

'Oo1f!'

'Nighty-night, soldier boy.'

Satisfied, I gazed down at the crumpled form on the floor. Now here was a good day's work if ever I saw one. But I wasn't finished yet. Not by any means.

I had no illusions. Mr Ambrose had no idea where I was. He could not come to rescue me from this hellhole. However, that didn't particularly bother me. Because that left the much more interesting option of rescuing myself.

Your plans are done, Dalgliesh! Watch out, here I come!

Bending down, I grabbed the fallen fake footman by the scruff of the neck and dragged him away from the window, so no one would catch sight of him from outside. Who knew, there might be other guards out there.

Pressing myself against the wall, I slowly approached the window, until I could peek out between the hide covering and the frame. Nothing. Not a soul in sight. No noise reached my ears, except for the occasional creak of a tree under the growing burden of snow.

Leaving only one man to guard the helpless damsel? Could any man truly be this stupid?

Yes, Lilly. They all could.

I smiled. Pride commeth before a fall, right?

Well, then let's make sure Dalgliesh falls hard!

Hurrying to the door, I took a peek outside. Nothing. No one. The snowy landscape was as deserted as Antarctica during penguin holiday season. I was about to dash outside when I suddenly hesitated.

No.

Think, Lilly, think!

It was biting cold outside. Besides, if I just ran away through the snow, I would leave tracks everywhere. When Lord Dalgliesh came back – and he would come back soon, I had no doubt – he would find my tracks and catch up to me easily. That was something I couldn't let happen.

Squinting, I searched the horizon for something, anything that could be helpful in my escape. A road, smoke from nearby village, a...

Wait a moment.

Was that water I saw sparkling in the distance?

Yes, definitely! There was a stream running through the countryside not too far away from the cabin – one that hadn't frozen over yet! A plan began to form in my mind. Hm...could it work?

Yes.

Turning, I hurried back into the hut and marched over to my fallen captor. For a moment I just stood there, thinking my plan over. Then I nodded, decision made, and stepped forward.

'Don't worry,' I told the slumbering soldier. 'I'm not going to make an assault on your maidenly virtue.'

With that, I grabbed his trousers and pulled them down. His jacket was a little bit more difficult, but eventually I managed to get that off, too. Soon I was clad in warm and practical, if slightly smelly, clothes. And as for soldier boy...well, just for fun, I removed his underclothes, too, and chucked them out of the window.

'Have fun searching,' I told him with a grin and dashed out of the door.

The snow was deep. It filled my shoes, tugged at my feet and made every step a struggle. But months of trekking through deserts and jungles with Mr Rikkard Ambrose had made me hard in a way I hadn't fully appreciated until now. Where a year ago I would have collapsed into the snow after a few hundred yards, I now gritted my teeth and sped up, sprinting forward.

I'm an ifrit! What's a bit of snow to me? Let's fly on wings of fire!

By the time I reached the river, I was panting, my nose felt frozen and my breath puffed out in thick clouds. But I had done it!

A smile tugged at the corners of my mouth. Now for the interesting part.

Let's see who's the smart one, Dalgliesh.

I stepped into the river.

~~**~*~*

The sound of hoofbeats woke me from the half-sleep I had fallen into. For a moment I panicked, thinking *Oh God, No! They have me!*

Then I remembered what I had done. I remembered the plan, and became very, very still.

The hoofbeats came closer and closer until, finally, they were like thunder in my ears. I resisted the urge to cover them.

Don't move, Lilly. Don't make a sound.

The thunder cut off.

The horses had come to a stop. I heard men dismounting and orders being shouted. The men were soldiers, that much was clear. Probably from the presidency armies, Lord Dalgliesh's personal band of merry minions.

'Jameson?'

At the sound of Lord Dalgliesh's sleek voice I couldn't help but drag in a sharp breath.

Calm, Lilly! Calm!

'Get the girl.'

'Yes, My Lord!'

'Carstairs?'

'Aye, Your Lordship?'

'Go and prepare the–'

But what exactly Carstairs was supposed to prepare we never found out. Because at that very moment, Jameson, who had entered the cabin, uttered a startled outcry. A moment later, he came dashing out again.

'Your Lordship! The girl! The girl, she...'

'She what? Speak, man!'

'She's gone!'

A deadly silence descended over the snow-covered fields. As a connoisseur of deadly silences, I could truly appreciate its fine qualities, particularly its soundless threat of murder and noise-free roar of rage.

'What,' His Lordship said very, very, calmly, 'did you just say?'

'The girl! She's gone! And, um, Sergeant Brewer...' The man cleared his throat. 'He's...well, you'd better see for yourself, Your Lordship.'

Hard steps marched past the soldier, into the cottage. I heard a fist slam so hard into a wall the whole building shuddered. Carefully, I peeked over the top of the log pile I was hiding behind – just in time to see Dalgliesh stride out again, red flecks of anger burning in his cheeks. The revolver in my hand suddenly felt very intriguing. Very heavy. Very significant.

For a moment I considered shooting him down where he stood. He was so close. Just one bullet, and Mr Ambrose and I would never have to worry again. One little shot...

...and his soldiers will gut you where you stand.

True. Blast!

Just then, the decision was taken out of my hands. Because in just that moment, Dalgliesh spotted the footsteps leading off, away from the cottage, towards the river. He whirled to face his men.

'After her!' he roared. 'Follow the tracks! She can't have gotten far! Find her, or I'll have your hides!'

Never in my life had I witnessed a detachment of soldiers mounting their horses this fast – not even the Queen's guards. In an instant, they were up on horseback and galloping across the snowy expanse, following my trail. The trail I had left while running towards the stream. The trail I had used to double back, walking backwards in my own footsteps.

I waited until they were a safe distance away, then rose with a smile from behind the log pile along one side of the cabin.

Checkmate, Dalgliesh!

I suppose I could have immediately set out in the opposite direction, but why hurry? Leaning against the wall, I stood there, smirking, waiting for them to disappear into the forest and thoroughly enjoying my victory. Outsmarting the enemy was fun under normal circumstances – but outsmarting the enemy when he was a pretentious, chauvinistic arse was simply sublime. I had to get myself kidnapped more often.

Just when I had arrived at that brilliant conclusion, I heard noise coming out of the woods. Frowning, I started to step out from behind the log pile to investigate – then stopped as I realised that the sounds were hoofbeats.

What? Was Dalgliesh already coming back? Had he seen through my ruse?

But no. The sounds were coming from a different direction. Besides...that sounded like a lot more riders than Lord Dalgliesh had had with him. Who in God's name would be riding through this arctic wasteland with half a company of men?

Making sure my revolver was cocked, I hunkered down behind the woodpile again. Whoever it was, if they'd come to take me, they would have a tough fight on their hands.

From my hiding place I couldn't see a thing of what was going on out there. With bated breath I waited as the thunder of hoofs approached. Horses whinnied. Tackle and weapons rattled. Then, finally, there came a voice:

'No one in sight, Sir. Should we go in?'

'Yes.'

Just one word. One small, insignificant word – but it turned the world on its head. I would have recognised that arctic voice anywhere. It made my wet feet feel toasty in comparison. A smile bloomed on my face, and all the tension to fight went out of me in an instant.

Nice of you to join me, Sir.

Trust Mr Rikkard Ambrose to do the impossible and find an unfindable place in the middle of nowhere. Warmth flooded through me. He had come for me! He had come to save me. Of course, I didn't actually need saving – but that was no reason to ruin his work. After all, he had obviously put so much effort into this rescue of his, I couldn't spoil it all for him by announcing I had already rescued myself, could I?

Closing my eyes with a smile, I leaned back against the woodpile. Yes. I'd stay here for a while. I would be considerate.

Plus, it would be great fun. I had never been able to listen to my own rescue before.

'If she's hurt...' That was Mr Ambrose again, cold as the ice at the heart of a glacier. 'Bring Dalgliesh to me. Alive.'

Bravo! An admirable amount of bloodthirsty vengefulness. Very good stuff so far, Mr Ambrose, Sir. Do continue.

'Yes, Sir!'

I heard the sound of men sliding off their horses and readying their weapons. Then...footsteps. The creak of a door, and finally – silence.

Very silent silence.

For quite a bit.

'Um...Sir?'

'Yes?'

'She's not here.'

'What?'

'She's not here, Sir. The only person who's here is, um...a naked man.'

Silence.

Even more silently silent than before. And cold. Oh, so cold. I grinned from ear to ear, safe in the knowledge that no one could see me behind the log pile. Oh, my rescue was turning out to be fun!

When Mr Ambrose next spoke, his voice was so icy, it nearly froze the water in my boots.

'What did you say?'

'A, err...naked man, Mr Ambrose, Sir.'

A few more moments passed without a sound. Then I heard someone sliding off the back of his horse, and the thud as his feet hit the ground. Somehow – don't ask me how – I knew who it had been. There had just been something so deliciously threatening and final about that thud.

'Out. Of. My. Way.'

'Yessir! Immediately, Sir.'

The brisk sound of marching feet, then again the creak of the door. From inside the cottage, I heard the delicious sound of a boot hitting a villain in the bollocks. Ah, what music to my ears...!

'Where is she? Where?'

'Nnn...what? I don't...'

Thud!

'Arg!'

'Where? Speak!'

I had to resist the urge to clap. As dramatic rescues went, this really was a prime performance. It almost made me wish I were still bound and helpless to see the final scene. Almost.

'Anderson! Renshaw! Get in here, and bring rope! Everyone else, spread out! Search the woods!'

I dared to peek over the pile. Two men were dismounting, hurriedly taking a coil of rope from one of the packhorses. They entered the cabin. The rest of them scattered to shouted commands in all directions. It wasn't long before they had disappeared into the forest. From inside the cottage, meanwhile, came the sounds of a naked man being turned into a casserole.

Time to make my entrance.

Rising from behind the log pile, I sauntered over to the lonely three horses remaining in front of the cabin. One of them I instantly recognised as the magnificent animal from the stable of the marquess that Mr Ambrose had ridden during my riding lessons.

'Hello there, you ugly beast,' I greeted him in a whisper and reached out to pat his head. The stallion promptly lunged and tried to bite my hand off.

'Yes, I missed you, too. But no time for sentimentality today.' Grinning, I grabbed the saddle and swung myself up on the horse. 'I think it's time we left, don't you?'

'Whee hee hee.'

I supposed that was stallionish for 'Of course, you silly hairless ape!' So I wasted no more time. Slipping two fingers between my lips, I took a deep breath and gave an ear-piercing whistle.

Inside the cottage, everything went deadly silent.

A moment later came racing footsteps, and Mr Rikkard Ambrose's face appeared at the window, eyes widened almost half a millimetre.

I gave him my prettiest smile. 'What are you waiting for, Sir? Let's go!'

CONFESSION BY INSTALMENTS

For a moment, one single, solitary moment, Mr Ambrose didn't move. Then he disappeared from the window, and a moment later, the door was torn open – literally. The flimsy thing flew right off its mouldy hinges and clattered to the floor somewhere inside. Mr Ambrose didn't seem to care. He was striding across the snow-covered yard with singular purpose, all his focus, all his icy energy, all his power concentrated on one thing – me.

He stopped a few paces away.

'Miss Linton.'

Just those two words. Nothing more. But the meaning vibrating in every syllable...

I swallowed.

'You took your time, Sir.'

His eyes met mine, delving, devouring, claiming.

'You seem to have managed well enough on your own.'

'Yes, I did, didn't I? Maybe I should just ride away and leave you here. It wasn't a particularly good rescue, you know.'

'Miss Linton?'

'Yes, Mr Ambrose, Sir?'

'Get off my horse.'

I smiled. 'I don't think so. I think I'll–'

But that was as far as I got. Because in the very next moment, Mr Rikkard Ambrose crossed the remaining distance between us. His arms lunged up. His foot found the stirrup. And the next thing I knew, he was half dragging himself up, half dragging me down. He didn't wait for either of us to make it the whole way before his lips claimed mine.

'Silence!' he growled against my mouth.

I didn't usually hold with men telling me to shut up – or telling me anything, for that matter. But with him kissing me like that...I might just make an exception. His mouth was a searing brand on mine. Waves of heat coursed through me, interlaced with shivers all over my body. How a man this cold could ignite such a fire inside of me was a mystery to me – but he did. Oh, how he did.

'My little *ifrit*,' he breathed against my lips.

'You should take your own good advice,' I shot back. 'Shut up and kiss me!'

I would never have thought Mr Rikkard Ambrose was one for taking orders. But this one he obeyed, fast, hard, and fierce. Strong arms encircled me, pulling me against a chest so hard you could break a chisel on it, nearly squeezing all the air out of me. In his kiss, his embrace, and every hard line of his body, I could feel the tension, screaming to be released. The realisation hit me like a boulder in the face: he had been scared. Scared for me.

I hugged him close and pressed my face into his chest before he could read the knowledge in my eyes.

'Thank you,' I murmured. 'Thank you for coming for me.'

In response, his grip tightened even more. 'I had no intentions of finding a new secretary. Do you know what vacancy advertisements cost these days?'

Glancing over his shoulder at the small army of riders approaching from every direction, I privately thought to myself that it would probably cost less than an escort of three dozen heavily armed men. However, I didn't voice this thought aloud. There were more important things to take care of right now.

Like continuing to kiss him?

Well, yes, that too. But first...

Lifting my face from his chest, I looked straight into his eyes. Our faces were so close that our foreheads touched. It felt...right.

'Let's get out of here!' I suggested.

'Agreed.'

Letting go of me, he took hold of the saddle, vaulting up onto the horse behind me. A short gasp escaped me as I felt him settling in so close, his chest pressing into my back. I had never felt anything like it. Even after all we had already done, this felt strangely intimate. A hundred times more so when his arms came around me, clutching me close.

My ears burning with embarrassment, I looked around. All the riders had returned by now and were gazing at me and Mr Ambrose with big, big eyes. It was clear that they knew Mr Rikkard Ambrose. It was also clear that they weren't used to seeing him sitting on horseback with his arms wrapped around a woman.

'Miss Linton,' my dear employer informed them in a tone cold enough to give frostbite, 'is a gently bred lady of good family and impeccable reputation. She would never do anything so rash as to kiss a man in public. If anyone were to suggest differently, I would be...displeased. Do we understand each other?'

Mesmerised, the men nodded.

'Adequate. Well, gentlemen? What are you waiting for? Ride!'

And before I could point out that I had been first on the horse and as such should be in charge, thank you very much, his hands grasped the reins.

'Gee-up!'

We raced off across the plain, snow spewing up right and left, a storm of crystals sparkling in the cold air. Around us, the riders followed suit, slowly forming a protective circle as we approached the woods. Leaning back, I relaxed into Mr Ambrose's hard chest. It felt nice, having someone to lean on. With a twinge of pain I realised that I had never had this before. Oh, I'd had my friends, and my little sister, but nothing like this. This felt different.

His arms around me tightened in silent agreement.

'How did you find me?' I whispered.

Somehow he understood me, even over the thunder of the hooves.

'I had sent one of my mother's servants with a letter to Newcastle requesting reinforcements from my agents and additional hired personnel as soon as Dalgliesh arrived,' he explained, his voice clipped. 'They arrived shortly after...after you...'

'After I disappeared,' I finished the sentence quietly.

He nodded. 'The room didn't look as if there had been a struggle. I surmised that the maid had been in league with Dalgliesh, and that she would be aiming to make a quick getaway after getting paid. So I sent three of my men to lay in wait on the road to the closest port city, and another three on the road south to London.' Even though I couldn't see his face, I could almost feel the cold glitter in his eyes. 'It wasn't long before she appeared.'

A smile tugged at one corner of my mouth. 'You have her?'

'Karim does. He's explaining the errors of her ways to her.'

'Oh.' That corner of my mouth curved up another inch or so. 'Oh dear.'

'Indeed.'

We fell silent then. But that wasn't a problem. Silence wasn't bad. In fact, cantering across the snowy expanse of the plain with Mr Ambrose's arms wrapped around me, snow swirling around us like miniature diamonds, it was bloody wonderful. I nearly made me forget that my wet feet were about to freeze.

'Bridge ahead, Sir!' the silence was broken by one of the riders. The man pointed ahead and, following the direction of his arm with my gaze, I saw a small bridge spanning a half-frozen river. The little thing had clearly seen better days – in the Middle Ages. Its weathered stones were covered by ivy and moss, and the arch seemed to sweep towards the sky with a sort of rheumatic charm: *Look here! I may be seven hundred years old, but I'm still in as good a shape as ever!*

'Developed an interest in medieval architecture, have you, Mr Ambrose?' I enquired.

'No. This is where we are meeting up with Karim and the other men.'

'The other men?'

'The maid could not provide any information on whether Dalgliesh had already removed you from the hut she saw you in. So I sent some men to Dalgliesh's closest holding, just in case.'

Dear me. He really had gone all out with this rescue. Carefully, out of the corner of my eye, I glanced up at the stern face of Mr Rikkard Ambrose. It was impassive and cold, just as immovable as ever, and yet, and yet...there was something in his eyes. Something that hadn't been there before. And I didn't mean a stye.

'Halt!'

Mr Ambrose raised a hand. Only a few yards away from the bridge, our cavalcade came to a stop. In an effortless move, Mr Ambrose slid out of the saddle, taking me with him. If I'd imagined him doing something silly and romantic like catching me in his arms, however, I was disappointed. I landed solidly on my own two feet.

How fabulous that I was a feminist and would never, ever expect such a thing!

'Spread out!' Mr Ambrose commanded. 'Dalgliesh's men may follow our trail and decide to attack. If they do, I want ample warning. Form a perimeter. Keep your guns handy, and be ready to fight.'

'Yes, Sir! You heard him, men. Go!'

The riders scattered, leaving Mr Ambrose and me alone at one end of the bridge.

'Come.' Jerking his head towards the moss-covered stone arc, Mr Ambrose strode forward. He stopped only when he was standing at the apex of the bridge. Resting his hands on the stone railing, he gazed out over the ice of the river. I stepped up beside him, hands under my armpits to protect them against the biting cold. A stiff breeze bit into my face, and a shiver ran down my spine.

'Bloody hell! You couldn't have found a warm spot to wait, could you?'

'At the time, Miss Linton, I had slightly more pressing matters on my mind.'

Like whether or not you would survive. He didn't say it, but he didn't need to. I heard the words as clear as a bell.

Silently, he lifted one arm, extending it towards me. Without even thinking about it, I scuttled closer, snuggling against him, his arm wrapped around my shoulder. Good God...! How could such a cold man feel so incredibly warm?

For a while we just stood there, gazing out across the icy river sparkling in the light of the sinking sun. The sunset was alive with fire, painting the entire expanse of ice and snow a glowing red-golden colour. It made the world look just like I felt: on fire in the grip of ice.

'Miss Linton?'

I resisted the temptation to glance up at Mr Ambrose's face. To judge by the sound of his voice, things might be visible there that he would not want anyone to see.

'Yes, Mr Ambrose, Sir?'

'While Dalgliesh had you in his power, did he...do anything? Hurt you in any way?'

The arm around my shoulders tightened to an almost painful degree. I didn't complain. Instead, I only pressed myself against him closer.

'No, he didn't harm me.' In order to keep him from starting a war in the middle of the English countryside, I decided it was probably better not to mention Dalgliesh's plans with regard to certain of my fingers. 'But he did talk quite a lot.'

'Whatever he told you was probably lies.'

I took a deep breath.

Here goes nothing...

'Oh? So you didn't run away from home as a boy because of an argument with your father, then?'

I felt him stiffen even more. Cold suddenly radiated from him in icy waves.

'It was somewhat more complicated than that, Miss Linton.'

Why? I screamed inside. *Why and how? Explain! I'm here for you! You can trust me!*

I wanted to ask all of that and more. But the tone of his voice made me think better of it. Whatever had happened – Dalgliesh had not told me the truth. Or at least not the whole truth. Half-truths could be so much more dangerous than lies, sometimes.

Later, Lilly. Later.

Reaching for his hand and giving it a squeeze, I leaned my head against him. 'I said it once already, I believe, but...thank you. I might have got out of there by myself – but then again, I might not have. If Dalgliesh had come back with enough men and searched the woods...'

I let the sentence trail off into a shudder. I didn't really want to imagine what might have happened then.

He hesitated a moment – then squeezed my hand back. When I glanced up at his face out of the corner of my eye, it was rigid and harder than ever. So hard, in fact, it looked close to shattering.

'I...had to come.'

My heart rate picked up. 'Really?'

His arm around my shoulders tightened once more, as if wanting to make sure I was really there. 'Yes.'

There was a moment of silence. Then...

'I am not a man who often expresses his emotions, Miss Linton.'

'You don't say?'

'But I must admit I was...somewhat concerned for you.'

I had to work hard to keep a smile from my face.

'Somewhat concerned? Dear God, really?'

Abruptly, he turned towards me, his eyes blazing with cold fire. 'Dammit! Do not joke, Miss Linton!'

I looked up at him, the picture of innocence drawn by a five-year-old with absolutely no artistic talent. 'I wouldn't dare!'

Stepping towards me, he reached out, until one of his hands gently touched my cheek. 'I...' He swallowed, and tried again. 'I might be slightly...irrationally infatuated with you.'

Warmth spread deep inside me. And on my face, a grin did. 'Irrationally infatuated? Dear me!'

His jaw clenched. 'All right, all right! I may even have certain...impulses towards you that border on caring about you.'

'You don't say?' I raised an eyebrow at him. 'Well, I am so glad to hear that you feel a certain amount of *friendship* towards me.'

His dark gaze pierced me accusingly. But I was enjoying this far too much to stop. I wouldn't make it easy for him.

'Friendship is not quite the right word, Miss Linton,' he bit out between clenched teeth, every word like a shard of burning ice. 'My impulses towards you...they might go slightly beyond the platonic.'

'Oh, so they are Aristotelian?'

'Mr Lin–' He swallowed, hard. 'I mean *Miss* Linton, we are not discussing philosophy here!'

I batted my eyelashes at him. 'Indeed? Then pray tell, what are we discussing?'

'I...I...'

'You can say it, you know,' I told him. 'The word isn't poisonous.'

'I...have feelings towards you.'

'Clearly. I knew that from the first day from the way you shouted at me and pelted me with threats.'

'Not *those* kinds of feelings!'

'What kind, then?'

'I feel...affection towards you.'

'You're nearly there,' I encouraged him, my smile widening. 'Just four little letters. The word starts with L. Go on. You can do it.'

'You're enjoying this, Miss Linton, aren't you?'

'Very much so.'

'Oh, to hell with it!' Dropping his hand from my face, he grabbed both my shoulders roughly and dragged me towards him. His mouth took mine in a fast, fierce, bruising kiss. It went on and on until I thought my lungs would burst and my mind catch fire. Finally, he broke away, and with the remnants of his breath whispered: 'I love you!'

IS YOUR PULSE WORKING, MY LOVE?

When Karim returned with an escort of armed riders a quarter of an hour later, Mr Ambrose and I were standing at the stone railing, a proper distance between us, studying the frozen river with an interest which rivalled that of two professional limnologists.[14] What we had been doing two minutes earlier...well, that was another matter. But nobody needed to know about that. Especially not Karim, who worked so hard to preserve the innocence of his eyes.

Smiling, I turned to greet the big man.

'Greetings, oh Prince Fragrant Yellow Flower in the Happy Moonlight. Shall we return to your ancestral palace of Gobbledygook in the principality of Rubbish?'

'*Sahib*,' my favourite walking mountain enquired with unmoving features, 'may I shoot her?'

'No!'

Mr Ambrose's order came perhaps a bit faster and more forceful than it would have done a day ago. But neither Karim nor anyone else seemed to notice. I noticed, though. I noticed a lot. And the warmth blossoming inside me wasn't the least bit dampened when he added: 'It would be a waste to exterminate her when we just spent so much money to reacquire her.'

Karim gave a reluctant grunt of agreement. With a hand signal, he called our guards from their positions. Mr Ambrose lifted me onto the stallion's back and then swung himself up behind me.

'Can I take the reins this time, Sir?'

'No.'

'I thought you loved m–'

A hand clapped over my mouth, cutting off all sound.

'Don't you dare!' he hissed. 'Don't you dare say it aloud! Someone might hear!'

'Mmnmmmh?'

'If you say it out loud, I will make your life a living hell.'

Which is different from my usual work schedule as your secretary how exactly?

It's too bad that you can't use smart comebacks when someone is holding a hand over your mouth. So, instead, I nipped his finger.

'Mr Linton!'

Dear me...we would really have to work on this gender issue. Otherwise, I might have to view his recent confession in an entirely new light.

Slowly, as if he were still afraid I might utter forbidden words in front of his men, he let his hand drop from my mouth.

'Let's get going, men. To Battlewood Hall!'

And he gave his mount the spurs. The horse sprang forward and I was jolted back against Mr Ambrose – to which I by no means objected. Stretching up towards him, I placed my lips right next to his ear and whispered: '*Love*.'

His arms tightened around me. 'You are incorrigible.'

'Well, then start to encourage me.' I nipped his earlobe. 'It's about time you did.'

He was silent for a moment. Then...

'Maybe.'

---

[14] Limnology: the study of rivers.

Eh? Agreement from Mr Rikkard Ambrose? Was I dreaming?

'Mr Ambrose?'

Silence.

'Mr Ambrose? Is something wrong?'

Again, no answer. My neck began to prickle. Something was wrong. Not because of the silence – no, that was to be expected. It was the sort of silence that worried me. Thoughtful. Planning. Scheming. It was the silence of a man deciding the future.

Oh, Lilly, don't be so overdramatic! Silence is just lack of noise. You can't honestly pretend to know this one sounds different from another, can you?

Shaking my head, I shoved my anxious thoughts aside. This was no time to be suspicious! What dire plans could Mr Ambrose be hatching, after all? He had just come rescue me. He loved me. He might even – with a little persuasion – give me a day off now and again. What could he possibly be plotting?

~~**~*~*

'Miss Linton?'

'Mmmh...'

'Miss Linton, wake up.'

'Nnnn. Nnmmph.'

'Wake up, Miss Linton.'

'Nmmm...'

'Mr Linton, wake up right now! That is an order!'

My head snapped up. 'Yes, Sir! Which file do you need, Sir? I– oh.'

Blinking, I took out the winter landscape rushing past around us. Over the thunder of hooves, I heard a choked sound from the left. I threw a suspicious glance at Karim, who had his lower face hidden behind one big paw. The corners of his eyes were suspiciously crinkled.

'What is the matter?' I yawned, stretching my arms and half turning to glance up at Mr Ambrose. 'Getting tired of holding me, were you?'

'No. We have arrived.'

'Arrived? I don't see–'

Just then, we crested the last hill and before us stretched the magnificent sight of the Battlewood Hall. I sucked in a breath. Of course, I had known that Battlewood was magnificent before, but only from up here, seeing its glory in entirety, could I truly appreciate the beauty of the place.

'It's magnificent,' I whispered.

'It is acceptable.' Mr Ambrose's voice was cool and detached. 'Though not as large as my private country house.'

I nearly fell off the horse.

'*You* have a country house?'

'Why so surprised, Miss Linton?'

'Because maintaining those things is more expensive than paying King Midas' annual tax bill!'

'Oh, I have found a way to make things a little more profitable.'

I would have pounced on that and demanded more information if not, at that very moment, a shout had sounded from the manor steps.

'Rick! Miss Linton!'

That voice! Was that...

My eyes flicked to the direction the shout had come from.

Yes!

A grin spreading over my face, I jumped down from the horse and, not paying any heed to Mr Ambrose's protests, raced down the hill towards the small figure running up towards me caring not in the least if her dress got wet or muddy. A moment later, I slammed into Adaira Louise Jannet Melanie Georgette Ambrose, daughter of the The Most Honourable The Marquess Ambrose, and hugged her so tightly I probably risked squeezing the breath out of her. Oh, how I had missed this girl!

'Miss Linton! Oh God, Miss Linton I'm so glad you're safe!'

And she, apparently, had missed me.

'There, there,' I muttered, wiping her tears away. 'Don't do that at this temperature! You'll turn into an ice sculpture.'

She hiccupped, giggled, and pulled out a handkerchief to blow her nose.

To heck with my plans to become friends with this girl! We already were. End of story.

Or maybe the beginning of one.

The thought made me smile.

Behind us, someone cleared his throat.

'When the two of you have finished this superfluous display of exuberance,' the arctic tones of Rikkard Ambrose cut through our girl moment, 'I shall be taking Miss Linton to the house. She needs rest and a change of clothes.'

'A change of – oh.' Adaira seemed only just then to notice the ill-fitting trousers and coat I had somehow managed to wrestle onto my body. 'Oh. Yes, I see what you mean. Get her inside without mother seeing, will you? I'd like her to survive into the next year, and the sight might be too much for her heart.'

'I shall do my best. Come, Miss Linton.'

Taking me by the arm with surprising gentleness, Mr Ambrose was just about to start leading me off towards the house – but then Adaira seemed to remember something.

'Wait!'

'What?' Mr Ambrose turned back to her – and she slapped him, hard, on the arm.

'Ow! What the-'

'That's for taking so long! You had me so worried!'

His left little finger twitched. 'Your concern is duly noted. Now, may I depart, or do you wish to visit further punishment upon me?'

'Not just now. But I'll come with you in case I change my mind.'

'Indeed.'

Without further comment, Mr Ambrose turned and marched me off towards the back of the house. Karim and his men followed as inconspicuously as a giant bearded bodyguard with turban, sabre and an escort of forty mounted man can. Not very.

'What in God's name is going on here?' came a stunned voice from beyond the circle of armed men around me. 'Who are you people? Leave! Get off this property immediately! This is the House of the Marquess–'

'–of Ambrose,' finished Mr Ambrose's cool, composed voice. 'I know.'

'M-master Rikkard?'

'Indeed.'

'Master Rikkard, who are these people?' The crowd parted, revealing the started face of Elsby, the steward. 'What do they want? Why–'

Then he caught sight of me.

His eyes widened to the size of dinner plates. Only with the admirable restraint of a domestic servant who had trained his whole life to bear the shenanigans of the upper classes with perfect dignity did he manage to keep his jaw from dropping to the floor.

'Miss...Miss Linton?'

'I'm so glad to see you, Elsby,' I told him with a smile, and tugged at the dirty trousers peeking out under my dress. 'I feel that I am in need of a change of clothes. Would you be so kind as to have a maid bring something appropriate to my room?'

'Of course, Miss. Immediately, Miss.' The steward bowed and was already turning around when Mr Ambrose's sharp command held him back.

'Elsby!'

'Yes, Master Rikkard?'

'Not. One. Word. To. Anyone.'

'Certainly, Master Rikkard.'

Taking my arm in an iron grip, Mr Ambrose pulled open a back door and rushed me into the house.

'Concerned for my reputation, are you?' I whispered up at him.

'No. For Karim's.'

'Oh, that's so sweet!'

My armed guard surrounding me in a protective shield, I was escorted swiftly to my room. Mr Ambrose, Adaira and Karim stayed with me the whole time, and if any servants caught sight of my circle of guards, I noticed nothing of it apart from the squeals they made as they were shoved out of the way. To be honest, I was glad for it. The exhaustion of the last day was finally catching up with me. I guess kidnapping takes its toll on you. I just about managed to stagger along with Mr Ambrose supporting me on one side and Adaira on the other.

Finally, we came to a halt in front of a familiar door.

'Open,' Mr Ambrose commanded, and Karim hurried to obey. I was dragged inside like a very tired, badly dressed sack of potatoes. Ignoring Adaira's protestations that she should be the one to help me, and what in God's name did her brother think, entering a lady's room like that, Mr Ambrose picked me up and carried me the last few steps to the bed. More gently than I would have believed him capable of, he lowered me to the mattress.

A moment later, Adaira appeared beside me.

'Oh, my poor dear! Are you all right?'

'Of course,' I wanted to say. 'Why wouldn't I be all right?'

But what came out sounded more like 'O-of ck-ckoco...cor...'

That was when I realised that my teeth were chattering.

'Oh Lord! She's going into shock!'[15]

'F-feet,' I managed. 'Off...f-feet...!'

'She's hallucinating!' Bending forward, Adaira began to gently stroke my forehead. 'Don't worry. Your feet haven't fallen off. If you don't see them, that's just in your imagination.'

'I believe what she is trying to say,' Mr Ambrose commented, 'is that her feet are cold and she wants us to take her wet shoes off.'

'Oh. Right.'

Karim stepped forward with a determined expression, but Adaira instantly held up a hand. 'Oh no you don't, big boy! Out!' She waved at the men I could just about see, gathered at the doorway, through the haze covering my eyes. 'All of you, out! This is lady's work!'

The men retreated faster than you could say 'Jack Robinson'.

Well...all except one.

'Have I missed something?' Adaira cocked her head at her brother. 'Are you a lady?'

He met her gaze implacably. 'No.'

'Well then get ou–'

He lifted a finger. One finger. That was all it took to silence her. Holy moly! I had known a whole lot of families in my life, and a whole lot of people with amazing talents. But never in my life had I seen a man who could shut his little sister up with just one look. I had to get him to teach me that trick. Maybe I could use it on the twins.

'Rick, I really don't think–'

'Not another word,' Mr Ambrose cut her short. Striding past her, he knelt at my feet. Yes, Rikkard Ambrose, *the* Mr Ambrose, the most powerful business mogul in the British Empire, knelt at *my* feet. Granted, it was for the purpose of removing my wet boots, but still...

'Let him stay,' I croaked.

Adaira looked at me, then at her brother, then back at me. Rolling her eyes, she knelt beside my other foot. Soon, the wet things were off, and my feet, along with the rest of me, were wrapped in thick woollen blankets. Dimly, through the thick veil exhaustion had cast over me, I could hear Adaira ordering servants to bring hot broth and wood for the fireplace. Mr Ambrose was a comforting presence, sitting just about as far away as propriety required, his

---

[15] In case anyone is wondering why modern medical terminology is used here: the term 'shock' is quite old, and was first employed by French surgeon Henri François Le Dran in 1743. He had observed the phenomenon while operating on wounded soldiers. His work was translated, and soon the term was used throughout the English-speaking medical world.

hand clasping mine in a firm grip. Slowly, safe in the knowledge that all was well now, I began to sink off into darkness.

'Karim?'

The cold voice seemed to come from very, very far away...

'Yes, *Sahib*?'

'Tell the men to get some rest. Be ready to ride in three hours, with provisions for a one week journey.'

'Yes, *Sahib*.'

Journey? I found myself frowning in half-sleep. Why would we go anywhere? Why would we do anything now that we were safe and well?

But before I could even start to ponder the matter, I was swept away into the realm of sleep.

~~**~*~*

When I awoke, the morning sun was shining through the frost-coated windows. A tall, dark, figure was standing in front of the largest arched window, the dawn painting a red-golden halo around him. It was probably the only time ever that he would remotely remind me of an angel.

'Good morning, Sir,' I croaked.

He stiffened at the sound of my voice. Slowly, he turned around to face me. His cool gaze swept over me in a way that made me shiver – and it had nothing whatsoever to do with icy feet. There was something new in his eyes when he looked at me. The same kind of look he wore when gazing at gold, banknotes and London real estate. A look that said: *You're mine. You just don't know it yet.*

'Miss Linton.' Striding across the room, he reached out and snatched up my hand.

'What–'

'Silence!'

Shoving up my sleeve, he pressed a thumb to my wrist. I waited for a moment or two – but he didn't do anything. Was he checking my pulse?

He was!

A moment later, he let go of my wrist and started wagging a finger in front of my eyes. I followed the motion instinctively, and he gave a nod to himself and started feeling my skull for bruises.

In a flash, I realised what he was doing. He was checking me for injuries. How did he know how to do this? There was still so much about him I didn't know.

'You know...you could just *ask* if I am all right.'

'Yes. I could.'

He left off my skull and continued with my arms and hands. I had no idea if he knew what he was doing, but what the heck? I just sat there and let him do it. It wasn't exactly as if I was opposed to letting him touch me.

Finally finished with his examination, he let go of me and took a step back.

'You are well.'

A smile tugged at the corner of my mouth. 'I could have told you that myself.'

He didn't smile. 'I had to make sure.'

Something tugged at my heart, and I had to swallow. 'Thanks.'

'You've been through a lot – but you're strong. Strong enough.'

I blinked. 'Strong for what?'

Pulling back a chair, he settled himself down behind a table in the middle of the room. Sitting like that, gazing at me with that cold, sea-coloured gaze, it almost felt as if I was Mr Victor Linton again, back in his London office, and he was the man who ruled my life.

'Strong enough for the journey, Miss Linton.'

'Journey? What journey?'

'Karim!' At Mr Ambrose's call, the door opened and the Mohammedan entered, grim-faced.

'You called, *Sahib*?'

'Is everything ready for the journey?'

'Yes, *Sahib*.'

'What journey?' I insisted. A cold tingle went down my back.

'Ready the men.' Dismissing Karim with an imperious wave, Mr Ambrose turned his full attention back to me.

'For the last time, Sir,' I whispered. '*What journey?*'

'Why, the journey to Scotland, of course, Miss Linton.'

'We're back at Battlewood, where we're supposed to be. What in God's name do you want in Scotland?'

Mr Ambrose nailed me to the chaise longue with his arctic eyes. His reply was one short, precise word. But it was enough to freeze my blood and rob my lungs of breath.

'Marriage.'

TAKEOVER NEGOTIATIONS

I sat there for a full five minutes, staring at him in silent shock, wondering if I'd heard right. Finally, Mr Ambrose pulled out his pocket watch, let it snap open and gazed at the clock face.

'Will this hibernation take long, Miss Linton? We have to get going if we want to reach the inn halfway between here and Gretna Green before sundown.'

Slowly, very slowly, I opened the mouth that didn't feel like mine right now. 'Marriage?'

The word echoed as if someone else had spoken it on another world, millions of miles away. It couldn't actually apply to this place. To us. To me.

'Matrimony, Miss Linton. Also known as wedlock. A common social custom in the United Kingdom of Great Britain and Ireland, if I'm not mistaken.'

His words helped me shake off some of the shock.

'I'm not going to marry you!'

His eyes narrowed infinitesimally.

'No?'

'No, Sir! Most definitely absolutely a hundred and twenty per cent no!'

If I had expected a reply along the lines of 'Argh, argh! How could you? You have shattered my heart! I shall live the rest of my life in hermitage in the woods and pine for you among the pines!' I would have been severely disappointed. Mr Rikkard Ambrose was no Romeo or Tristan. He simply steepled his fingers and regarded me over their tips with icy concentration. When he spoke, his voice was as cool and composed as ever, and ten times as implacable.

'Wrong.'

I blinked. 'Did you just tell me that I was wrong?'

'Indeed.'

'Fascinating. So you know more about what I'm going to do than I do, Sir?'

'Likely, since the same is the case with most subjects, Miss Linton.'

My hands clenched into fists. All right...if he had been planning to get on the top ten of most ruthlessly chauvinist proposals, he was off to a good start.

'Why on earth would I want to marry *you*?' I growled.

Maybe because you love him, Lilly? a little voice inside suggested.

True. But he didn't know that yet. And if he stayed on this course, hell would freeze over before I'd tell him!

'Why wouldn't you?' He cocked his head quizzically, as if any woman on the street would instantly be willing to marry him.

Which was probably true. Damn!

'Well, for starters,' I ground out between clenched teeth, 'you haven't even asked me!'

'And I'm not going to.'

'*What*?'

Dark, sea-coloured eyes bored into me with a force that could make a king's knees buckle. 'Why ask when I already know it's going to happen?'

The bloody arrogant son of a...! How dare he! How dare he...

...be right?

No! I told my inner voice. *Shut up! He's not right! He's not!*

I wasn't going to marry anyone. Never! Husbands had complete power over their wives. Power the like of which tyrants only dreamed of. Images flashed through my mind of countless reports I'd read, stories I'd heard from my friends, of women being dominated, tyrannised or even beaten by the men they had bound themselves to. I clenched my teeth. Not that I believed Mr Ambrose would ever raise a hand to me. But dominate and tyrannise? Hell, yes! That was his favourite pastime!

Well, but if he's doing it already, why not make it official?

Shut up! I snapped at that annoying inner voice of mine as, for just a moment, the gruesome pictures of newspaper headlines were replaced with an image of Mr Ambrose's hand in mine. *Shut up, shut up, shut up!*

Slowly, Mr Rikkard Ambrose rose from behind the table and started to stalk towards me.

'Why?' he demanded.

'Why what?'

'Don't play dumb with me, Miss Linton. Why won't you marry me?'

'What does it matter? I simply won't! The reasons are of no importance!'

'Oh yes, they are! A no is just a problem to be solved. *Tell me!*'

His command slammed down on me with all the cold force of his voice – the powerful voice of a man who knew how to make men obey.

Well...how fortunate for me that I wasn't a man, then.

'No!'

He took another step closer. His eyes roamed my face, searching for clues with perfect attention to detail.

'You're afraid.'

Crap!

'No, I'm not!'

Another step closer. He had almost reached me when suddenly he veered sideways and began to circle me. I felt like a shipment of prized goods being evaluated for purchase, or a company analysed before the big takeover. Well...maybe, to him, I was.

'What are you afraid of, Miss Linton?' his whisper came from behind me, cool and in control of everything. In spite of this, no, because of it, it was the most seductive thing I'd ever heard. 'Just tell me. Problems exist to be solved. Let me solve yours. Marry me.'

'Marriage *is* the problem!' I snapped. 'I will never marry!'

'So...' He appeared in front of me again, his dark eyes glittering with knowledge. *Knowledge is Power is Time is Money*. His words echoed in my mind as I stared up at him, unable to break his gaze. 'It's not marriage to me you object to. It's marriage on principle.'

Bloody hell, he was quick! Why did I have to fall in love with someone who wasn't just too smart for his own good, but mine as well?

Hard hands slammed into the chaise longue on either side of me, caging me in. Leaning down, Rikkard Ambrose brought his perfect, chiselled face within a few inches of mine.

'Marry. Me.'

'No!' Quickly, I ducked under his arm and jumped to my feet. Taking a few hasty steps backward, I threw my arms into the air. 'Why would you want to marry me, anyway?'

His eyes narrowed infinitesimally. 'Humility? From you?'

'Ha! You wish!' My eyes narrowed as well. And not just a bit. 'I know that I'm fantabulous. I'm just not sure why you would agree. Knowledge is Power is Time is Money, remember? A marriage with me won't bring you power or money, that's for sure. And I'll probably take up lots of your time, particularly at night!'

'Miss Linton!'

'That leaves knowledge.' I took a step forward, one corner of my mouth curving up. 'Is that it? Would you like to know me, Sir? In every sense of the word?'

The only warning I got was a growl an instant before he pounced on me. His fingers buried themselves in my hair and pulled me helplessly towards him. His mouth hit mine in an explosion of a kiss. A hard kiss. A dominant kiss. It proved every word I'd thought and spoken. And still...I couldn't stop. We kissed and kissed and kissed until the world was sparkling with imaginary stars and the blood was burning in my veins.

When we finally broke apart, my knees felt weak and I had to cling on to him to remain upright.

'Why?' I demanded. 'Why me?'

His face was a mask of stone and ice. How could he look as cool and composed after a kiss like this?

Easily. By being Rikkard Ambrose.

'Why?' I repeated in a whisper.

'For simple reasons,' he told me, his voice just as cool and composed as his face. 'I had always planned to marry at some point in the future. Contrary to my preferences on the matter, I shall not live forever, and I need an heir to my fortune. You seem as capable of producing one as any other woman of marriageable age.'

Why, thank you for the compliment, Sir. You are too kind.

'Besides,' a muscle in his throat moved as he swallowed. 'After what I told you on the bridge...'

He left the sentence hanging in the air.

I promptly grabbed it and rammed it into the ground. 'You mean the fact that you love me?'

'Shh!' He let go of me as if I were on fire. Hurriedly taking a step back, he glanced around to see if anyone was in hearing range. 'Silence, Miss Linton!'

'What?' I blinked. 'You mean about the fact that you're in love with me?'

'I said silence!' Dear God, was it my imagination, or did Rikkard Ambrose actually look nervous? He did! Rushing to the door, he ripped it open, glanced outside and slammed it shut again. Was he checking for people listening at keyholes? Oh my Lord, this was too good! A grin tugged at the corners of my mouth.

Capping my hands around my mouth, I took a deep, deep breath. 'Hello? Anyone around? Mr Rikkard Ambrose loves me! He is head over heels in love with me and wants to marry me! Anyone interested? He loooves me! Would anyone like details? No? Good, but I'll repeat it anyway just in case anyone hasn't heard yet! He looooommmph!'

A masculine hand slapped down across my mouth.

'Mmm! Mmmph!'

'Miss Linton,' he enquired in a very calm, very controlled voice. 'Do you know the meaning of the word "discreet"?'

When he carefully removed his hand from my mouth, I told him with a cheeky smile: 'Yes. It means "separate".'

Cold fire flashed in his eyes. 'You...! We'll be lucky if no one heard you.'

'Don't worry,' I reassured him. 'The walls of this house are at least as thick as your head.'

Sliding his grip from my mouth to my chin, he turned my head to face him. The cold fire was still burning bright there.

'I want you. I even...well, you remember what I said on the bridge.'

I batted my eyelashes at him. 'That you *love* me?'

'Do not push me, Miss Linton. *Don't. Use. That. Word.*'

His tone was such that, for once, I did as suggested.

'I want you,' he repeated. 'I even...care for you to some extent.'

Some extent my rosy smelling foot!

'So why not marry me? My offer is the best one you are ever likely to receive.'

Oh, thank you so much for pointing that out. That was really wonderful to hear.

'It would be useless to deny these facts,' he told me. 'Marriage is the logical conclusion. Once we are wed, you will belong to me fully and completely. I will owe you my protection, and you will owe me your love and obedience. It is the perfect agreement. Why will you not consent?'

I gazed up into his cold, calm, unbelievably beautiful face and wondered how a man this intelligent could be so dense.

'You just listed all the reasons,' I whispered. 'There's more to life than belonging to a man. I will not sign my freedom over to anyone – not even you.'

Especially not you. Because you're the one person that might be able to make me forget to regret.

His grip tightened. His eyes bored into me with renewed force, trying to subdue me with sheer force of will – and nearly succeeding. 'Marry me!'

I swallowed. I had to gather all my strength to squeeze out the one syllable that saved my life and chipped a tiny, but very important piece off my heart.

'No.'

Then, suddenly, a grin curved up one corner of my mouth. 'There's always an alternative, you know.'

He blinked. Mr Rikkard Ambrose actually *blinked.*

'Alternative?'

'Yes. We could try living in sin.'

Only on very few occasions had I been privileged enough to see something akin to a facial expression flicker over that stone mask he called his face. Never before had it been as sweet as this one.

'*I beg your pardon,* Miss Linton?'

'You have it,' I told him generously. 'So, would you like to take my clothes off now?'

The temperature in the in the room instantly shifted. But did it go up or down, or all over the place? I had no idea. His eyes were suddenly burning into mine in an entirely new way, and shivers were shooting up and down my spine. I was hot and cold and everything beyond, all at once. When his hands dug into my arms, pulling me hard against his chest, my breath hitched.

'Have you lost your mind, Miss Linton?'

'I don't know, Sir. Would you like me to check my pockets?'

His sea-coloured gaze devoured my eyes, my face, my entire body. 'I am a gentleman, Miss Linton. I have done many things in my life – fought, threatened, even killed when it was necessary. But never have I ever taken advantage of a woman.'

One corner of my mouth quirked up. 'Only because you thought it would be a waste of your precious time.'

'Well yes, but–'

'Thought as much.'

His grip tightened even more. For a moment, it became almost painful. Almost. 'My motivation is not the issue here!'

'Isn't it?' Slowly, I leaned toward him until my breath was skimming over his skin. I felt him stiffen under my hands. 'There's no need for promises or lifelong commitments. You want me. I want you, and have given up wondering why. Let's do this. Right here. Right now.'

'No. Marry me!'

'No. Seduce me!'

'That,' he ground out between clenched teeth,' is what *you* are doing to *me*, Miss Linton.'

'Oh? Well... I guess I am.' I grinned. 'Is it working?'

'No!'

'Too bad.' Riding up on my tiptoes, I brought my mouth to his throat, skimming my lips over his skin, up to his ear. 'Are you sure?'

A muscle in his jaw twitched with the effort to remain immobile. I kissed his neck, and his entire body shuddered. 'I. Am. A. Gentleman.'

'What,' I whispered, sliding one hand up to the top button of his tailcoat, 'if I don't want you gentle?'

Something snapped. Maybe something in him. Maybe something in both of us. In an instant, I was pushed back against the door, the hard surface heating beneath me. Grabbing my hands, Mr Ambrose slammed them against the wood.

'These are too dangerous to be allowed to roam free,' he growled.

Breathing heavily, I gazed up into his mesmerising eyes. 'I could say the same of you, Sir.'

'No, you couldn't.'

'Oh? Why not?'

'Because you can't say anything while I do *this*,' he told me, and claimed my mouth with a kiss. My knees buckled. If he hadn't been holding me upright, I would have fallen flat on my face. This was a kiss unlike any we had shared before. We had kissed with need; we had kissed with passion. We had even – when Mr Ambrose had temporarily taken leave of his senses – kissed with tenderness. But never ever before had he kissed me in a way that sent a message: *you're mine. And it's only a matter of time before you realise that.*

He tore his mouth away and stared at me, a cold ferocity in his face that made me shiver inside.

'Marry me.'

'No.' My eyes were just as fierce as his, and just as full of fiery need. 'I'm free, and that's how I'm going to remain! But...' Stretching up, I leaned into him, running my lips along his collarbone. '...that doesn't mean we can't finish what we started.'

His hands tightened around my wrists. 'Don't! Don't, I...'

'Just say yes,' I whispered. 'There's no need for a ceremony. Just you and me, and a few hours that will remain our little secret forever.'

Through my clothes and his, I could feel his heart pounding against me. He wanted this. Wanted me. Badly. I nearly had him. Rising up further, I skimmed my lips over his jaw, towards his mouth, and–

–and suddenly he was gone. I stumbled forward, barely able to keep standing. Blinking through a haze of need, I just saw the ends of his tailcoat disappearing through a door at the other end of the room. Then it slammed shut, leaving me alone.

He had run.

Mr Rikkard I-Can-Vanquish-Anything-Or-Anyone Ambrose had run from me, little nineteen-year-old feminist secretary me. Dear Lord. I wasn't quite sure whether I should feel angry at him or proud of myself. Panting, I leaned back against the door – just in time to have the doorknob jabbed into my generous derriere.

'Hello?' came Lady Samantha's worried voice from the other side. 'Hello, is someone in there? Miss Linton? Adaira? The door won't open! Is it jammed?'

THE ANNOUNCEMENT

'Hello?' The doorknob rattled against my behind. 'Hello? Is anyone in there?'

I jumped away from the door as if a bear had bitten me in the butt. And, I supposed, in a way it had. As the door opened and Lady Samantha's motherly, radiant face appeared in the doorway, all I could think was:

OhmyGodohmyGodohmyGodIjustofferedtohaveanintimateaf-faiwiththissweetlady'sson!I'msogoingtohell!

And I didn't even believe in hell.

But when Lady Samantha smiled at me and a moment later hugged me close, that sort of made me believe a tiny little bit in heaven.

'Oh, my dear, I'm so glad you're back! I hope the Sultana is all right?'

It was good she was still hugging me. That way, she didn't see my jaw drop open.

'The...what?'

'The Sultana, dear! Adaira told me how you had to leave suddenly, because the Sultana of Bakavāsa had arrived in the country for a visit, and you had to be there to greet her, since she was an old friend of your mother's.'

'Oh, she did, did she?'

'I never knew that you moved in such exalted circles, dear.'

'Neither did I.'

'Pardon, what did you say?'

'I said, *I'm a little bit shy.*'

'Oh, that's so adorable.' She gave me a last hug before letting me go. 'Look at you! You look all flushed and pretty. Was the journey bracing?'

'Um...oh yes.'

And so was having my mouth ravished by your son.

'The Sultana is well, I trust?'

I managed to get a smile on my face. 'The Sultana of Bakavāsa is as well as she's ever been.'

'Oh, I'm so glad to hear that, my dear. I had to admit, I was slightly worried.'

'Worried?'

'Yes, I...' Lady Samantha glanced aside, looking almost too guilty for such a sweet soul. 'I understood that you had to go greet your mother's old friend, of course, and I would never have asked you to do differently, but...I really hoped that you wouldn't be long. I'm so glad you managed to return in time for the Christmas ball.'

'You are?'

'Yes.'

She peeked up at me.

'Has my son come to see you since your return?'

Suddenly, the atmosphere in the room was prickling. I wet my dry lips. *Bloody hell, bloody hell, bloody hell, what to say?*

'He came to see me.'

'I thought perhaps he might. Did he say anything?'

You mean apart from commanding me to elope with him?

'Not much.'

That much at least was true. His mouth had been otherwise engaged most of the time.

'Miss Linton...' Again, Lady Samantha glanced up at me. 'I hope I'm not being too presumptuous when I say that it would make an old woman very happy to see you dance with my son at the Christmas ball. I couldn't wish for a better gift.'

My breath caught. Was she hinting...

No.

It couldn't be.

But still...it sounded very much as if she was giving the two of us her blessing.

Oh Lord! How was I ever supposed to tell this sweet lady that her son had just proposed to me, and I had turned him down? I couldn't! It was that simple. I could tell Mr Rikkard Ambrose no without a second thought, but not his mother.

'I'll save a space on my dance card for him,' I promised. *Among the three dozen other empty places that will probably be there.*

Abruptly, Her Ladyship looked up, and in her eyes, I saw her heart bared. A mother's heart.

'And in your heart, Miss Linton? Will you save a space for him there, too?'

The blood drained from my face – then rushed back in a flush of heat. What was wrong with me? I never blushed! Never!

'W-what do you mean?'

You stuttered! You just stuttered!

She gazed up me with a sweetness that was more deadly than the coldest stare Mr Ambrose had ever given me. 'I think you know what I mean, Miss Linton.'

Oh crap.

I swallowed.

'Your son is...very dear to me,' I managed somehow. Don't ask me how. 'I care for him a great deal.'

'Has he asked you?'

By the tone in her voice I knew she wasn't talking about reserving a dance at the ball.

'No,' I told her, my ears turning red. *He just ordered me.*

She gazed at me for a moment longer – then seemed to reach some private conclusion, nodded to herself and took my hand, squeezing it gently. 'I'm really glad you're back, dear. I have a feeling things are going to work out very well.'

And, with that cryptic statement, she turned around and left the room.

~~**~*~*

'Attention, please, my Lords, Ladies and Gentlemen.' Lady Samantha picked up a fork and delicately struck it against a wineglass, evoking a pure, serene sound. 'I have an announcement to make.'

The whole table fell silent.

We were sitting at breakfast – Adaira, her mother, me and all the other guests. The only ones missing were iceberg senior and iceberg junior. I was just thanking God, the fates and any other deities within listening distance for the latter, when the French windows were thrust open and, among a swirl of snow and cold air, Rikkard Ambrose marched into the breakfast parlour. Shutting the French windows behind him, he strode to the table and took the empty seat right opposite me.

Oh crap.

'Um...well, as I was saying, my announcement...' Lady Samantha attempted a warm smile. It was no easy feat in the same room as Rikkard Ambrose, whose mere presence seemed to suck up all the warmth in a fifty-yard radius. 'We're having the Christmas ball tomorrow evening, on Christmas Eve. Isn't that wonderful?'

Mr Ambrose reached up, picked two nuts out of a bowl in in the middle of the table and closed his hand around them. His other hand came down in a lightning-fast move. There was an ear-splitting crack, and everyone flinched.

'Err...yes, Your Ladyship,' Major Strickland managed, watching Mr Ambrose calmly dissect the shattered nuts out of the corner of his eye. 'Most wonderful indeed.'

'We shall have such a merry time,' the marchioness enthused. 'I have hired the best musicians for the occasion, a quartet straight from Paris. They've played before King Louis Philippe and Emperor Ferdinand of Austria.'

'Then why,' Mr Ambrose asked, his voice as cold as a winter night, 'were they desperate enough to come here?'

Shoving the nuts into his mouth, he grabbed another pair.

Lady Samantha cleared her throat and tried to regain the attention of her audience. It wasn't easy.

'The celebrations will extend from the official opening of the Christmas ball over Christmas Day and Boxing Day.'

There was another crack. Mr Ambrose had broken another nut. This time, however, I'd be willing to bet my bowler that it was unintentional.

'*Boxing Day?*' he enquired, cold eyes raking his mother. 'You follow that...*custom* here?'

Lady Samantha held his gaze. 'We do.'

Giving an involuntary shudder, Mr Ambrose turned away. Part of me almost pitied him. Boxing Day – so called because of the Christmas boxes filled with presents that employers traditionally gave to all their faithful employees – was, to put it mildly, not Mr Ambrose's favourite day of the year. I remembered the one occasion on which one of his hundreds of clerks had dared to ask what he would be getting for Boxing Day, and Mr Ambrose had reacted by—

Well, some memories were better repressed.

'Now, as to the Christmas ball...'

Instantly, I forgot about my fork, and my attention snapped to Lady Samantha. So did the attention of every other lady in the room, particularly the hyenas.

'My husband is not feeling particularly well. So, this year, the Christmas ball will be opened by my son.'

Slowly and deliberately, Mr Ambrose raised his gaze to meet his mother's. '*What* did you say?'

She met his gaze head-on. Dear me...I would never had thought the little old lady had it in her. 'I believe you heard me. There are so many charming young ladies present.' Lady Samantha's gaze swept over the assembled young women in the room, lingering just an instant on me. 'I'm sure you will find someone here that will suit you perfectly.'

At that, the eyes of the harpies practically started glowing. They fastened on Mr Ambrose with ravenous intent.

Mr Ambrose wasn't fazed. Cold eyes reviewed the collection of ladies arrayed before him. They went from one to the next and the next – until they reached me, and swept over me as if I didn't even exist. Budding hope that I hadn't even realised had begun to rise inside me was crushed under a mountain of ice.

What did you expect, Lilly? You turned the man down! Did you think he was going to ask you to dance after that? For what? Being turned down again?

As if he were reading my thoughts, Mr Ambrose's gaze suddenly snapped to me, and our eyes met.

Would I? Would I turn him down? For a marriage, yes, but for a dance? I suddenly realised that I wouldn't. I would happily spend a dance or two in Mr Ambrose's arms – even if it only was for the chance of stomping around on his feet a little.

Our eyes met again, and a shiver raced down my spine.

What is he thinking? What is going on in that granite head of his?

'By the way...' Lady Samantha's voice interrupted our duel of eyes. Everyone looked over to her.

'Yes, mother?'

'Elsby has informed me that a large number of...unconventional guests have invaded the servant's quarters.' She glanced at me – or rather, as I realised a moment later, behind me. I half-turned and saw four of the men who had been in my rescue party standing there in ill-fitting servants' livery. 'May I ask the reason for this?'

Once again, Mr Ambrose's cold, sea-colored eyes flicked to me. 'A...package needed delivering.'

Package? *Package?*

'Dozens of men for one single package?'

'It was a very important package.'

Well, thank you so much! Now I feel much better.

'And now that the delivery has been accomplished, will they leave?'

'Not just yet. They will accompany us on our way back south after Christmas is passed. One can never be too careful. The highway can be a dangerous place.'

Lady Samantha hesitated – then nodded. 'Very well. You are right. Your...friends are welcome to stay until then.'

The rest of the meal passed mostly in silence. Oh, don't get me wrong, the other ladies and gentlemen were quite loquacious, and the hyenas tried to draw Mr Ambrose into conversation more than once. They didn't seem to comprehend what I had known for a pretty long time: Mr Ambrose and conversations? Not a feasible mix.

But between Mr Ambrose and me, silence reigned. Silence that was punctuated only by the occasional glance out of the corner of an eye, and forceful use of cutlery. Our behaviour didn't go unnoticed. Lady Samantha threw more than one curious glance in our direction, and Adaira – well, she didn't content herself with glances. Her sea-coloured eyes were as piercing as the points of Poseidon's trident. I could practically hear her whisper in my ear: *what is it? What's happened between my brother and you? Spit it out!*

Luckily, spitting was against table manners. Still, her scrutiny was nearly as intimidating as that of Mr Rikkard Ambrose. When the dinner finally came to an end, I literally jumped at the chance to get away. I only mumbled a hasty excuse to Lady Samantha, then I was on my feet and heading towards the door, towards freedom–

–when a strong, hard hand closed around my wrist.

'Miss Linton. A word?'

Oh, that cool, collected voice...

What is he thinking?

He wanted a word! With me! Was he going to ask me to open the ball with him?

But when I turned around and saw the icy determination in his eyes, I knew Mr Ambrose hadn't come to ask anything. He had come to demand.

'Last chance, Miss Linton.' His voice was too low for anyone to overhear – but everyone was watching. Everyone. Especially the hyenas. Oh, and Lady Samantha. And Adaira. Spiffing! 'Have you reconsidered my offer?'

I raised an eyebrow at him. 'Have you reconsidered mine?'

Good God! I'm asking him in front of a room full of people including his sister and mother if he'd like to dance the fandango de pokum with me!

'No.'

I gave him my best 'kiss my generous butt' smile. 'What a shame.'

With one tug, I pulled my hand free of his grip. He gazed at me for a moment longer – then whirled around and stalked out of the room, the tails of his coat flapping behind him like raven's wings.

I stood there for a moment, unable to move, gazing after him.

That moment was enough for the huntress to catch up to me.

'What was all that about?' a familiar voice hissed into my ear.

'Oh. Hello, Lady Adaira. What a lovely morning it is, don't you think?'

'Really? Talking about the weather?' She raised an eyebrow. 'Is that the best you can do? I would have expected a more imaginative evasion tactic from you.'

To be honest, so would I. But right now, my brain isn't working very well.

She stepped forward, her sea-coloured eyes, so terribly familiar, boring into me.

'What happened between you and my brother?'

I smiled. 'Don't worry. I didn't seduce him and rob him of his virtue.' *Yet.* 'We've merely had a...difference of opinion.'

'Ha! And I am Father Christmas.'

'Well, now that you mention it, I think I see the beginnings of a white beard growing on your face.'

Adaira was not deterred so easily. One small hand took hold of mine and squeezed gently, caringly – and suddenly I wanted to tell her. I wanted to have a shoulder to cry on. My usual shoulders, attached to my little sister and four best friends, were nowhere in the vicinity, and Adaira was here, and she was strong and understanding, and...

Could I tell her? Would she understand, or would she blame me?

Leaning forward, she pierced me with her forceful gaze and put an arm around me. 'Tell me! What has that brother of mine done to make an arse of himself this time?'

I breathed a sigh of relief.

Thank you! Thank you God, for sending me a girl with the right perspective on life!

'He...he...'

I tried to get the words out. But with dozens of curious eyes still on us, they just wouldn't come. The tension of the last few days had built up inside me. I longed for the dam to break and the flood to burst out of me, but not here. Not now.

Instinctively, Adaira seemed to understand. Her grip on my hand tightened, and she pulled me towards a door that lead to the hallway.

'Come. I know a place where we can talk. And besides...' A mischievous grin spread across her face. 'If my brother has done something to deserve your ire, Miss Linton, I know just the right way to let off some steam.'

A Flapdoodle in the Snow

'Aah...' Sighing, I straightened and gazed contentedly at my handiwork. 'You were right, Adaira. This is a marvellous way to let off steam. Let me guess – when we're finished, this will depict...'

'Yes, it will. Let's just hope *he* doesn't find out.'

'We're at the back of the house, behind three rows of hedges. He won't even know where we are. Plus even if he found out, he can go eat my parasol!'

'A very commendable sentiment.' She grinned at me. 'I have often wanted to make him eat a parasol – or a cow, or a bucket full of rusted nails. However, last time I saw you and my brother together, I had the impression that your feelings towards him were, how shall I put it, of a more tender nature?'

I ground my teeth. 'Tender my foot! He...he...!'

'What did he do?'

My clenched fist slammed into the half-finished snow artwork we were building. It felt very satisfying. 'He told me he loved me!'

'How atrocious. I can see why that would upset you.'

'No! No, that's not it!'

'It isn't?

'No! I'm in love with him, too, curse him!'

'You are?' An expression of puzzlement crossed over her face that only the little sisters of attractive older brothers can produce. She shrugged. 'To each her own, I guess.'

I punched the snow again, then grabbed some more to fill out the holes I had made in our wintery masterpiece of art. We continued sculpting in silence for a while. Finally, Adaira said: 'Well, if that's not what you're angry about...what is it? Are you angry that he couldn't keep Dalgliesh from taking you?'

'What? No!' I made a dismissive gesture. 'That was nothing! I didn't even need his help to get away. I freed myself and was just about to start on my way back when he arrived.'

'You...you did?' There was an unholy amount of glee in Adaira's voice. Her eyes suddenly sparkled more brightly than the snow around us. 'Dear me.'

I had a feeling that Mr Ambrose would be hearing quite a few comments on this subject from his little sister in the days to come.

Good. Very good indeed.

'Yes. It's not about the kidnapping. It's not about him telling me he loves me on the ride back. But when we had returned, he...he...' Righteous anger made me choke on my words. Adaira made soothing noises, and I managed to gather myself enough to get out the words: 'He waited till the next morning – just one day after he swore that he loved me – and then he *asked me to marry him!*'

Silence.

Not cold silence. Not stony silence. No, this was a 'Yes,-and-what's-the-punch-line?' silence.

It took Adaira a moment to realise there wasn't one.

'Oh. How, um...atrocious? Horrific?'

I punched the snow in front of me, trembling, with…rage? Fear?

'I know, right? He said he loved me! How could he! How could he do this to me!'

'Um, yes. I must say it's really quite shocking. I mean, from love to marriage, how could anyone make that leap? It's an outrage.'

'Exactly! And that's not the worst of it!'

'It isn't?'

'No! His mother – your mother – wants it too! She approves of me!'

'My goodness! How scandalous. Though I must admit I understand the feeling.'

'There! There, you see?' I jabbed a finger at her, accusingly. 'Even you want me as your sister-in-law! This marriage madness is spreading like the plague!'

'My apologies. I simply cannot help admitting that you are by far the least despicable candidate for sister-in-law that I have ever met.'

'Gah!' Pulling at my hair, I gave the half-finished snow sculpture a good kick. 'Blast, blast, blast! Everyone is infected by this insanity! And do you know what's the worst?'

'No. What?'

'Even I am tempted! I! I should know better than anyone else that this can only end in a catastrophe – and still, I keep having these flashes of pretty churches, and wedding dresses, and him and me together, and I think I'm going insane! And it's all his fault!'

Adaira patted my back. 'Deplorable! That miserable cad! I'll help you eviscerate him.'

'Thank you! You are a good friend.'

'Just one thing…'

'Yes?'

'If you could explain to me why exactly you don't want to marry him, that might help me understand what you've been going on about for the last five minutes.'

I stomped on the ground, sending a cascade of glittering crystals into the air. 'Don't you see?'

'Err…no, not really. He loves you. You love him, hard as that may be to understand. So, why not make it official?'

'Because!' My foot slammed into the ground again. This time the snow flew so high it filled my shoe. Right now, I didn't care. 'Because it's marriage we're talking about! Marriage! Have you had both eyes and ears open? Have you heard the whispers, read the papers? Don't you know what some husbands do to their wives?'

'Rick would never–'

'–hurt me, I know. But that's not the point, Adaira.' Taking a step towards her, I took her hands and looked straight into her eyes. 'Do you know why I took the job as your brother's secretary? Do you know why I've been running after him for over a year now, through Egypt and Brazil and God knows where else?'

'I've had my suspicions, but I don't really know, no.'

'I did it because I want to be free! I want to be my own woman, go where I want, do what I want, be who I want to be. I don't want to be an appendage to someone else!'

'But you won't be! Rick–'

'–is a man. A powerful man, who is used to being in charge. And marriage is a contract. Do you know what it is I'd be signing up for?' Pulling a small, leather-bound book out of my pocket, I waved it in the air. 'I wasn't absolutely sure myself. I didn't want to listen to rumours and newspaper gossip columns. So I borrowed this from your mother's library. The Book of Common Prayer. It has the standard wedding ceremony in there, as prescribed by the Church of England.'

With trembling fingers, I opened the book at the page I had marked earlier. 'Do you really think that when the vicar steps in front of me and asks me *Wilt thou have this Man to thy wedded Husband, to live together after God's ordinance in the holy estate of Matrimony? Wilt thou obey him and serve him?* I will be able to answer with a "Yes"? Do you really think that when the vicar stands there and tells me, *Wives, submit yourselves unto your own husbands, as unto the Lord. For the husband is the head of the wife, even as Christ is the head of the Church: and he is the Saviour of the body. Therefore as the Church is subject unto Christ, so let the wives be to their own husbands in everything,*[16] I will be able to just stand there and meekly swallow it?'

Panting, I lowered the book. Adaira was looking at me with big eyes, dumbstruck.

'If you think that,' I whispered. 'You don't know me at all.'

She hesitated a moment – then nodded. 'You're right.'

My eyebrows shot up. 'I am?'

'Yes. Down with matrimony!' She slammed her fist into her palm, then lowered her voice and added: 'But for heaven's sake, don't let mother know I said that!'

A smiled tugged at the corners of my mouth. 'I won't.'

'And I hope you won't be offended if one day I choose to marry anyway?'

'Not in the least.'

'Because, you know...there are quite a lot of men out there who probably wouldn't stand on the letter of the contract.'

'True.' I gave her a weak smile. 'But Mr Rikkard Ambrose is not one of them.'

She nodded solemnly. She knew her brother more than well enough to know that a contract with him was not to be undertaken lightly.

'And do you know what's most important?' I asked her, my voice totally serious. "He knew all this, Adaira. He knew how I felt about marriage, he knew that I would die before giving up my independence. And still – one day after

---

[16] The latter part of this isn't just taken from the Book of Common Prayer, but from St. Paul's Letter to the Ephesians 5:22-24 in the Bible. It was taken from the latter by the writers of the Book of Common Prayer and inserted in the standard marriage ceremony, and quite accurately reflects social norms in the nineteenth century. This goes some way to explaining, I think, why Lilly might be somewhat opposed to the concept of matrimony.

telling me he loved me, he asked me to become his wife. No, he didn't even *ask* – he *ordered*! Can you understand now why I would be a teensy-weensy bit annoyed with your dear brother?'

Adaira considered for a moment – then nodded. Bending down, she lifted up a compact ball of snow and slammed it on top of the figure we had been moulding. It was a tall figure, made of snow pounded so long it was almost as hard as ice. An old black top hat sat upon its head. For eyes, it had two sea-coloured pebbles, and the mouth was a thin line that looked as if it almost never opened.

'I think we did a really good job.' Cocking her head, Adaira regarded our masterpiece. 'He looks just like the original.'

'He has a carrot for a nose,' I pointed out.

'Like I said – just like the original.'

I really loved this girl.

Pulling a parasol from behind her back, she held it out to me. 'Want to do the honours?'

Really, really, really loved her.

'Nothing would please me more.'

I snatched up the parasol. Focusing my gaze on my hapless victim, I raised the deadly weapon above my head.

'You...you...you....'

'Son of a bachelor?' Adaira suggested. 'Foozler? Flapdoodle?'

'...you have known me for over a year now! How could you do this? How could you ever think this is what I want? What I need?'

'Oh. Pardon. I thought you were aiming for an insult. Don't let me interrupt.'

Dragging in a deep breath, I stabbed the parasol downwards. The old top hat flew away into the distance. And so did the head. 'Take that!'

'Good one! Now get him in the gizzard!'

'And that! And that! Ha! Got anything to say to that? No, of course you don't, because you never ever talk! And when you do you *don't - talk - sense*!'

'Ha! Right through the middle! Keep going, girl! Keep going, you're nearly done!'

'There! And there! Take that you...you...foozler!'

'You're welcome.'

The snow man Ambrose – unsurprisingly – was proving remarkably stubborn. But he was only hanging on by a thread. Panting, I raised the parasol for one final blow. 'Take that, you...you...flapdoodle!'

The parasol came down. Snow exploded in a silver-white cloud all around me. Adaira let out a burst of laughter, dancing in the glittering confetti. I joined in, and soon we were both dancing around in the snow, laughing like little girls. Good God, this had been fun! This had been just what I needed.

When my laughter had subsided enough for me to speak, I demanded: 'What...what in God's name is a flapdoodle?'

Adaira gave another giggle. 'How should I know? The coachmen don't often explain their language to young ladies.'

'A pity.' I wound my tongue around the word. 'Flapdoodle...I kind of like the sound of it. I'll have to find out.'

'I can save you the trouble, Miss Linton,' came a very familiar cold voice from behind me. We froze. 'That particular expression describes a man whose reproductive organs are no longer in working order.'

Oh crap...

ALL IS FAIR IN LOVE AND CARROTS

Adaira cocked her head, looking down at the remnants of the snowman Ambrose in front of us. 'We really did do a great job, didn't we? It even talks.'

'I,' Mr Ambrose said from behind us, his voice a few degrees colder, 'am not amused.'[17]

The words made the hair on the back of my neck stand up and travelled down my spine like fingers of velvet frost. I swallowed. Slowly, I turned to face him. There he stood, as tall and indomitable as ever.

Keep it together, Lilly! Keep it together!

'What are you doing here, Miss Linton? What is the meaning of all this snow?'

He knows. He already knows. But he wants me to say it.

I racked my brain for a rational, sensible, adult explanation of why we were here. Since there apparently wasn't one, I gave up and went with the truth.

'Oh, we were just amusing ourselves, you know. Passing the time.'

'Indeed?' His gaze bored into me, daring me to say it.

'Indeed, Sir.'

'Doing what?'

The pile of snow that had been the snowman Ambrose's head chose this strategic moment to crumble. The dilapidated black top hat fell off and rolled a few yards before coming to rest in front of Mr Ambrose's feet. He gave it a look. One of *those* looks. Honestly, I was surprised the poor hat didn't spontaneously grow legs and run to hide behind the nearest tree.

'I see.'

Adaira, I noticed, had begun to inch away from the evidence of our little snow escapade. Trying to escape, was she? I had to commend her initiative, but I could have told her it wouldn't work. This was Rikkard Ambrose we were dealing with. He lifted his eyes from the offending top hat and nailed her to the spot with just one icy look.

'You. To your room.'

'What? You can't do that! You're not my father!'

'Indeed I am not. If I were, you would most likely not obey. Now – go!'

Poor girl. She had no chance. Her legs ran away with her, and she just had time to throw me one last supportive look before she disappeared into the manor house.

---

[17] Historians have debated for a long time whether this quote was indeed created by Queen Victoria. Now we know – she pinched it from Mr Rikkard Ambrose.

Finally, Mr Ambrose turned away from his sister, and our eyes met again. My mouth felt dry, and I cleared my throat.

'I...I can explain–'

That was all I got out before he crossed the distance between us with three long strides and pulled me against him. His lips crashed down on mine, taking my mouth with a cold ferocity that made me shiver inside. His nose brushed mine, and it didn't feel at all like a carrot.

Well...this wasn't the kind of explanation I had planned, but it would do just fine in my opinion.

'You...!' Breathing hard, he broke away just long enough to glare down at me, then reclaimed my lips and started to kiss the life out of me. 'You're impossible! Unlike any other woman I've ever...You're impossible!'

'Does this mean you've reconsidered my offer after all?'

'No!'

The word was a ferocious growl against my lips. I pulled a face – which is not easy thing to do while being kissed by Rikkard Ambrose, believe me. 'You're being unreasonable about this.'

'I, unreasonable? You're the one who is suggesting that I...that we...'

I waited – but he couldn't even say it. Living in sin apparently didn't appeal to him for some reason. Strange. I would have thought he'd jump at a cheaper alternative to marriage.

'Just think about it,' I coaxed. 'There would be no commitment, no pressure, no need for a really, really expensive ceremony–'

'That will not happen!' he hissed. 'Either you will be mine completely, or not all.'

'Why?'

His hands slid into my hair, holding me fast. 'Because I am a gentleman.'

'And a chauvinistic tyrant.'

He did not deny it.

'I heard you and Adaira talking at the end.'

'And?'

'And you were talking nonsense!'

'Really? So you did not intend to demand my obedience at the altar, then?'

He looked almost surprised. As surprised as a stone statue when someone asks it to be more flexible. 'Of course I will! What's nonsense is that you would object to the idea.'

I felt fire spark inside me. 'You...you insufferable flapdoodle!'

Tightening his grip on me, he shoved me back until I was pressed up against the remnants of the snow Ambrose. Cold bit into me from behind, while icy fire burned me from the front.

'I could easily demonstrate the incorrectness of that insult,' he growled, 'if the marriage contract were signed.'

'Forget contracts! Forget promises! Show me here and now!'

I didn't care about the cold. I didn't care about the snow. I had one Ambrose behind me and one in front. And, all right, one was headless and made from oversized snowballs, but still! There was only so much a girl could stand before catching fire.

'I'm not going to say it again!' Using my hair like reins, he pulled my face forward until my lips were nearly touching his. I desperately wanted to close the last bit of distance between us, but he wouldn't allow it. He was too strong. 'You know what I want. You know what you want, and what you'll have to do to get it.'

I met his gaze head-on. 'And I'm not going to give you my answer again! You know it already, and knowledge is power is time is money, right?'

I saw something flicker in his eyes then – something I had never seen there before. It wasn't exactly confusion, and neither was it exactly anger. Such useless emotions were foreign to Mr Rikkard Ambrose. What I saw was realisation. The realisation that right here in front of him was something he wanted and couldn't have.

I might have laughed had I not felt exactly the same.

My heart gave a painful tug. *Blast! Why him? Why does it have to be him? Why not someone simpler? Someone who would jump at the chance of a clandestine affair?*

The answer to that question came a moment later when he roughly pulled me towards him.

Not to kiss me.

Not even to glower at me, or give me a reprimand.

No, he just wrapped his arms around me and held me close. And suddenly, for one moment, my heart overflowed with warmth, and all was right with the world. That moment stretched into two moments, then into three. That was some premium time-wasting we did in those moments. For once, Mr Ambrose didn't seem to mind.

'How did you even find me back here?' I whispered into his chest. 'We came back here to be alone.'

He made a derisive noise in the back of his throat. 'You're never alone.'

'What?'

'Did you think after what happened with Dalgliesh I would be taking any further risks? My men have been watching you since we returned to Battlewood.'

I thought for a moment whether I should protest against this. I was, after all, an independent woman, who was very well capable of watching out for herself, right?

Then I thought about Lord Dalgliesh and his smile, sharp as a knife.

No. Wrong.

I couldn't watch out for myself. And neither could Mr Ambrose. We would have to watch out for each other to survive. And if we had help – all the better. There was only one thing I had to make sure of...

'Err...when you say your men have been "watching" me...do you mean all the time?'

Like when I am getting ready for bed, for instance?

If he said yes, Mr Snowman Ambrose wasn't going to be the only one to lose his head!

Somehow he seemed to read my meaning on my face. His arms tightened around me, holding me so close I could hardly breathe. Who knew lack of oxygen could feel so nice?

'Do you think I would ever allow something like that to happen?' His voice was so cold. So terribly cold and ruthless. How come it made me feel so wonderfully warm inside? 'You're mine. No other man will ever see you, let alone touch you.'

Holy...that was so proprietary, tyrannical and chauvinistic! For him to take that tone with me, as if I were already his, was completely egotistical and unacceptable–

–*sweet and wonderful, and please, God, let him say it again, because it sounds so magical on his lips.*

No! No, absolutely not! He had spoken as if my saying yes or no to him didn't matter. As if he were in charge, and his loving me, his wanting me, was more than enough to settle the matter. I couldn't accept that! I was going to protest. I was going to–

'If any other man ever caught a glimpse of you like that,' his cold voice whispered in my ear, 'do you know what I would do?'

I shivered, and forgot all about protesting.

'No.'

'I don't yet know either, Miss Linton.' Out of the corner of my eye, I saw a muscle in his jaw twitch. 'And that should scare you. I have always known what I would do to my enemies. A bullet, clean through the skull, a watery grave, a few sessions with Karim in a remote underground room – there is not much I have not done. And yet, all that seems insufficient when I think of you and another man together. Keep that in mind.'

Lifting my face from his chest, I looked up straight into his icy, sea-coloured eyes.

'And you had better keep *this* in mind.' Raising an arm, I pointed to the sad remnants of Mr Snowman Ambrose. 'You're not the only one who doesn't know their limits.'

Silence hung heavily between us – a silence charged with ice and fire and anger and love. Our eyes were fastened to each other as if we were magnets, unable to let go. Hot need flared up inside me, a need to cross the distance and finally do what had been hovering as a dark promise in the air between us for months now. I could see the same hunger in his eyes. But I could also see that he wasn't going to do anything about it. Not yet. Not without his ring on my finger.

So, instead of devouring Mr Ambrose, I did the next best thing. Bending down, I picked up the fallen snowman's carrot and bit off the tip.

'Hm. Not bad. Bloody hell, I'm hungry! Building a snowman is hard work.'

I caught Mr Ambrose giving me a look and raised an eyebrow. 'What? Why are you looking me like that? It's not *your* nose I'm nibbling on.' A sudden grin spread over my face. 'Or is that the problem? Would you prefer that?'

'Miss Linton!'

I held out the carrot to him. 'Want a bite?'

'No.'

'Come on. Vegetables are good for you.'

He gave me another look. Shrugging, I took another bite of Ambrose's nose.

'All right, if you prefer.'

We weren't standing as close anymore as we had been. Without really noticing, we had put a little distance between us – just enough of a safety radius so we couldn't touch anymore. But we still watched every movement the other made, every flicker of emotion in each other's eyes. For a while we just stood there like this, while I nibbled on my carrot, and Mr Ambrose exuded Ambroseness. We kept eyeing each other, trying to discern what the other was thinking, while not entirely sure what we were thinking ourselves.

Finally, I decided to ask.

'So...what now?'

Silence.

Absolute silence.

How wonderful. Was Mr Ambrose back to normal? Had he gotten this wedding nonsense out of his head?

Suddenly, out of the blue, I felt a painful twinge in my chest.

Wait a minute, Lilly...you do want him to get it out of his head, right?

Of course I did!

Do you? Do you really?

'Shut up!'

Only after the words were already out of my mouth did I realise I had spoken aloud.

Mr Ambrose cocked his head. 'I didn't say anything.'

'I was talking to myself.' I raised an eyebrow. 'That makes for much more interesting and varied conversations than the ones I usually have with you.'

His left little finger twitched. Other than that, I got no answer. I met his gaze, challenging him.

'So, what do you say? What about the two of us? What's going to happen?'

His silence was really answer enough. We each wanted different things from the other. Neither of us was the type to give up. The lines had been drawn. Really, there remained only one thing to say: let the battle begin.

I nodded.

Mr Ambrose nodded.

The air between us crackled with tension. Who would make the first move?

We might have found out if not, at that very moment, a man had come dashing out from the woods, waving his hat in the air in a signal that I had seen Mr Ambrose's men use before. Instantly, Mr Ambrose stiffened. In a second, he had placed himself between me and woods, sweeping me behind him.

'What is the matter?' I demanded.

'I would very much like to know that myself, Miss Linton. He's signalling danger. Stay where you are.'

The man ran towards us, coming to a panting halt a few yards away. Trying desperately to speak around his panting breaths, he supported himself with his hands on his knees.

'Speak up, man!' Mr Ambrose demanded. 'What is it?'

The man glanced up, his face grim. He didn't bow to his employer. He didn't waste time with greetings or honorifics. He just rasped one single word.

'Dalgliesh!'

DARK PROMISES

Had Mr Ambrose and I been arguing? I suddenly couldn't remember or care. That one word, that name, tipped the whole world on its head. Our eyes met, and it was as if our disagreement had never existed. Suddenly, Mr Rikkard Ambrose and I were on the same team, and we would fight fiercely till the end.

The end of anyone who was against us.

Oh Lilly, a voice whispered in my head. *It doesn't really matter whether you want to bind yourself to him or not. You already are. And you don't even want to get free.*

Squashing that rogue thought with all my might, I stepped up beside Mr Ambrose and took his hand. He gave mine a squeeze, and I squeezed back. No words were spoken – and yet, for once, I knew exactly what he was thinking.

I turned to the man who had come to warn us. 'Fetch Karim. Tell him to come quickly and... no. No, don't tell him that.' An idea popped into my head and, suddenly, insanely, I had to smile. 'Tell him it wasn't me who invented Prince Fragrant Yellow Flower in the Happy Moonlight – but I know who did, and I might be willing to tell him.'

The man blinked at me. 'P-pardon, Miss? Prince who?' His gaze flickered to Mr Ambrose in an are-you-sure-she-has-all-of-her-marbles way.

He returned the man's gaze with implacable force.

'Do as she says.'

The man paled, turned on his heels and dashed off through the snow. Glancing over at me, Mr Ambrose cocked his head. 'I believe Karim will be coming to meet us very quickly indeed.'

'Yes, Sir. I believe he will, too.'

'You have learned quite a lot about how to handle a man.'

'Indeed I have, Sir.' Smiling, I lifted one eyebrow at him. 'And don't you forget it.'

He gave me a long, long look. 'I shall endeavour not to.'

Mr Rikkard Ambrose extended his arm to me like the perfect gentleman he would never be.

'Shall we?'

Without thinking twice about it, I slipped my arm into his.

'We shall.'

And we set out towards the house, leaving behind a sad pile of snow, an old top hat and a half-eaten carrot. As we proceeded along the garden path, more people joined us. Men of all sizes and ages, but all with the same hard, sharp, sensible look in their eyes – a look that I had seen every time I looked at one of

Mr Ambrose's hired guards. Halfway to the house, a big shadow rushed out from behind a hedge and planted himself in front of me.

'*Who?*' Karim demanded. 'Who was it that brought shame upon me? Whoever it was, I shall rip them apart! I shall fight them to the death and then I shall take their dead body and–'

Further description of what the poor, unsuspecting bodyguard intended to do with his employer's little sister was cut off by one of Mr Ambrose's trademark arctic stares.

'Not now, Karim.'

'But *Sahib*, the insult to my honour–'

'–will still be just as insulting in an hour or two. There is not time right now. Dalgliesh is here.'

Karim had just been about to open his mouth to protest again – but at hearing that, he shut up. His hand shot to the sabre at his belt, and his eyes turned into slits. I had a feeling that whatever he had planned for the inventor of Prince Fragrant Yellow Flower in the Happy Moonlight, it was nothing compared to what he'd like to do to Lord Daniel Eugene Dalgliesh.

We didn't enter the house through the usual back door. With as many as there were of us, it would have taken ages for us to file inside. Mr Ambrose unlocked the French windows on the terrace, and his small private army marched into the beautiful drawing room, sticking out like a forest of sore thumbs.

'Where exactly did you get those keys?' I enquired. 'Did your father give them to you?'

His face was a mask. 'I like to be prepared for every eventuality.'

'Dear me! Copying your own relative's keys? I'm shocked!'

And I was. Shocked that I hadn't thought of the idea first. Once I got home, I would have to see how I could get my hands on Aunt Brank's key ring. That could come in handy.

We moved through the house at a swift pace, our circle of guards never loosening or falling behind. Just as we stepped into the entrance hall, a door at the other side of the hall opened and Adaira, accompanied by her mother and a few curious guests, stepped out to meet us.

'Ah, Rick! There you are.' Lady Samantha looked very relieved. 'Have you heard?'

'Yes.' Mr Ambrose's voice was cold enough to freeze a desert at noon. 'One of our guests has seen fit to return.'

'Indeed.' Lady Samantha glanced away. 'I will be welcoming him. Will you come with me?'

'Yes.' His gaze slid over to Adaira. 'But she won't.'

His little sister's spine stiffened as if strapped to a posing stand.[18]

---

[18] Back in the Victorian Era there were no cell phone cameras that could take photographs with just one easy click. Cameras were in a very early stage of development, and instead of one quick flash, the exposure of a photograph could sometimes take minutes, or in very early cases even hours. This led to the invention

'I won't stay behind! I'm not a child, and I won't be treated as though–'

A normal older brother might have taken this opportunity to point out that yes, she was indeed a child, which would lead to further denial and an eventual row that would rock the walls of the house. Mr Ambrose just snapped his fingers, and a contingent of his guards formed a line in front of Adaira, keeping her from going anywhere unless she wanted to ram head first into her brother's hirelings.

'I'm going to get you for this!' came a determined, if muffled, voice from behind a wall of muscle. 'Just you wait!'

Ignoring his little sister completely, Mr Ambrose turned towards the front doors and started forward. I followed suit, nearly running to keep pace with his long strides. Out of the corner of his sea-coloured eyes, he glanced down at me.

'I suppose I can't talk you out of accompanying me?'

'No.'

'And if I order my men to keep you here, along with my sister?'

'Then I will find a way to let Her Majesty's Treasury know about some of your more creative bookkeeping methods.'

He made a not-very-polite noise in the back of his throat. I smiled up at him broadly. 'Either you let me go with you, or you're not going at all. It's your choice.'

Another indistinct noise. Then...

'All right, Miss Linton. Let's go. Karim?'

'The men are ready, *Sahib*. Nothing will happen.'

'That had better be true.'

We stepped outside onto the porch just in time to see a magnificent coach drawn by four beautiful white horses rolling down the driveway. It was accompanied by a small cavalcade of horsemen, dressed in luxurious livery. The whole scene screamed 'fairytale prince' – until the coach rolled to a halt, the door opened, and Lord Daniel Eugene Dalgliesh stepped out. The servants dismounted. Under their tailcoats, I saw the brief glint of sabres and pistols.

Karim gave a discreet hand signal. Without any of the guests or Lady Samantha noticing, Mr Ambrose's guards moved closer, placing themselves halfway between us and His Lordship.

With long, leisurely strides, Lord Dalgliesh crossed the snow-covered ground between us. He was smiling and didn't even seem to notice the tension in the air – unless you took a good look deep into his eyes. They coldly assessed the situation, sweeping over Mr Ambrose and his mother, me and Karim as if we were just pawns on a chessboard. His gaze lingered for a second on me, and I could feel Mr Ambrose stiffen at my side – then it continued on, to take in the many men in badly fitting livery that were scattered all around us, watching the scene with emotionless professionalism.

'My Lords, Ladies and Gentlemen.' Lord Dalgliesh bowed, his eyes never dipping a millimetre, staying focused on Mr Ambrose and his men. 'I am delighted

---

of the posing stand, a wooden construction with straps attached to which people were strapped in order to help them stand in a certain pose for a long, long time.

to see you all again. My sincerest apologies, Marchioness, for my delay in returning to your lovely home.'

'Your apology is accepted.' Lady Samantha nodded graciously. 'However, may I ask why you left in the first place? Your departure was rather sudden and unexpected.'

'I'm truly sorry.' His eyes flicked to me for just an instant. 'I had some business to take care of.'

'I see. Well, I am..." Lady Samantha searched for the right word – but she didn't find one, so she went with a wrong one. "...glad that you could rejoin us for Christmas. The great ball is this evening, and some of us were beginning to fear you would miss it.'

Again, Dalgliesh's steel-blue eyes flickered to me, boring into me like diamond drills – then they swept to my left and right, where there stood at least a dozen men, their hands casually hidden under their jackets, no doubt holding deadly weapons. They didn't take their eyes off His Lordship for one moment.

'I am afraid I must disappoint you in that regard, Your Ladyship.'

'You must?' Lady Samantha had never sounded so happy to be disappointed.

'Yes. The business I was speaking of...' Once more, he speared me with his gaze. I ignored him. 'It did not go entirely as expected. There are unforeseen difficulties. I will have to return to London, to develop a new strategy.' He smiled, and it was deadly smile, meant solely for me and Mr Ambrose. 'What is it they say? Patience is a virtue.'

To me, it didn't sound like a virtue just then. It sounded very much like a threat.

'Well...' Lady Samantha cleared her throat. 'I wish you the best of luck with your business, Your Lordship.'

Thanks so much. I appreciate you wanting me to get kidnapped by a psychopath, Your Ladyship.

'Thank you.' Lord Dalgliesh made a deep bow, a smile twisting one corner of his mouth. 'You don't know how much that means to me. I so very much look forward to being a guest in your beautiful home again at some point in the future. I will do everything in my power to ensure that day comes soon.'

With those words hanging darkly and ominously in the air, he turned around and strode back to his coach. One of his henchmen opened the door for him. He climbed in. The coachman cracked his whip. Just as I was about to relax, Lord Dalgliesh leaned out of the window, catching my eye. Almost imperceptibly, he lowered his head in a mocking little bow. The gesture needed no translation.

Till next time.

As he withdrew and the coach rolled away down the driveway, I couldn't suppress an involuntary shudder.

~~**~*~*

Sighing, I closed the door of my room behind me and leaned against it. He was gone! Finally, he was out of sight and out of mind!

All right, it wasn't over yet, not by a long shot. Dalgliesh would be planning his next grand move at some time in the future, now that he knew I was Mr Ambrose's weak spot. I would have to be prepared. Still, for now at least, I would have a little peace.

Not that Mr Rikkard Ambrose took so cheerful a view of things.

'The guards are staying,' he'd told me in an undertone while we were watching His Lordship's carriage drive away. 'This might be a ploy to lull us into a false sense of security.'

I had tried to argue with him a little bit, just for the fun of it – but in truth, I could have sung with joy! The guards were staying? Did this mean that he still cared, even after I'd turned him down? Did it?

Or was it just that he didn't want to lose to Lord Daniel Eugene Dalgliesh?

Right now, I couldn't find the energy to care! Lord Dalgliesh was gone, and Mr Ambrose wasn't going anywhere. I would have plenty of time to figure out what was going on between the two of us. With a tired sigh, I tottered over to the bed and sank down on it. Time for a little break. After all, there was no hurry. Most of my problems were over, and the ones that weren't could wait for a little while, right?

Wrong.

In that exact instant, the door burst open and a dervish danced into the room. A dervish that looked suspiciously like Lady Adaira Louise Jannet Melanie Georgette Ambrose. She made a last whirl and then came to a stop in front of my bed, beaming down at me.

'Isn't this just fantabulous? Dalgliesh is gone! Really, absolutely one hundred per cent gone! And Mother has given me *carte blanche*! Oh, we're going to have so much fun!'

'Fun?' I blinked up at her. 'Fun with what?'

'With finding the right dress for you to wear! After all, you want to look your best for the ball tonight, don't you? For the ball, and...' She winked. She *winked*! '...and for my brother?'

Oh blast!

Groaning, I sank back onto my pillow. My problems weren't over. They were just beginning.

INSIGNIFICANT OTHER

'Crap, crap, crap!'

'Miss! I must protest! Your language...!'

'Oh, pardon. I meant horse dung, of course. Or do you prefer faeces?'

The sputtering shop assistant bustled away to bury her scolded ears in folds of muslin. Behind me, Adaira disguised her giggle as a cough.

'You do have a rather colourful way of expressing yourself.'

'Well, colourful is good, isn't it?' I held up the brilliant orange ball gown against my front. 'What do you think?'

'Um...I think maybe not in this case. Try that one.'

I glanced around, and was nearly blinded. Adaira was holding up a brilliantly gleaming dress that was, from neckline to hem, a shiny golden colour.

She grinned at me. 'I bet he won't be able to take his eyes off you in this.'

I returned her smile with one eyebrow raised. 'I see you know your brother well.'

'Indeed I do. So, what about it? Are you going to try it on?'

'Hmm...thanks, but I think I'll politely decline. I don't really wish to spend the entire evening with him fiddling around on an abacus, trying to figure out how much my dress is worth.'

'But you do want to spend it with him.'

I glanced down, biting my lip. Usually, I was a pretty plucky girl. I didn't easily get afraid. But when it came to answering questions like this one...

'Yes.' The word was hardly more than a whisper. 'Yes, I do.'

'Hm.' Adaira tapped her chin. 'So...you want to spend time with him. You want to be with him. But you don't want to marry him.'

'Yes.'

'That's a pretty tough conundrum.'

'Yes.'

'Especially considering the fact that my brother, for some mysterious reason, is the most eligible bachelor in the entire British Empire and there are droves of unmarried young women hunting him wherever he appears.'

'Yes.'

'It probably won't be long before one of them gets their claws into him, and she'll give him compliments, and money, and will do anything in her power to–
'

'Adaira?'

'Yes?'

'Shut up and get the next dress!'

'Yes, Ma'am!'

We continued to rifle through racks of ready-made dresses, balls of cloth and other finery. It felt extremely strange. All my life I had been on the outside looking in, wondering why other girls put so much effort into dressing up and looking pretty. Now I was on a desperate quest to do exactly the same. And why? To catch the attention of a man, in the hope that he might perhaps maybe perchance possibly if I was very, very lucky dance with me.

How the mighty have fallen.

Fallen indeed.

Fallen in love.

It was a terrifying feeling, and even more terrifying was to acknowledge it. I wanted – no, needed – Mr Rikkard Ambrose. Needed him with a bone-deep intensity that surpassed even my love for solid chocolate. But I had rejected him. He was not the sort of man to take that lightly. What if, with him, it was everything or nothing? What if, now that I had refused his offer, he no longer wanted me? It was a scary thought. But even scarier: what if he still did?

What if he asked me to dance tonight? What would I tell him? What could I possibly say? *Hello there! I'm sorry I don't want to marry you, but would you like to just live in sin with me instead, because I'm head-over-heels in love with you, you stone-faced son of a bachelor?*

Already tried that. It hadn't worked out so well.

So...what else could I say?

Baby steps, Lilly. Baby steps. After turning a man down like a ton of bricks, he most likely isn't inclined towards a passionate affair. First get him to dance with you. That is, if you can get him to unclench his teeth. Then worry about what to say to him.

All right.

Get him to dance with me. Get him to dance with me. Get him to dance with me. The words repeated over and over in my head, but I still had no clue how to do it.

I needed to attract his attention somehow. I needed just the right dress, the right make-up, and, most of all, the right style. I needed to become so stunningly beautiful that he couldn't possibly resist me. But...how?

You need help organising a demonstration for women's rights? I'm your girl! You need someone for a bit of target shooting? Great, I'm in! But dressing up? As a *female*?

Where did you even begin?

'Adaira, please!'

Desperately, I stared at the endless racks of clothes stretching in front of me. 'What am I supposed to do? What could I possibly wear that would attract his attention?'

'Well...' Turning in a circle, she gave the clothes all around a thoughtful look. 'You could always ask the tailor if he could stitch you a dress made from five-pound notes.'

'Adaira! This is serious!'

'I know. And I know my brother. If you want him to be unable to take his eyes from you, and to tear your dress off the moment the two of you are alone, that's the way to go.'

'I want him to tear my dress off because he wants *me*, not because he wants the dress!'

'Oh.' She clucked her tongue. 'Well, that's a little more tricky.'

'Serious suggestions. Please.'

There must have been something in my tone. Or maybe Adaira just knew exactly how I felt about her brother, because she instantly stopped teasing and started searching. She hadn't been joking when she said her mother had given her *carte blanche*. Without hesitation, she went through the most expensive dresses in the shop, everything from the latest London creations to rare and insanely expensive imports from Paris. Apparently, Lady Samantha had a quite definite preference as to which among her lady guests she would like to see as her daughter-in-law. Poor dear. I just didn't have the heart to tell her that I had turned him down already. Oh, and there was the little fact that I really, really didn't have enough money to pay for a ball gown, myself.

It would be rude to turn down her generosity, right?

But I wouldn't overdo it. Unless I really were to appear in a dress stitched from banknotes that he would get to keep, Mr Ambrose wouldn't be impressed by expensive fashion anyway. I needed something simple and elegant. Something that screamed 'I'm classy and cheap!' (the latter in the literal sense). I needed something perfect just for him.

But what kind of dress could that possibly be?

'Lilly!'

'Yes?'

Pulling my eyes from the décolletage of a dark red dress (much too generous for me, thank you), I turned to see Adaira emerging from a rack that featured fine, yet simply-cut dresses in interesting colours. She turned to face me and, smiling the devious smile I was starting to love, held up a dress into the light.

'What do you think of this?'

I stared – then I started smiling, too. 'Adaira, you are a genius!'

~~**~*~*

All was set. My clothes were bought. My secret weapons were sharpened and polished. My emergency stash of solid chocolate concealed in a hidden pocket. There was only one thing left for me to do: go completely and utterly barmy.

Ishegoingtoaskme? Ishegoingtoaskme? Blastblastblast! Ishegoingtoaskme?

The words hammered against my skull from the inside, needing to get out. I stalked through the halls of Battlewood, unable to sit down or even stand still, and every time I caught a glimpse of him, I wanted to grab him by the collar and demand: *'Well? Well, you bloody son of a bachelor? Are you going to ask me to dance with you? Are you? Do you still care?'*

But I didn't.

Because, for one, that would be utterly undignified. And for another, *he* would bloody well have to ask *me*! I wasn't going to ask him whether he was going to ask me, no Sir!

But...

But...

But what if he was going to ask someone else?

The hyenas were everywhere. They were prowling the halls of Battlewood, stalking every single one of Mr Ambrose's steps, just waiting to pounce on him.

Okay, maybe I had taken the metaphor a little bit far. But you get my meaning. Every single one of them acted as if she were the only one Mr Ambrose could possibly choose, as if she had a special right to him that no one had better doubt. Snide comments flew through the corridors like flies in the summer. Eyes were suddenly filled with greed and hatred, tongues were coated with poison. Over the course of the day, nearly half a dozen incidents occurred that, had the participants been men, would have ended in deadly duels. Everyone hated and mistrusted everyone else. There was only one thing that all of them agreed on, one thing united them all: their hatred and mistrust of me.

'So, my dear Miss Linton...' Lady Eveline glanced up from her embroidery and gave me a smile that was just as fake as her needlework. She was stitching daisies on a field of green. My corpse pierced with three dozen needles would have been a much more honest representation of her true artistic vision. 'What excuse will you give for not attending the Christmas ball?'

I returned her smile with one just as insincere. Years spent in the company of my aunt had made me an expert. 'Whatever makes you think that I'm not going?'

'Oh, nothing, it's just...' She gave a little laugh. 'I met a few gentlemen in London who had the "honour" of dancing with you at a ball or two. Let's just say they found the experience quite memorable. The bruises on their feet especially impressed themselves quite firmly on their recollection.'

Blasted, blood-sucking little witch! If I ever meet you in a dark alley...!

'Is that so?' My smile widened. 'I myself met quite a lot of gentlemen in London, but strangely enough none of them ever mentioned you. I suppose you must be easy to forget.'

Her hand jerked and she stabbed a needle into her finger.

Bingo! Score one for you, Lilly!

Now, if I could only make her stab herself in the heart instead...

'Tell me, Miss Linton,' came a sugary-sweet voice from behind me. 'How do you manage to be so plain and ordinary, and yet so self-assured? I really admire that about you. How do you do it?'

...there would still be two dozen more just like her left.

'Oh, it's quite easy.' With a beaming smile, I turned towards Lady Caroline. 'I stand in front of the mirror every day and tell myself "I shall not behave like a horrible hag today." You should try the method some time. It might do you a world of good.'

The friendly smile bled from Lady Caroline's face.

'You don't actually think you have a chance, do you?'

I raised an eyebrow. 'A chance with what?'

'Not what. Whom.' Her eyes narrowed to slits. And hers weren't the only ones. All around, gazes turned predatory. Guess who was the prey? 'You can't honestly think he'll pick *you*!'

He already has, you witch! In more ways than you can imagine.

I shrugged. 'Well, you never know. As they say in Spain ¡Vete a freír espárragos!'[19]

Her brow furrowed. 'What?'

I only smiled.

'Don't fool yourself.' That was Lady Caroline again, her voice like venom. 'A girl like you, with no title, no money, no nothing – he won't go near you with a ten-foot pole at that ball. Leave now, and spare yourself the humiliation of standing alone in a corner all night.'

'Excellent advice. Why don't you take it yourself?'

---

[19] A Spanish phrase which literally means 'Go fry asparagus!' Regarding its not-so-literal meaning...well, that is not quite so polite. I'll leave you to figure that out for yourself.

Blood rushed to her cheeks. Huzzah! My comeback reflex was still working as well as ever.

Unfortunately, it didn't do much good. They started to encircle me, approaching slowly, their fans drawn as if they were weapons.

'We are only concerned for your feelings and your reputation,' another lady told me with a smile you could have used as a bone saw. 'Wouldn't it be better for you to leave this place now, before you completely embarrass yourself?'

'To be honest...' Leaning forward, I slid my hand under the coffee table that stood between us. Invisible, it shot forward under the table top, grabbed her hand and bent back her forefinger. A quick twist was all it needed.

Her face paled.

'I think I'd rather stay. I can handle anything that comes at me. Don't you agree?'

Sweat appeared on her forehead. She gave a jerky nod. All her friends stared at her as if her hair had suddenly turned into spaghetti.

'Well, this has been fun, ladies.' Rising to my feet, I let go, and the hyena collapsed back in her chair, staring up at me with wide eyes. 'But I've got to run. Goodbye, or as they say in Spain, ¡Vete a la mierda!'

And I walked away with my head held high. Dear me... my recently gained Spanish vocabulary was really proving useful.

~~**~*~*

My boost of confidence had disappeared by lunchtime. True, I could hold my own against the hyenas. If I wanted to, I could lie in wait for Lady Caroline, hold her at gunpoint, tie her up and take her to the nearest farmer who needed a new scarecrow. But what good would that do?

Well, it would be tremendous fun.

All right, it would, but *apart from that* what good would it do? What did she or Lady Dorothea Asquith or Lady Eveline Maria Westwood or any one of those women really matter? After all, tonight, and every night after that, there would only be one person whose decision would count. And he was not wearing a dress or pelting me with snide little remarks. In fact, he hadn't spoken a word to me since Dalgliesh had left. And right now at the dinner table, he seemed determined to continue this policy.

Lady Samantha – bless her optimistic soul – had seated the two of us next to each other. It felt like sitting next to an undertaker's cold storage room – except that corpses would probably have been a lot more chatty. The arctic, ear-piercing silence radiating off of him was enough to make my bones shiver. If I needed an answer to the question whether he'd forgiven me for saying no to him – here it was.

Once or twice I glanced up at him, trying to catch his eye. I might as well have tried to catch a Siberian tiger with my bare hands. He didn't even seem to notice I was there.

But I knew better.

He noticed. He just didn't care to do anything about it.

Bloody hell! This can't be happening! Is he really that angry? Is he really going to ask someone else?

I couldn't bear to imagine him with any of these women. Dancing, holding hands, their bodies so close...

Swiftly, I sat down the glass I'd been holding. Another moment and I would have shattered it, so tight had my grip become.

Control yourself, Lilly! This isn't helping. You're next to him. Use the time. Find out what's going on in that stony head of his.

'Well, Mr Ambrose...' Putting on my best and most polished social smile, I turned towards him. 'I'm so looking forward to the Christmas ball. It's going to be so much fun.'

Silence.

Cold, hard, unforgiving silence.

All right. Another approach. What about a direct question? He'd be forced to answer then.

'Your mother has done a wonderful job decorating the house and making everything perfect for Christmas so far, don't you agree?'

A moment of silence, then...

'Indeed.'

Hooray! An answer.

Only not one that was particularly helpful.

'Do you think the ball tonight will be equally splendid?'

He made a noise in the back of his throat, somewhere between a 'yes', a 'no' and a 'go boil your head in vinegar'.

'By the way, since we're on the subject...'

I paused with bated breath, waiting to see if he'd pick up the bait.

He didn't. Damn!

'Since we're on the subject, have you made any plans yet?'

'Yes.'

My heart made a leap. 'Really?' *Too eager, bloody hell! You sound too eager, Lilly!* 'What are they?'

'Building a boot factory in Sunderland.'

I blinked. 'Pardon?'

'Boots, Mr Linton. Attire for feet generally made from leather.'

'I know what boots are!'

'Indeed? You never cease to amaze me.'

'I wasn't talking about your business plans for the next quarter! I meant what are your plans for tonight?'

Please say they involve me. Please, please, please.

'Well...' Spearing a piece of roast lamb on his fork, Mr Ambrose raised it to his lips and took a deliberate bite. I was seized by a sudden, slightly disturbing envy for roasted lambs. 'I suppose I will have to attend that ball of my mother's.'

Yes, yes yes! But with whom? With whom, damn you?

'Are you looking forward to it?' I asked, more as a way of keeping the conversation going than as an actual question. I knew his answer would be something like 'as much as I enjoy being stabbed repeatedly in the eye with a rusty pitchfork.'

'Very much indeed, Miss Linton.'

I nearly choked on a bite of Yorkshire Pudding. *'W-what?'*

'I believe I spoke perfectly audibly, Miss Linton.'

'Did I hear correctly? You are *looking forward* to a ball? An evening festivity that involves lots of dancing with females and no making money?'

'Indeed. You cannot spend all your time making money.'

Oh God. Was the world going mad?

'Besides...there will be a lovely young lady at the ball with whom I intend to dance the first dance.'

My heart nearly stopped.

You had better bet talking about me, Mister, or I'll...I'll...

'When do you intend to ask her?' I enquired, my voice no more than a whisper.

Nonchalantly, he sliced off another bit of roasted lamb and popped it into his mouth. 'Oh, I already have.'

What?

Slowly, my boiling hot mind followed the logical steps. He had already asked someone. He had not asked me yet. Ergo: he had asked *somebody else.*

Breathe, Lilly! Breathe! And above all, do not stab him through the heart with your pastry fork, no matter how tempting it may be!

'You...have, have you?'

'Indeed, Miss Linton.'

Indeed! If I hear that blasted word one more time...!

My hand tightened around the fork. Who was she? Who was the little witch who was trying to steal him away from me? I burned to ask him, burned to torture it out of him – but I couldn't. Doing so would mean admitting that I cared, in a bone-deep, heart-wrenching, soul-torturing way. And no way in hell was I prepared to admit that.

But I couldn't just sit there and say nothing!

'Do I know the lady?' I asked with the admirable nonchalance of a charging rhinoceros.

'Oh yes.'

Tell me her name! Tell me her name! Tell me her name, blast you!

Of course he didn't.

But he did say something else.

'And I must admit, Miss Linton, I'm quite fascinated by her. I've known her for quite a while, but since arriving here at Battlewood she has impressed me with her charm, her fiery spirit and her intelligence.'

Did he have a death wish?

'Oh, and it's generally thought that she is quite beautiful, too.'

Yes, he did. A big one.

I rammed my fork into a piece of Yorkshire Pudding, imagining that it was the head of Mr Rikkard Ambrose. I would have liked to imagine it as *her* head, but unfortunately, I didn't know what *she* looked like. Not yet. When I found out...

'Congratulations,' I ground out between clenched teeth. 'It sounds like you have found a very fitting lady for the first dance.'

'Oh, I intend to spend a lot more time with her than just one dance.' Taking another deliberate bite of roast lamb, Mr Ambrose gazed coolly out of the window as if I weren't even there. His face was a hard, impassive mask of stone. 'She's going to play a big role in my future life – one far beyond that of dance partner.'

My fork fell on the plate with a clatter.

What. Did. He. Just. Say?

FIRST OR FOREMOST

I tried everything to find out who it was. Everything. Questioning. Cajoling. Blackmail. Pleading. Death threats. Beard-removal threats. Nothing worked. Not even the latter on Karim. Nobody seemed to know who this mysterious lady was who had conquered Mr Ambrose's affections in one swoop, or if they knew, they weren't telling me.

The little witch certainly knew how to be sneaky! How could she do this, whoever she was, without me hearing a single word about it? Not a whisper even! I had no suspects. None of the hyenas had behaved out of the ordinary. In vain did I look for a smug smile or self-satisfied strut. Whoever she was, she knew how to keep a secret.

Well, she would have to, Lilly, wouldn't she? After all, she managed to steal the heart of the man you love right under your nose.

I just couldn't understand! How could he? Only this morning he had *proposed marriage* to me, for heaven's sake! And now he was already after somebody else? Weren't rejected romantic heroes supposed to brood and stew and pine for their one true love? But he probably considered that a waste of time. The Rikkard Ambrose new efficient romance method: one proposal per day until an accepting target is found. Ha!

'Worthless, faithless, fickle son of a bloody bachelor!' I growled, punctuating each word with a gunshot – not at him, mind you, but unfortunately only at the shooting targets in the range behind the house. Thick snow covered the targets and, with the sun setting, there was hardly enough light left to shoot properly, but right now I didn't care. I just needed *something* to shoot at. Whether I actually hit the intended target was secondary.

'Blasted, block-headed bastard! Feeble-headed flapdoodle! How could he? This isn't how it's supposed to go! He's supposed to love me!'

Which might have been a little easier if you'd accepted his offer of marriage, don't you think?

'Shut up!'

Sometimes, an inner voice of reason was really, really annoying. Especially when she had a point. I could have accepted his offer of marriage, and I could have been happy. But...could I have been me?

I didn't think so.

'Damn him! He's supposed to understand this! He's supposed to love me!'

Bam! Bam!

Two shots went off, and two holes appeared in the snow-covered target to the left of the one I'd been aiming at.

Damn him! Now he was even affecting my aim. Was there no part of me he would leave untouched?

A bit redundant, that question, Lilly, don't you think? If there were any part of you untouched by him, would you be standing out here in the snow while everyone's inside preparing for the big dance? Would you be shooting at targets you can't even properly see? And would that little bit of moisture that you're not prepared to call a tear be running down your cheek?

Swiftly, I reached up, wiping the moisture from my face. Then, as if drawn by seductive magic, I turned my head to glance back at the house. Lights were starting to appear in all the windows. Music began playing. I wanted to stay out here in the cold, stay alone and safe, away from Mr Rikkard Ambrose – but I couldn't. I couldn't resist his pull, and I couldn't resist seeing the girl he had chosen instead of me.

Damn my curiosity! And double-damn my love!

Firing a last shot, I whirled away from the targets and started towards the house. Within minutes, I had changed into my new ball gown – what a waste of money! – and collected my dance card. The gloves I had worn against the cold outside I discarded. The revolver I kept. Just in case I'd come face-to-face with *her*. Plus, I was not so overtaken by mindless jealousy as to forget that Lord Dalgliesh might still have spies among the staff. Safe was better than sorry.

I glanced at myself in the mirror just once. It was bittersweet. I'd chosen the gown with hope in my heart. Now that there was only despair there, the sight hurt. But I had never been the sort to shy away from pain. Particularly not the kind for which I had only myself to blame. Straightening my spine, I stepped out of my room and started down the corridor. The sweet, discordant sound of musicians tuning their instruments drifted up the hallway towards me, and I let it lead me to my destination.

Lady Samantha was waiting at the entrance to the ballroom, officially greeting a few lady friends. When she looked up and saw me, her eyes widened slightly. I knew why, but I resisted the temptation to hug myself and hide as much of my dress from the world as I could. I would not be ashamed of myself or my choices.

'Hello, dear.' Lady Samantha's voice was softer even than usual. She reached out and grasped my hand. 'I'm so glad you came. You look...beautiful.'

Her eyes slid up and down, taking me and my dress in once again – but she said nothing more. In that moment, I loved the little old lady.

'Thank you.' *If only your opinion were the one that really mattered.* I gave her a sad smile. 'But not beautiful enough, I think.'

'Whatever do you mean, my dear?'

'Didn't you hear?' One corner of my mouth curled up in a sad little smile. 'He picked someone else for the first dance.'

The marchioness gave me an odd look. If I didn't know better, I'd almost say she was amused. But that couldn't be, surely.

'Um...why don't you go in, dear? The ball will start soon, and I am quite certain that you shouldn't miss a minute of it.'

With that strange statement, she gave me a gentle push towards the door. Shaking my head in confusion, I entered. What had all that been about?

The moment I stepped into the ballroom, Lady Samantha's odd behaviour was driven out of my mind. The place was magnificent. There was no other word for it. Magnificent. Hundreds upon hundreds of candles on majestic chandeliers illuminated the gigantic hall, casting it into a golden light that really wasn't even necessary, because the place was already golden. Golden and white and silver and every other pure and precious colour you could think of. Exquisite paintings covered the walls and ceiling where they weren't gilded, depicting gods and titans and ancient heroes. Images which should have clashed with the occasion – but somehow they didn't. Somehow, that mystical scenery of ages past dancing in the shadows created the perfect contrast to the giant tree rising in the middle of the room, in the centre of the light.

The tree *he* had put there.

The thought was like a dagger through my heart. Except that a dagger would have ended all of this. The blasted thought just hurt like hell. Damn!

But if I was still alive, at least that meant I would still get a look at *her*. My curiosity was stronger even than my desire to crawl away into a corner and die.

Quickly, I let my gaze drift around the room – but he wasn't here yet. And if he wasn't, she wouldn't be either. Ladies almost always entered the ballroom on the arm of their escort – if they had one. And whoever this girl was, she would most certainly be walking in on the arm of Mr Rikkard Ambrose. None would be stupid enough to miss that chance. Quickly, I let my gaze slide over the faces of the ladies who were already here. I spotted Lady Caroline, Lady Dorothea and Lady Eveline and felt a surge of satisfaction.

So...they're here without him tonight, are they?

My satisfaction disappeared abruptly when I remembered that so was I.

'My Lords, Ladies and Gentlemen?'

All eyes snapped to a liveried servant who had appeared at the entrance of the ballroom, holding a staff. With his instrument of authority, he pounded the polished floor three times, making clear what his duty was tonight.

'It is my great honour and pleasure to welcome you to the Christmas ball at Battlewood. Please greet the man who will be your host for tonight. Lord–'

A hand shot out, wrapping mercilessly around the man's wrist and squeezing. A few cold, whispered words floated through the air, too low to be understood.

'...um, *Mister* Rikkard Ambrose.'

And there he was. Rikkard Ambrose, as he lived (and maybe even breathed if he wasn't made of stone). He towered in the doorway, more perfect and beautiful than he ever had been. And on his arm, walking proudly beside him with a broad smile on her face was...

I blinked.

Then I looked again, just to be sure. But I hadn't made a mistake. If there was one young lady in this house that I'd recognise even with a bag over my head, it was Lady Adaira Louise Jannet Melanie Georgette Ambrose.

His sister.

He had come to the ball with his *little sister*!

I remembered what he'd told me about his dance partner at lunch. Suddenly, his words appeared in a slightly different light.

I'm quite fascinated by her. I've known her for quite a while, but since arriving here at Battlewood she has impressed me with her charm, her fiery spirit and her intelligence. She's going to play a big role in my future life.

I was going to kill him.

Slowly.

Painfully.

And then I was going to resurrect him and kiss him till he suffocated.

Wait...maybe you should rethink that, Lilly.

Indeed?

Yes. Perhaps you should kill her, first.

What a wonderful idea! I searched my treasure trove of Spanish and Arabic swear words for a word that was bad enough for my dear friend Lady Adaira, the traitorous little witch, but found nothing. The little vixen had known all along! And she had let me stew in my own over-romantic juices for the fun of it! Oh, when I got my hands on her...!

Maybe I should team up with Karim. He probably knew lots more torture methods than sweet little me, and would be more than willing to help avenge himself on the creator of Prince Fragrant Yellow Flower in the Happy Moonlight, Heir to the Principality of Rubbish. Maybe he'd even lend me his sabre.

In just that moment, Lady Adaira glanced up and spotted me. Smiling, she dipped into a perfect curtsy – and then winked at me.

She *winked* at me.

Oh, that was too much! She was...she was...

...impressive? Admirable?

No! No, horrible! Outrageous! A disrespectful, mad little imp!

The difference to you being?

I'm sure I would have found a satisfactory answer to that question if not at that very moment, the musicians had started playing, and Mr Ambrose had swept his sister off onto the dancefloor.

Oh my God.

He could dance.

I mean *really* dance.

The other guests were just as stunned as I. They drew back in hushed silence as he and Adaira whirled across the parquet, dancing with the grace and elegance of two professional dancers. They were like fire and ice, like water and stone. She moved with a fae-like fluidity, he with a precision that calculated every step, every twitch of every muscle. And I?

For just one moment, I didn't feel envy or anger or anything like that. I saw the light in her eyes, and the intensity with which Mr Ambrose looked at her. He might not have always been the big brother she wanted or needed. He might have been far away for years upon years. But Rikkard Ambrose always paid his debts. This was his apology. His way of saying sorry without uttering a word. Tonight, he made her shine, for all the world to see.

Dammit! Where had my blasted anger gone? Where was my desire to strangle her?

Things weren't any better than they had been ten minutes ago. All right, so he wasn't dancing with a mercenary little witch who wanted to snatch him away from me, but so what? He wasn't dancing with me, either, and by the looks of it, he had no desire to do so. There was only one thing left for me to do. Only one thing that would soothe my wounded heart and make me feel marginally better.

Slowly, the other couples began to join them on the dancefloor. As the ballroom started to fill with music, the sound of dancing feet and flowing silk, I retreated into a corner. Inconspicuously, I slid my hand into my dress and pulled out my salvation.

'I knew it,' I sighed. 'I knew I was going to need this.'

And I took a big bite from my emergency solid chocolate ration.

~~*~**~*~*

In general, balls were just about the most sophisticated form of torture you could have devised for me. They inflicted a maximum of suffering with a minimum of screaming and broken bones. This ball was a little different. Usually, I was in the company of my aunt, who insisted on towing me onto the dancefloor and thrusting me into the arms of partners she considered suitable. This time, I was without such a lovely, helpful companion. Plus, due to Lady Samantha's matchmaking preparations, there were plenty of young ladies present who were much more eligible than me, and the fact that most of them were also eligible for the hag-of-the-year award didn't seem to deter most of the gentlemen present. Many of the young officers especially, all younger sons who had gone into the army because of a lack of inheritance, were looking for an heiress to catch – which I was most definitely not.

So, for once, I was being left alone. I could sit peacefully in my corner and munch my solid chocolate. Nobody even approached to ask me to dance. How great! I was being left in peace for once in my life. Wonderful. Fantastic. Stupendously, remarkably marvellous. I was so lucky tonight.

Nnng! Lilly, who are you trying to fool?

253

Without my being able to prevent it, my eyes slid to the dancefloor, searching. But in vain. If Mr Ambrose was still there, he was hidden by the whirling figures of dozens of other guests, having the time of their life. Smiles shone everywhere. Here and there, a happy laugh rose over the crowd. Everything seemed to sparkle with that very special golden shine that only a happy gathering at Christmas could produce.

A gathering I wasn't part of.

Merry Christmas, Lilly. Very merry Christmas.

Sighing in misery, I took another bite of solid chocolate.

The night dragged on. Once in a while, the dance music ceased and the dancers could rest their feet while the musicians struck up a popular carol. Some people were so merry, they actually sang along. Personally, I didn't particularly feel like singing about joy and good cheer. If there were a carol about misery, murder and mayhem...now that would have been a different thing.

I thought the night had reached its all-time low – and then my solid chocolate ran out. It was like a dagger through my battered heart. For a moment, I considered leaving. But then I caught a glance of Lady Samantha through the press of people. I couldn't run out on her! Whatever might be said about her son, The Marchioness Ambrose had been nothing but kind to me during my stay at Battlewood. Leaving her Christmas party after my male alter ego had specifically asked for me to be invited and she had agreed against all odds, would be unaccountably rude. And while I had no problems with being rude to most of the world's population, she was a definite exception.

Finally, the candles started to burn low, and a liveried servant stepped in front of the musicians to announce the last dance. I sighed. In relief? In pain? I didn't really know. Either way, it was good that all this would soon be over. Maybe in sleep, I would be able to forget how much my heart was aching.

I was just about to rise and make my way to the door when a hand suddenly came down to rest on my shoulder. A strong, hard, familiar hand.

'Miss Linton?'

That voice...

I swallowed, my heart giving another agonising pang.

'Mr Ambrose.'

Slowly, I turned to face him. I thought I had prepared myself for the sight of him – but I'd been wrong. He was magnificent. The flickering light of the candles accentuated every hard line of his chiselled face, giving him a golden shine that somehow made him look like an angel descended from heaven. Only...the guardian or the avenging kind?

'What do you want?'

Taking a step towards me, he leaned forward and pinned me with his arctic eyes. Those unfathomable eyes, pools of dark, stormy water, drew me in, destroying any chance I had at resistance before I'd even begun to try.

'This is a ball, is it not?' Bowing just deep enough for our eyes to be on one level, he hit me with the full force of his commanding gaze. 'Miss Lillian Linton, will you grant me the honour of your hand for the last dance?'

Silence Broken, Words Spoken

I stared at him.

And then I stared at him some more.

Finally, Mr Ambrose cocked his head. 'An answer, Miss Linton?'

'Now?' My voice was half-growl, half-whisper. 'You've had the whole evening to ask me to dance, and you choose to do it *now*?'

'Yes.'

'Yes? *Yes*? That's all you've got to say for yourself?'

'Yes.'

And before I could think of a comeback to that magnificent statement, he had captured my arm with his and was leading me off to the dancefloor.

'Hey!' I protested. 'I haven't said yes, yet!'

Mr Ambrose gave me a cold look that told me he read more into my words than just one dance. 'I know.'

Oh dear...

He was angry. The kind of arctic anger which only Mr Ambrose and a Canadian blizzard were capable of. And in his anger, he was only more beautiful.

'The last dance, My Lords, Ladies and Gentlemen!' The liveried servant in front of the musicians clapped his hands and stepped into the shadows.

Mr Ambrose held out his hand to me. Before I could think about it, my fingers had already closed around his.

What is happening? He's been an arse to me! Why should I do this? Why should I...

The remainder of that question slipped out of my mind when I was whirled around with consummate skill, and dipped back. A strong arm came up behind me to catch me just before I fell. Breathing hard, I gazed up into the stunningly perfect face of Mr Rikkard Ambrose.

'Shall we?'

I felt as if I were dreaming. Only...was this a dream or a nightmare? Was he only doing this to humiliate me further? To get his revenge for my refusal?

But it wasn't revenge I saw burning in his eyes. It was the cold fire of desire.

'I feel that I am making an objectively true statement,' he whispered, 'when I say that you look beautiful.' His eyes slid up and down my form, caressing every curve, and I shivered under his scrutiny. 'Especially in *that dress*.'

Ah yes. The dress.

I felt heat burn in the tips of my ears. Suddenly, my choice of gown didn't seem like such a good idea anymore.

'Adaira picked it,' I hurriedly asserted. Well, it was mostly true.

'Indeed?' He leaned forward, his gaze becoming somehow even more intense. My knees felt as if they would buckle any second. 'And did she decide on that colour, too?'

'No,' I muttered, glancing down at the ball gown that was a fascinatingly deep, dark sea-coloured shade somewhere between blue, green and grey – the exact same colour as his eyes. 'That was my decision.'

'I see.' So quickly I had no time to protest, he pulled my hand to his lips and kissed it. When it was over, the only evidence it had ever happened was the burning brand on the back of my hand. Tingles travelled up my arm, and somehow, it felt as if I'd been permanently marked. 'It's...adequate.'

'Why, thank you so much for the compliment, Sir.'

'You're welcome, Miss Linton.'

The musicians struck the first notes of the dance. Breathless, I felt Mr Ambrose's arms tighten around me. He was really going to do it. He was going to dance with me.

'Why?' I demanded in a whisper.

Why did you do this? Why the last dance, not the first? Is that all I am to you? An afterthought?

He seemed to read all those silent questions in my eyes. Twirling me into the first move of the dance, his cold gaze speared me with the force of a crashing glacier.

'The first dance for the first woman I knew, the last one for the last. You may not have been the first woman in my life, Miss Linton – but I promise you, you will be the last. There won't be anyone else as long as I live.'

For a moment, I forgot to breathe. Good God that was...

That was so Mr Ambrose. Ignoring me the whole evening, and then trying to pass it off as romantic.

And do you know what the worst thing was?

It *worked*. It *bloody worked*, curse him! And oh, how very well! All I wanted to do right then and there was to throw my arms around his neck and kiss him until I passed out. And he knew it, too, dammit! There was victory in his eyes, victory and power.

Instantly, I felt the fire of rebellion rise in my belly. 'The last woman in your life, eh? So does that mean you intend to remain celibate for the rest of your life, Sir?'

He met my eyes head-on, not a hint of shame on his granite face as he said, 'Not at all, Miss Linton. Quite the opposite, in fact.'

I felt heat rise to my face. Blast! That had backfired! Quickly, I glanced around.

'Mr Ambrose! Remember where you are!'

'I know exactly where I am. I'm in a ballroom at Battlewood Hall dancing the waltz, and you are in my arms.'

Before I could reply, he whirled me around to a trill in the music, and suddenly, I was bent backward again, and he was leaning over me, his hot breath caressing my skin.

Breathe, Lilly! Breathe!

'Well, *you* may feel like I'm the one,' I whispered. 'But what if I don't? I could decide to take another lover any time. Ten, in fact. Ten dozen, if I wanted.'

If I ever stopped loving you.

In a flash, he pulled me up again and whirled me the other way, his hands pulling me along like magic.

'Over my dead body, Miss Linton!'

'That could be arranged!'

His eyes narrowed infinitesimally. 'Interpreting emotions is not my forte, Miss Linton-'

'You don't say.'

'-but can it be that for some reason you feel aggravated?'

At first I wanted to snap back at him, to thump his thick head against a wall, anything – but then I took a deep breath and did something a thousand times harder: I told him the truth.

'Yes. There is a reason.' I lowered my head, so he wouldn't see my face. 'You didn't ask me for the first dance!'

There was a moment of silence. Then...

'You didn't give me any reason to believe I would get it if I asked.'

'What?'

Incredulous, I stared up into his dark, ice-cold eyes, and for a moment saw something there I had never seen before. Was it...could it be *hurt*?

No! No, that couldn't be! For it to be hurt, Mr Ambrose would have to be able to have real feelings!

Feelings like love, you mean?

Good point.

I wet my lips, trying to find the right words. 'Just because...just because I said no to marriage doesn't mean I said no to everything. I want you. I need you. You make me crazy, and sometimes I want to kill you – but I couldn't imagine my life without you.' One corner of my mouth quirked up. 'Especially without that monthly pay cheque of yours.'

It was a joke, meant to lighten the mood. So his next words hit me like the blade of a dagger, sharp, hard and cold.

'That's all you want me for? My money?'

The cold demand shoved past all my defences straight into my chest. I was about to retaliate with a barrage of insults of my own, when I saw that uncertain shimmer in his eyes again, and suddenly the truth began to dawn on me.

'That's what all this is about?' My voice was no more than a whisper. 'You think I don't love you?'

Whirling me around, he pulled me close until our faces were only inches apart. A muscle in his jaw twitched.

'It's a reasonable conclusion to come to, don't you think? I asked you to marry me. I asked you to be mine, to have and to hold, to love and to cherish. And you said no.'

'But that doesn't mean I don't...! How would you even get the idea into your head that...? You know how I feel! Of course you know! I mean, I told y-'

The word stuck in my throat as I realised something.

I had never told him.

He had told me about his feelings. Mr Rikkard Ambrose, the living incarnation of stubborn silence, had wrenched open his jaws and confessed his love to me – and I had forgotten to say 'Ditto!'

Oops.

'Ehem...Well...' I cleared my throat. 'I may have made a slight oversight.'

'Indeed, Miss Linton?'

'Indeed, Sir.'

Around us, the musicians struck up the last chords of the dance. We turned into a final whirl, and then, suddenly, the dancers were slowing down, and the first candles at the edge of the dance floor were guttering out. The night was coming to an end.

'Well, Miss Linton?' His face even more beautiful now that it was half-cast in shadow, Rikkard Ambrose stared down at me with enough intensity to make my bones melt. 'What is it that you've forgotten to tell me?'

I opened my mouth to reply – but in that very moment, the music ended, and the last candles guttered out. Laughing voices disappeared out of the room, down the corridor, and a moment later we were alone in the darkness, broken only by thin slivers of moonlight.

The end.

The end of the ball. The end of the night.

The end for us as well?

I cleared my throat.

'I...I should go.'

Cast in shadows as it was, the chiselled face of Rikkard Ambrose was even more of a mystery. He didn't display one single emotion.

'Yes. Yes, you should.'

Neither of us moved.

'Like right now. We should leave right now. The servants may see us if we stay here alone. There will be talk. We should leave, Mr Ambrose.'

'Yes. Yes, we should.'

Still, neither of us moved. Still, we kept staring at each other.

'Why aren't you leaving, Mr Ambrose?' I accused.

'Why aren't you, Miss Linton?'

Silence.

A silence full of words that were dying to be spoken. Some had already died and ascended to heaven on beams of moonlight.

'Miss Linton...I...'

'Yes?'

Slowly, torturously, he reached up, brushing his hand against my cheek.

'Lillian...'

My whole body quivered under his gentle touch. Images flashed through my head, silly ideas, crazy ideas, wonderful ideas, all of them completely impossible. I couldn't! I simply couldn't! But...

'Lillian,' he said again, and once more touched my cheek.

Just a simple little touch.

And I broke.

'Not here.' Hidden by the spreading shadows, I swiftly reached up to catch his hand and give it a gentle squeeze that meant so much more than a simple touch. 'Not here.'

What the heck? What are you talking about, Lilly? You have to move! If his mother sees you...

And then I was moving.

Only...it wasn't away from him.

Strong, familiar hands took hold of me, and swept me off the dancefloor, straight into a shadowy alcove. Before I could ask him what we were doing there, he had pulled aside a curtain, revealing a small door leading out of the ballroom.

'How–'

'The advantages of growing up in a place,' he cut me off. 'Come.'

'Anywhere!' I heard a breathless whisper. Was that girlish promise in the dark me speaking? No. I could never be so foolish and reckless!

Lilly, have you met yourself?

There was a tidal wave building inside me, one strong enough to sweep away the greatest of rocks and the most monumental icebergs. And my heart danced atop the waves, lost in the storm. All I could do was be pulled along as he drew me down the corridor faster and faster, towards the inevitable end. Halfway to my room we slid around a corner, bumped into a wall and slammed into each other. His arms came up around me to catch me, and suddenly we were kissing, and just for a second, I didn't care where we were or what we were doing, or who might walk in on us.

Even his mother?

All right, maybe I did care.

'We...we can't do this,' I whispered against his lips. 'Not here.'

'Agreed,' he told me, and kissed me so hard I saw stars.

'We have to stop,' I told him, and kissed him back so hard he probably saw £ signs.

'Indeed.'

'Then why aren't you stopping?'

'Why aren't you?' he asked, and kissed me again. Damn him! And damn me, too, for letting him! For desperately wanting more!

In dire need, I reached for a special weapon—the magic word.

'Please,' I whispered.

I felt his body shudder.

'Miss Linton...!'

'Please. I need more. But...not here.'

A growl erupted from his chest, and his grip on me tightened. But even that didn't work. Okay. Time for my last resort. Time for the *real* magic word.

'Now!'

He growled, and suddenly, I was moving again. I did my best to control my grin as he swept me through the dark hallways of Battlewood, but I didn't have much success. The magic word had worked! We moved faster than ever, Mr Ambrose pulling me along, arm in an iron grip around my waist. I was more than eager to keep up, but with his long strides eating up the ground as if it were nothing, it wasn't easy. Finally, he simply swept me up in his arms and carried me along. I gave a half-yelp, half-sigh of pleasure. I didn't even think of protesting, that's how far gone I was.

'Impatient, Sir?' I murmured against his chest.

'You know what they say.' Penetrating the darkness, cold, dark, sea-coloured eyes met mine. 'Knowledge is Power is Time is Money.'

How was it possible that those words made my insides heat? They were the coldest, most callous, calculating words that had ever been invented in the history of humankind, and yet, and yet...

It was him. It was Mr Ambrose, and the fact that the words came from his lips. That tidal wave inside me rose up again, ready to swallow me whole.

Just then, out of the corner of my eye, I saw a flash of dark brown through the shadows – and Mr Ambrose stopped.

'We're here.'

Here? Where?

Oh, right. My room. I had been so captivated by his eyes that for the moment I had completely forgotten where we were going.

Slowly, he set me down. I reached behind me and felt the smooth wood of the door at my back. The logical part of my brain screamed at me to find the damn doorknob, get inside and lock the door, but I couldn't. Mr Ambrose stood so close...I could feel his icy energy radiating off him, could feel his arctic gaze burning into me. If only I could see his eyes. If only I could read his expression. But it was far too dark for that.

Something thudded against the wood to my left, and a second later to my right. I couldn't see, but I knew: they were Mr Ambrose's arms, caging me in with his hands on either side of the doorframe. There was nowhere for me to run, no way for me to escape him.

As if I really wanted to.

'Now...where were we, Miss Linton?'

He moved closer. I couldn't really see it in the shadows, but I felt it. Felt him. I swallowed, suddenly feeling a bit weak in the knees. 'Um...well...'

'Ah, I remember.' His voice was smooth as a freshly polished iceberg, and ten times as dangerous. It was a voice that could make kings quiver in their boots. 'You were just about to tell me how you feel about me, Miss Linton.'

'Was I?'

'Yes. You were.'

His tone was hard. Uncompromising. Commanding.

I swallowed again. My throat was bone dry. Why in heaven's name was this so hard?

'How about,' I whispered, standing up on my tiptoes until my eyes were on a level with his, 'if I just show you?'

And I kissed him.

Not with fire.

Not with passion.

With love.

Softly.

Slowly.

Silently.

And Mr Rikkard Ambrose, the arctic iceberg in human form, melted under my touch. He made a sound in the back of his throat I had never heard before – a needy sound.

Mr Rikkard Ambrose *needing* something?

Oh, sure, he *wanted* lots of things – money, power, the one hundred and seventy-hour work week – but *need*? He'd never really needed anything before. Yet to judge by the way his arms slid around me, pulling me so close I could hardly breathe, he needed me now. He needed me with a vengeance!

Breaking away from his mouth, I placed another gentle kiss on his cheek. The words began to tumble out of me, and there was nothing in the world I could have done about it.

'I.'

One more kiss, on his other cheek.

'Love.'

And a third that I somehow, stretching up farther than I would have thought possible, managed to press on his forehead.

'You.'

His arms tightened even more, cutting off my air completely. I didn't mind in the least. Oh, exquisite, fantabulous suffocation! Wouldn't it be spiffing to die this way? Why care that my life would be over, as long as I was in his arms?

'Again!' His voice was more cold and commanding than I had ever heard it – and I loved it! Loved him. 'Say it again!'

That was Mr Rikkard Ambrose. Always get two for the price of one.

'I love you.'

His lips claimed mine for one fiery, fierce, heart-wrenching second. 'Again!'

A laugh escaped me, echoing in the dark hallway. It was a laugh that felt lighter and happier than any in my life. 'Again? How many times until you've had enough?'

His hand captured my chin, turning my face straight towards him. Through the shadows I could just barely make out the dark, sea-coloured pools of his eyes. 'What makes you think I'll ever have enough of you? Now...' Leaning forward until his forehead touched mine and his eyes were burrowing into my soul, he whispered: 'Say. It. Again.'

Feeling a wave of need sweep over me, I gazed into those dark eyes – and the words left my mouth before I could catch them.

'Come inside, and I will.'

The offer hung in the air between us, heavy with meaning. Inside. Into my bedroom.

For a long moment there was nothing but silence. Then...

'Miss Linton!'

'Yes, Mr Ambrose, Sir?'

'You can't seriously be suggesting that I...!'

Standing up on my tiptoes, I pressed a gentle kiss to his cheek.

'Oh yes, I can.'

His body shuddered under my touch.

'I know what you're trying to do!'

'Do you?' Slowly, I let my lips slide from his cheek, down over his lips, onto his throat in a gentle caress. 'Do you really?'

Because I didn't. Someone else had taken control of my body. Someone brave and fearless not just on the outside, but on the inside, too. Someone who wasn't afraid to grab what she wanted when it was right in front of her.

Mr Ambrose slammed his fist into the wall. 'I can't! I'm a gentleman! A gentleman mustn't....a gentleman can't...'

'And I am a lady,' I heard myself tell him. 'I know we mustn't. I know we can't.'

'I have to leave.'

'I know. Me, too.'

'Then go! Go now, before it's too la–'

His words drowned as I reclaimed his lips. Fumbling for the doorknob behind me, I twisted, and kicked the door open. Half-dragging, half falling, I pulled him into the room. Under normal circumstances, I wouldn't have been able to move him an inch. But right now...

I had just admitted to loving a man. And he loved me back.

Circumstances weren't normal.

Not at all.

'It's already too late,' I told his shadowy form towering above me in the darkness. 'It's been too late for a good, long time.'

'I must leave.' His protest was nothing but a raspy whisper now. 'Right now! It's time to say good night.'

I pressed my forehead to his. 'Oh, it will be a good night, all right. A very good one.'

Under my touch, I could feel his entire body harden, his muscles tensing deliciously. Capturing his face in my hands, I leaned forward, until our lips brushed against each other. 'I love you.'

All I got in return was silence. Silence and that soul-piercing, dangerous look of his.

'Well?' I swallowed. I needed to hear him say it again. 'Do you still love me, too?'

'How about,' he growled, taking hold of me and pushing me backwards towards the bed that held such a dangerous, delicious promise, 'if I just show you?'

LOVE IN THE MOONLIGHT

How about if I just show you?

My own words, thrown back at me, echoed in my head like the harp of a fallen angel. Did he really mean what I thought he meant?

This can't be happening. Those words can't have come from the lips of Mr Rikkard Ambrose. He never wanted to before! He never...

But then a sliver of moonlight cut through the darkness, falling upon his stone-hard, serious face – and I knew. I knew I had heard right. I knew that those delicious words wouldn't be the only incredible thing to come tonight.

The backs of my legs hit the bed. Suddenly I was falling. The soft down engulfed me and I lay on my back, gazing up at Mr Ambrose towering above me.

'Lillian.'

My name on his lips was a plea. A command. It was everything and more.

Reaching up with one trembling hand, I touched his chest and licked my lips, tasting the unfamiliar word before I spoke it.

'Rikkard.'

He moved. Or did I? It was hard to tell when a moment later we collided with a force too great for any heart to survive. Clutching at each other, we rolled across the king-sized bed, hands tugging at each other's clothes, lips seeking lips.

This is crazy! This can't be happening! Not with Mr Rikkard Stone-Cold Ambrose!

But if this wasn't him and me, who then? Some strange doppelganger with a pounding heart alive with love? If so, who was the man above me? The stone-hard, powerful, perfect man whose hands were tearing at my clothes in a frenzy? Surely it couldn't be the one I truly wanted.

'Lillian!'

That voice, breathing my name...

His voice.

'Please!' And that had sounded like my voice. 'Please! I need you!'

Yes, it had really sounded like me. But I would never admit such a thing.

Then came the broken whisper out of the darkness:

'I need you too, Lilly.'

All right, that proved it. Whoever this was who was quickly and efficiently tearing off my clothing, it was *not* Mr Rikkard Ambrose.

Or at least that was what I thought until his lips brushed my ear and whispered: 'I love you.'

I shook under the force of those three words. Such unimportant words, my mind had always told me – until that moment. In that moment, my world shattered and reformed, and suddenly they were more important than anything else. More important than solid chocolate. More important than life. More important than my desire for a raise.

'Love you, too!'

There was that voice again, that voice sounding just like mine. But why did it sound so breathless? Maybe it had something to do with the mouth leaving a trail of burning kisses down my throat?

'Please, Sir... Please, now.'

'Yes.'

Strong, familiar fingers found the neckline of my dress, encountering resistance. A ripping sound came out of the darkness. Was he tearing off clothes? Was I? Was it a freak storm?

I didn't really care, because the storm of desire rising inside me was strong enough for both of us. The night around us was silent and black as pitch, but inside of me, a fire was burning, and the mingled sounds of our gasps fanned the flames with every breath we took. Cloth tore. Silk brushed my skin as my dress slid away to disappear, torn and discarded, into the shadows. Cool air tickled me and, instinctively, I pressed myself closer against him, feeling...

Bare skin.

Bare skin over strong, hard, muscles.

A heady feeling rushed up inside of me. This was actually happening! This wasn't just a bit of hanky-panky in the office, or a kiss in the heat of the jungle. We were together, in a bed, on the verge of...

I couldn't quite think the word. Not yet. But I could feel it. Feel the need burning inside me. Feel his skin burn into mine with a heat I would never have thought this iceberg capable of.

'Lillian.'

A thrill raced down my spine. Would I ever get tired of the sound of my name on his lips?

A moment later, his mouth claimed mine and gave me the answer: yes! There were so much more interesting things for his lips to do than talking. Hot things. Needy things. Things that left me panting and pleading for more.

'Please...!'

'Soon.'

Breaking the kiss, he reached out with one hand and cupped my face in the gentlest gesture I had ever seen him make, except perhaps the time he'd handled that Ming vase worth over two hundred thousand pounds.

Bloody hell! Was I feeling jealous of a piece of pottery?

I was!

Ha, just you wait, you stupid little vase! I'll show you! I bet you couldn't do this, could you?

My hands flew up into the shadows. Grabbing him by the lapels, I jerked him down towards me. His supporting arm slipped and he toppled onto the bed. We rolled over until I came to rest on top, where I belonged.

'What are you doing?' he demanded.

'What do you think?' Pressing a heated kiss to the corner of his mouth, I took a tighter hold on his lapels, and tugged. There was a ripping sound and buttons scattered in all directions.

'Miss Linton!'

My cheek pressed softly against his, I whispered, 'You called me Lillian just now.'

There was a moment of silence. Then, in a voice that was slightly hoarser than usual, he said:

'That will take money to repair!'

'Deduct it from my salary. I don't care!' Moisture pricked the corner of my eye, but right now, that didn't matter to me. Right now, I didn't need or want to keep my defences up. I let the single tear trickle down my cheek, unashamed. My hands curled into the last layer of cloth that lay between us, and tugged it off. 'It was worth it. You're worth it.'

Silence.

And not the cold kind.

The dumbstruck kind.

As it extended and spread through the darkness like a blanket of snow, enveloping us, I suddenly realised something: that just now had probably been the first time in a very long time that anyone had told Mr Rikkard Ambrose he was worth it – worth anything.

Oh, I was sure he got more compliments than there were stars in the sky, from sycophants and lickspittles who wanted to ingratiate themselves with the richest man of the British Empire. But a truly heartfelt compliment from someone who knew him and cared?

When was the last time he had heard one?

Better question, Lilly: when was the last time that someone who really knows him was crazy enough to care?

'You are!' The words spilled out of my mouth before I could think twice about them. Grasping his face, I moved closer until even in the darkness, I could see into his eyes. 'You are worth it! You may be a stubborn, chauvinistic, cold-hearted, ruthless, self-righteous son of a bachelor–'

'Don't flatter me too much, Miss Linton.'

'–but you're a good man. Well, to me, anyway. Sometimes. Mostly.'

'Are you quite sure that you are in love with me?'

'Yes!'

'Just checking.'

Instead of answering, I kissed him again. Long and hard and with all my heart. Then, slowly, I let my lips wander. First over his cheek, then across his stone-hard jaw, and further down to where, usually, his ten-year-old mint-condition tailcoat was to be found. Now there was no tailcoat. No nothing. There was only him.

And he...

He was really truly mine?

I got my answer when strong arms slid around my shoulders, pulling me closer until my cheek was cradled against his rock-hard chest.

Safety.

Warmth.

Love.

Never in my life before had anyone made me feel like this – like a small child, and at the same time like the strongest most beautiful woman alive. I couldn't keep the smile from tugging at the corners of my mouth. Was this real? Was Mr Ambrose, Mr Rikkard Stone Face Ambrose actually making me smile?

He was. And it felt wonderful in more ways than I could have dreamed of. I had expected the intoxicating rush of this encounter, had expected to feel heat and need and passion – but never in a million years would I have expected how close it would make me feel. Close to him. Close to his heart.

Let's not forget his body, shall we?

Good point.

Tentatively, I reached out. Feeling almost like a naughty child touching an invaluable artwork, my fingers brushed against his chest. He was so hard, so smooth, I might really have thought he was a sculpture hewn from stone if I hadn't felt him tremble beneath me.

'I'm sure,' I repeated, my words a whispered breath against his skin. 'I love you.'

His arms tightened around me. 'Adequate.'

I couldn't help grinning like a fool. My greedy fingers continued to explore. I couldn't see a thing, couldn't catch a single glimpse of his perfection – but that didn't matter. Because no matter how perfect he might look, how chiselled his muscles might appear in bright daylight, it was nothing compared to how they felt, bare to the touch. Heat rose inside me to meet his ice and stone. I wanted more. Touch more. Feel more. It wasn't enough. It would never be.

'Corset!'

My breathless demand was hardly audible, but he caught it. A second later, his fingers were at the back of my corset, tearing open lacings as if they were no more substantial than cobwebs. The bloody cumbersome thing fell away, and I was free! Free to move, free to feel, free to do terrifying and wonderful things.

'Come!'

I didn't have the best track record when it came to obeying commands coming from Mr Rikkard Ambrose – but that one I obeyed without hesitation. Gripping his broad shoulders as if they were a lifeline, I closed the distance between us, just as he grabbed me to do the same. We clashed like ice and fire, like rock and not-so-solid chocolate. With only a thin chemise between us, his chest dug into me almost painfully hard. Almost. And if there was a bit of pain, it was the kind that only made you want more.

'Miss Linton...you are...!'

His voice trailed off, and the silence said more than a million words could ever have. His hands slid up under my chemise, worshipping me, tentatively exploring every single inch. In every touch, I could feel the truth: I was his love, and he was mine.

'I know,' I whispered to my man in the shadows. 'I feel the same.'

Safely wrapped in darkness, I let my fingers travel farther and farther, clinging to him while his strong arms held me and his hands continued to worship me. His body was like a beautiful landscape made from bedrock. Hard ridges and shallow dips, smooth plains that I wanted to kiss a thousand times. I revelled in every single inch. Felt them. Claimed them. And as I did, slowly a realisation began to sink in:

He's real, Lilly. He's really real, and he's yours.

Tentatively, I moved both my hands until they were lying lightly on his chest. The strong beats of his heart under my hands fired my blood, making my own heart thump faster with a feeling for which there was only one word.

Love.

It was love. Both in his heart and mine. And whatever the morning brought, I wanted this night with him.

Bending down, I pressed a gentle kiss on his chest, eliciting a groan from deep inside him.

'Miss Linton...Lillian–'

'Shh!' Quickly, I covered his mouth with a single finger. I didn't want to hear if by chance he had any more reasonable, well-thought-out objections to our night together. I was not in a very reasonable mood. 'Remember what they say? Silence is golden.'

'And you,' he told me, his sea-coloured eyes finding me even in the pitch-black darkness, 'are diamond.'

His words nearly made my heart burst. Bending down, I retaliated in kind, pressing a gentle kiss just above his heart.

That did it. Whatever restraint he'd still possessed before was gone. A growl erupted from his chest, and suddenly I was on my back, Mr Rikkard Ambrose was above me, gleaming in a sliver of moonlight. Holy Mammon! If I'd thought he was beautiful before, that was nothing compared to the sight of him hovering above me, the remnants of his shirt hanging in tatters around his waist, muscles shining in the silver moonlight. The storm in his eyes had abruptly turned into a hurricane, ready to devour anything that came into its path.

Me! Me! Take me!

The words were as clear on my face as they were in my head, and Mr Rikkard Ambrose – he was not one for wasting time. Ravenously, he plunged down and claimed my mouth in a searing kiss. Capturing both my wrists with one powerful hand he pinned them to the bed, taking charge, riding the wave of passion rising in us both. I bowed under him, losing my mind and my body. Losing them to him, and never wanting them back.

'Tell me you're mine!' he commanded.

'I'm yours!' *For tonight. Just tonight.*

'Tell me you want this!'

It felt like a command. It sounded like a command. But from the way his free hand reached out of the shadows to caress my cheek, I knew it wasn't. He was asking in the only way Rikkard Ambrose could.

Turning my face into his hand, I pressed a soft kiss onto his palm.

'Yes.'

With a primal noise of satisfaction, he slid his hand around the back of my neck and pulled me up for a kiss that rocked me to my core. I hardly heard the ripping noise, hardly noticed a thing until cool air touched my skin and I realised: *It's done. The last barrier between us is gone.*

He released my hands.

Silence fell. Reverent silence. Silence filled with love.

Reaching up, I tenderly caressed his face.

'This...this is my first time. Will you do something for me?'

Even through the darkness, I could see the storm roiling in his eyes. 'Anything.'

'Oh. Good.' Quickly, I reached over to my bedside table, pulled one of the little items I had in stock for just such an eventuality out of the drawer and pressed it into his hand. 'Put this on, will you?'

WRAPPING THINGS UP

Silence.

Complete, utter, icy silence.

For quite a long time.

Then...

'Miss Linton?'

'Yes?'

'Is that...is that a–'

'Yes.'

His hand snapped shut around the little thing and crushed it.

'Hey!' I protested. 'It took me quite a while to make that!'

On the other hand, I had over thirty more, just in case. Hey, I'm an optimist, all right?

Reaching into the drawer again, I pulled out a replacement and dangled it in front of his face. I could tell he didn't particularly like the view.

'Miss Linton. Do you mean to tell me that before we engage in amorous congress, you wish me to...to...'

'...wrap up your belly-tickler? Yes, that was the idea.'

'Miss Linton!'

'What?' I raised an eyebrow, even though in the dark he probably didn't see it. 'You didn't think that I'd let you get me pregnant and then end up marrying you after all, although I don't really want to, did you?'

Silence.

Silence which, in this case, spoke volumes.

'You did! You bloody son of a bachelor! You were banking on me getting pregnant!'

'Banking has always been one of my favourite occupations.'

I thumped his chest. 'Be serious!'

'I always am, Miss Linton.'

And he was. He absolutely was. Getting me pregnant to get me to marry him – that scheme had Rikkard Ambrose written all over it.

'That's what you were trying to do?' I whispered, something tugging at my heart. 'You were really trying to get me pregnant?'

In the midnight moonlight, he met my eyes without blinking. His gaze was perfectly steady, cool and unashamed.

'Of course. It was a perfect solution for my problem.'

'Your problem?'

'You.'

'Me?'

Reaching out, he cupped my face with a tenderness that made my heart ache. 'You're everything I want. Everything I need. I have to have you. No matter what I have to do, you will be mine.'

A part of me wanted to slap the devious, chauvinistic part of a bachelor – but the problem was, the bigger part of me felt exactly the same about him. I wouldn't be able to survive without him. Besides – if he weren't a devious, chauvinistic son of a bachelor, he wouldn't be Mr Rikkard Ambrose.

Time to take the reins, Lilly!

Through the shadows, I smiled at him. 'So...you want to marry me?'

'I think that by now I have made that abundantly clear, Miss Linton.'

'And there's no other way you'd be with me tonight? No other way I could convince you?'

His face was as solid as bedrock. 'No.'

'Are you sure?'

'Absolutely.'

Reaching out, I cupped him, too – only not his face. I went a little bit lower.

'Ah!'

'Are you really, really sure?'

'Miss Linton...!'

I smiled into the darkness. 'Yes, Mr Ambrose, Sir?'

'I am the one in charge here! You cannot manip–aahh! – manipulate...oh...'

He was probably going to say more on the subject of what I could and couldn't do – but my kiss shut him up mid-sentence. Shuddering, he melted beneath my touch as I whispered words against his lips that no one but the darkness was ever meant to hear.

Well, when I say 'melted'...

Most of him did.

The most important part didn't. It remained quite solid and substantial, in fact.

'Miss Linton! I order you to dispose of that...item immediately! I will not allow – aaa...!'

'You were saying?'

'Ohh...'

'Bloody hell! Hold still, will you? How am I supposed to get it on you if you keep wiggling like that? Let's try again...'

'Aaargh! Ouch!'

'Oops! Um, sorry. I missed.'

'I noticed!'

'Well, at least I know what you told me back in South America was true. You do still have your balls.'

'Miss Linton!'

'All right, all right. I'll get a move on.'

'You do realise that people have been thrown in jail because of these things?'[20]

---

[20] This is a historical fact. While specific laws against contraception only existed in America during the 19th century, not in England, there were anti-obscenity laws in England which were sometimes used to combat contraception. For instance, when Annie Besant and Charles Bradlaugh published the contraception guide *Fruits of Philosophy* by American physician Charles Knowlton, they were sentenced to six months in prison for publishing obscene material. While the sentence was later

I grinned into the darkness. 'Sounds great. I know a comfy police station in London where we could share a cell.'

'Miss Lin–'

I pushed down.

'–aaah!'

'There. That wasn't so bad, was it?'

'No comment.'

'Don't worry.' Leaning towards him, I pressed a light kiss on his lips. 'It'll get better from here, I promise. I'll be gentle.'

He groaned. Capturing my face between his hands, he held me fast, unwilling to let me go. 'I actually believe you. Sometimes what you do to me frightens me.'

'Likewise,' I whispered. 'Likewise, Mr Ambrose, Sir.'

The time for jokes and games was past. Gazing into the shadowy pools of his eyes, I knew that now it was time for just him and me, and what we were about to do. Wordlessly, he gathered me up in his arms, lifted me, and gently laid me in the exact centre of the bed – the same position, I could see in his eyes, that I occupied in his heart. He leaned down. I stretched up, clutching his broad shoulders.

'I'm going to have to hurt you,' he whispered.

That was Rikkard Ambrose. Straight to the point. Brutally, beautifully honest.

'I know.' I smiled. 'Don't worry. You have lots of practice. I'm sure you'll manage.'

'Miss Linton, this is no joke! I don't want to hurt–'

'I'll whack you over the head tomorrow if it makes you feel better.'

This time he kissed me to shut me up, and I let him. I let him do much more than that. Strong hands encircled my ankles, parting them as far as they would go. He leaned down until his forehead pressed against mine, and other parts of him pressed against me, too.

'Ready?' he demanded.

'For you?' My smile widened. 'Never and always.'

That night, Mr Rikkard Ambrose wasn't silent. That night, some talented person whose name I won't mention managed to make him scream.

~~**~*~*

When I awoke the next morning and started to blink the sleep out of my eyes, for a moment, I didn't remember where I was. My bed suddenly felt unusually hard, and during the night, it seemed to have grown two clamps that

_____

overturned, it does demonstrate the enormous prejudice against contraception during that time period. On the flipside, the trial caused the book to become an instant bestseller in Britain, with over 200,000 copies selling while the trial was going on, so things probably didn't go as the prosecutor had intended.

were tightly wrapped around me. Hard, warm clamps that wrapped around me tightly and felt suspiciously like the bare arms of a–

I jerked upright.

Or at least I tried to. But apparently, Mr Ambrose's slumbering arms were exactly like the rest of him awake: grabbing anything and giving away nothing for free. His arms tightened around me as if I were the key to the vaults of the Bank of England.

'Hey! I'm not a big jewel or a bag of money! You can let go.'

He gave a sleepy grunt of protest, and his grip tightened.

Blast! Even asleep that man was stubborn as a slab of rock! Pushing at his iron-hard arms, I tried to slip out of his grasp – but it only tightened farther, nearly squeezing the breath out of me. Wheezing, I used my one free arm to prod his shoulder.

'Hey! Wake up! You're strangling me.'

'I am awake,' he told me, making me jerk.

'Good God! Then why are you squeezing me half to death?'

'Because.'

'That's not an answer! Why won't you let go?'

Pressing close from behind, he placed a searing kiss against my neck that made me shiver.

'Because this is where you belong. With me. Bound forever.'

I felt heat rising to my ears. Holy Moly! Why, after everything we had done last night, would *that* make me blush?

Well...

Because what we had done last night had been under cover of darkness. It had been safe – my own little secret, tucked away in the shadows. Now I was wide awake. A new day was dawning. Sunlight was streaming in through the windows and falling on me and Mr Rikkard Ambrose, tangled up together in my own bed, inside his parents' home.

All right, there probably was reason to blush. But no need to let *him* see it.

I jabbed him in the ribs.

'Oof!'

His arms loosened, and I slipped away, throwing him a smile over my shoulder. 'Thank you.'

Giving me a cool look, he rubbed his ribs. 'Was that really necessary?'

'No, but it was fun. I might do it more often in the future.'

Grabbing a sheet and wrapping it around me, I rose from the bed to survey the room. The bed was in chaos. The drawer of the bedside table hung half-open, my severely diminished stash inside peeking out for anyone to see. A vase on a nearby table had somehow toppled over. One of the curtains, which I must have grabbed in one of the night's more energetic moments, was torn in several places. And stretched right across the bed, wearing about as much clothing as Michelangelo's David and looking a hundred times as tempting, lay Mr Rikkard Ambrose, his sea-coloured eyes gazing up at me from under his lashes.

I glanced at the clock in the corner. Hm... ten thirty am wasn't really that late, was it? Maybe I could crawl back into bed a little and we could –

'Good God! It's ten thirty already!'

Ah. Apparently, Mr Ambrose had noticed the time, too.

Half a second later, an Ambrose-shaped blur shot past me and started gathering up discarded clothes from all over the room. Deducing that the fun times were probably over for now, I started to look for clothes as well. However, my search was far less successful.

'Come on, move!' Mr Ambrose's voice came from inside his shirt as he pulled it over his head. 'What are you waiting for, Miss Linton?'

I held up a chemise which was torn from top to bottom down the front. 'For this to mend itself. But I'm afraid I'll have to wait a long time for that.'

A stone-faced head popped out at the top of the shirt. He regarded my chemise critically. 'Hm. You should really take better care of your clothing.'

'*I* should take better care? *You* tore it in half!'

'Exactly. Next time, take it off before I'm forced to resort to extreme measures.'

'Oh no, Mister! You're not getting off as easily as that!' Taking a step towards him, I waved the tattered remnants of my undergarment under his nose. 'You love me, don't you? Well, prove it! Pay for a replacement!'

He froze.

His entire body stiffened. His face stayed as stony as ever, but I could see the struggle underneath. A single muscle in jaw twitched, and his teeth were clenched. He was clearly engaged in a titanic battle with himself.

I sincerely sympathised. I really did. On the one hand – the woman he loved. On the other hand – spending money. It really was such a terribly tough decision.

'Your salary shall have to suffice.'

Oh. Not that tough, after all, apparently.

'Or you can simply sew your own new clothes,' he suggested, bending and picking up something from the floor. Rising, he dangled the crumpled, stained little object in front of my face. 'You seem to be talented at sewing.'

'Oh.' My ears turned fiery red. 'Those were kind of an exception.'

'You don't say.' Turning away, he continued to dress himself. 'Tell me, Miss Linton – where exactly did you learn about these objects? Where would you acquire such specialised knowledge?'

'In a whorehouse.'

'*Pardon?*' Freezing in mid-motion, he slowly turned around to spear me with icy eyes. '*What* did you say?'

'Oh, not through participation. My lessons were purely theoretical.'

'For the sake of the male patrons of that establishment,' Mr Ambrose told me in a voice as cold as the heart of a glacier, 'I hope that is true.'

He looked so cold, so ruthless, so...adorable.

Before I could think better of it, I had thrown myself at him, and my arms were around him, hugging him close. Snuggling my face against his solid chest, I drank in his warmth.

'Miss Linton! We do not have time for such frivolities. Cease this immediately!'

'Yes, Sir!' I grinned up at him, and squeezed harder.

A moment of silence, then...

'You still have not let go, Miss Linton.'

'Yes, Sir!'

He gazed at me for a moment, apparently not sure what to say – and then he put his arms around me and pulled me close. In that moment, I wouldn't have exchanged places with anyone, up to and including the Queen of England.

'In my past, when someone declined a business offer of mine,' he told me, his voice so low I nearly didn't catch the words, 'I have never in my life made a second proposal, let alone a third. Never.'

'Um...yes. And?'

'Marry me.'

'Oh.'

Leaning back until I could look into his eyes, I cupped his face in my hands. 'You know my answer. You know I can't.'

His eyes were hard as bedrock at the bottom of the sea. 'And you know I can't take no for an answer. Not as long as I know that you love me.'

Taking my hands in his, he slid them from his jaw to his lips and pressed one tender kiss on each palm. Just for an instant, his face softened a tiny little bit.

'Just imagine what it would be like.'

'Oh, I have. Trust me, I have.'

'You would rather be my secretary than my wife?'

I tried to smile at him, but I only managed to lift one corner of my mouth a little. 'Well, with the former job I at least get one day off a week.'

His face hardened again – and yet, the emotion in his eyes didn't vanish. On the contrary. It burned with a cold fire bright enough to devour my soul.

'I won't give up. Not ever.'

Why didn't that surprise me?

'I'm flattered. But for now...do you think it's possible you could focus your energies on finding some clothes for me? I've already been quite impolite to our hosts by missing breakfast. I think your mother wouldn't approve if I show up to lunch wrapped in a rumpled blanket.'

'Indeed. That would be impolitic.'

'And draughty. So...' I batted my eyelashes up at him. 'My lady clothes are all stored in my other room, a long way down the corridor. Do you think you can find something for me?'

'Hm. Well, I suppose I can lend you something of mine. If you promise not to damage it.'

'Thank you, oh gracious master of the double standard.'

Giving me a look, he strode to the connecting door and disappeared into his room. I dropped the blanket back onto the bed and followed him.

'Nothing I can find among my things will probably fit you very well, Miss Linton.'

'I had deduced as much from the anatomic measurements I undertook last night, Sir.'

'Indeed?'

'Yes. I was planning to to use your clothes to go to my other room and fetch some of my men's clothes from there.'

'Adequate suggestion. Here.' He pulled a few clothes out of the wardrobe and turned. 'Take thi–'

That was when he caught sight of me.

Without the sheet.

Without anything.

'Thank you.' Doing the best curtsy you can do in your birthday suit, I pulled the clothes out of his unresisting hands. 'With a tight belt, I should be able to make these fit.'

Silence.

Well, except for the footsteps.

Wait – *footsteps*?

'Hello?' The knock coming from the door made me jump ten feet in the air. But it was the voice that nearly gave me heart attack. The voice of the very last person I wanted to enter this room right now. 'Hello, Ricky? Son, are you awake?'

Oh crap.

THE LAST DAY

Things went very, very fast. One moment I was standing in front of Mr Ambrose, a bundle of clothes in my bare arms, the next, the man who had sworn eternal love to me pushed me over onto the carpet–

Thud!

'Ouch!'

–and shoved me under the bed.

'Nng!'

Who said gentlemanly chivalry was dead? You simply had to admire a gentleman who assisted a lady with such swiftness. And the moment I was out from under this bed, I would show him my admiration with a swift kick in the butt!

Right now, however, the only things in sight were his feet, and the rather smelly, dusty carpet. God, how long had it been since this thing had been cleaned? I would have to have a word with the chambermaid.

Click.

The door opened and another pair of feet, this one wearing pink shoes, entered the room.

'Ah. Good morning, Mother.'

All right – butt kicking postponed.

'Rick! Are you all right, my son?'

'Certainly. Why wouldn't I be?'

'Well, you didn't show up for breakfast, and now I find you here looking all flushed and hot. Do you have a fever?'

I glanced down at my lack of ladylike – or indeed any – attire. *Yes, he definitely has. But not the kind you are probably referring to, Your Ladyship.*

'No.'

'Are you sure? Let me feel your forehead. Lie down on the bed for a minute and–'

'No! The bed is perfectly fine! And so am I.'

'Oh. Um...very well.'

'Stop beating around the bush, Mother. We both know you are not here because I missed breakfast. It wouldn't be the first time, and it won't be the last. What do you really want?'

There was a pause.

'Very well. You're right. I did have another reason for coming here.' Another pause. 'I noticed you danced with Miss Linton last night.'

Oh, yes, he danced with me all right! We danced fandango the pokum quite a lot...[21]

'Correct.'

'The two of you...get along well?'

'As well as an employer can get along with the immature younger sibling of his secretary.'

My mouth dropped open.

Oh? So I was an immature younger sibling, was I? I'd show him immature!

Snaking my arm out from under the bed, I tickled the back of his knee. He flinched and shifted to shield me from his mother.

'So you have no – how should I put this – plans with regard to Miss Linton?'

'Plans?' Reaching a bit higher, I pinched him in the butt. He flinched again, then gave the bed a kick so a blanket fell down and shut me in. Damn him! 'I have no idea what you mean, Mother!'

In that moment, I was so very tempted to lift the blanket, wave at Lady Samantha and chirp 'Good morning, Your Ladyship.' So very, very tempted. But if I did that, there probably wouldn't be any way to get around the marriage thing. Mr Ambrose would drag me to the altar with a lasso, if necessary.

'Oh. No plans at all?' There was no way I could miss the humongous mass of disappointment in Lady Samantha's voice. I almost felt bad for not throwing away my feminist principles and tying myself to a dictatorial chauvinist for the rest of my life. Almost. 'Are you sure?'

'Absolutely. Miss Lillian Linton is nothing but a silly, immature girl with a tendency towards temper tantrums.'

Bloody hell, he was a master dissembler! He sounded so convincing, you would never guess he didn't believe what he said.

Wait a moment...he *didn't* believe what he just said, right?

If he actually meant that, if he...oh, just you wait until I get my hands on you, Rikkard Ambrose!

'I have no plans to be married in the foreseeable future, Mother. It would take a rare woman indeed to change my mind.'

Oh. All right, maybe I wouldn't strangle him after all.

---

[21] A Victorian expression for making love rather energetically.

'Since you are here, Mother, I might as well take this opportunity to tell you–

Oh, really? You think *right now* is the best opportunity to talk to your mother, do you?

'–I'm leaving Battlewood.'

What?

'What?'

'Adaira requested–'

Ordered, more like.

'–that I come for Christmas. I have done so. Christmas has passed. The ball is over. I'm returning to London. I have business to take care of.'

'But...you...your father–'

He cut her off brutally. 'If you thought that this little invitation would suffice to make me forgive him, think again. He hasn't earned my forgiveness, and neither have you. You want to know why?' Beyond the blanket, I could see the shadowy outline of his feet shift, taking a step towards her that would have had princes and kings quaking in their boots. 'Ask my employees. I make people *work* for what they earn. Hard.'

Yep. I can attest to that.

'Rick...I'm sorry. So sorry. Your father and I...we...'

'Don't bother. I have heard enough excuses to last me a lifetime.'

'Please, will you stay just a little bit longer? Stay and talk to him? Once? That's all I'm asking, please. Just once.'

There was a long moment of silence.

And another one.

And a third one, that lasted even longer.

Finally...

'Perhaps.'

~~**~*~*

The last days at Battlewood Hall flew by. I – or should I say Mr Linton – spent most of it with Adaira, taking long walks in the garden, planning vendettas against Adaira's enemies in the neighbourhood and exchanging embarrassing details about her brother. We stood beside Lady Samantha as she saw off one guest after another, and gave marks on which disappointed girl made the sourest faces at Mr Ambrose. And all the while, Mr Ambrose didn't give a single hint that he intended to go upstairs to see his father. And his father most certainly did not seem willing to come downstairs to see his son.

Maybe they would get to talk to each other if the house collapsed?

Finally, the day of departure dawned. Rolling over in my (Ambrose-free) bed, I gazed out of the window. The sun was shining bright through the window. Snow still covered the landscape, but it had slowly begun to melt. *And maybe*, I thought as I felt a twinge in my heart, *the snow isn't the only thing that's melting away.*

We were leaving this place. Times were changing.

'Mr Linton! The sun is up! Why are you lazing about? Let's go! Knowledge is power is time is money!'

I smiled. Well, maybe not too much.

Sliding out of bed, I dressed in women's clothes and grabbed my parasol. My 'brother' Mr Victor Linton had already left yesterday, after a tearful goodbye from Lady Samantha and lots of barely suppressed giggling from her daughter, to prepare for Mr Ambrose's arrival in London. His journey hadn't been very long, and had only consisted of a three-mile circle back to the rear of Battlewood Hall. Lilly Linton's journey would be a little bit longer. The road to London would be tough this time of the year.

Breakfast passed in a friendly mood with lots of lively chatter (between Lady Samantha, Adaira and me) and icy silence (between Mr Ambrose and Mr Ambrose). It was really quite impressive how he managed to give himself the cold shoulder, as well as everyone else in the room. I didn't let myself be offended, though. I knew exactly what was behind his especially arctic mood.

Breakfast came to an end and the servants rushed in to clear the plates.

'Darling?' Lady Samantha cleared her throat. 'If you want to before you leave...It's time to go see your father.'

Mr Ambrose raised his eyes from his plate and speared his mother with the glacial gaze that was reserved for debtors and people calling him 'darling'.

'Please,' she said, giving him big, blue puppy dog eyes.

Still, his gaze remained ice-cold and unmoved.

I kicked him under the table.

'Aargh!'

'Yes?' Lady Samantha, whose hearing was apparently optimistic enough to mistake 'aargh' for 'yes', perked up. 'You'll do it?'

My dear employer threw me a look that told me I would be paying for this later. I didn't particularly mind. I had recently discovered a rather interesting way of clearing debts with him.

'Yes. Yes, I will.'

'Oh, Rick! Thank you! Thank–'

'Have the coach readied for departure,' he cut her off. 'This won't take long. I'll be back in a few minutes.'

And, rising to his feet, he marched off towards the grand staircase leading up to his father's chambers.

For a moment, the three of us sat in silence. Then Lady Samantha folded her napkin and rose with a worried little sigh.

'Well, I think I'd better go and make sure that the carriage is ready.'

I waited until the door had closed behind her, then quickly jumped to my feet, too.

'Well, I think I'd better go and–'

'–listen at the keyhole to find out what my brother is saying to Father?' Adaira finished with a small, innocent smile.

I grinned at her. 'If I didn't already have six of them who're nothing like me, sometimes I'd think you could be my sister.'

Like a pair of dust devils, we raced off towards the staircase. Except for my short foray up the stairs when I'd needed a good vantage point to shoot at Lady Samantha's latest guest, I'd never been upstairs before. It was a different world. Whereas the lower levels of the house clearly bore signs of Lady Samantha's influence, with pink cushions, pink flowered wallpaper and vases that held roses which were – surprises, surprise – pink, the upstairs was dominated by paintings and busts of austere-looking gentlemen, massive dark wood furniture and a general air of impending doom that proclaimed 'Danger! Male Ambrose in residence!'

Clearly, this was the domain of The Most Honourable The Marquess Ambrose.

'What now?' I whispered.

'Father's study is over there.' Adaira pointed down a corridor lined with portraits of noble ancestors giving us disapproving looks.

'How welcoming.'

'Yes, Father is really warm and fuzzy.'

We proceeded through several majestic rooms and down high hallways. Finally, Adaira raised her finger to her lips – which either meant I still had some breakfast stuck on my lip, or we were approaching our goal and I should keep quiet. I went with the latter. Cautiously, I stuck my head around the last corner – and instantly pulled it back.

'There are two goons in livery standing in front of the door!'

'Drat!' Adaira bit her lip, thinking. 'Maybe...no, that won't work. But perhaps...yes!' She snapped her fingers. 'Come with me!'

And she drew me through a door leading off to the side, into a small salon with the ugliest turquoise-beige flower-pattern wallpaper I had ever seen in my life.

'What are we doing in here?' I enquired. 'Planning emergency redecorating?'

'No, of course not! Although, now that you mention it, that would actually be a great idea. No, we're here for this.'

And she pointed to a set of French doors opening on a balcony.

I needed no further explanation. In an instant, I was at the doors and outside in the fresh air. The balcony – praise the architect – had a solid stone railing, perfect for hiding two curious girls. And as luck would have it, the window to the neighbouring room stood open a crack. Fate clearly approved of eavesdropping.

Unfortunately, the wind didn't seem to share fate's opinion. It was blowing hard, making both of us shiver and, more importantly, drowning out half of the words that came from next door. But the other half, the words that we heard...

Oh boy.

AU REVOIR

'Son.'

'Father.'

Translation:

I would like to murder you with a rusty axe.

Yes, thank you. The same to you.

'So you came.'

'Indeed.'

Silence.

Silence colder than ice.

Silence colder than the primordial cold before fire was invented.

'Well?' The two voices were alike, but never in a million years would I mistake Mr Ambrose for his father. His father's voice was cold and ruthless in a way that made me want to scrub myself. Mr Ambrose's voice was cold and ruthless in a way that made butterflies dance in my stomach. 'I am waiting, Father.'

'Waiting for what?'

A noise as if from a shifting glacier came from inside. I thought for a moment Mr Ambrose had truly turned into an iceberg – but then I realised that he was just cracking his knuckles. 'A "thank you" would not be a bad idea, to start with.'

'Me? Thank *you*? You, who have dragged our family name into the mud?'

'I dragged you *out* of the mud, father! Out of debt, and despicable poverty! You and the rest of our family! Do you remember where I found you? Do you? You should be thanking me on bended knee!'

'Insolent boy! You will show me the respect due to your–'

The winter wind howled, cutting off whatever Mr Ambrose was supposed to show respect to. It didn't matter. I could have told the Marquess he wouldn't do it. The only things Mr Rikkard Ambrose showed respect to were ones with the £-symbol on them.

Except maybe me.

Occasionally.

'Dammit!' Adaira whispered, glaring at the air, as if she could chase away the wind like that. 'Quiet down, will you?'

Amazingly, it did. The howl subsided into a whistle, and then vanished altogether.

'–going off to the colonies! Do you have any ideas of the stories that I heard about you? Wallowing in filth like a commoner, working for money with your bare hands–!'

'You should try it sometime. It might do you a world of good.'

'You will speak when you are spoken to, boy! I will not be lectured on life by an insolent lout whose breeding is no better than a primitive's! You will keep your mouth shut and–'

Suddenly, Ambrose senior was silenced. And this time, it wasn't the wind who was responsible. There was a thud, and a choking noise. Adaira gave me a wide-eyed, panicked look, which I'm sure I returned to her in equal measure.

'No.' Mr Ambrose's voice was as cold and as deadly as an adder's hiss. 'You keep your mouth shut and listen, Father. If not for my work and my money made by my filthy hands, your precious family, your life in this pretentious palace would be nothing. Gone. Vanished in an instant. You had better keep a civil tongue in your head next time we meet because if you do not, I will consider all debts between us paid, and you will be finished!'

There was a pause.

'You are an Ambrose!' ground out the old man. 'A man of noble blood! The son of a Marquess!'

'Believe me, I know. I have only been trying to forget for the last ten years!'

'Do you have no respect for what that means? What honour and duty rests upon your shoulders? You've soiled your family honour! Some of the things they say about you...the things you did out in the wilds...'

'What did they say, Father? What did the great Marquess Ambrose have to hear about his Prodigal Son?'

'Things too vile to repeat! I spoke to a man who saw you then. Saw what you were like. What you did...'

'There, there, now, Father.' Mr Ambrose said, deceptively soft. 'It wasn't as bad as people make it sound.'

'It wasn't?'

'No.' His voice abruptly hardened into granite. 'It was worse. It was a hundred times worse, thanks to you and Mother! It was blood and guts and bone-breaking work – most often literally. I have a scar across one finger, where a man broke it because I could not pay my debts. I have a burn on my head from a black powder explosion that nearly ripped my skull apart! And yet I'm still here, and my debtors and enemies are gone. You don't want to be one of them. I have seen a lot of things, and done a lot of things. Remember that next time you try to play the parent.'

The next thing we heard was the sound of a door slamming so hard the door-frame cracked.

I waited a moment, till a second door closed, then turned to Adaira with a tremulous smile.

'Well, that went well, didn't it?'

~~**~*~*

The Most Honourable The Marquess Ambrose did not come out of the house to see his son off. But that was all right. It was cold enough outside anyway.

Lady Samantha, wrapped in a thick fur coat that was almost larger than she was, stood at the bottom of the front stairs, Adaira beside her and the staff arrayed in two lines right and left. Tears were sparkling in the old lady's eyes, and errant snowflakes in Adaira's. I knew that the latter were melting snowflakes and definitely not tears, because she had assured me and her brother of that fact three times already.

'Don't you dare think I'll miss you,' she told him, lifting her chin to meet his eyes. 'You are rude and dictatorial and the worst big brother on this earth, and if you come back in a hundred years it'll be too soon!'

Mr Ambrose inclined his head about half an inch. 'My feelings exactly.'

'Good bye, Lilly!' Turning to me, Adaira threw her arms around my neck and hugged me hard enough to squeeze the breath out of my lungs. 'Come back soon, will you? I miss you already! You'll always be welcome at Battlewood.'

'Yes, Miss Linton.' Smiling shyly, Lady Samantha stepped forward and squeezed my hand. 'You're welcome here any time. Especially if your stay here....' Her gaze flitted to Mr Ambrose. 'Especially if your stay would be a longer one.'

Mr Ambrose made a noise in the back of his throat. 'If you are all quite finished fawning over my secretary's little sister, we have to be going.'

'That goes for you, too.' Undaunted by his frosty demeanour, Lady Samantha took his her son's hand. 'You're welcome here any time.'

'As long as you bring Miss Linton with you,' Adaira added, which earned her a stern glance from her mother and a grin from me.

'I shall endeavour to have her never leave my side,' Mr Ambrose shot back at his little sister. Only I noticed that when those words left his mouth, his eyes flicked over to me, and there was hunger in them. I had a feeling he wasn't just making a retort.

For the first time, I wondered what he had planned for me when we had returned to London. The thought alone sent a delicious shiver down my back. Yet, back in London there didn't just await endless possibilities – there also awaited infinite dangers. First and foremost among them my aunt and uncle. It had begun to dawn on me that my refusal of his marriage proposal might not seem as insurmountable an obstacle to Mr Ambrose as it appeared to me. After all, was it usually the girl who decided her future husband? No. It was her parents or her guardians. And if Mr Rikkard Ambrose, or better yet, Lord Rikkard Ambrose, son and heir of The Most Honourable The Marquess Ambrose, approached my dear aunt and uncle, asking for my hand...

Aunt Brank would probably be ready to chop it off with a meat cleaver and hand it over to him wrapped in fancy paper. And Uncle Bufford...

Our conversation would most likely go something like this:

Uncle Bufford: Do you like him?

Me: Yes, but–

Uncle Bufford: Is he rich?

Me: Yes, but–

Uncle Bufford: Good. Marry him. And make sure he pays for the wedding.

Me: But–

Uncle Bufford: Out, girl! I've got important business to attend to. I have lots of money to count.

Yes, that would be a very productive talk.

'Miss Linton?'

A familiar cool voice tore me from my thoughts, and I looked up into the dark, sea-coloured eyes of Mr Rikkard Ambrose. They were deep as the ocean, and just as alluring. I couldn't help but get lost in their depths.

Would he go to my aunt and uncle? Could he? Could he ever do something like that to me?

I remembered his confession, wrestled from his heart with brute force: *I might be slightly irrationally infatuated with you. I may even have certain impulses towards you that border on caring about you.*

Could a man who delivered such a passionate declaration of love just go behind my back?

Yes, he could, blast him!

But maybe, just maybe he wouldn't. And if he betrayed me, if he ignored my feelings and tried to entrap me against my will, I'd cut off his bollocks and dye his precious tailcoat orange!

'Shall we go?' Mr Ambrose extended his arm to me, and I took it like a perfect lady.

'Yes, we shall.'

Accompanied by sobbing (from Lady Samantha) mad waving (from Adaira) and lots of bows and curtsies (from the servants), we climbed into our coach. I immediately stuck my head out of the window and started waving, and when Mr Ambrose just sat stiffly in his seat, I grabbed his hand, stuck it out of the window and waved it for him.

'Miss Linton!'

'Oh, don't be a stick-in-the-mud! Wave goodbye to your sister and mother!'

'They are perfectly well aware that we are leaving. We do not need to indicate the matter via hand signals.'

'Sir?'

'Yes, Miss Linton?'

'Shut up and wave.'

Up on the box, Karim cracked his whip, and the carriage took off, rolling down the driveway. As soon as we reached the road, Karim gave Mr Ambrose's mean old coach horses free rein, and we raced along the highway, slush and dirt spraying up around us.

As we travelled south, the weather became warmer and the remnants of snow began to disappear. The warmer climate, however, did not appear to have an impact on Mr Rikkard Ambrose. He sat in a corner, brooding silently over some papers from his briefcase. Not that this was unusual behaviour for him, but still...it felt different. He didn't order me around, or utter threats against the Royal tax collectors, or any of the other things he normally did. I got a feeling that he was waiting for something.

But what?

I didn't have to wait long to find out.

'Why are we slowing down?'

I had been gazing out of the window at the passing trees – when, suddenly, they ceased to pass. The coach rolled to a halt and an earth-shattering *thud* came from outside, the kind of noise only caused by a mountain collapsing, or by Karim jumping off the box.

'Karim?' Mr Ambrose demanded, putting his papers aside. 'What is the matter? Why have we stopped?'

'There's a rider approaching, *Sahib*. He's hailing us.'

Mr Ambrose's hand slipped into his tailcoat, to the bulge I very much suspected was his revolver. 'Does he look hostile?'

'No, Sahib, I don't think so. He...he seems familiar. I'm not sure, but–'

'Yes?'

'It's Kenward, *Sahib*! It's Kenward!'

'Who is Kenward?' Leaning forward, I tried to peek out of the window, but to judge by the approaching hoof beats, I was on the wrong side of the coach.

'One of my agents, Miss Linton. I usually send him to businesses who have not been performing as they should. He's a quick rider. If he's here...'

Not bothering to finish the ominous sentence, Mr Ambrose pushed open the door and jumped out of the carriage. Quickly, I gathered up my skirts and, cursing the fact that I wasn't wearing trousers, I followed him outside, where I took up a position beside him. Standing straight, my hand close to my gun, just in case, I fixed my eyes on the rapidly approaching rider.

The man reined in his mount a few yards away and leapt down. His face was drawn as if he hadn't slept for days, and his knees were shaking from exhaustion. The horse didn't seem to be in much better shape.

'Thank God I spotted your coach, Sir,' the man panted. 'I thought you were still at Battlewood! I would have ridden straight there if–'

'Yes, yes, enough of that.' Impatiently Mr Ambrose waved his hand. 'Why are you here? What has happened?'

'It's Dalgliesh.'

Those words were enough to make an icy tingle of fear shoot down my spine and make my fists clench, instinctively preparing for a punch. I had known this would be coming. Dalgliesh himself had warned us before leaving: *I will have to return to London, to develop a new strategy.*

I just hadn't thought that developing a new strategy would happen so fast.

'What is it?' Mr Ambrose demanded. 'What has he done?'

Kenward, as his name apparently was, looked uncomfortable. He cleared his throat, then glanced at me.

'What?' I demanded. 'Do you need some cough syrup?'

'I believe, he is indicating that this is a sensitive business matter that we require privacy, Miss Linton.'

I looked around. 'But we're in the middle of an empty road. How much more private can you get?'

Leaning over, Mr Ambrose hissed: 'You are not currently dressed appropriately for the post of secretary, *Miss* Linton.'

'Oh.'

'Indeed.'

Apparently not in the mood to explain the intricacies of crossdressing feminists to Mr Kenward, Mr Ambrose stepped over to the man and leaned down so Kenward could whisper in his ear. The more he listened, the colder Mr Ambrose's face became. His left little finger started twitching in prestissimo. Then he suddenly straightened, teeth clenched tight.

'You're not serious!'

'I swear to you, Sir, it's true!'

'But there, of all places...How did Dalgliesh even know it?'

'I have no idea, Sir. But he obviously does. And he wants it.'

'Over his dead body!'

'But Sir, you'll hardly be able to get there in time, let alone–'

'Let that be my concern!' Mr Ambrose cut him off. 'You get back to London and make sure things run smoothly. I shall expect everything to be as if I'd run things myself on my return, understand?'

Kenward paled, but nodded. 'Yes, Sir! I understand, Sir!'

'Adequate.'

Without another word, Mr Ambrose whirled and marched back to the coach. I followed silently, burning to know what was going on, but instinctively knowing that now was not a moment for wasting time with questions.

'Karim!' Mr Ambrose slammed the knob of his cane against the roof of the coach. 'About-turn! Take us to Newcastle!'

My eyes went wide.

'Um...Mr Ambrose?'

'Yes, Miss Linton?'

'Newcastle as in "we were nearly roasted and stoned there"-Newcastle?'

'Yes, Miss Linton. And?'

'Nothing. Just curious.'

The drive wasn't long and, luckily, our reception to the city of Newcastle was distinctly cooler and less geological than last time. We drove straight through the city towards the waterfront, but only when the masts and sails of anchoring ships came into view did I understand what was about to happen.

I swallowed.

'Oh dear. This will be difficult to explain to my friends and my little sister.'

'What will?'

'Disappearing on another mysterious journey. I wrote to them, telling them I'd be coming back. I thought we were returning to London, you know.'

'You are.'

'I am? But–' And then it hit me. I began to understand what he really intended to do. What he had been intending to do ever since he met that messenger on the road. Wherever he was going, Dalgliesh would be there, too. It would be dangerous. And no matter how ruthless or cold-hearted Mr Rikkard Ambrose might be, he would never put someone he loved into danger.

'No!' I almost jumped out of my seat. 'No, you can't be serious!'

He cocked his head. 'There you go again, assuming I am capable of levity. How long will it take to cure you of this curious misconception?'

'You're not leaving me behind!'

'Yes, I am.'

'You are a bastard son of a bachelor!'

'Yes, I am. Albeit in the metaphorical sense only.'

'I love you!'

'Thank you.'

'That was meant to convince you that you can't leave me behind!'

'Oh. Well, in that case, it did not work.'

Reaching out, I grabbed his arm and held on so tight it must have hurt – but he didn't complain. He didn't even try to pull away. Our eyes met. 'Where are you going?'

Silence.

'Mr Ambrose, *where are you going?*'

More silence.

Loosening my grip, I slid my hand down his arm until my fingers gently brushed against his.

'Where?'

He glanced down at our joined fingers – then looked up to meet my gaze again.

'It's better if you don't know, Miss Linton.'

'No it isn't!'

'Will you ever stop arguing with me?'

My fingers tightened around his. 'Never.'

Funny. Why did that sounded like more than a promise to me? Almost like a...vow.

The coach rolled to a halt. Taking a deep breath, Mr Ambrose rose to his feet. 'Well, the continuation of our argument will have to wait.' And, slipping out of my grasp, he stepped out of the coach. I jumped after him, parasol ready to strike. I would force him to listen! I would beat it into his thick head that he couldn't just leave me behind like some dainty porcelain doll!

Karim awaited us outside, face even more wooden than usual, arms crossed in front of his massive chest. The moment he saw me, his posture tensed, and I could have sworn his beard stood on end with trepidation.

'Oh no.' Raising one hand, I waved a warning finger at Karim. 'Don't you dare! Don't you–'

'Karim,' Mr Ambrose interrupted me ruthlessly, 'Miss Linton is being stubborn.'

'What a shockingly astounding development, *Sahib.*'

'Indeed. It will be your duty to return her safely to London–'

'Hey! I'm not a package you can just return to sender!'

'–and watch over her while I am away.'

The Mohammedan's face betrayed only the barest hint of soul-deep suffering. 'Must I really, *Sahib?*'

'Yes.'

'Very well, *Sahib.* I hear and obey. For you, I would brave the fiery pits of hell.'

'Hey!' Threateningly, I raised my parasol. 'Watch what you're saying!'

Mr Ambrose and Karim ignored me completely, holding each other's gaze and nodding, in some strange male ritual of understanding.

'She shall be safe with me, *Sahib*.'

'Adequate. Then it is time.'

This was all going too fast. Far too fast. He couldn't go now! Not now that he and I...not now that we had just... He couldn't! And he definitely couldn't send me back with *just Karim* for company!

'Please don't do this!' I couldn't ever remember begging Mr Rikkard Ambrose for anything. I was far better at demanding. But I would beg now. I would beg to come with him, to be by his side and have his back! If I didn't, no one else would. 'Please!' Pushing aside a startled Karim, I grabbed Mr Ambrose and pulled him close. 'Please don't go without me. I can't let you...just please.'

In moments like these, I really hated and envied the ability of Mr Rikkard Ambrose to keep his face stone-hard and free of emotion.

'I can't. Dalgliesh will be waiting for just such a chance. Where I'll be going...He'll be lying in ambush.'

My grip tightened. 'And you think that argument will convince me to let you go?'

'No. It'll tell you why I cannot take you with me.'

My fingers were now wrapped so tightly around his arm they would probably leave permanent creases in his ten-year-old mint-condition suit. Strangely, he didn't seem to care. His eyes, deep, dark and bottomless as the ocean, didn't move from mine for a second.

'Miss Linton?'

I swallowed hard. 'Yes, Sir?' The well-rehearsed reply slipped over my tongue without my even noticing.

'Let go.'

'No, Sir.'

Reaching up, he cupped my face with his free hand. Not fair!

'Let go of me, *Mister* Linton. That is an order!'

It was like a stab to my heart. He truly didn't want me to come. Did that mean...did that mean he didn't want me anymore? At all?

I had rejected him, after all. Was it now time for him to return the favour?

Behind him, the shadowy form of a massive dark ship approached, sails flapping in the wind. Of course. Of course he would have a ship ready in any port of England, ready and waiting to do his bidding. Curse the man and his power and perfection!

'Karim?' Taking his gaze from me, Mr Ambrose locked eyes with his bodyguard behind me. 'Take care of her.'

'Yes, *Sahib*.'

With a thud, the gangplank of the ship slammed onto the pier. A crew member appeared at the railing, signalling Mr Ambrose. Without another word, he turned and strode off towards the ship. But then, just as he reached the bottom of the gangplank, he stopped and half-turned to look back at me, pinning me to the spot with his arctic gaze.

'Oh, and Miss Linton?'

'Yes, Sir?'

'If by any chance you think my leaving will alter your fate in the slightest –
think again!' His dark, unfathomable eyes flashed. 'I'm going to return. And
when I do, I will come for you. I am not someone who takes no for an answer.
You, Miss Lillian Linton, will be mine. Fully and completely.'

And with that, he whirled, gathering his black coat around him, and
marched onto the ship waiting to take him across the sea.

THE END

THREE CHAPTERS FROM

MR AMBROSE'S PERSPECTIVE

'Gone',
'After Her',
and
'Expressions of Superfluous Sentiment'

GONE

'God rest ye merry gentlemen
Let nothing you dismay...'

My finger froze halfway through the report I was trying to read. It was at moments like these that I was filled with gratification at being neither merry nor a gentleman. I had no intention whatsoever to rest.

And there are more than enough reasons to be dismayed.

My finger resumed its movement across the page—a page that detailed at least one such reason: Dalgliesh. The man had been busy. From what my agents in India had to report, far too busy for my liking.

'Away in a manger, no crib for a bed...'

For a moment, I considered sending Karim to find those carol singers, and fulfilling their dearest wish. Sending them away stuffed into a manger, preferably with the lid nailed shut, seemed like a very tempting idea at the moment. It would definitely allow me to finish my report in peace. However...the Christmas enthusiast was most likely a member of my mother's staff, and she usually didn't appreciate members of her household being stuffed into crates and shipped off to distant lands. She tended to get over-excited about a lot of things.

Such as what is between you and a certain lady?

Nothing. There was nothing there. I would remain cool, calm and collected. And there was nothing whatsoever a certain disrespectful, rebellious woman could do about that. No woman had the power to make Rikkard Ambrose do as she wished.

'Sir?'

My head jerked up to face the servant who was standing right beside me. How had he gotten there without my noticing?

A lack of vigilance. That's how.

Giving a jerk of my head, I nailed the young servant to the spot with my stare. 'Yes?'

The young man swallowed. 'Y-your mother was wondering where you are, Sir. She ordered me to fetch y—' Abruptly, he cleared his throat and changed the direction of his sentence. Wise decision. 'Um, she *requested* me to enquire whether you could spare her a few moments.'

Instinctively, my head jerked towards *her*. The woman who was the reason for my being here. The woman who was responsible for my lack of discipline, my mother's sudden interest in my affairs, and a host of other unpleasantly irregular events in my life.

'Go!' She waved her hand. A greeting or a dismissal? The former, surely. She wouldn't dare to dismiss me. 'I'll be perfectly safe! Mabel—it is Mabel, right?'

'Yes, Miss,' the housemaid curtseyed promptly.

'There, you see? Mabel is going to keep me company. If anything happens, I'll scream the house down.'

And she gave me a smile. The kind of smile that pulled at something deep inside me, and...

Ignore. Focus.

I felt a muscle twitch. 'It's a large house.'

'And I'm good at screaming, as you should know from experience. Go!'

For a moment, I hesitated—then realized what I was doing. Just sitting here, wasting time? What had happened to me? Abruptly, I rose to my feet. 'I shall be only a minute. In the meantime...' Fixing a look on the housemaid, I made sure she understood. Understood without words whom she was dealing with, and what would happen if anything went amiss. 'You are personally responsible for Miss Linton's safety. If anything happens to her in my absence, you will have me to answer to.'

~~**~*~*

I thrust open the door and marched into the room. My mother was just in the process of stitching a number of superfluous endothermic vertebrates on a scrap of silk—in other words, embroidering a handkerchief with birds. Swiftly and silently, I strode up to her.

'Mother.'

She jumped a foot into the air, almost stabbing her finger with her needle. My sister, sitting a few feet away, glanced up, looking as if she would very much prefer to stab me instead.

'Good Lord! Can't you knock?'

I gave her a cool look. 'The ability to do something does not imply the necessity.'

She nodded. 'Ah. So you're just bad-mannered. Good to know.'

Turning away from the young raven-haired harpy, whom I was seventy-five per cent certain was related to me, I focused on the easier target: my mother. She was looking up at me with a soft, longing look in her eyes. Soft, longing and *loving*.

Certainty: twenty-five per cent.

'You wanted something, Mother?'

'Yes, Rick. Um, I...' She fiddled with her needle, accidentally stabbing her birds to death multiple times, and turning the flower on the handkerchief from a rose to a porouse. 'I was wondering...'

'Yes?' My cool gaze swivelled back from the vertebrates to her—and promptly, her courage faltered.

'I was wondering if you would like to sit down?'

'No.'

'Oh.'

'Err...would you like a cup of tea?'

'No.'

'A biscuit?'

'No.'

'A kick in the butt?'

290

That last one had *not* come from my mother. My gaze turned to Adaira, who was smiling up at me with absolutely no shame. Hm. Maybe seventy-six per cent certainty.

'Sit down, you granite-headed ligger!'[22] she ordered me, with far too much determination for a little squirt of a girl who, only a few years ago, was dribbling gruel on her nappy. Females! You leave for a decade or two, and all of a sudden they think they're grown up and entitled to their own opinions. 'Mother wants to talk to you.'

'You don't say. I hadn't noticed.'

This was a waste of my time. I had to get back to my business. My documents. *Documents which just happen to be in the same room as a certain lady.*

Irrelevant. Ignore.

Clamping down on my urge to march out of the room, I perched down on the plush blue monstrosity that passed for furniture in my mother's eyes. I sank seven point thirty-two inches into the thing before decelerating and coming to a stop.

'Well, um...Ricky...'

'Yes, Mother?'

My mother's fingers started nervously stitching again. Only, she wasn't paying particularly much attention to what her hands were doing. Right now, the needle was in the process of adding a third wing to the bird's backside.

'Well...I was wondering how things...how things are going with you.'

'Not.'

She blinked at me. 'Pardon?'

'I'm not going. I'm sitting. While not getting any work done, I might add.'

My sister shifted in her seat and, with a dexterity that was almost enough to distract me, managed to kick me in the process. I put another scratch on the mental list of things to talk over with my little sister as soon as I managed to get her alone.

'No, what I meant was...' Blushing, my mother glanced sideways. Meanwhile, her nervous fingers added a fourth wing to the bird's bottom, and a beak to his left foot. 'I noticed you've been spending quite a lot of time with—'

No. Don't say it. Do. Not. Say. It.

'—Miss Linton lately.'

I regarded her for a moment in silence. Then...

'Indeed?'

Ayla gave me another kick. This time *without* pretending to shift in her seat.

'Go on, big brother! Spill!'

Reaching for one of the tea cups on the tray next to the sofa, I spilled a few drops of the contents onto the saucer.

'Sufficient?'

She glared at me with an expression I had once seen on the face of a hungry African hyena just before she leapt on her prey.

---

[22] Ligger: a British term for "freeloader", i.e. a person who likes other people to buy stuff for them, and doesn't like paying those other people back.

'Brother...'

I raised both shoulders precisely two millimetres. 'I prefer to deposit liquid in my stomach.'

Then, before my sister had any more chance to emulate raptor behaviour, I redirected my attention to my mother. Her eyes were still focused on me with deep love and concern.

Fortunately, I was immune to such distracting phenomena.

'Is there a...connection between you and Miss Linton?' she enquired.

'Certainly there is.' I took another sip of tea. 'She is my secretary's sister.'

My mother's busy fingers sped up. She was still adding wings to her embroidery. This time, it didn't appear to be attached to any bird, but flying free towards the sky. Her eyes seemed to be similarly inclined to avoid any contact. They were jumping from one corner of the room to another, never focusing on anything for long. She was working up to something.

Leave. Now.

'That's not what I meant, Rick. What I meant to ask was...Is there something developing there?'

'I currently have a number of properties in development. Several in London, some in Manchester, and a number in—'

'That...that wasn't what I'm talking about either.' Her hands sped up even more, starting to embroider a....tentacle? Or was it spaghetti? I was not entirely certain. 'I'm talking about you and Miss Linton.'

Miss Linton. Miss Linton, who was currently sitting upstairs, guarded only by a maid. A strange, cold feeling started to trickle down my spine. Not just any cold trickle—a cold trickle that *bothered* me. That was new.

I shifted.

Get a hold of yourself. She is perfectly safe. Feelings, whether yours or other people's, are not relevant in the matter.

'Rick!' Abruptly turning to fully face me, my mother gazed up at me. She was wringing her hands, and with them the four-winged, tentacle-armed, spaghetti-wielding birds. Pity. It had been the only mildly interesting piece of embroidery I had ever seen. 'I...know we're not particularly close, son. But...I'm your mother. I care about you. And this tendency of yours to shut yourself off from people who care for you, to be as cold and distant as an icy mountain.... Please, try to overcome it for my sake. Whenever I try to open up to you, you turn away and—'

From above, through the ceiling, I heard a sudden thud. My head whipped around.

'Yes,' Adaira commented from behind. 'Just like that.'

I didn't listen. My ears, my eyes, my entire being was centred on the ceiling. Had I just imagined it?

'Rikkard?' Someone took hold of my sleeve. My mother? Sister? The under-footman? The doorknob? Irrelevant! The question right now was: what had that noise been? 'This is just what I'm talking about! You need some warmth in your life, some emotion. There's a lovely girl upstairs, who I'm sure would be delighted to spend some time with you. It's Christmas, the time of love and companionship! This is no time to be rushing off to your next business meeting or some dusty documents that—'

Another *thump* came from upstairs, this time unmistakable.

'Excuse me,' I bit out, and tore my sleeve free of her grip. 'I have some documents to attend to!'

In three steps, I was at the door. Pushing it open, I rushed out into the corridor.

'Rick! Where are you going? You can't run away from things forever!'

If only that was what I was doing. But I wasn't running away. I was running towards something. Towards the only thing that mattered—besides my safe combination.

'Karim!' My command cut through the air like a whip. Moments later, a door somewhere in the distance crashed open, and thunderous footsteps approached. Moments later, a familiar mountainous figure appeared beside me. Never had I been so glad to see him. Or glad to see anyone. Or just glad, for that matter. I was *glad*. And *scared*. I was exhibiting *emotions*. What in Mammon's name was going on?

'Upstairs!' I bit out, taking the first three steps with a leap.

'The *Sahiba*?'

'Yes!'

More words weren't necessary.

We reached the upstairs landing in three point five seven seconds. Tearing down the corridor, I reached into my pocket for my revolver.

It won't be necessary. She'll be fine. She'll be fine. She must be fine!

If I gave the universe a firm enough order, it had to obey. It had to!

Or at least that's what I kept telling myself until the smell hit my nose. Leaping forward, I kicked open the door—

Only to find an empty room, filled only by the lingering odour of chloroform.

AFTER HER

Moving fast.

I had *always* had been moving fast. It was what I was best at. I went on and on and on, no matter if other people or some unfortunate mountain stood in my way. Yet never in my entire life had I moved faster than right in this second. Never had I moved faster than when I ran to her chair.

Her *empty* chair.

'Karim? Get in here!'

'I'm here, *Sahib*.'

Karim appeared beside me, his face expressionless, his eyes flickering around the room. He sniffed, dragging in air like a bloodhound.

'*Sahib*! That odour—'

'Yes.' My eyes swept across the floor—and halted. Kneeling, I snatched up the rag off the carpet and held it to my face, sniffing. Instantly, I started to sway.

'*Sahib!*'

I tore the rag away. 'It's all right, Karim!' I ground out. But it wasn't. It wasn't in the least. Chloroform!

A strong hand gripped my shoulder. 'Are you all right, *Sahib?*'

'The maid!' Shrugging off his hand, I straightened and peered into the corners of the room. 'Where is she?'

Both mine and Karim's eyes were drawn to the stinking rag in my hand. My fingers clenched around it, balling up into a fist.

'*Bhens ki aulaad!*'[23] Karim cursed.

'Find that maid!' My words were ice and steel and death, all melded into one single weapon. 'Find that maid, and make her rue the day she was born.'

'As you command, *Sahib.*' Striding to the door, Karim tore it open—then hesitated. 'And what are you going to do, *Sahib?*'

My fingers clenched even more tightly around the stinking cloth in my hand. The cloth that, not-so long ago, had been pressed to the face of...

No. Don't think. Act!

'I'm going after *her!*'

When I stormed into the entrance hall twenty-seven seconds later, my mother and my sister were both waiting for me. Words were coming out of my mother's mouth. Meaningless words. What was she saying?

'Listen, Rick. I'm really starting to get worried. You're always working, always rushing around, never stopping a minute to relax or talk to—'

Dashing past her, I kicked open the front door, and marched outside.

'Well,' I heard my little sister's voice from behind. 'That was a scintillating conversation, wasn't it? I can hardly wait till the next time we sit down as a family and—'

That was when the front door fell shut behind me.

'Renshaw!' I bellowed. 'To me! Now!'

The man in question dashed out from behind a nearby bush. A bush from behind which he had been standing guard—without noticing a thing!

Strangulation is not the best solution. Strangulation is not the best solution.

'Where are the reinforcements I requested?' I growled.

Renshaw straightened. 'Only half a day's ride or so away, Mr Ambrose, Sir. I got a message from Perkins yesterday, saying that—'

'Forget the letter! Get someone on the fastest horse in the stables and send them to meet Perkins. He is to get his posterior here yesterday, understood?'

'Yes, Sir! Of course, Sir! But...' He cleared his throat. 'What if your father's stable master isn't amenable to our taking the animal?'

'You are familiar with the hole at the back of the stable? The one through which the stable hands shovel dung onto the dung heap?'

'Yes, Sir?'

'Good. If he should resist, make sure the stable master becomes familiar with it, too. Very, very closely.'

'Yes, Sir!'

---

[23] Son of a buffalo!

'And once you've sent out the messenger, gather all the remaining men you have and meet me at the oak behind the summerhouse, armed and ready to go.'

'Yes, Sir!'

When I reached the oak, my horse was already saddled and waiting. Just as I swung myself into the saddle, the dozen or so able-bodied men I had been able to place among my father's staff came galloping around the corner of the house. Quite a few, I had thought until recently. Not enough, I now knew.

'Spread out!' I commanded. 'She's been taken! I want her found!'

Nobody dared to risk their jobs and necks by asking whom I was referring to. They knew. I knew.

How is it that when I say the word 'her' these days, it always means one woman?

The answer was as simple as it was terrifying.

Because she's mine!

'Johnson, Higgins and Higgins! You go west. Ellerson and Gold! To the east!' I barked out more orders, gave more directions. Finally, I stabbed my finger towards the oldest of the men—one of the gardeners, who looked about as comfortable on a horse as I would have at a charity ball. 'Stay here, and report to Karim and the reinforcements. Send them after us the minute they arrive.'

'Yes, Sir!'

Not wasting another second, I gave my horse the spurs. Snow sprayed up into the air. The empty stretch of white before me turned into a blur. Behind me, I heard my men shouting for me to wait.

Wait?

Wait?

I had shipped people off to the Sahara for less idiotic suggestions. Once again, I spurred on my mount. Faster! *Faster!*

Somehow, faster wasn't fast enough.

The northern English countryside was something I had never really contemplated before. It was simply there, like grass on the ground, birds in the sky and creditors at the door. But now...now it was everywhere. Too big. Too silent. Too empty. So infernally empty! One hill after another after another...

What if I don't reach her in time? What if she—

Another man might have turned to God at this point. Another man might have prayed, and promised all kinds of things if only she would be safe.

I?

I wasn't good at promising things. Threatening was more my department.

You had better be all right, Mr Linton! Do you hear me? You had better be!

'Sir? Sir, please wait!'

If you're not all right, I'll cut ninety per cent of your wages and make you reorganize all seven levels of my subterranean archive! Do you hear me? All seven levels!

'Sir! Please, Sir!'

I spurred my horse on again. Faster!

The land had never been so empty. Spreading out, my men and I followed trail after trail leading away from the manor. Why in Mammon's name did my infernal father have to have so many people coming and going? Butchers, woodcutters, huntsmen...what were they all doing here? Nobody in their right mind needed that much firewood! Body heat was more than sufficient for heating. And who needed to eat meat if there was bread and water available?

'Another trail, Sir!' One of my apparently less incompetent men came galloping up, gesturing east. 'There's someone over there, beyond the woods.'

'About-turn!' Jerking my hand in a signal to the riders that were farther away, I whipped my mount around and sent it galloping off towards the trees. Through the foliage, I caught sight of someone on a horse and—

And there was something slung over the back of that horse. Something lifeless.

Gritting my teeth, I forced my horse to run its heart out and whipped my revolver out of my pocket. Blood pounded in my ears, faster and faster. One hundred sixty beats per minute. One hundred seventy. One hundred eighty. Snow-laden trees flew by, blocking my view—but I knew what was behind them.

Something lifeless slung across the horse!

The last few trees flashed past me. Suddenly, there he was: the rider! I crossed the last few yards in an instant. In a flash, I had my gun up.

'Freeze!'

The farm boy did freeze. So did the horse, as well as the seven-inches-tall canine the boy held in his arms. The dog watched me with enlarged eyes.

'I...errr...um...ng...'

Slowly, the boy's eyes travelled from the tip of the barrel of my revolver to my hand. I met his eyes—then my gaze travelled down to the sack of hay hanging over the back of the horse.

A sack of hay.

'Woof?' The little dog enquired. 'Woof, woof?'

I cleared my throat.

'Dog inspection. Show the paws.'

Very, very cautiously, the boy raised first the small canine's paws, then his own. The dog's were considerably cleaner.

'Adequate.' I motioned with my gun. 'Carry on.'

'Y-yes, Sir!'

Wheeling his horse around, the boy raced off in the direction from which he'd come. A moment later, three riders burst through the trees, behind me, weapons out.

'Mr Ambrose? Mr Ambrose, Sir?'

'False alarm.' My words were clipped and hard as stone. 'Head back and spread out!'

Immediately, they did as ordered. We had just cleared the trees and started to spread out across the white expanse of nothing when a sharp whistle echoed over the landscape. My head snapped around towards its origin, and I saw one of the men waving. Jerking his hands in a quick signal, he pointed westwards. My head snapped around in the direction of his gesture. What was he going on about? There was nothing there, except—

I stiffened.

My hand shot down to the saddlebag. Pulling it open, I took out a telescope and lifted it to my eye. Focusing on the horizon, I let it travel from left to right, searching, searching...

Yes. *There.*

I had seen dust clouds in the desert often enough. Whenever a rider galloped through the waste, dust was hurled up into the air, forming a cloud warning any one of their arrival. A cloud just like the cloud of snow rapidly moving towards us.

'Men! Gather round! Weapons out!'

If that was Dalgliesh and his men, if he had hurt her, I would...!

...have a problem. It looked as if he had at least thrice as many men as I.

As if something like that had ever stopped me in the past.

Reaching for my revolver once again, I twirled the cylinder, making sure it was locked and loaded. The cloud of snow was racing closer rapidly.

'Retreat between the trees,' I bit out. 'Take cover! You and you. Get off your horses and find two trees to climb. At the first sight of a rifle, you shoot!'

They didn't even waste time saluting before starting up the trees. I myself didn't retreat between the trees. I stood just at the edge, clearly visible to the approaching riders, drawing their attention away from my men. Right out in the open—except for the big boulder right next to me that, if necessary, would work adequately as a cover.

'Get ready.' My command came out low. Too low to be heard over the thunder of the approaching enemies. Still, my men knew what to do. Behind me, I heard the click of hammers sliding into position.

Folding my arms, I hid my gun beneath my sleeve, raising it almost high enough to shoot. The first hints of faces were becoming visible in the white cloud racing closer. My grip on the gun tightened. Any moment. Any moment now...

'*Sahib!*'

The gun dropped.

'Karim?'

A big, black shape loomed up among the swirls of white. Moments later, the massive bodyguard shoved past the other riders, cantering along on the back of a poor horse that, while a giant beast to any other rider, looked like an exhausted little pony beneath the huge Mohammedan. And not just because he was heavy, no. Because he had something slung over the back of the horse—and it was most definitely *not* a wheat sack.

You've got her?

I didn't dare utter the words out loud. But my eyes conveyed it clearly enough. Leaping from the horse, Karim grabbed the lifeless form from the back of his mount and lowered her to the snowy ground. In front of me, I saw the slim, somewhat sour face of the traitorous housemaid.

He had her.

Just not the 'her' I really wanted.

Of course, you fool! Of course he would bring the maid. You sent him after that traitor.

Enough time wasted.

'Why is she unconscious?' I demanded.

Karim's brow wrinkled. 'I am not certain, *Sahib*. I did not harm a hair on her head. When I caught up to her, I simply grabbed her by the throat, held the tip of my sabre in front of her eyes and threatened to eviscerate her with my bare hands if she did not tell me everything she knew. She didn't even give me a chance to enact any of my threats. She just lost consciousness for some mysterious reason.'

He shook his head at the strange ways of English women.

'Did she tell you anything before she collapsed?' I demanded.

'No.'

'I see.' I would not let such a little thing as unconsciousness stand in my way. Time to get down to brass tacks. Especially since any other sort of tax was simply intolerable. 'Johnson! Bayard!'

'Yes, Sir?'

'Hold her!'

'Err...Yes, Sir, but why do you want us to—'

'That's why,' I told them, scooping up two handfuls of snow and, unceremoniously, dropping them right into the traitor's décolletage.

'Iaaaaaah! Ah! Uh! What...?'

The girl jerked, flopping from left to right, trying to throw off the snow. Blinking, she stared up at the faces of the two men leaning over her, blocking her view of the sky.

'G-gentlemen! Oh, thank God! It was only a nightmare. Good Sirs, you won't believe this, but I had the most horrible nightmare! I dreamed that a savage attacked me in the middle of the English countryside and—'

That was the moment when Karim stepped into her field of vision.

'Yaaaaaah!'

'She did that the last time I approached her.' Karim frowned. 'What does it mean? Is it a British expression?'

'P-please...' Crawling backwards, the traitorous maid tried to get away from Karim—and came up against something hard and horsy. Looking up, she gazed straight into the grinning maw of a stallion. 'Aaaaaah!'

'No,' I told my bodyguard. 'It's a cowardly expression.'

The maid turned from left to right, trying to find a way out. But wherever she turned there were the boots of men, the hooves of horses and snow, endless, cold, harsh snow. Finally, she found a way and started scrambling forward frantically—until her fingers came up against two polished black shoes. Slowly, her eyes rose higher and higher until they met mine.

She gulped.

'P-please...'

Grabbing my walking stick, I whacked her outstretched arm away and pinned her to the ground.

'No! You don't get to ask! You only get to answer. Now tell me...' I pressed a little harder with the stick. Just hard enough to bring my—and its—sharp point across. '*Where is she?*'

'I...I...err...'

She lay there, silently opening and closing her mouth, unable to get a word out.

Unacceptable.

'Karim?'

The Mohammedan stepped forward, back straight, arms crossed. 'Yes, *Sahib*?'

'She's all yours.'

~~*~**~*~*

The hoofbeats of the horses thundered in my ears. They pounded wildly, out of control—and yet, it was nothing compared to the absolutely steady and regular beat in my head that counted down the distance.

Three point five miles...

Three point four...

Three point three...

Would I be in time? Would she still be there?

She has to be! And if she isn't...

I had ways of forcing the world to be as I wanted it to be. And if some blood was spilled in the process, that would be more than acceptable.

Three point two miles...

Three point one...

Out of the blank nothing of the landscape appeared a tiny black dot. Slowly, it started to grow, then faster and faster, until—

'There it is, Sir!' Bayard jabbed his hand forward. With the other one, he was holding a telescope to his eye. 'The hut she told us about.'

Very quickly, and very succinctly. Karim could be extremely persuasive.

'Faster!'

'But Mr Ambrose, Sir, the horses—'

'—have to learn about work ethic. I said faster!'

The hut raced closer, faster and faster. When I was finally close enough to make out details, I clenched my teeth.

Hoofprints in the snow.

Leading to *and* away from the cabin.

If she's gone, if they've taken her, I will...!

I didn't finish the thought.

Because I truly did not know what I was going to do.

Take revenge?

Kill Dalgliesh?

Be...heartbroken?

Irrelevant. Ignore. Concentrate on her. Take action!

Heartbroken.

Destroyed.

Irrelevant! Ignore!

The last bit of distance between us and the hut vanished in a blink. Tugging at the reins, I brought my horse to an abrupt halt. Johnson came to a stop beside me.

'No one in sight, Sir. Should we go in?'

I jerked my head in a nod. 'Yes.'

Three men dismounted and, dashing towards the cabin, pressed themselves against the wall. Slowly, they inched towards the door. For a moment, they hesitated. Their eyes flicked to me as they waited for the order. I met Johnson's gaze, ice in my eyes.

'If she's hurt...' Never before in my life had my voice been so cold. It seemed to come from far, far away, deep underneath the Arctic Ocean. Which was where I wanted to put a certain peer of the realm. 'Bring Dalgliesh to me. Alive.'

Johnson nodded.

'Yes, Sir!'

They cocked their weapons, and Johnson raised his hand, three fingers extended.

Three...

Two...

One...

Crash!

The door was kicked in, and the three men rushed in side, weapons levelled.

There was a moment of silence. No shots. No shouts. No nothing, except a long, long, silence. Finally, Johnson cleared his throat.

'Um...Sir?'

Expression of Superfluous Sentiments

I stared at the naked man. Not something I made a habit of doing, under normal circumstances. But at this precise moment...

This moment wasn't normal.

'Where. Is. She?'

The naked man on the ground refused to answer, most likely due to the fact he was unconscious. I had never been one to accept excuses.

Drawing back my foot, I brought it forward to solidly collide with the main part of the man's male anatomy.

Thud!

'Aargh!'

'Where?'

'Nnn...what? I don't...'

Thud!

'Arg!'

'Where? Speak!'

No answer. Not an acceptable result. Not anywhere at any time, but most especially not now—when it was all about *her*.

'Anderson! Renshaw!' I called. 'Get in here, and bring rope!' *And some sharp implements.* 'Everyone else, spread out! Search the woods!'

And if you don't find her, don't bother to come back.

The words didn't need to be spoken. My eyes conveyed them perfectly. Anderson and Renshaw came hurrying into the hut with one rope each slung over their shoulders. My other men scattered like dust in the wind. Very determined, very deadly dust.

'Who in God's name do you think you are?' the man on the ground howled as my men twisted his arms behind his back and started to tie them together. 'I'm a soldier of the presidency armies, and—'

I whirled to face him, cutting him off with a single, razor-sharp glance.

'If I were you,' I told him, every word a well-paced splinter of ice, 'I would not mention the name of that band of blaggards again. Unless you want certain portions of your anatomy permanently removed.'

The soldier swallowed and closed his mouth. Adequate. He'd live at least a little while longer.

'Get him out there on a horse. Karim will interrogate him while the rest of us go after Dalgliesh and find out what's happened to Miss—'

Just then, a strange sound cut me off. A shrill, discordant whistle reminiscent of a choking nightingale.

Or...almost.

Without knowing exactly why, I turned and strode towards the window. Outside, my horse stood waiting for me. And on the back of my horse...

'What are you waiting for, Sir? Let's go!'

Her.

It was *her.*

On *my horse.*

'Look, Sir!' One of my men appears beside me, completely redundantly pointing at the female sitting there as if she had no cares in the world. 'She's safe!'

Yes. She was safe. Safe on *my horse.*

My feet started moving before I knew what was happening.

What the...?

Under normal circumstances, I welcomed initiative, but I preferred it from my employees, not my body parts! Still...right now I didn't particularly care. The only thing standing in my way was a hut's flimsy door. One good, hard kick, and it flew right of the hinges, sailing into the snow.

And there she was.

Instantly, I started forward again. Moments later, I stood before my horse, gazing up at the most impudent smile I had ever seen. So impudent it has to be wiped off right now.

Preferably with a kiss.

Where did that thought come from?

Well, wherever it did, it had better go back there straight away!

'Miss Linton.' My voice sounded cold and distant like the whistling wind on a winter night. Just goes to show how deceptive sound could be.

'You took your time, Sir.' Her voice was warmth. Welcome. Fire burning just beneath the surface.

Our eyes met and held.

'You seem to have managed well enough on your own.'

And you're sitting on my horse.

She cocked her head, thoughtfully. 'Yes, I did, didn't I? Maybe I should just ride away and leave you here. It wasn't a particularly good rescue, you know.'

She wouldn't dare!

That thought flashed through my mind before I remembered who I was dealing with. Inconspicuously, I sneaked up my hand to grab hold of the reins. Just in case.

'Miss Linton?'

Her smile widened. So fiery. So fierce. 'Yes, Mr Ambrose, Sir?'

Kiss it. Kiss her.

'Get off my horse.'

She cocked her head. 'I don't think so. I think I'll–'

Enough!

With one step, I crossed the remaining distance. My arms shot up towards her and, stepping into a stirrup with one foot, I launched myself up at the same moment I hauled her down. Just to get her down from the horse, I told myself. Just to get her down from the horse. Just to get her down from the—

Our lips collided.

No. No. No.

Yes. Yes. Yes!

'Silence!' I growled. But was it at her, or at the voices fiercely arguing in my head? In my...heart?

What are you doing? This is madness! Remember. Calm. Control. Get away from her, before it is too late! Before—

And then she started to kiss me back.

I had received a lot of kisses in my life. Of course, most of them had come from French business partners who wouldn't let a little thing like an icy glare that threatened evisceration stand in the way of their treasured social customs. But still...it should count, correct? I had experience. This should be nothing out of the ordinary. Easy to deal with. Simple. Average.

So soft. Her lips are so soft...

So what? I owned a pillow factory!

And they could take a leaf out of her book. Or from her lips. Or...

No! Mine! All mine!

'My little *ifrit!*' The words were out of my mouth before I could hold them back. But...did I even want to?

'You should take your own good advice,' she shot back at me. 'Shut up and kiss me!'

And for once I did what I had never ever done before. I did what I was told. Sliding my arms around her, I pulled her against me, hard, and kissed her.

Kissed her for five seconds. Ten. Fifteen. Time. It suddenly seemed like such an insignificant little concept now that she was safe. Here. With me.

What happened to getting her off my horse?

She happened.

'Thank you,' her whisper drifted to my ears. 'Thank you for coming for me.'

A tug. Painful. Deep in my chest.

Just a pulled muscle. That's all. A pulled muscle.

Statistically speaking, it did seem remarkable, however, that those pulled muscles always seemed to appear whenever I was in the vicinity of Miss Lillian Linton. A statistic worthy of investigation.

'I had no intentions of finding a new secretary,' I told her. 'Do you know what vacancy advertisements cost these days?'

Her face slowly rose from where it lay against my chest and I felt a sudden impulse to clutch her back against me.

Mine!

Then our eyes met, and I saw what I had been hoping to see. Whatever had happened, whatever Dalgliesh had done to her, it hadn't broken her. It hadn't even bent her. I saw fire in her eyes, burning more brightly than ever before.

Nonsense! Eyes cannot burn! It is a physical impossibility!

Except perhaps with her.

Her chin rose. 'Let's get out of here!'

It sounded suspiciously like an order. And for some inane reason, right then and there, I didn't mind.

'Agreed.'

Not wasting another millisecond, I pulled myself fully up into the saddle behind her. Very close behind her. A little gasp escaped her lips, and I felt my body stiffen in response.

Concentrate. Ride.

On second thought, thinking about riding might not be the best idea right now.

The horse. *Just ride the* horse.

Not listening to my head, my arm snaked around her, pulling her roughly against me. Her ears heated approximately three point five degrees, turning an intriguing shade of red. Was it because of me, or...

I glanced around.

My men were back from their scouting mission. They were gathered all around. Looking. At me. At me and her.

'Miss Linton,' I spoke, my voice at zero temperature, 'is a gently bred lady of good family and impeccable reputation. She would never do anything so rash as to kiss a man in public. If anyone were to suggest differently, I would be...displeased. Do we understand each other?'

Heads nodded like mechanical marionettes.

'Adequate. Well, gentlemen? What are you waiting for? Ride!' Reaching around her to grab the reins, I gave a snap of my wrist. 'Gee-up!'

Our equine transport accelerated immediately, rushing off across the plain, sending snow flying up right and left. The ice crystals danced in the air, and they were...

Beautiful?

It was simply frozen water. How could a phase of matter be beautiful?

Instinctively, my arm tightened around her.

Thunder enveloped us. Glancing to the side, I saw my men catching up and surrounding us from every angle. There were dozens of men around us, not to speak of the horses, and the animals that hid in the forest. But right then and there, it felt like the only two people existing in this world were she and I.

And that's an objectively stupid feeling. Most importantly, because it is a feeling. *Stop! Think, don't feel!*

It suddenly didn't appear as easy as it always had. Not with her in my arms. I was just about to try and start to fight down my irrational emotions—then she turned, and looked up at me.

'How did you find me?'

By removing anything in my way. Permanently.

'I had sent one of my mother's servants with a letter to Newcastle requesting reinforcements from my agents and additional hired personnel as soon as Dalgliesh arrived. They arrived shortly after...after you...'

'After I disappeared.'

My head jerked once in the affirmative.

'The room didn't look as if there had been a struggle. I surmised that the maid had been in league with Dalgliesh...' –*the little fool*– '...and that she would be aiming to make a quick getaway after getting paid. So I sent three of my men to lie in wait on the road to the closest port city, and another three on the road south to London. It wasn't long before she appeared.'

'You have her?'

Another woman's voice might have contained concern or fear for another female, even though that female had stabbed her in the back. Not her. All I could hear was determination for vengeance.

Maybe she's not such an illogical choice after all.

'Karim does. He's explaining the errors of her ways to her.'

'Oh.' A corner of her mouth quirked up and I felt the sudden urge to reach out and touch it. 'Oh dear.'

'Indeed.'

I didn't reach out. Instead, I just held her. I held her as we raced across the snowy fields, in the cold, on horses that had cost a lot of money, with people who had cost a lot of money to hire, all to retrieve a woman who could bring me no possible monetary gain, and...and I had never been...

What was the word?

Happier.

What in Mammon's name is going on?

'Bridge ahead, Sir!' a voice suddenly tore me from my thoughts. Glancing up, I saw one of my men pointing ahead, at a small bridge spanning a half-frozen river. A bridge I hadn't noticed.

Again!

Since when did I have to have other people alert me to my surroundings? *Simple. Since her.*

It was correct. She was interfering with my mind. She was turning everything on its head. First my office, then my life, and now, my...my...

I had to get rid of her!

Instinctively, my arm tightened around her, and I urged my horse forward, towards the bridge. Towards safety.

'Developed an interest in medieval architecture, have you, Mr Ambrose?' the impudent female in front of me enquired.

'No. This is where we are meeting up with Karim and the other men.'

'The other men?'

'The maid could not provide any information on whether Dalgliesh had already removed you from the hut she saw you in. So I sent some men to Dalgliesh's closest holding, just in case.'

Just in case. Hire men, just in case. Pay money, just in case. What is happening to me?

'Halt!'

Was it a command to my men or to myself?

Raising a hand, I brought my men to a stop. Not letting her go for a minute, I slid out of the saddle, setting her down on the ground.

'Spread out!' I commanded. *And that only applies to my men, Miss Linton, not to you.* 'Dalgliesh's men may follow our trail and decide to attack. If they do, I want ample warning. Form a perimeter. Keep your guns handy, and be ready to fight.'

'Yes, Sir! You heard him, men. Go!'

The riders galloped off in different directions, leaving her and me alone in front of the bridge.

'Come.' I nodded at the bridge. Taking a firm hold of her hand, I strode forward until we stood in the very centre of the bridge, far away from either riverbank. The safest point. In the icy cold, I could almost feel her, warm and soft, standing only inches away. The urge to turn my head to the right, to look at her, was almost irresistible.

Almost.

I didn't turn. Instead, I looked out over the ice of the river. Out of the corner of my eyes, I saw her slide her hands under her armpits. Was she cold?

And why precisely do you care?

A stiff breeze swept over us, and I forced my eyes forward again, pretending I was alone. Pretending I was at the prow of a ship, sailing far, far away from any—

'Bloody hell! You couldn't have found a warm spot to wait, could you?'

Did you really think you could pretend for long around her?

'At the time, Miss Linton, I had slightly more pressing matters on my mind.'

Such as whether or not you would survive, for instance.

But now she *was* safe. Now she was standing right beside me. And she was cold.

Without even giving it a thought, I lifted one arm, offering.

Offering something for nothing. Something really is wrong with you.

305

Without a word, she slid under my arm, pressing her body close to mine. And it suddenly occurred to me that, perhaps, I was not offering something in return for nothing. Perhaps I would be receiving something very valuable in return.

Time ticked by. We just stood there, looking out over the ice-covered river. One minute. Two minutes. Three. With every passing moment, the warmth between us spread, blossoming from a pile of embers into a crackling fire. Four minutes. Five.

Say something!

Why? Why should I want to say something?

Because! Because you have to know she wasn't...

I swallowed, hard.

'Miss Linton?'

'Yes, Mr Ambrose, Sir?'

'While Dalgliesh had you in his power, did he...do anything? Hurt you in any way?'

My arm around her shoulders tightened as one great, terrifying question pounded in my mind.

What will you do if she answers yes?

Well, for the sake of Dalgliesh and everyone in my way, let's hope I would never find out.

Her lips parted—but no sound came out. Tense like wire, I awaited her answer.

'No, he didn't harm me.' *You're in luck, Dalgliesh. You get to live another day.* 'But he did talk quite a lot.'

I had just been about to relax a little. At her words, I was suddenly again stiff as a board.

'Whatever he told you was probably lies.'

There was a pause. Normally, it was I who made people uncomfortable through long silences. Being on the receiving end of this method was...unexpected.

'Oh? So you didn't run away from home as a boy because of an argument with your father, then?'

Did I think I had been tense before? I had been mistaken. My arm tightened around her shoulders like a vice, as if I wanted to keep her from running away. Maybe that was exactly what I wanted.

'It was somewhat more complicated than that, Miss Linton.'

She was silent again for a little while. But this time the silence somehow wasn't uncomfortable in the least. Instead, it was...warm. Reassuring.

Soft fingers touched mine. I sucked in a breath and instinctively started to pull away—then stopped. Her smaller hand closed around mine and gave a single, simple little squeeze.

One.

Just one squeeze.

That was all.

That was enough. More than enough. Something inside me shifted.

'I said it once already, I believe,' came her soft voice from beside me, 'but...thank you. I might have gotten out of there by myself—but then again, I might not have. If Dalgliesh had come back with enough men and searched the woods...'

She didn't finish the sentence.

Fortunately.

If she had, I didn't know whether I would have been able to stop myself from swinging myself back onto my horse and riding out there to join my men. Join them in the quest to find Dalgliesh, get a hold of him and squeeze his throat until—

Until what?

Until he was dead?

That might be a worthy goal, but spur-of-the-moment strangulation was not the way to a achieve it. There was only one thing I should squeeze right now. One thing I wanted to squeeze. So I squeezed Miss Lilly Linton's hand. It felt right. It felt as it belonged in mine.

'I...had to come.'

The words fell out of my mouth as if it were a gash, a wound I couldn't close. One that I didn't *want* to close.

'Really?'

'Yes.' I hesitated for a moment. But even now that all those insane, irrational words were falling from my lips, I couldn't do one thing: procrastinate. My mouth snapped open again, and words started pouring out. 'I am not a man who often expresses his emotions, Miss Linton.'

'You don't say?'

She was making fun of me? She dared to make fun of me *now* of all times? Now, when I was getting ready to...?

What exactly was I getting ready to do?

My mouth seemed to have quite definite opinions on the matter. Without my say-so, it started speaking. 'I must admit I was...somewhat concerned for you.'

'Somewhat concerned? Dear God, really?'

She was making fun of me. And, to judge by the sparkle in her eyes, she was having considerable fun doing it. The insolent little...!

I whirled to face her, my eyes alight. 'Dammit! Do not joke, Miss Linton!'

She blinked up at me, so sweet, so innocent, so completely full of colloquial manure. 'I wouldn't dare!'

Stepping forward, I reached out until I had captured her face with my hand. The logical, cold part of my mind was shouting commands to let go, to step back, to keep silent—but for once, I could not keep my mouth shut. Words kept pouring out. Words from deep in my chest where, once upon a time, there had been a living, beating heart. 'I...I might be slightly...irrationally infatuated with you.'

She put a hand to her chest. 'Irrationally infatuated? Dear me!'

My jaw clenched hard. How could she still be ridiculing me? I was tearing myself open for her!

Admittedly, I was doing it with a precision scalpel, creating an opening of roughly two point twenty-one millimetres, but that should be enough for anyone, shouldn't it? It was perfectly clear what I really meant!

But all she did was stand there, grinning up at me with a knowing smile, her head cocked in that way that made me want to...made me want to...

'All right, all right!' I snapped. 'I may even have certain...impulses towards you that border on caring about you!'

There! If that wasn't romantic, I didn't know what was.

'You don't say?' She raised an eyebrow. She. Dared. To. Raise. An. *Eyebrow.* 'Well, I am so glad to hear that you feel a certain amount of *friendship* towards me.'

Friendship.

Friendship?

I did my best to nail her to the spot with the pure force of my eyes—a skill that had me served well during many a business negotiation. Right here and now, it didn't even put a dent in her grin.

'Friendship is not quite the right word, Miss Linton,' I squeezed out between clenched teeth, every word a curse and a plea at the same time. 'My impulses towards you...they might go slightly beyond the platonic.'

'Oh, so they are Aristotelian?'

Was it legal to sue a woman for damages for excessive verbal torture?

I would have to put my legal team on that.

'Mr Lin-' I swallowed, biting back the address, which, by now I had to admit, was nothing but a farce. One I was more than ready to dispense with. 'I mean *Miss* Linton, we are not discussing philosophy here!'

She batted her eyelashes at me. *Batted her eyelashes.* Oh yes indeed, my legal team would be getting work soon. 'Indeed? Then pray tell, what are we discussing?'

'I...' My voice failed. I just couldn't bring myself to do it. It was such an illogical concept. Such a madness! 'I...'

'You can say it, you know,' she was kind enough to inform me. 'The word isn't poisonous.'

Isn't it?

I had a feeling she was going to be the death of me.

'I...have feelings towards you.'

She inclined her head sombrely. 'Clearly. I knew that from the first day from the way you shouted at me and pelted me with threats.'

Someone had told me once that counting down from ten helped to calm people. So far, I had never had a need to test the theory. Now, however...

Ten...nine...eight...

Do not strangle. Repeat. Do not strangle.

...seven...six...five...

Repeat. Do not strangle. This is an order.

...four...three...tw—

Oh, Bugger!

'Not *those* kinds of feelings!'

She blinked up at me, eyes so innocent, so warm, like molten chocolate. 'What kind, then?'

'I feel...affection towards you.'

'You're nearly there.' Her smile widened. 'Just four little letters. The word starts with L. Go on. You can do it.'

My eyes narrowed to slits. 'You're enjoying this, Miss Linton, aren't you?'

'Very much so.'

'Oh, to hell with it!' Dropping my hand from her face, I grabbed hold of her and pulled. A moment later, my lips were on hers, and I was kissing her. Kissing her as if my life depended on it.

Which it does.

This girl...no, this *woman* had turned my ordered world upside down. And somehow I knew that, if I tried to force it back right side up again, it would be empty. And most likely, I wouldn't be able to lease the empty space out for three shillings per square yard.

Breaking our kiss, I gazed down at my little *ifrit*, and whispered, 'I love you!'

...THE MIDDLE...

ABOUT THE AUTHOR

 Robert Thier is a German historian and writer of historical fiction. His particular mix of history, romance, and adventure, always with a good deal of humour thrown in, has gained him a diverse readership ranging from teenagers to retired grandmothers. For the way he manages to make history come alive, as if he himself lived as a medieval knight, his fans all over the world have given him the nickname 'Sir Rob'.

For Robert, becoming a writer followed naturally from his interest in history. 'In Germany,' he says, 'we use the same word for story and history. And I've always loved the one as much as the other. Becoming a storyteller, a writer, is what I've always wanted.'

Besides writing and researching in dusty old archives, on the lookout for a mystery to put into his next story, Robert enjoys classical music and long walks in the country. The helmet you see in the picture he does not wear because he is a cycling enthusiast, but to protect his literary skull in which a bone has been missing from birth. Robert lives in the south of Germany in a small village between the three Emperor Mountains.

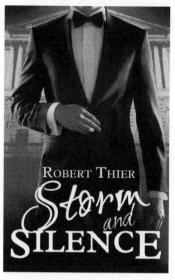

Storm and Silence

Freedom – that is what Lilly Linton wants most in life. Not marriage, not a brood of squalling brats, and certainly not *love*, thank you very much!

But freedom is a rare commodity in 19th-century London, where girls are expected to spend their lives sitting at home, fully occupied with looking pretty. Lilly is at her wits' end – until a chance encounter with a dark, dangerous and powerful stranger changes her life forever...

The award-winning first volume of the *Storm and Silence* series! Winner of the *People's Choice Award* and *Story of the Year Award* 2015.

ISBN-10: 3000513515   ISBN-13: 978-3000513510

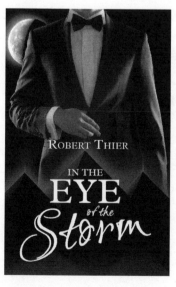

In the Eye of the Storm

Egypt... land of romance, mystery, and exploding camels. Lilly Linton thought she'd be ready for anything after one month of working for her boss – cold, calculating businessman Rikkard Ambrose. But when they embark on a perilous hunt through the desert, she has to face dangers beyond anything she has encountered before: deadly storms, marauding bandits, and worst of all, a wedding ring!

Can the desert's heat truly be enough to melt the cold heart of Britain's richest financier?

The long-awaited second volume of the acclaimed *Storm and Silence* series.

ISBN-10: 3000513515   ISBN-13: 978-3000513510

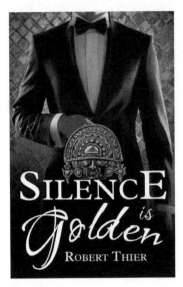

Silence is Golden

Silent. Cold. Chiselled perfection. That is Rikkard Ambrose, the most powerful business mogul in Great Britain.

Free-spirited. Fiery. Definitely *not* attracted to the aforementioned business mogul. That is Lilly Linton, his personal secretary and secret weapon.

The two have been playing a cat and mouse game for months. So far, Lilly has been able to fight down and deny her attraction to Mr Ambrose. But what happens when suddenly, the dark secrets of his past begin to surface and they are forced to go on a perilous journey into the South-American jungle? A journey they can only survive if they band together?

Volume three in the award-winning *Storm and Silence* series.

ISBN-13: 978-3962600587

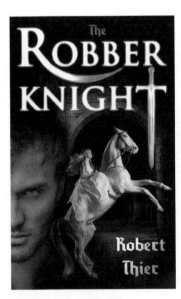

The Robber Knight

When you are fighting for the freedom of your people, falling in love with your enemy is not a great idea.

Sir Reuben, the dreaded robber knight, has long been Ayla's deadliest enemy. She swore he would hang for his crimes. Now they are both trapped in her castle as the army of a far greater enemy approaches, and they have only one chance: stand together, or fall. Welcome to *The Robber Knight*—a tale full of action, adventure, and romance.

Special Edition with secret chapters revealed and insights into Sir Reuben's mysterious past.

ISBN-10: 1499251645   ISBN-13: 978-1499251647

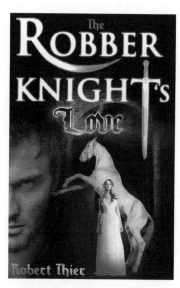

The Robber Knight's Love

Ayla has uncovered a terrible secret: the man she loves is in fact her worst enemy. As a mighty army gathers to destroy her and her people, she must ask herself: will he join them to destroy her? Must she cut him out of her heart to survive?
Or is there another way—a way to forgiveness and...love?

Special Edition with secret chapters revealed and insights into Sir Reuben's mysterious past.

ISBN-10: 3000536590   ISBN-13: 978-3000536595

WARNING! Fairy Tales

WARNING! Please be advised that this is not a bedtime story about sparkly fairies and pink unicorns. This book may contain graphic descriptions of poisoned apples and witches' ovens. It is not appropriate for supernatural beings under the age of 377 (excluding vampires and werewolves).
DISCLAIMER: Wicked Witches Inc. and Evil Stepmother Enterprises are not responsible for any maiming, mass murder or permanent insanity resulting from the reading of this book.

The first volume of Robert Thier's *WARNING! Fairy Tales* series.

ISBN-10: 3000547118   ISBN-13: 978-3000547119

WARNING! Fairy Tales 2

WARNING! Please be advised that big bad wolves, wicked witches, and harmless-looking little girls are roaming the pages of this book. It may contain graphic descriptions of wolf teeth and grandmothers with big ears. This book is not appropriate for supernatural beings under the age of 388 (excluding anyone wearing a red hood).

DISCLAIMER: *Wicked Witches Inc.* and *Evil Stepmother Enterprises* are not responsible for wolf bites, vampirism or witch curses incurred during the reading of this book.

The second volume of Robert Thier's *WARNING! Fairy Tales* series.

ISBN-13: 978-3962600013

WARNING! Fairy Tales 3

HEALTH WARNING! Reading this book may cause sudden attacks of magical metamorphosis. It may cause a fast and furry transformation into a beast, a troll, a vegetable, or, in a worst-case scenario, a cute little blue bird. No curse-breaking via kiss of true love guaranteed.

DISCLAIMER: *Beastly Beasties Inc.* and the *Royal Society of Enchanted Princes* are not responsible for any acquaintances, personnel and/or random bystanders accidentally transformed into furniture. Furniture polish and feather dusters must be purchased separately.

The third volume of Robert Thier's *WARNING! Fairy Tales* series.

ISBN-13: 978-3962600020

Upcoming Titles

At present (2018), the titles listed above are Robert Thiers's only books published in English. However, book three of the Robber Knight Saga, *The Robber Knight's Secret*, as well as his latest project, *Black Diaries*, are being edited for publication. Keep updated about the books' progress on the internet.

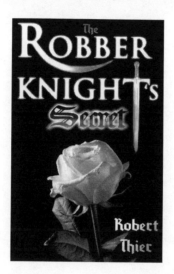

Website: www.robthier.com

Facebook profile: www.facebook.com/robert.thier.161

Facebook page: http://www.facebook.com/TheSirRob/

Twitter: http://twitter.com/thesirrob

Goodreads: www.goodreads.com/author/show/6123144.Robert_Thier

Made in the USA
Columbia, SC
02 May 2021

37255526R00198